SISTERS OF THE NIGHT

THE SOUL OF AN ANGEL

SISTERS OF THE NIGHT

THE SOUL OF AN ANGEL

Chelsea Quinn Yarbro

Illustrated by Christopher H. Bing

AVON BOOKS NEW YORK

This is a work of fiction. Names, characters, places and incidents either are the product of the author's imagination or are used fictitiously. Any resemblance to actual events, locales, organizations, or persons, living or dead, is entirely coincidental and beyond the intent of either the author or the publisher.

AVON BOOKS, INC.
1350 Avenue of the Americas
New York, New York 10019

A Swordsmith Production
Edited by Leigh Grossman
Associate editor: Lesley McBain
Consulting editor: Jeanne Cavelos
Interior design by Kellan Peck
Copyedited by Nancy C. Hanger

ISBN: 0-380-97401-0

Library of Congress Cataloging in Publication Data:

Yarbro, Chelsea Quinn, 1942–
The soul of an angel / Chelsea Quinn Yarbro ; illustrated by Christopher H. Bing.—1st ed.
p. cm.—(Sisters of the night)
I. Title. II. Series: Yarbro, Chelsea Quinn, 1942– Sisters of the night.
PS3575.A7S6 1999 98-47261
813'.54—dc21 CIP

First Avon Books Printing: April 1999

AVON TRADEMARK REG. U.S. PAT. OFF. AND IN OTHER COUNTRIES, MARCA REGISTRADA, HECHO EN U.S.A.

Printed in the U.S.A.

FIRST EDITION

QPM 10 9 8 7 6 5 4 3 2 1

www.avonbooks.com

— AUTHOR'S NOTES —

The sixteenth-century Venetian Empire, the Most Serene Republic, reached from northern Italy along the Dalmation coast to Greece and was the major European rival to the expanding Ottoman Empire. Made powerful by her merchants and protected by her formidable navy, la Serenissima Repubblica was the foremost Catholic presence in the Adriatic, the Mediterranean, the Aegean, and the Black Seas.

Trade routes known as Galleys connected Venice to ports throughout Europe and the Middle East. From the Greek island of Corfu—which Venice controlled—the Galleys not only reached all major Mediterranean Basin centers, but connected Venice to Russia at Tana on the Sea of Azov (the Galley of Romania) and northern Europe at Antwerp, Bruges and London (the Galley of Flanders).

The Zucchar family is typical of the wealthy upper middle class in Venice, having much in common with the Burghers in the north and the traders in the east. As is typical of many Venetian families, the final vowel of the name is dropped. In the Venetian dialect *ce* and *ci* are pronounced not *chay* and *chee* as in standard Italian, but *zhay* and *zhee*, so Fenice is Fay-NEE-zhay (phoenix); Artemesia is Ahr-tay-MEE-shah (Artemis); Eloisa is El-OY-za (Heloise); the family name, Zucchar, is ZOO-kar.

This one is for
British Columbia's vampirologist extraordinaire
Robert Eighteen-Bisang
and his
Transylvania Press

— PROLOGUE —

Venice, 1569

My passion, like a river in flood
Races over the fields to the vast sea
And will not be held back.
—Lodovico Ariosto

In the Campo Sant' Angelo, the house of Gaetano Zucchar was glowing with lampshine as the twilight fog drifted in over Venice. Not even the services at Sant' Angelo itself, nor those at San Stefano, across the canal, intruded on the family celebration or disrupted the steady stream of guests arriving by foot and in gondolas to join in the great event.

"Lionello!" his father cried, lifting his glass to his youngest son, who was about to make his first voyage. "A fair wind, calm seas, and good fortune!" Gaetano was a burly man now becoming portly since he had given up going to sea in favor of his sons. He had a fleshy face, a neat beard and close-trimmed dark hair. He was dressed elegantly, as befitted a merchant of his standing. The gold-and-silver braid along the wide, turned-back sleeves of his dogaline glistened, and the revealed silver satin lining was luminous as pearl.

All the guests echoed these sentiments before they drained their elegant glasses, for the Zucchar family could afford the finest in wine and in drinking vessels, and delighted in displaying their riches to the world. Zucchar merchant ships had been plying the Adriatic for more than a century, and never more prosperously than in the last twenty years, when their wealth had doubled and doubled again.

Lionello grinned, his young face just showing its first beard. "I have my brothers for an example. How could I not succeed?"

This was met with a roar of approval. Those guests lingering over their sweetmeats and candied flowers surged to their feet to honor the young man's valor; the rest drank again in tribute to Lionello.

From her place at the family table, Fenice Zucchar stared longingly at her brother, wishing fervently that they could trade places—that it was *she* who was about to sail, and that *he* was the one getting a new tutor for Greek. It was all so unfair, she thought darkly, just because she was female, to be deprived of the opportunity to go about the world as Lionello was about to do. She did not care that her envy of him was a sin, or that no woman in their family had ever gone to sea; she longed for adventure with the deep-burning passion of a saint for martyrdom. Nothing had ever been so important to her as getting to sail to the remote places of the world—not her learning, not her reputed beauty, not her chance at a husband. Her dreams were of distant cities and tumultuous seas, not jewels and children.

Lionello regarded his family with a fond, brave smile. "I must thank my father for entrusting me with our enterprise," he said, his voice cracking once from nervousness. "And I thank my mother for her guidance and good counsel. I thank my brothers"—here he nodded to the only one present, Febo, who lifted his glass in salute—"for showing me the way. When Ercole returns, I know he will have added to our treasures. And you, Febo, will do the same." He looked toward his sisters and his smile softened. "To Bianca, Fenice, Artemesia, and Eloisa, what can I do but promise that I will bring you gauds and trinkets from the ends of the earth?"

All his sisters but Fenice raised their glasses: Fenice stared down into her wine as if she had just been rebuked. She did not want to be given such trivial prizes; she wanted to get them for herself. Belatedly she picked up her glass.

"As this is Lionello's last night ashore for some weeks, let us be certain he enjoys it," Gaetano Zucchar called to all his guests. "There are musicians to play for you, jugglers to entertain you, and the company of friends to make the evening happy."

With this as permission, the entire party rose from the dinner tables and trooped into the main hall of the extravagant house. It was not the Ca' d'Oro on the Grand Canal, but it was one of the most splendid of the merchants' houses in all of la Serenissima; everyone knew that the Zucchar family was among the wealthiest families in Venice, and treated them accordingly.

Bianca, walking just ahead of Fenice, remarked over her shoulder, "What do you think? Will we see Lionello again before the Nativity?"

"It is not yet Lent, and you are thinking about the Nativity?" Fenice said, not wanting to be reminded of the fine long voyage Lionello was embarking upon. "That is months and months away."

"Well, Ercole should have been back this week, and now we know he will not arrive for at least another ten days," said Bianca, keeping her head down to conceal the purple, arrow-shaped birthmark on her jaw that marred her otherwise pleasant but unremarkable features.

Fenice's eyes brightened. "Can you imagine? Fighting off a corsair and outrunning him to Corfu? It must have been marvelous, to battle and win. How proud I am of him. I wish I had been there."

"Do you jest?" Bianca challenged her. "Corsairs are deadly fighters, and had our brother not won his fight, he would be at the bottom of the sea by now, or in some Turkish slave market."

If she meant to frighten Fenice, she did not succeed. "I know. That's what would make it exciting. Think of it, Bianca! Only your sword and your wits can save you. Now, *that* is something worth doing. Sewing a straight seam, well—" She gestured her scorn.

"For Our Lady's sake, Fenice," Bianca said, shocked at such unsuitable sentiments. "You're almost thirteen. It's time to stop longing for impossible things."

"Tell me really, Bianca," Fenice said, tugging her sister aside and lowering her voice, "wouldn't you love to sail with Lionello? Or Ercole? Or Febo? Don't you ever dream of the places they tell us about?"

"Of course not," said Bianca, pulling her brocaded sleeve out of Fenice's grasp. "And neither should you."

"Oh, Bianca!" Fenice exclaimed. "I never thought you were so paltry."

"If being paltry means not to hanker after the inappropriate, then I deem it an honor to be paltry." Bianca stood straighter, mustered as much dignity as her sixteen years would allow, and walked away from her tempestuous sister.

Fenice made a face at Bianca's back, then stepped into the main hall; she paid no attention to the gilded lamps that provided the brilliance in the room, for she was used to them, and to the tall paintings depicting her father and his brothers setting out to sea with Poseidon to help them and angels to guide them. The display of candles was an extravagance that even the Zucchars rarely indulged in, and Fenice stood admiring them for some time, her expression distant, as if she saw something more than light in the dancing flames.

"How does it happen that you are alone?" asked a voice beside her.

Fenice turned to see her father's friend, Rocco degli Urbanesei, standing near her; as always, he was dressed in great elegance, his sea-blue giaquetta embroidered in gold with pearls to set off the slashing, which revealed the fine white silk of his camisa beneath. His upper hose were deep blue, full-cut and slashed like his sleeves, with more billows of silk revealed. She was so startled that all she could do was stammer out the polite phrases she had been taught to use with guests; she had not mastered the handling of her elaborately pleated skirt well enough to risk curtsying, though she knew it was the correct thing to do. "Signor degli Urbanesei," she said as she regained her poise.

"You look quite as splendid as any of the ladies in this hall, young Fenice," he said, treating her as if she were two or three years older and entitled to gallantry; he licked his lips fastidiously, then smiled.

"Then you have not looked at the others very closely," Fenice responded.

Rocco degli Urbanesei laughed aloud. "You must not apologize for your pertness. Some would chide you for it, but in one so young, it is refreshing."

"Refreshing," Fenice repeated as if she did not quite understand the word; what did he mean by that, she wondered.

"Why, yes. Young ladies too often strive to be simpering copies of their elders, but not you. Your artlessness makes you all the more enchanting. In a year or two you will be breaking hearts with your love of wildness." He held out his hand for her to lay hers upon. "Come. The others want to dance. Shall we give them room for their entertainment?"

"If you wish." As Fenice allowed him to lead her away from the center of the floor, she cast a yearning glance at her brother.

"You will miss Lionello," said Rocco degli Urbanesei, following her gaze. "How you must worry for him. You will pray for his safe return every day he is gone." His expression was indulgent, avuncular but with something less remote in it.

Fenice laughed. "Not I: I never fear for my brothers," she said, and added, "I wish I could go with him."

This admission evoked an indulgent chuckle from Rocco degli Urbanesei. "You have no notion what he will encounter. You imagine it is all like the fine tales you heard as a child, but it is not. Being on the sea is—"

"Dangerous. Yes, I know," said Fenice. "Why else should anyone bother with adventures if there were no dangers to be overcome?"

"You are so fierce," Rocco said with an indulgent smile. "No corsair would dare to fight you."

"And why not?" she demanded hotly. "Am I so unworthy of steel?" She knew she had said too much but was unable to stop herself from adding, "I would have to fight twice the number my brothers have, so that everyone would know I am in earnest."

Rocco degli Urbanesei shook his head, his smile turned to a smirk. "How could anyone doubt that, Signorina Fenice?" He laid his hand on her shoulder, addressing her from the vantage point of his twenty-nine years. "But do not say so much to the other guests. Most of them would misunderstand you."

"And you do not?" she asked sharply.

"Why, no. I recognize the high spirits of youth. I recall my own sisters hanging on every word I had for them at the end of a voyage, and I know the dreams they had of the places I had been, like some great romance by Ariosto. If I said I had ridden a hypogryph, they would have believed me." He removed his hand.

"Would they? I am not so easily gulled," Fenice stated and then walked away as the musicians struck up a festive tune. She looked about for Lionello, wanting to find him, to entreat him to take her with him, though she knew he would never agree to anything so audacious.

Aurelio Pirenetto, who was only a year older than Fenice and looking out of place in his new, grown-up finery, stumbled on the shallow steps, flushed deeply and mumbled an apology to anyone who had noticed. He caught sight of Fenice and his color intensified.

Fenice paid him no heed; she was preoccupied with her own, private dream of far-flung exploits; and with the full determination of her youth, she swore to herself to achieve them.

A short while later her brother Febo found her sitting in an alcove, an unaccustomed frown on her face. "So this is where you disappeared to," he said lightly. "We are supposed to be gathering to give Lionello his holy medals for his voyage."

"Must we?" Fenice asked plaintively.

"Of course we must," said Febo, wise enough not to try to cajole her out of her unexplained wrath. "What if some ill should befall him, and we failed to arm him with his faith?"

"Do you really think it would make any difference?" She knew he would say nothing of her doubts to anyone because he shared them.

"It doesn't matter what I think. The family expects this of us, Fenice."

"Oh, all right," she said, "if we *must* be sensible, then I'll come with you." She got up from the low upholstered bench and started toward him. Suddenly tears welled in her eyes. "But, oh, Febo, I wish I were leaving, and not Lionello."

Febo's voice softened with his features. "I know, I know, piccolina; I know. You remember the maps we made when we were children? You still want to go to those faraway ports, don't you?" He bent and kissed her shining dark hair. "Perhaps one day you will." He said this to console her and to take the heat from her soul, with no larger purpose.

"Yes," she said as the seeds of intent took root deep within her. "Yes, Febo. One day I will."

VENICE

1572–1573

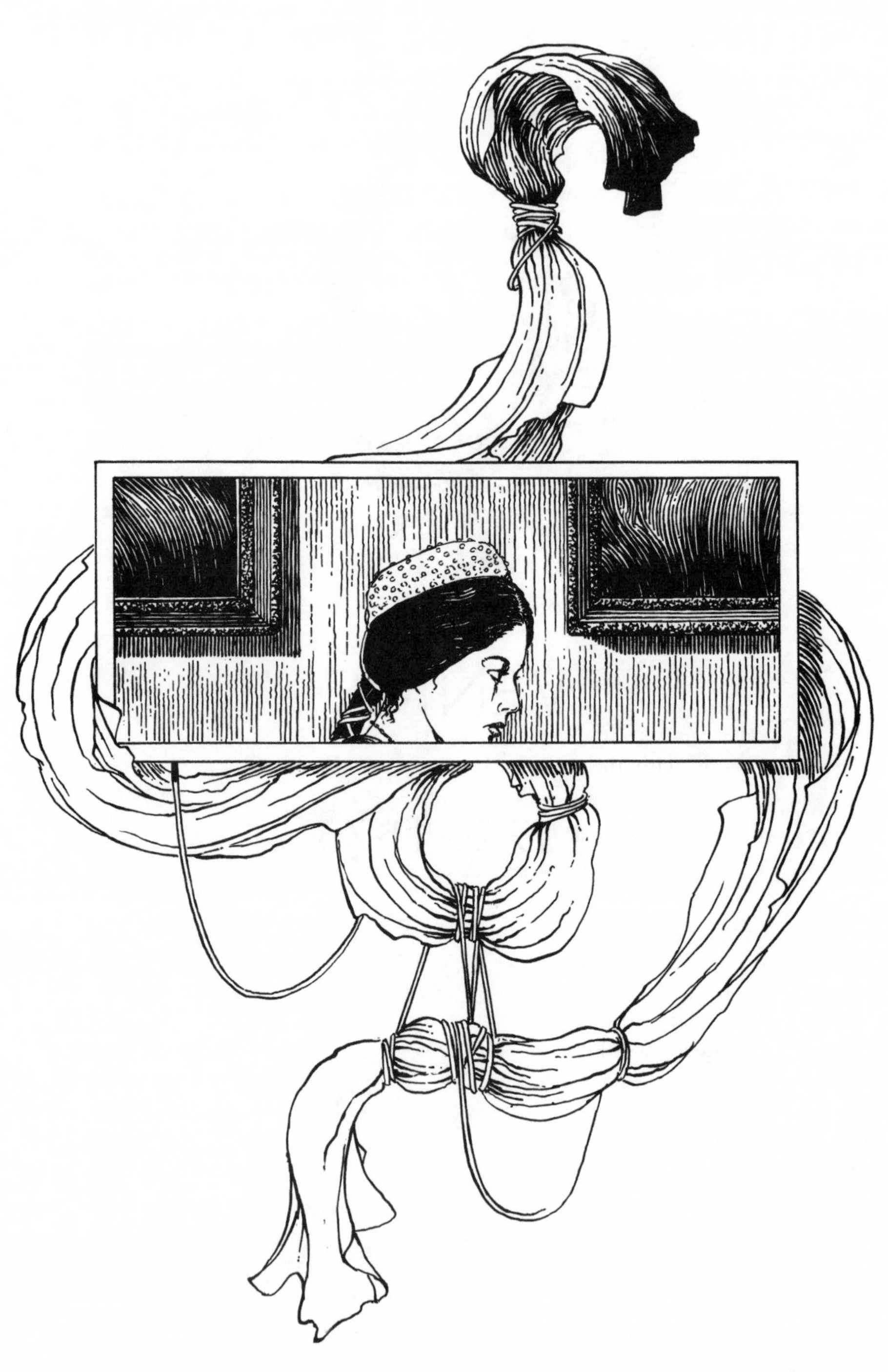

I live upon a lonely, gloomy, sea-girt rock
Like a mourning bird that seeks not food or water . . .
—Vittoria Colonna

— I —

Lionello's successful completion of his third voyage gave Gaetano Zucchar an excellent reason for celebration; he liked displays and occasions and he was afforded an excellent one now—two of his sons were in Venice, a rare occurrence.

"It will provide you another opportunity, Fenice," he informed his daughter as she left her tutor's supervision that late September afternoon, "to decide between your suitors. You are sixteen; it is time you chose your husband." He sat in his study with the windows open on the canal behind him; rosy-gold light streamed in, striking his desk and the Oriental carpet.

"But I don't want to marry yet, Padre Mio; I told you that months ago," she said with a rush of energy that animated her pretty vixen's face. Her changeable eyes seemed suddenly dark and lustrous, and her lovely bowed lips became stern. In the last two years she had gone from a gangly filly of a girl to a slender, lovely young woman with a cloud of crimped dark hair framing her pert features more beautifully than the jeweled chaplet she wore. "A year or two won't make that much difference. Many girls wait until they're older than I am, so they will be wiser in their choices. I will be much calmer when I am eighteen." She gave a twitch to her brocaded skirt and favored her father with a beguiling glance.

Gaetano Zucchar sighed and asked himself if this task were not better left to his wife; doggedly he persevered. "Fenice, no one wonders that Bianca is still unmarried, though she will be twenty soon. They know that women with birthmarks do not often find acceptable husbands. But you have no such excuse, and for the sake of your sisters, it is time you married. Think about them, for a change. You know they will not be pledged until you are married. It will not be possible to make matches for Artemesia and Eloisa while you are single."

As much as she wanted to, Fenice could not make herself laugh. "Padre Mio," she said, her voice wistful, "I am not ready."

"Do you tell me you will not consider any man?" he asked, his good humor beginning to fray. "Do you intend to defy me?"

"No. Of course not," Fenice soothed. "But I pray you will not make such demands on me for yet awhile." Once she was married she knew all chance for adventure would be gone forever, and she was not ready to relinquish her dream.

"The men who have spoken to me are honorable men," Zucchar warned Fenice with as much vehemence as he could summon up for his most beautiful, most perplexing daughter. "They will respect your reserve, but they will not wait forever while you cast about for someone you might like better."

"But, Padre Mio, I want to be sure I will not be discontented," Fenice said, and smiled in such a way that the dimple in her cheek deepened. "You have said yourself that there is no greater disaster in marriage than a discontented wife."

Gaetano Zucchar sighed; he had indeed made such an observation many times. "I would not want that for you, of course," he said, looking directly at her and thinking as he did that she was right to take her married state so seriously; far too many girls married lightly and rued their choices. He could not bear to think of Fenice becoming one of that unhappy sisterhood. "Very well; I will not press you for the time being. But if you will not make up your mind in good time then you and I must talk again." He leaned forward and kissed her forehead.

"Thank you, Padre Mio. You are very good," said Fenice, feeling a little breathless, as if she had managed to escape a close pursuit.

"And who is to say," he went on as Fenice curtsied to him and prepared to leave him alone in his study. "One of your brothers may find the enterprising man you seek and bring him back to Venice for you."

"If he did, I would not want to be married already," Fenice said mischievously from the door. She slipped out into the hall, hurrying along toward the family dining room; it was not yet the hour for supper, but Fenice knew that bottles of wine and fruit juice would be set out along with sugared sweetmeats. She was always thirsty after spending the afternoon mastering Greek and geometry, both of which she found dry and dull. Only the knowledge that she would need Greek on her travels and that geometry was crucial in navigation kept her at her studies.

She found Ercole in the dining room ahead of her, seated under the huge portrait of their father painted by Titian two decades ago. The resemblance between father and son was striking. At twenty-four, Ercole was Fenice's oldest sibling, a grown man with a curly dark sea-captain's beard and sunburned skin. He had put on his Venetian finery—a giaquetta of blue-green brocade piped in gold with double-bell slashed sleeves, simple upper hose of the same brocade as his giaquetta, and fitted hose in a lozenge pattern in blue and yellow. He held a cup of wine in one hand and a cluster of grapes in the other. He nodded to Fenice as she hesitated in the door. "Well, Signorina Spitfire, how goes it with you today?"

For an uncharitable moment Fenice wondered why her father did not urge Ercole to marry—he was much older and he would be glad of a wife to come home to. She made herself smile as she came in. "It goes today as it does every day," she told him as she went to pour wine for herself. "You would be hard-set to choose among them, month upon month."

Ercole laughed. "At least you haven't turned into one of those primping, artificial creatures every other family seems to be infested with." He watched her as she went and sat down at her customary place at the table.

"You're being awfully harsh, aren't you?" She wanted to hear his answers and so did not touch her wine while he spoke.

"No, I don't think so," Ercole said after a brief, thoughtful pause. "Most girls turn from fine, spirited youngsters with wit and charm to giggling, tittering magpies who have nothing better to do than carp at their maids and condemn the lace in a ruff." He took a long draught of wine. "You know I'm right. Think of Evangelina Tempesta. When she was fourteen she would come to meet her brother at the docks when he returned home no matter what the hour or weather. She did not need to dress in her finest satins, with her hair crimped and her handkerchiefs perfumed—she was content to wear homespun if it meant she saw him more quickly. Now that she is seventeen, she will not stir abroad before midafternoon, and only then with a mask and her grand clothes revealing what the mask is supposed to conceal and she will not go near the docks while ships are unloading for fear of smirching her fancy clothes. Everything that was admirable in her has been replaced by vanity." He pointed a finger at Fenice. "Promise me you won't turn into something like her."

This admonition surprised Fenice, who took a deep, steadying breath before she said, "All right; I promise." She wondered if Ercole were entirely sober, for she had not known him to show such vehemence before.

"Good for you," he approved, glaring into his cup.

Fenice sipped her wine contemplatively. "You'll be leaving again soon, won't you?"

"In ten days, God and the winds willing. I will be back not long after Epiphany." He waved his hand to show how confident he was. "Now that the Turks have been routed from our seas, I need not worry that they will pursue me like seaborne wolves."

"Lepanto stopped them forever," said Fenice, a glow of excitement growing in her that had nothing to do with the wine. "It must have been a wonderful battle."

"Wonderful," he said as if he had never heard the word before. "It was bloody slaughter is what it was. Men and ships broken and burning, thousands of galley-slaves drowning where they were chained as their decks ran with blood." He shook his head. "No, it was not wonderful. I saw the aftermath and I thank God I did not see the battle."

"But the Turks were defeated," said Fenice with emotion. "You cannot say it was a small thing that we have made the seas safe from them."

"The cost, Fenice, the cost," said Ercole with a terrible fatigue. "Not the ducats, though enough of them were paid, but the lives and the souls of the men." He drained his cup and went to fill it again. "May you never know what battle is."

Had Ercole not looked so suddenly bleak, Fenice might have argued with him; as it was she decided they should speak of more pleasant things. "You go only to Constantinople this voyage, don't you?"

"Yes. There is a shipment of silks coming along the Old Silk Road that was supposed to arrive in the summer but which was delayed. I am going back to get it, and a load of pepper." This last was a significant achievement and he allowed himself a moment to gloat over it. "Six full-measure barrels of pepper."

"Six full-measure barrels," Fenice marveled. "What did you trade for such a treasure?"

"Glass," said Ercole with feigned indifference; he knew he had increased the family fortunes dramatically. "Goblets and plates."

"Oh, *Ercole!*" Fenice shrieked with pleasure. "Pepper!" Of all spices, pepper was by far the most prized. She went silent and regarded him with an expression of disfavor. "You were going to tell us about it before you sailed, weren't you? Or was it going to be a secret?"

"I've told Papa," said Ercole, and his cheeks reddened above his beard. "I don't want anyone to be disappointed in case something occurs on this voyage."

"How could we be disappointed?" Fenice asked, and answered for him, "Yes, I know. It could all be lost, or someone might steal it, or pay more for it. I know. But isn't it exciting to have managed six full-measure barrels—of pepper!"

"It's exciting," he conceded, and drank more of his wine. "And if all goes well, we will be able to afford to purchase another ship next year." He smiled with self-satisfaction. "You know how that would benefit us."

Fenice was an apt enough student to know how the addition of a fourth ship to their fleet could enlarge the family's burgeoning wealth. She lifted her cup to show her approval but could not conceal a wistful hope that such a ship—however impossible—would be hers to sail and command. Her expression became remote as she made herself set her dream aside. "We would be richer than we are."

"Wouldn't you like that?" Ercole was turning playful. "Think about how your suitors would flock to you then. You would only have to crook your little finger and half the young men of Venice—and some of the old ones, too—would come running."

"What a good bargain!" Fenice marveled sarcastically. "Any husband I want, for only a fraction of the family's wealth." She tapped her finger on the table as if she had just remembered something. "You will have to reserve enough to buy Artemesia and Eloisa husbands, too. You can't squander it all on finding one for me."

"Fenice, for pity's—" Ercole said. "It's not like that at all. Our money means that you are not going to have to marry a man who does not suit you. You have the luxury of marrying happily."

She drank more of her wine, not trusting herself to speak. She was not being sensible; she knew it, but there was nothing she could do to change her feelings. The life that she had been born to did not include the kind of adventure her brothers had and, barring a miracle, never would. She finished her wine and was about to get up when she impulsively said, "I wish I could be like you, Ercole."

He glanced at her in mild surprise. "Hum? That's thoughtful of you."

"Would you like that? Would you like me to go voyaging with you?" She hoped he could not hear the forlorn note in her voice.

"You're a hoyden," he said affectionately. "What sort of brother would I be if I encouraged you in such wildness?" He shook his head as if trying to imagine how such an arrangement would turn out. "I wouldn't be able to show my face in half the ports on the Adriatic."

"Do you think so?" That did not seem reasonable to her, but she supposed he knew what he was saying. "What about beyond the Adriatic?" she asked, recalling her geography lessons. "What about the Black Sea?"

"Minx!" he accused her laughingly. "You might as well be nine still. Go pester your tutor with such questions. But mind," he went on a bit more seriously, "you keep such questions between you and me."

"And Febo," she said. "He says it would be great fun to show the world to me."

"Febo would," said Ercole, trying to be stern. "You were a pair when you were children. Always into mischief."

Fenice curtsied to her brother and left the room, relieved to have got away without another lecture about husbands; she had had her fill of them for the day.

Just over a week later Fenice's mother summoned her to her sewing room. Rosamonda Zucchar was a handsome woman; even at thirty-nine her russet-colored hair under a lace shadow-coif had not faded much, and her skin was gently lined, promising an attractive old age. She was fashionably plump and she shone with vitality. She was dressed simply in a simarra of light, gray-green silk over a linen sottana embroidered in a pattern of seashells. Soft felt slippers made her feet look very small. She was working at her embroidery frame by the window and indicated to Fenice to sit down on the stool opposite her.

"What is it, Madre Mia?" Fenice asked, unable to keep the apprehension from her voice.

"Are you comfortable, Fenice?" her mother inquired as if she were entertaining a guest.

Fenice's anxiety increased; her mother usually showed the greatest kindness to her children when she wanted to influence them in some way. "Comfortable enough."

"Very good," said Rosamonda, and continued to set perfect stitches in the bench-cover she was working on the frame. After a short silence, she began as if she were returning to a topic of discussion rather than initiating it. "Of course, when my father arranged for me to marry Gaetano Zucchar, I hardly knew him. I had to rely on my father's concern for me and judgment of character. As you are aware, I was fortunate in his choice."

"Yes, Madre Mia," said Fenice, who wished she had some reason to flee.

"Your father and I have long had good cause to thank my father for his decision. I was fourteen when we married, and unsure of the world. I would not have known how to choose a husband had I been given the opportunity. You're sixteen now, and by the time I reached your age, Ercole was a year old." She held up her hand to keep Fenice from speaking. "Your circumstances are not mine. You need not remind me. But you are old enough now to decide whom you will marry. Your father has spoken to you about this; he told me about it. But I thought that perhaps I could allay your fears if we talked about the two men who are most persistent in their attentions. By their actions, they show how they value you."

"Like a load of cargo," said Fenice. "Ercole told me that we have money enough to buy me any husband I want."

"Well," said his doting mother fondly, "Ercole is a man, and not always wise in these matters, even if what he told you is true. You could look among the court of the Doge if you wished to marry into the nobility. There are any number of noblemen's sons who would be glad enough for a bride with a dowry like yours." She stitched a moment, and added, "Younger sons, to be sure, but nobly born, if that is what you would like."

"Lord of the fishes, no!" Fenice cried impulsively.

"Fenice, do not swear. It is not becoming in a woman to use such terms." The admonition was an automatic one, lacking heat or dismay.

"Madre Mia, please don't make me marry yet. I'm not ready." She knotted her hands in her lap. "I know you were younger than I am when you married and it turned out well. But your husband is not one of my suitors."

"Fenice!" Rosamonda clicked her tongue in disapproval.

"And that's my *point,* Madre Mia. I know who you mean by the two most persistent men who call upon me, and neither one of them can hold a candle to Padre Mio." She lifted her chin. "I would like another year or two before I marry. Marriage is so . . . so final."

"You make it sound like a death sentence," said Rosamonda, chuckling a little. "And it is nothing of the sort."

"For you and Padre Mio, perhaps. But do you really think Rocco degli Urbanesei or Aurelio Pirenetto are cut of the same cloth as your husband? Rocco likes pretty things, and as long as I suit his taste for beauty, he would treat me well, as benefits a valued possession. He has so many trophies in his house, he would like a living one to set beside the rest. The trouble would come once I was no longer what he fancied. He would go elsewhere to complete his collection."

"There is some truth in what you say," Rosamonda allowed. "It would be your task to attach his affections so that he would not stray later."

Fenice did not dignify her mother's comment with a response. "And Aurelio—he does not know where he is two days out of three. He is lost in his thoughts and those endless designs of galleys he does. Not that his work is not important. The Armory has high regard for him, and doubtless his contributions will keep la Serenissima the strongest navy on the seas. I don't mean to say he has done nothing of any worth. But he forgets to lace his giaquetta and half the time his sleeves don't match."

"But he is fond of you, piccola," said Rosamonda sensibly. "And unlike Rocco, you may be sure his attention will never wander."

"How could it? He would not know I was there most of the time." Fenice gave an exasperated snort and did not apologize for her rudeness. "And I have heard that Italo Foscar is going to marry Cristophina Tedesco, so the only noble younger son I would find to my liking is not available to pursue. No other suitor has presented himself, so I suppose you are right and I will have to take either Rocco or Aurelio."

"No man is wholly without some fault, Fenice, and no woman is perfect," Rosamonda reminded her. "You would not want perfection in a husband."

"Not perfection," Fenice agreed, "but a complementary temperament. Is that too much to want?"

Rosamonda did not say anything for a short while, then remarked, "You are making things difficult for your sisters, waiting so long to choose. They must wait upon your choice, and they are not as pretty as you are." She stopped her embroidering and regarded Fenice thoughtfully. "It is that Bianca is still at home, isn't it? You do not want to marry before she takes the veil. You need not hesitate on her account. Her determination to be a nun is known to most of our friends, and your marriage will not be seen as a slight to her. In fact," she added with a slight nod, "Bianca would probably be glad to be able to celebrate one wedding while not in Orders, so she might take leave of the world joyfully."

"So I owe Bianca a wedding?" Fenice demanded. "So she can revel before she becomes a nun? Bianca never reveled in her life!"

"Well, yes, that is so." Rosamonda was unperturbed. "But you are the eldest, in regard to marriage, I mean. And you are the beauty, so you must make the most of the gifts God has bestowed on you."

"Madre Mia, please!" Fenice felt her cheeks grow hot.

"Figlia mia, you have always had a clever mind; that was one of the reasons you have been tutored so long. Turn your learning to good use now. You may establish yourself well as the wife of a great man and live comfortably for the rest of your life." She made no concession for her daughter's embarrassment. "You have a lovely face, your skin is good, your eyes are well-spaced and their changeable color is attractive as well as unusual, and your hair is beautiful, so dark and wavy. You are a trifle slender and your bosom is not deep, but having a child will change both those minor infelicities for the better. You have two very good opportunities to marry, and you are more than old enough." She folded her hands. "I will not make my wish imperative, not yet. For now, let me only ask you to think about everything I've said. If you decide that you will accept one of these men, then we may both be thankful for your good sense."

"And if I do not?" Fenice asked as a chill went through her.

"I can't imagine that will happen. You're much too sensible." She patted her daughter's hand. "There. Now we both can feel better."

Fenice made an incoherent reply: whatever she felt, it was not *better*. She wondered if men crossing the Bridge of Sighs felt as abandoned as she did. Clenching her jaw in an effort to keep from weeping, she rose, curtsied to her mother, then unceremoniously fled.

Febo returned to Venice three days after Ercole left; Lionello would be outward bound the following day, so family festivities were private, conducted with elegance in spite of the smallness of the company. For part of the evening Fenice played her long-necked chittarrone, picking out melodies she knew Febo was particularly fond of as a tribute to him.

At the end of the evening, when the household had finished their thanksgiving prayers, Febo pulled Fenice aside as they were about to retire to their rooms. "All right, piccolina, what's wrong?"

Fenice avoided his steady gaze. "Nothing. The weather is so dreary—"

"And it's not the only thing," said Febo. "You're drooping like a sail in the doldrums." He planted himself squarely in front of her, determined and handsome, his features a more rugged version of her own, his clothes lavish as befitted a successful merchant. "You might as well tell me. I'll find out on my own if you don't."

Because he was her favorite brother and they had always been allies, it made it harder to answer. "It's nothing," she insisted.

"Don't lie to me, Fenice. I know you too well for that." He waited, and when she did not speak, he said, "You're upset. I can see it if the rest can't."

She was about to cry and she hated herself for the weakness. "I . . . can't."

"Don't tell me you're lovesick," Febo said, and was surprised when she blanched. "All right, not lovesick. What is it then? And don't say nothing again, for I won't believe you."

She pulled off her chaplet and frowned. "It's time for bed."

"Not yet," he said. "You aren't going to undress here in the corridor, so don't take on those airs with me." He shook her arm, but gently, and his voice changed. "Come on, Fenice. Can't you see I'm worried about you? Are you ill?"

"No." She faltered. "It's that . . . that they want me to . . . to get married." The last word came out in a wail.

To Fenice's chagrin, Febo laughed. "Is that all? I would think you'd be overjoyed."

"Febo!" Anger went through her like a blade. "Not you, too?"

"What's wrong with getting married?"

She was disgusted with her tears and impatiently wiped them away with the edge of her hand. "Everything!"

"Everything?" he echoed. "Why everything?" He pulled her closer to him as if to shield her from herself. "Tell me, piccolina."

"It's that I'm . . . sixteen. And they . . . Padre and Madre, that is . . . they want me to choose a husband," she complained and recognized how absurd she must sound. "I know I'm supposed to want to get married, but Febo, oh, I don't."

He could not keep from asking, "Why not?"

Now she was crying in earnest. "I thought you'd understand."

"Tell me; I'll try," he said, putting his arms around her. "Fenice, I do hate to see you so unhappy. What can I do to help?"

"Tell them," she burst out. "Tell them not yet."

"Our parents," he guessed. "That you do not want to marry?" She nodded against his rolled-and-padded shoulder. "Can I give them some reason?"

She made herself answer. "It's just that . . . once I'm married . . . there's no more adventure. I will be as confined as if I were in prison. After I am married, everything in my life will be laid out for me and I will have to do what is expected of me until I die."

"It is women's lot in life, piccolina, and one that many would be glad to attain." He knew this would mean little to his sister. "I have seen how women live in other places; you cannot know how very fortunate you are."

"If I could travel and see for myself, I might," she said, wanting to strike out as she spoke, but not at her favorite brother.

He stroked her hair. "But you know you will have to marry someday; you've known it all your life."

"Yes, but not yet," she pleaded. "I haven't *done* anything. I haven't *gone* anywhere. Once I get married, I never will."

"Would that be so terrible?" he chided her gently.

"Yes! *Yes!*" She felt her eyes well with new tears.

He let her cry herself out, saying nothing while she railed against her fate in short, furious bursts that held more emotion than sense. When her sobs had turned to sniffles, he took a step back from her. "All right. I'll talk to Padre, but I can make you no promise that he will heed what I say. It's useless to talk to Madre. All she thinks of these days is how to have her children marry advantageously. She yearns for grandchildren, and nothing will change that but having some."

"Then let Ercole marry, or you, or Artemesia. Why must it be me?" Fenice sounded cross and she put her hand to her mouth. "I didn't . . . Febo."

He laughed once. "Sons are not like daughters, Fenice, and well you know it. When her daughter has a child, Madre will know it is also hers."

"No, sons are not like daughters. Everyone is pleased when the sons travel and bring back treasure from distant ports. Daughters are expected to stay at home and marry." She shook her head so that her long dark hair whipped around her. "It is wrong."

"You wouldn't say that if you had actually been to sea," he told her.

"But I haven't," she said, making no excuse for her resentment. "And perhaps you're right and I would be content to remain here after going somewhere. Who knows, I might lose all my desire to go about the world, or to seek adventure in distant places. But I will not have the chance to find out, will I? I can watch you sail, and Ercole, and Lionello, and never realize how fortunate I am to be allowed to remain in Venice."

He could not deny the point she made. "If I could take you with me, Fenice, I would." It was an impulsive remark, made to assure her of his sympathy, but she seized upon it.

"Would you? Oh, Febo, would you? Will you tell Padre you will take me with you, just once, just one little voyage, even if it's only to Ragusa?" Her eyes which had been dark as slate now shone green-gold.

There was no question of such a venture; he was certain of it even if she was not. Still, to give her some hope, he said, "I'll try to arrange something."

She smiled up at him. "Oh, Febo, you are the best of my brothers. You always were and you always will be." She kissed his cheeks and favored him with a lopsided grin. "Just one little adventure, that's all I want. Something that I can remember when I am so bored I think I will go mad. You'll do that for me. I know you will."

Febo was disquieted by her sudden change from melancholy to delight, but he was too grateful for it to question it closely. "It's late, Fenice. It's time you were abed."

"Yes, yes it is. And I shall have such sweet dreams now. Ragusa isn't far and we don't have to worry about corsairs since Lepanto." She regarded him. "I am so grateful to you, Febo."

"Padre hasn't said yes yet," he warned her, finding her mercurial change hard to address.

"You will persuade him. I know you will. Because you understand. The others think that I am not in earnest when I say I want to see the places you have seen and learn the things you've learned. But you know I am entirely serious. If I loved you for no other reason, that would be enough." She kissed his cheek again and went down the corridor to her door, waving at him before she went inside.

Gaetano Zucchar stopped Febo in mid-plea. "Out of the question." His study was gloomy this morning; fog had wrapped Venice in its gelid embrace, leaching the shine from the gold of her domes and shrouding her canals in treacherous mists. The sea was very still; all sounds carried eerily, from the cries of vendors on barges to the prayers of the priests at Sant' Angelo.

"She has her heart set on it," said Febo. "She will not be content until she has seen something more of the world than our city."

"Then let her husband take her as a wedding gift," said their father.

"You know that will not happen. She is right on that point: once she marries, she will be here for the rest of her life." Febo smiled engagingly. "Who would want to live anywhere but Venice? No one, you think. But Fenice will not know that until she has seen some of the world for herself."

"You are probably right," said Gaetano with a gusty sigh. "And if society were not so censorious, I might consider what you request. But how could her reputation survive such a madcap antic as travel?" He sat forward, his elbows on the desk, his big hands wrapped around themselves. "It is difficult, very difficult, raising daughters. Everyone says sons are more of a trial, but sons can do so much more without the world looking on them askance. Girls must be guarded and guided diligently, or they destroy their chances for a good life."

"Giuseppina Barbarigo was not—" Febo began.

"Giuseppina Barbarigo was married to one of the Console, and her nephew was Doge. She cannot be compared to Fenice. And that was more than a century ago, when the world was less . . . less squeamish than it is now." Gaetano shook his head. "What sort of father would I be if I indulged her enough to ruin her chances? If it were Bianca, that might be different. Bianca is not the sort of woman people gossip about, and if they did, it would mean little to the Church, especially since our dowry of her vocation is generous. The Church would welcome her repentance, if she had anything to repent. But when a girl is a beauty, then the worst is always suspected of her, and Fenice is a beauty; everyone knows she is. Because God smiled on her, she must guard herself and that gift. Fenice would not have two acceptable suitors once she did anything so capricious as travel. She would be fortunate to get a younger son without prospects if she went off for so much as two days."

"Do you think you could explain it to her?" Febo asked. "I don't think I can, and I know she is chafing at the restrictions imposed on her."

"Her mother should have done it," said Gaetano, sounding ill-used. "I will try to make her comprehend my refusal."

Febo was about to rise when he said, "You could send me on a longer voyage. That way, by the time I return, she may well be married, and the whole matter resolved. There will be nothing she could ask of me, and I will not have to deny her." His voice took on a persuasive note that had proved useful in negotiations from Alexandria, in Egypt, to Tana at the limits of the Black Sea. "I hate to disappoint her. If I am far away, I cannot do it. It would make her less likely to try . . . oh, any kind of escapade."

"You don't think she would—" Gaetano broke off, too shocked to go on.

"She might, with me. But if I am gone, then she may be more resigned to what must come to her in life." Febo tugged at the top of his boot. "I cannot help but feel that I have betrayed her, encouraging her all those years to yearn for something she could never have. I am sorry, Padre Mio."

"How could you know?" Gaetano asked, dismissing his son's worries with a single wave of his hand. "Children like excitement; if Fenice had left her wishes behind with her youth . . . But she didn't. I don't know how to deal with her, and that's God's truth."

"Marriage will change her. Once she marries, she will find adventure enough." Febo tried to make light of his suggestion, but then added, "If you force her, make her choose too quickly, she may rebel and do precisely what you would not like."

Gaetano nodded slowly several times. "So. A long voyage for you—the Galley of Barbary and Northeast Africa together, perhaps," he suggested, combining two trade routes that would lead from Cyprus and Beirut to Algiers in Africa and Malaga in Spain, "and another six months for her to make her choice. Artemesia will be furious, but I suppose it is the best we can do." He saw a lift to Febo's brows. "Oh, yes. Artemesia has a suitor. And at fourteen, she is more than ready to marry. As long as Fenice delays, Artemesia will be upset."

Febo was on his feet now. "God send you good judgment, Padre Mio," he said, giving the words more meaning than they usually held.

"Amen," responded his father, crossing himself.

"Febo, no," said Fenice when he told her of the plans their father had for his next voyage. "I was hoping they would send you . . . oh, to Constantinople, or . . ."

"No, that is for Lionello, when he is next in port. At least it is not the Galley of Flanders," said Febo. "Our strength is to the south and east, not the west and north." He bent and kissed her head. "You will manage on your own well enough, sorella mia." He looked about the study where she had been engaged in reading a Greek account of the war between Venice and Genoa. "Grim tales for a pretty girl."

She frowned at him. "You sound like Ercole."

"Never say so," he protested in mock dismay. Then he came and sat across from her, taking her hand and looking at her with concern. "You have let yourself be seduced by these stories, Fenice. I admire the wild soul in you, but it does not serve you well in this world." His face seemed suddenly older than his seventeen years. "I would not have you suffer any hardship, for all the gold in Turkish hands."

"But I don't mind," she said, leaning forward and lowering her voice. "If you think sewing and learning Greek and writing long translation is no hardship, you have forgot what the classroom is like."

He was not persuaded. "That may be tedious, but it is no hardship." His words became more urgent. "You are letting yourself imagine things that . . . are not true, or possible."

"I imagine only what I hear from you and Ercole and Padre Mio. Are you saying you lie?" She tugged her hand away in indignation. "Well? Do you?"

"No. But you do not hear with real understanding—" he began, only to be interrupted.

"Then take me on a voyage, a short one, so I will know how to grasp what you tell me." She made a gesture of frustration. "It would not take much, a few days and I would be satisfied."

Febo regarded her skeptically. "Would you really?"

She felt her face grow hot. "Of course," she lied.

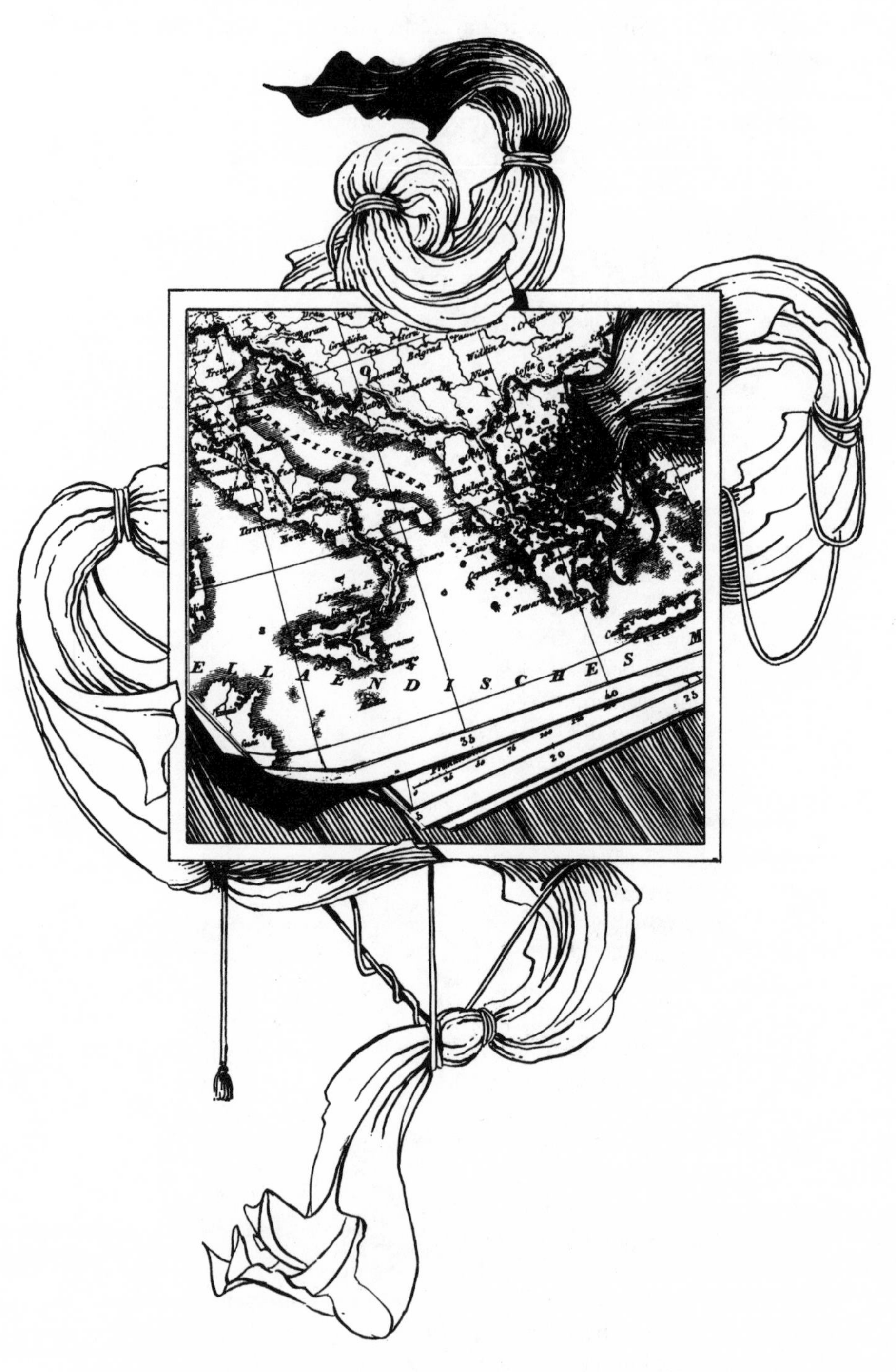
Treviso
Belgrad
Widdin
Sofia
Nicopolis
ADRIATISCHES MEER
Catanzaro
ELLAENDISCHES M

. . . Then you became
A stranger to love, and my
Youthful passion turned to scorn . . .
—Torquato Tasso

— II —

When Febo had been gone three weeks, Artemesia's suitor called upon Gaetano Zucchar for an unorthodox meeting: very carefully and with a great many digressions, he explained that he wanted to marry Artemesia before her older sister was wed. Umberto Dandin was a studious young man of eighteen from a very high-ranking merchant family, soberly dressed and grave in his deportment, and so Gaetano did not refuse him out of hand. "I will have to consider your request," he said, trying to make himself sound encouraging; he did not want to have two daughters upset with him.

Umberto accepted this response with a slight bow. "I know the notion is extreme, but given the recalcitrance of Artemesia's older sister, I cannot wait upon her whim in order to make my devotion known to you."

The stiffly formal phrases irked Gaetano. He thought Umberto a stick, but he knew Artemesia was determined to marry him, and since his family was so important, he had no reasonable response other than to accept this offer. "A betrothal of a year is customary," he reminded Umberto.

"And, under the circumstances, I think all such distinctions should be closely observed," said Umberto, sounding more like a pedant than a man in love to Gaetano's ears. "You may rely on me to maintain the decorum society demands."

"Yes. Very prudent, I am sure," he said, trying to discern what it was in Umberto that had so captivated Artemesia.

"I am deeply aware of the awkwardness of the situation, and you may rest assured I will do everything in my power to ensure it is not made more difficult by any plans for our wedding." Umberto did not touch cheeks with Gaetano as a way of showing his intended reserve in the coming months. "I will not ask that my courtship receive any special tokens of authorization. It would too much demean your older daughter."

"That it might," said Gaetano, doing his best to like the young man. "But you will dine with us on Friday, will you not? We keep to home on Fridays and so the occasion would be appropriate. I know Artemesia will be pleased."

"Then I will anticipate that honor with gratitude," said Umberto, and very correctly took his leave.

The next day Ercole returned, five weeks late, with a damaged ship. But his cargo was nearly intact, including the six full-measure barrels of pepper, which turned the family evening at home on Friday into a grand celebration for the Zucchars.

Gaetano had invited Rocco degli Urbanesei and Aurelio Pirenetto along with Umberto Dandin to be part of their festivities, which, as acknowledged suitors, they might attend without any untoward gossip resulting. All three men had accepted the invitation and now sat on the side of the men's table reserved for guests, facing Gaetano and his sons Ercole and Lionello. Of the three guests, Rocco was the most elaborately dressed, while Umberto was less so, both in style and color. Aurelio looked as if he had put on the first clothes that came to hand.

At the women's table Fenice took pains to be certain she sat directly opposite Ercole so she could watch him as he told about his travels; there were no women guests present to impede her view. She was eager to hear all he had to relate; it was difficult to hold her tongue, for she wanted to ask him at once about his voyage.

Ercole had acquired an interesting scar on his cheek as well as a gold earring. Sitting down to dinner—his hair and beard newly trimmed, in his second-best clothes, the giaquetta particolored in deep green and golden brown, the upper hose full-cut of rust-colored brocade, his underhose knit in Florentine stripes of green and rust—he still retained something of the wild sea with him, as if his finery were nothing more than an unconvincing disguise. He drank down his Lachrimi Cristi, filled his goblet again, and began.

"You know that I did not get back to Venice as quickly as I had intended." He put his elbows on the table amid the remains of their feast; he looked across to the table where the women sat and smiled at his mother and sisters. "I was glad of your prayers, you may be sure of it. I certainly had need of them."

"But what *happened?*" Fenice prompted him, unable to contain herself any longer. "You were more than a month late, on what was supposed to be a short voyage. Was it corsairs?"

"Corsairs are not the only hazards on the sea, Fenice," said Ercole with a wise nod of his head. "On the third day out, the seas came up, a storm following close behind. For two days we were battered about by the waves and the wind. Storms can do more damage than cannon fire. One of our sails was so badly torn that it was nothing more than rags when we finally brought it down." He stared off toward the window as if seeing the incident afresh. "There was a ship off our bow the first day, but she went down, and we could not save any of her crew; it was Cordolce's *San Zaccharia*, more's the pity.

More than once I feared we should join her. Then the winds slackened and the skies cleared and I knew we had won through."

Lionello looked at his oldest brother, his expression a fine combination of admiration and doubt. He put his elbows on the table and propped his chin in his hands.

At this deliverance, Rosamonda crossed herself and indicated that her daughters should do the same. "The Lord between us and danger," she whispered.

Knowing he had his family's rapt attention, Ercole went on. "About a third of the glass we had on board was broken in the storm; to lighten our load, I had it thrown into the sea. Some of our food was ruined, too, which meant that we had to put into port for provisions sooner than I had intended. When the storm was over, I made for Corfu as fast as the ship could safely travel." He drank again. "Corfu is a gem in the sea, with olive trees crowning the crests of her hills. After such a storm, she was as welcome a sight as the Gates of Paradise. She is as Venetian as she is Greek, and we did not go there as strangers." His smile was raffish. "When one has been delivered from the jaws of death, one seeks the joys of life with renewed gusto."

At this, Gaetano shot Ercole a warning glance.

"We had the most urgent repairs made, and I restocked the ship with food and water, and we made for Cyprus, our original destination. It may be lost to the Venetian Republic, but they do not disdain our ducats." He paused in his recitation to touch the scar on his cheek. "One of the men was caught stealing from our cargo. He had hidden two silver plates in his bedroll—you remember the German silver?—and I had to fight him to get it back." He fingered the scar again. "It was quite a battle. The man had a knife and he knew how to use it. I had a club. It is not so quick and it does not cut like a knife, but I knocked his brains out of his head to end it." He realized he had said too much as he saw the horrified expression in Rosamonda's eyes.

"Ercole!" she admonished him. "That is quite dreadful."

"Very good," Lionello approved.

"He was trying to kill me, Madre Mia. He had already nicked my face; he had been aiming for my eye. I would be wearing a patch now if he had succeeded in his plan." He waited while she considered this. "If I had not killed him, think what the rest of the men might have done. In Cyprus, I could not hope for justice from the conquerors had I tried to have the sailor taken into custody. And I would not have been able to sleep safely for a single night. As it was, the men saw that they could not overcome me, and that ended it."

"But still, figlio mio, you should have—" She broke off. "No. I do not know what you have to do while on the sea. I will not tell you how you are to manage."

Fenice hung on every word of Ercole's story. She had not heard anything so exciting for months. "What did you do with his body?" she asked, caught up in his tale.

"Fenice!" her mother said.

"Well, I don't think they hang bodies from the masts of ships until they rot, the way they do over city gates."

"No, Fenice. We throw such offal overboard to feed the fishes." Ercole smiled a little. "And then we eat the fishes."

Umberto Dandin was sitting so stiffly that Gaetano wondered if he had been cast in bronze.

"How can you say such things in this company?" he asked.

"Why should I not?" Ercole countered. He had drunk just enough wine that he was feeling reckless.

"Ercole, don't!" Artemesia protested, coming to the aid of her suitor. "He's right; what you're saying is most upsetting."

"I can tell you, it upset *me*, to have someone try to kill me," Ercole declared. "It was the nearest-fought challenge in my life. But I won. That is the only thing that matters. And when I discovered his theft, two more men admitted they had stolen silver as well. They confessed without any threat of repercussion, which I am pleased about. I had them both flogged but I did not kill them." He reached out to refill his goblet. "They understood. And the rest of the men, as well."

"About the voyage," Gaetano suggested. "You reached Cyprus. What then? Was there trouble? Did the Turks try to—"

"The Turks demanded fees as they always do. I had enough for them. But I had to make up for the glass we had lost. So I went to the Venetian quarter of the harbor, to see if I could arrange credit for the purchase I was going to make. I wanted our cargo secure." Ercole picked up a slice of candied orange and popped it into his mouth.

"Not the pepper!" Fenice cried as the rest of the family waited for his answer.

"No; not the pepper—the brasses I had already traded for," said Ercole. "Not that the pepper would not have secured me more credit, but I did not want word of my purchase getting about, for there are many who would have loved to take that prize for themselves." He winked at Fenice. "Would you have done any differently than I did?"

"No," she said, her cheeks glowing and not from wine.

"You see?" Ercole exclaimed, directing his gaze to Artemesia. "One of my sisters is made of steel." He grinned. "I had the funds I required to buy all the cargo waiting for me, and I made all haste to claim it. For once we sailed without any trouble—the seas were calm and the winds were fair. We made our voyage in good time, and when I arrived, the barrels were waiting and were transferred with nothing more than a single bribe. I was anxious to be away again, and I was glad the authorities did not detain me for more than a day. This was not the blessing I thought it was at the time, for I neglected to undertake as thorough an inspection of the ship as I would have done otherwise. Word of our cargo was spreading and I knew it would not be wise to linger in port for very long. I was so determined to get away in good time that I overlooked the safety of the ship."

"You mean you had a stowaway?" asked Gaetano, his brow coming down in disapproval. "That is not like you, Ercole."

"No. It was worse than that, I regret to say. I would have welcomed a stowaway compared to what I did have: we had a slow leak in the hold." He let this dramatic announcement hang on the air.

"You never did," said Fenice, certain he was jesting. "How could you make such an error?"

"Pride, my dear sister, foolish pride, and impatience to be in Venice again." His tone was lightly mocking, but behind it, Ercole was abashed at so inexcusable a mistake.

"Go on, Ercole. Tell us all," said Gaetano, his face intent as he listened to his son.

Lionello scowled into his wine. "Pride is a sin, Ercole."

"Well," said Ercole, hesitating now he had revealed his fault, "we were two days out to sea when the ship began to wallow. I knew we had to be taking on water somewhere, and I put half the crew to looking for the trouble. We found it at last, belowdecks, and did what we could to put tar enough on it to keep from foundering, but it was apparent that we should have to get repairs long before we could reach Venice again. We did not want to turn back with such a valuable cargo aboard, and we dared not try for Crete. So we began to look along the small Greek islands, and found one at last where the fishermen were willing to help us."

"What island was it?" Fenice asked, recalling all the hours she had spent learning her geography.

"It was not much larger than Torcello," he said, referring to one of the larger islands at the northeast end of the Venetian Lagoon. "Quite near Milos; the name escapes me. It isn't one you hear of often . . ." He pinched the bridge of his aquiline nose. "It has quite a fine ruin on it, marble pillars and damaged statues . . ." He drank more wine as if it would reveal the name. "Confound it. Well, it will come to me. Anyway, the fishermen there helped us mend the seams as best they could."

Fenice was leaning forward, her face eager, alight with excitement. "Did you have to fight for your cargo? Did the fishermen try to keep you on their island?"

"No," said Ercole, dampening her interest at once. "No, of course not. They would not try even if they wished to. The fishermen helped us with the ship, we paid them for their labor, and then they brought their priest to bless our voyage. We were treated very well by them; without them we would have gone down, I am convinced of it. I had the sailors—those that could swim—take the time to inspect the hull after the ship was afloat again, looking for bubbles. Probably a good thing, too," he added darkly. "We encountered rough seas as we came north. For a time I feared we would have to put in at Trieste instead of coming on to Venice, for the winds were driving us eastward. But then the weather changed and we arrived safely home."

"But late," said Rosamonda, frowning. "When all three of my sons are at sea, I am not easy in my mind."

"And who is to blame you?" Ercole asked with a fond smile. "We rely on our women to pray for us and keep us always in their thoughts. Your care is the star that guides us home."

"If you took us with you, you would have our company as well," Fenice said audaciously.

"For San Michele!" Artemesia burst out. "Fenice! How can you say such things?"

Fenice turned her changeable eyes on her younger sister. "Be candid with me for once: have you never wanted to go to sea? To find all the places we're only told of? Wouldn't you like to see the minarets at Alexandria and Tyre? Or the ancient temples on Rhodes? Or the palaces of Constantinople? Or the markets at Trebizond?"

"Fenice!" her mother admonished her. "Think what you are saying, child."

Rocco degli Urbanesei laughed indulgently.

"I am saying what the rest of you have thought. I know you have," Fenice responded with an accusing glance at her sisters. "Maybe not Bianca, but Artemesia and Eloisa, you must have dreamed of these places."

"You would," said Lionello.

Artemesia shook her head, glowering at her sister; Eloisa smiled shyly.

"There. At least Eloisa is willing to admit it," Fenice said. "And don't tell me again it is dangerous—I don't care a fig for danger."

Ercole's somber words caught the attention of all. "You should. Danger is nothing to be laughed at, Fenice, much as you would like to think it is. Danger puts your life and your very soul at risk."

"I *know* that," Fenice protested. "I do not think danger is a light thing. When facing enemies and the sea, anyone might quail, no matter how courageous he may be. But I am not a coward. I think it must be the most alive thing in the world to do, to be on the brink of death and to triumph." She saw the disapproving look in her father's eyes. "Forgive me, Padre Mio. I cannot lie about what is in my heart."

"And would that half my sailors were as brave," Ercole declared. "Most of them were preparing to drown on our last two days at sea." He discovered he was once again out of wine and refilled his goblet. "I am afraid, Fenice, that even a short stay at sea would wipe away all gallantry for you. It is not as wonderful as you think it is."

"Then take me with you, and I will show you," she said, doing her best to ignore the disapproval of everyone seated at the tables.

"Ha!" Lionello scoffed.

"Fenice, you will not speak of such things," said Gaetano firmly. "Ercole, tell me how much you lost because of your oversight."

"Not as much as I feared we would. I threw some of the brasses overboard, but we lost less than ten percent of the cargo, and not one corn of pepper."

He was justly proud of this and let his smile show it. "And the ship can be saved as well. It will be costly, but not prohibitive. So in the end, we prosper."

"We have already ordered a new ship," said Gaetano. "The pepper will more than pay for the new vessel and for repair of the old." His satisfaction was so apparent that Rocco degli Urbanesei rose to his feet to honor him.

"All success to the Zucchars," he proclaimed, looking directly at Fenice.

"All success," the rest dutifully responded.

"And to adventure," said Fenice, and drank her own pledge.

When Fenice encountered Ercole the next morning, he was nursing an aching head. They stood on the balcony together and looked toward San Stefano across the canal. The mist was beginning to lift, showing the buildings in all their splendor.

"This is the most beautiful place in the world," Ercole said after a long silence. "We are fortunate to live here and to be made rich by our city. I wish you would believe that."

Fenice shrugged. "If I had seen something of the world, I would probably agree with you. As I have not, I must suppose you are telling me the truth. Yet it is possible you are only saying what you wish me to hear. Until I have the opportunity to see for myself, I have no way of judging." She walked the length of the balcony and looked toward the Grand Canal. "If I traveled, I am sure I would miss this place."

"More than you can imagine," Ercole concurred. "I have often spent nights dreaming of the sun shining on the domes of San Marco, and the sound of Italian being spoken, and I have longed for the taste of good Venetian cooking and Tuscan wines." His laughter was rueful. He put his hand to his bloodshot eyes and peered at her. "What makes you so . . . determined to travel? You are the only girl I have ever known who wanted such things."

"I am the only one who admitted it, you mean," she countered with an impish smile. "You think because no female says she wants adventure that she does not? What cravens you must suppose we are."

"Nothing of the sort," said Ercole, a bit too quickly to be convincing.

"You do not lie well, Ercole," she told him sharply. "I would wager you one full barrel of pepper that at least half the females in Venice have yearned, at least once in their lives, to go to sea as their men do. They may not say so, but you cannot doubt that they dream of it. Febo understands; if he were here, he could make you understand what it is I am seeking."

"Febo," said Ercole, "has goaded you on in your ambitions. He never thinks that you are in earnest."

"That he has, and I am grateful to him for it," said Fenice, a trifle too hotly. "Little though you may think it, he knows how much I value my dreams."

"You think the others share your dreams? Because you have them?" Ercole suggested.

"Yes. I am not so different as you think, except that I speak my mind." She swung around to look at him, unaware of how fetching she was with the sun on the soft ruff framing her face. "Why should I be so unlike you? We are from the same family, and our family has been going to sea for nine generations."

"So we have," Ercole said. "And we have made our fortune. The sea is the source of our wealth. But we have lost ships and men as well. Think of Marcantonio Zucchar, who went down near Sicily with all his cargo. It took us ten years to recoup those losses. And what about—"

"Alvise?" she suggested sweetly. "I know our history as well as you do. Alvise lost two ships and was taken by the Turks to be a slave. That was seventy years ago. Alvise was betrayed by his pilot. We all know that." She tossed her head.

"Do not think such things cannot happen again." Ercole sat on the railing of the balcony, rocking a little as if still on his ship. "Fenice, I know Febo encouraged you in your love of excitement. It is just what he would do. But he has not served you well if he has promised you anything more than your dreams."

This time her temper flared fiercely. "Do not say anything—*anything*—against Febo. No one in this family knows what I feel but Febo. I wish he were here now. But he is on a long voyage, and we will not see him for a year." Her voice and eyes were desolate at this prospect.

"And by then, you will have other matters to occupy your thoughts," said Ercole, and then wished he had remained silent.

"What matters?" Fenice demanded.

"Well, you know," said Ercole, hedging.

"No. I do not. Tell me what you mean," Fenice said, and waited.

Ercole tried to make the best of it, aware that she would not accept another half-answer. "Just that by then you will have chosen between your suitors and Febo will be able to greet you as a married woman. That will please him more than any adventure you may hanker for. Put your dreams aside if you wish to be happy in life. It is for the best; Febo would say the same." His voice dropped as he saw the irate shine in her eyes that were now dark as storm clouds; he did his best to mollify her, chuckling as he said, "Unless you escape first."

Fenice did not trust herself to speak. She put her hands on the roll at the top of her skirt and glared at him. Then she turned on her heel and went into the house, leaving him alone on the balcony listening to the singing from the cloister across the canal.

The house of Marin Pirenetto was overflowing with company. Elaborate arrangements of food and drink were put out on tables in half the rooms on the main floor, and lamplight glistened in all the windows facing the Grand Canal. Marin Pirenetto himself welcomed his guests—the gaudy, rich merchant-elite of Venice—to his celebration at Advent. His second wife was known to be near delivery of their first child and so she did not come down from her apartments; instead his three sons from his first marriage shared the duties of host: Arrigo, Aurelio, and Andrea stood at the head of the stairs leading up from the Pirenetto landing, each in their finest clothes, each handsome in his own way, swelling their father's bosom with pride and making others envious of the great success of the family.

Arriving by gondola with her family, Fenice was able to exchange only a few words with Aurelio; she was dressed in a new simarra of rich bronze-green brocade studded with tourmaline, over a sottana of gold damask. The chaplet covering her dark hair was gold fretwork edged in seed pearls. The rest of her family was as elaborately clothed as she, Artemesia's garments being the simplest as she was too young for jewelry—a Spanish-style ropa in deep blue velvet piped in silver over a sottana of dove-gray silk. Lionello remained at home, preparing to leave in the morning.

To crown the evening, the Doge himself, Alvise Mocenigo, arrived halfway through the evening to honor the Pirenettos.

"The brilliant designs of Aurelio will keep our navy the master of the seas, and no Venetian can deny his importance to our Republic." The Doge held out a gold chain to Aurelio, who blushed and stammered as he received it.

"My son is overcome with your honor," said his father, saving the occasion with his customary grace. "The Pirenettos are forever grateful to Venice for our place in the world."

Aurelio, feeling his brother Andrea tug on his sleeve, managed to say, "A great honor . . . not one I deserve . . . most humble . . ." He bowed.

"Thus a great man," said the Doge, and went on into the depths of the house to join the other guests.

"For San Marco," whispered Arrigo, taking the chain from Aurelio and putting it over his brother's head in a quick, impatient gesture. "You would lose your way in the reception hall if it weren't for the furniture." The oldest of the three Pirenetto sons was twenty, tall, and arrogant, and known for his cutting words. However much satisfaction he might take in this recognition of his younger brother, he showed little of it to Aurelio.

"That I would," Aurelio said, not wanting to fight with Arrigo on such a marvelous occasion. Andrea, who was not quite fourteen and a gangly youth, still fussed with the stiff, pearl-studded sleeves of his giaquetta. "How much longer do we have to stay here? I'm hungry."

"Now that the Doge is here, we may join the rest," Marin announced, and signaled to his sons to come into the main rooms of the house. "Aurelio, Gaetano Zucchar and his family are here already. You will want to show them the chain the Doge bestowed on you."

"Yes. I will," said Aurelio with a marked lack of enthusiasm.

"You have received a great honor, figlio mio," Marin went on, to encourage his bashful son to act. "Your friends will want to share in your occasion of regard."

"Especially Fenice," said Andrea with a broad wink.

"But . . ." Aurelio cleared his throat. "I will show them," he said as if declaring his intention to go to war.

"Very good," said Arrigo curtly, his patience with his preoccupied brother exhausted. "I saw Marcellina Venier arrive earlier. I am going to make myself pleasant to her. The Venier family could use a little new blood, and it might as well be Pirenetto." He flashed a calculating smile and was gone into the glittering tide of guests.

Aurelio watched his confident brother vanish among their guests, and made himself plunge in after him. He went in the direction of the music room, for he had seen the Zucchars go in that direction.

Gaetano Zucchar found Aurelio before Aurelio found him. "There you are—the hero of the evening," he exclaimed as he approached. "May God bless you as the Doge has done!"

"Amen to that," echoed Rosamonda Zucchar as she came to her husband's side. "Your recognition is richly deserved, Aurelio."

Aurelio could feel himself reddening again, and so he looked around for Fenice: as one of her acknowledged suitors he knew he could attach himself to her for the evening; she would fend off well-wishers for him. "I knew you would like to see this," he said a bit breathlessly as he came up to her.

"Oh, yes," said Fenice, smiling at him to put him at ease. "You have done so much for the Arsenal; it is fitting that the Doge should honor you." Two of the brooches joining his right sleeve to the giaquetta were not fastened and she set about putting him to rights. "There," she said when she was finished. "You look . . . tidier."

"Thank you," he said in real gratitude. "Arrigo has been making remarks about that since the first guests arrived."

"Well, if he remarked on it, he might have done something to fix it," said Fenice, reminding herself of why she did not like Aurelio's older brother. "He might have closed the brooches as readily as I did."

"Not Arrigo," said Aurelio darkly.

"No," Fenice agreed after a moment. "Probably not."

Aurelio looked around with his usual distracted air. "Would you like to walk out to the loggia?"

This abrupt invitation was so like Aurelio that Fenice thought nothing of it. "If you would like to, yes."

He offered his hand to her. "Come. I . . . I need a little time to . . . to gather my thoughts."

Fenice laid her hand on his, suppressing the urge to smile at him; she felt an urge to protect him come over her, and wondered if that was what her mother meant when she spoke of love. Fenice remained unconvinced. "You are well-attended tonight," she observed, and when she received no reply, she was not surprised. She permitted Aurelio to lead her haphazardly through the guests to the loggia at the Grand Canal.

The wind was cold, coming with winter's icy teeth to grapple with the city in the lagoon. Standing near the boat landing, both Fenice and Aurelio shivered. Finally he spoke. "I really don't like these grand events."

"They are . . . oppressive," said Fenice, trying to find the words that would best please Aurelio.

"Yes. They are." He turned to look at her. "You don't like them, do you?"

Fenice heard the eagerness in his question, and answered him as kindly as she could. "Well, they can be trying, but I enjoy fine celebrations if there are not too many of them."

"Oh," he said, looking downcast.

"This is one of those I do enjoy," Fenice went on, hoping to take the sting out of her candor, "in large part because it honors you."

"Oh," he said, more brightly.

"If any other man had received a chain from the Doge tonight, he would be in the middle of the throng, boasting and preening. You are not like the rest, Aurelio," Fenice told him. She glanced at him speculatively. He was so willing to try to please her, and he was obviously fond of her; she wished she could be satisfied with his good heart even though her own was not engaged. Why could she not be content with his devotion? Why did she have to crave adventure and the sights of distant lands? Why was his earnest kindness not enough?

"Does that matter?" he inquired, doing his best not to sound anxious.

She answered truthfully. "Not to me."

"But you must," Artemesia said as she faced Fenice in their mother's sitting room; twilight came early now, so that lamps and candles were lit as Vespers began in Sant' Angelo; it was a week since the festivities at the Pirenetto house, and Aurelio had called at the Zucchars' every day since. He had left less than an hour ago and now the women of the household were closeted together. "I do not want to wait until I am as old as you are to marry."

"Then don't," Fenice responded with a smile and a bow, as if Artemesia were her guest, not her sister. "You can marry before I do. I don't mind." She swung around to her mother. "Madre Mia, truly. It is fine for Artemesia to marry now."

Rosamonda had been playing songs on the virginals, but stopped, her face revealing only mild irritation. "Fenice, you are being deliberately provoking. We have been over this countless times. You know that it would be improper for Artemesia to marry before you do. And do not," she warned, her tone becoming sharper, "remind me that Bianca is not yet wed; she will enter her Order in the summer, so her single state has no bearing on the rest of you."

"*Mama!*" Artemesia protested. "Tell her she must marry. Aurelio or Rocco would welcome her decision. I am tired of asking Umberto to delay."

"Artemesia," said Rosamonda, "you are behaving as if you were still in the nursery. You must learn to moderate your manner." She then turned to regard Fenice. "Not that Artemesia is being unreasonable."

"I told you," Artemesia said, preening. While Fenice was with Aurelio, she had spent an hour that afternoon with Umberto Dandin and was still flushed with pleasure. Although she was not as pretty as Fenice, or as Eloisa promised to be, she had a neatness about her that gave her an attractive air. She dressed with restrained taste, knowing that she would appear better in contrast to simplicity than to opulence, which she left to Fenice and her mother.

"It would be very strange for Artemesia to be allowed to marry before Fenice, and well you know it. It is not as if either of your suitors, Fenice, are merchants gone to sea and not to return for months," said Rosamonda, as if speaking to young children. "It would lead to suspicions you would not like. There would be talk, and the rumors would damage your happiness, Artemesia, for it would be supposed that you had . . . had not been chaste when you married, and that haste was required to preserve your reputation."

"But I could say I am the one who is reluctant to wed," Fenice offered. "It is nothing more than the truth."

"No woman of sixteen is reluctant to marry unless she has a religious vocation," Rosamonda said with authority. "And it is known you have no such vocation, Fenice. Therefore you would do your sister a disservice if you were to speak so."

"But Madre Mia," Fenice began only to be interrupted.

"Your father and I will discuss it. Whatever he decides will be final." She folded her arms and stared at her puzzling daughter.

"I wish you could understand," Fenice said quietly as she went to the window and looked out into the darkness. "I wish I could make you understand."

"And so do I," Rosamonda said, surprising both Fenice and Artemesia. "For then I would know how to help you give up these mad dreams of yours. *Che pazzia.*"

She sighed. "They aren't mad, not to me."

Rosamonda sighed. "No. That is what troubles me." She began to play again, and after a short while, Fenice came back to her mother's side.

A week before the Nativity, Fenice accompanied Ercole to the Basilica di San Marco for Confession and a Mass celebrated for Lionello and Febo. She needed to ask Heaven for Febo's swift return, for she was sure no other member of her family would support her continued refusal to choose between Rocco degli Urbanesei and Aurelio Pirenetto, and she could feel her conviction eroding under the constant demands of her family.

Passing through the tremendous doors of the domed basilica, she noticed the four bronze horses high above her in their niches. She tugged at Ercole's sleeve and whispered to him, "Even those statues have traveled more than I have."

Ercole patted her hand. "They are spoils of war. Would you want to be carried off by force? I doubt it."

Fenice had to shake her head, but thought it was unfair of Ercole to discourage her so. She had only intended to remind him that travel was an essential part of Venice. She kept back her annoyance with her brother; she did not want him changing his mind about escorting her through the city.

Crossing herself and kneeling to the altar before she went to the confessional, she had to admit she did not want to be kidnaped—that was not adventure. She made her way to the confessional, paying little attention to the massive mosaics around and above her: she had seen them so often that they were now almost invisible to her. Entering the confessional, she crushed her voluminous skirts before she recited the ritual phrase, *Forgive me, Father, for I have sinned,* and began to enumerate her lapses from grace; she said little about her obstinacy regarding marriage: try as she would, she could not think of it as sinful to reject what she knew must make her unhappy.

"Is there nothing else, my daughter?" the priest asked. "Have you revealed everything?"

"I have often prayed we will have no more explosions; is that wrong?" She had the satisfaction of knowing all Venetians worried about the gunpowder depots even though they had been moved to distant islands, away from the city itself.

"There is no harm in such prayers, my child," the priest assured her. "Is that the whole of it?"

"Well," she said tentatively, "sometimes I dream about fighting Turks."

"All good Christians have such dreams. Why do you assume you should confess it? It is a virtue to defend the True Church and our Catholic faith."

Fenice considered her answer carefully. "It troubles my family that I want to do such a thing. They fear I am . . . that I am making myself less a woman through my aspirations."

"If you defend the Church, you have not erred," said the priest soothingly. "It is the grace given to women to become eunuchs in the eyes of God for such aspirations."

It was on the tip of Fenice's tongue to deny that she had any religious vocation, to try to explain that it was not love of God that fired her imagination, but the hunger for travel and excitement; Bianca would be the nun, not she. But she realized the priest had said *eunuch*, not *nun*, and she held her breath as she considered the possibilities in his choice of words. "Thank you, Father," she whispered in contained excitement. She hardly heard the penance he assigned her, and she left the confessional with unseemly haste, as if she had been released from captivity.

Ercole was startled at her appearance as she joined him at the chapel where the Mass was being celebrated for their brothers. "What is it?" he inquired in an undervoice, noticing the brightness of her eyes and the flush in her cheeks.

Fenice shook her head as she knelt beside him. She could tell no one about the idea she was nurturing deep within her; only Febo would know of it, if he returned before she had to act. For now, she enjoyed her delicious secret, hugging herself with delight as the Mass continued.

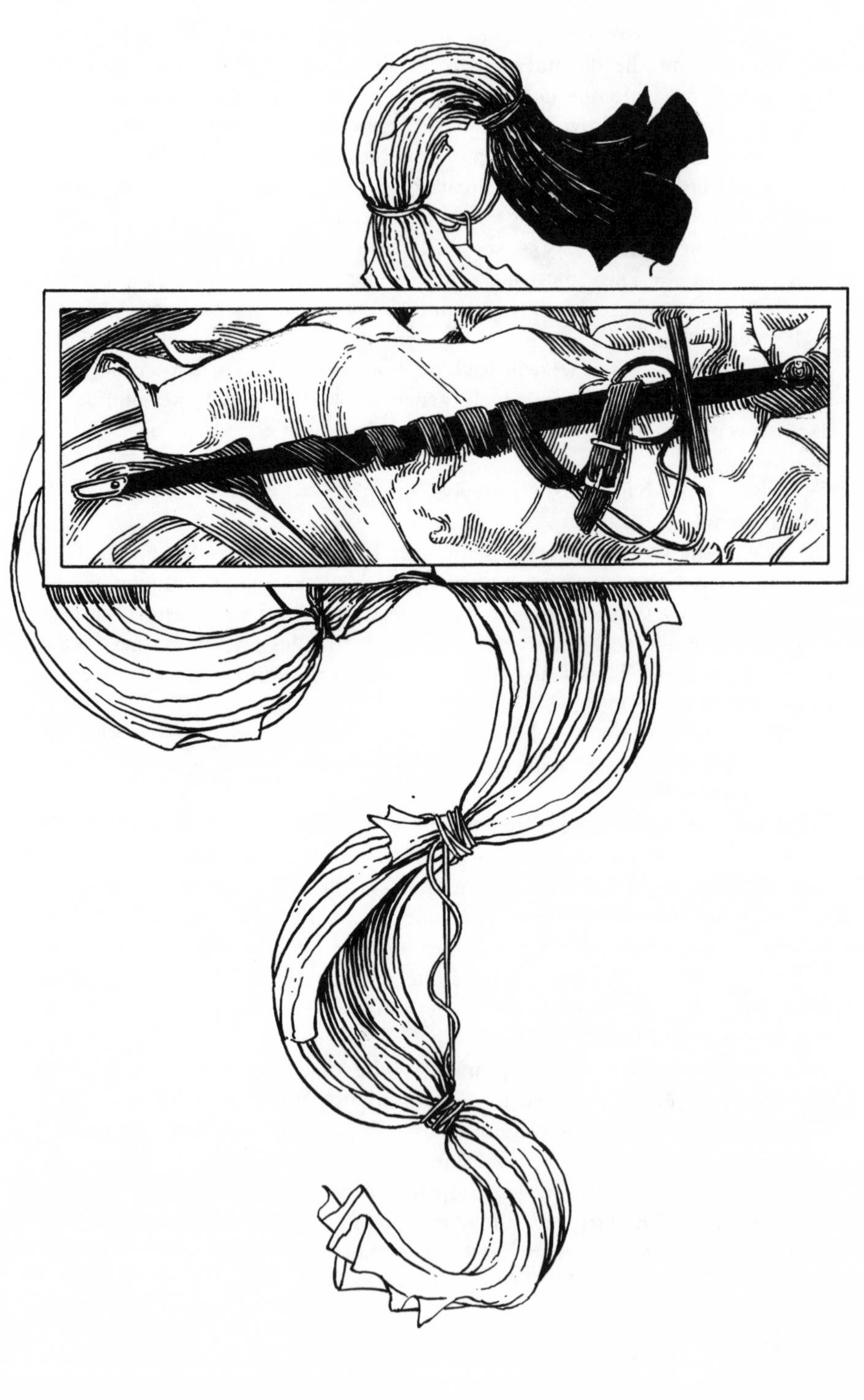

If any woman were so craven
As to falter in fear . . .
—Lorenzo de' Medici

— III —

"More gifts?" asked Eloisa as she saw Fenice come into the withdrawing room where the women sat in the afternoons. "You are being very generous this year. I can hardly wait for Epiphany." It was a dank winter day with a steady mizzle falling as the light waned; lamps and candles held the gloom at bay, and a good-sized fire glowed in the hearth to stave off the persistent chill.

Fenice cast off her hooded cloak and held her parcels as if to protect them from her sisters: Bianca and Artemesia turned toward her, their needlework abandoned for the moment. "I cannot show you. Not yet." Some of the items they would never see, she reminded herself, and it would be unwise to let them be discovered. "They're surprises."

"You are caught up in the season," said Artemesia, her observation not completely approving.

"Yes," Fenice said with a smile as she carefully set the parcels beside her cloak. "This is likely to be the last Nativity I spend within this family, and I believe I should make the most of it."

Artemesia shrieked and ran to hug Fenice. "Is it? You've chosen? Do you mean it? Truly?"

Fenice disengaged herself from Artemesia's embrace. "No, I haven't chosen yet," she said, trying to soften the blow as best she could. "But I know I must do so, and soon. Our parents have been lenient, but they will not remain so." That afternoon, Rocco degli Urbanesei had come to call upon her and to remind her that he was a very patient man; she had been able to banter with him for a while, but had excused herself, claiming the press of holiday duties.

"But before the next year ends, you will—?" Artemesia persisted, her face bright with hope.

"Before the next year ends, it will be settled, I promise you; my choice will have been made," she said, provoking another squeal of delight from Artemesia. "You and your Umberto can marry come Advent next year. Will that suffice?"

"Do you mean it? You aren't just playing with me?" Artemesia asked, holding herself in check while she waited for Fenice to answer.

"No, I am not playing. My situation will have to be settled soon; I know it. And you will be free to marry." Fenice saw her mother's dawning look of relief as Artemesia flung herself into Fenice's arms.

"Oh, you are the *best* of all sisters!" she cried, laughing and weeping at once. "How good of you! Madre Mia, did you hear?"

The smile on Rosamonda's face banished any trace of rancor in her remark. "I should think they heard you in Udine," she said, and rose from her chair to come and embrace her two daughters. "This will make your father very happy. He has been truly worried that you would try to hold out for another year. Which of the men is to be your husband?" The question came too quickly.

Fenice took a step back. "I have given myself until spring to make up my mind," she said, knowing she would have to put her plan into effect by then or lose the chance entirely. "It will be either Rocco or Aurelio."

"We know that," said Eloisa with the bored attitude of a youngster emerging from childhood. "But which one?"

"When I have determined that, I will tell you," said Fenice, her mind filled with possibilities that had nothing to do with either man.

"You might find a new suitor between now and then," said Artemesia, pulling away from Fenice. "Then you will wait another year and I will have to wait, too." She flounced over to the one settee in the room and sank down on it with a gesture of despair. "You want another suitor, that's it, isn't it?"

"No, not really," said Fenice, confused by this unexpected accusation. "I am not going to tell you that Rocco and Aurelio are the men I would choose for myself if it were for me to choose. But as I do not know any other man I like better—"

Rosamonda looked troubled now. "You are not saying that you do not want to marry either man?"

"No . . . no," said Fenice. "It is not so simple as that. I know how much Artemesia longs for her Umberto; I wish I could feel that way about . . . oh, anyone. But as I do not, I must make the best choice I can, and hope I am wise." She went to the settee and put her hand on Artemesia's shoulder. "I will not make you postpone your happiness beyond a year. You may tell Umberto and our father I have said so."

Unable to conceal her doubts completely, Artemesia glanced up at Fenice. "You will not change your mind? In a month you will not say you need another year?"

"Not even if I find a splendid suitor; if I do he will have to woo quickly," she answered with a faint smile. "By the time the *Signor Tiziano* is ready to go back to sea, I will have made up my mind." This mention of Ercole's ship gained the attention of Rosamonda again.

"You will have to be married while Ercole is away. This will not trouble you?" She did not give Fenice time to answer. "I know. You want Febo to be in port when you marry. He has always been special to you."

"Yes; that's it," said Fenice, hoping her lie was not apparent. "I want Febo to be with me when I marry."

"The *Bonaventura* is supposed to return in May," said Artemesia. "You could be married by July." She leaped up from the settee and went to hug her mother. "And I will be married by Advent next year! You're right!"

"If Umberto agrees," said Eloisa, not willing to join her sister in a display of enthusiasm.

"What do you know of it, brat?" Artemesia challenged her younger sister with a flounce of her skirts. "You are not old enough to understand what we speak of."

"Yes I am," said Eloisa stubbornly. "You want him to show he can wait for you as long as he has to. It's just the same as Seraphina Trevisan. She thought Pietro de' Noventi would accept anything she demanded of him, and so he married Drusilla Lando, after waiting two years for Seraphina."

"Eloisa!" Rosamonda said, her expression severe.

"You're just saying that to . . . to upset me. Umberto is nothing like that," said Artemesia, her cheeks flaming.

"No, of course he is not," said Rosamonda, determined to keep the joy of her daughter unhampered. "Eloisa, curb your tongue."

"He is nothing like Pietro de' Noventi," Artemesia insisted, tears mounting in her eyes. "He knows what his word must stand for. Pietro never did."

"No, Umberto is not like Pietro, you need have no fear on that account," said Fenice, laughing at the suggestion that the punctilious Umberto might have anything in common with the rascally Pietro. "Artemesia, I only hope your Umberto will not become stodgy before you have your first child. He is the most correct suitor I have ever seen."

Torn between her wish to uphold her suitor's honor and her hope that Umberto might be more spontaneous, Artemesia could only frown. "I have found the man whose life is blameless and who is loyal. If that makes him stodgy, I will not complain," she said staunchly.

Eloisa, satisfied that she had been able to make her opinion felt, giggled and bolted for the door. "I'll get two sets of new clothes for the weddings, won't I? Then I'll have suitors, too," she called from the corridor beyond.

With the youngest sister gone, Fenice became more serious; she took Artemesia's hands, saying, "I hope you will have a long and happy life with Umberto. You do not know how much I envy you, finding a man whom you can choose without doubts."

At this, Rosamonda said, "Doubts. What woman does not have doubts when preparing to marry? I have often thought that women have more reason to select their spouses with care than men do. Men may always take a mistress if they are displeased with their wives. But women must remain faithful or lose all. I can understand why such a man as Umberto is has claimed your heart, Artemesia. And I find I can share Fenice's doubts about her suitors." This revelation startled both her daughters.

"Madre Mia," Fenice said, feeling a touch of chagrin at the deceit she was practicing. "I had not supposed anyone knew—"

"If I had to choose between them, I might find Aurelio the more promising," said Rosamonda with a bluntness that astonished Fenice. "He is lost in his thoughts most of the time, and he will never remember when to come to dinner, but he will not stray in his affections, nor think of what he might have with another." She pursed her lips. "Rocco is not as . . . as sensible."

Fenice laughed at Rosamonda's choice of words. "Sensible. That is one way to see it."

Artemesia stifled a chuckle. "Rocco is richer, and more gallant."

"For now," said Rosamonda. "Rocco has expensive taste. Aurelio will be given more honors by the Armory and the Doge, and money will follow his honors. In ten years, their situations might well be reversed. And Aurelio's family is well disposed to him, unlike Rocco's; his mother sees him only four times in a year and only because she must. If he has earned the enmity of his mother, what does this tell us about him?"

"It may tell us nothing more damning than that his mother is a bitter old woman, shunning all her family—which she does, and everyone knows it—because her husband never returned from his voyage to Antioch, where he kept a second family," said Fenice, repeating the rumor that had been circulating among the merchant families for years.

"Yes," said Rosamonda. "We all know this; but what if we are wrong?" Now that she had broached the matter, she said, "I have never been completely easy in my mind about those rumors." She took a deep breath. "And since you have not lost your heart to either man, you may wish to arrange to call upon Tomasina degli Urbanesei, to discover if there is anything that you might need to know in order to make a proper assessment of her son's character."

Fenice cocked her head, and studied Rosamonda's face. "You have had this on your mind for some time, haven't you?"

"Yes." Rosamonda went back toward the virginals. "I know your father is not much concerned about these matters, but I have felt qualms for . . . several months." She sat down and began to play. "I will, naturally, accompany you on such a mission. It would not be suitable for you to go alone."

"And you can explain it to Padre Mio if we discover anything to Rocco's discredit." Fenice was able to smile. "I have always thought you were more clever than Padre Mio, and so you are, Madre Mia."

"Clever is as clever does," said Rosamonda, smiling in spite of her best intentions. "Suppose we arrange to make the call part of our Nativity visits? It is appropriate to include a suitor's family."

Artemesia, who had been listening with a degree of shock, said, "I would like to be included. Truly. I would."

Rosamonda shook her head. "You know that would not be acceptable, figlia mia. You have no connection to Rocco but that he courts your sister."

"But—" Artemesia began only to be cut off.

"Content yourself with planning your own nuptials, and leave this to Fenice and me." The admonition was kind but firm; Fenice and Artemesia knew it was useless to try to change their mother's mind. She continued to pick out a dance tune on the black-and-white keys, adding, "I will send a servant with a note in the morning. Now go ready yourselves for supper."

"Yes, Madre Mia," said Fenice, gathering up the parcels she had brought with her into the withdrawing room, wrapping them in her cloak. As she started to the door, she added, "You are very good to me, Madre Mia."

"It is easy to be good to good daughters," said Rosamonda, settling the matter with a wave of her hand; she watched Fenice and Artemesia leave, then gave her attention to her playing.

The swordsmith looked speculatively at Fenice as she swung the stiletto in an experimental arc; on this cold, blustery day many people thronged the markets of Venice, making the last of their Nativity purchases, for the reverential devotions would begin in two days, and then the markets would be closed except for those on the Giudecca, where all non-Catholic Venetians lived. "It's a true blade," he said in defense of his work. "That short sword, the one with the feather quillons, that is also a fine weapon."

"My brothers captain ships," Fenice said, as if to account for her interest in these weapons.

"The *Signor Tiziano*, the *Bonaventura*, the *Stella d'Aurora*, and the new one, the *Impresa*, those are the Zucchar ships; they are modified round ships with a bank of oars and a narrowed hull, for speed and maneuverability as well as hold room for cargo. They have plied all the Galleys but the Galley of Flanders. The Galleys of Alexandria, Northeast Africa, Beirut, and Romania are their sea lanes. All Venice knows them." The swordsmith achieved what was supposed to be a benevolent smile, but with his hard-featured visage was more of a sneer.

"Yes," said Fenice, not quite pleased by this recitation. She glanced at the servant who accompanied her. "I like the stiletto, and I think I should purchase that short dagger as well." Both weapons were more easily concealed than the short sword.

"The sheaths are an additional price, and blades of this quality are not cheap, and I do not haggle," the swordsmith warned before he told her the full price.

It was more than Fenice had wanted to pay, but she made herself nod in acceptance. "I have it," she assured him as she opened her purse and brought out the four gold and three silver coins the swordsmith required.

As he made parcels for her to carry, he said, "That's two of your brothers accounted for; what for the third?"

Fenice frowned at the man's familiarity with the family business, but reminded herself that Venice was known for its close-knit society, and so replied, "Febo will not return until May. He will have gifts aplenty then."

"Of course," said the swordsmith, and handed her the parcels which she gave to her servant to carry. "God and the Angels bring you a prosperous year."

"And you," said Fenice as she made her way toward other stalls and shop-fronts along the narrow way going past Santa Maria del Giglio to the bridge leading to the newly built Palazzo Pisani and on to San Stefano; as she neared the campo between Santa Maria del Giglio and San Samuele, Fenice stopped as if she had just remembered something. Signaling to her servant, she said, "Enrico, I may have left the necklace for Artemesia at the goldsmith's shop. I know it is an imposition, but would you go and see? It is not among my parcels, for it is wrapped in blue cloth." She knew that she was asking the man to leave her on her own—a serious lapse—but she smiled broadly and hoped this would make him disregard the impropriety of her request.

"It isn't fitting, Dona Fenice."

"I will stay here. There are stalls I can visit, just along toward San Samuele." She smiled more broadly. "If you would rather, I will go into the church . . ." The suggestion trailed off. "I paid well for that necklace. I would not like it to be lost."

This last consideration finally persuaded Enrico. "Very well. But stay at the stalls or go into the church. If you are not in either place when I return, your father will beat the both of us and we will deserve it."

"You are very good to me, Enrico," she said, and watched as he hastened to retrace his steps to the goldsmith's shop in the shadow of the Doges' Palace. As soon as he was over the bridge to Santa Maria del Giglio, she set about her private tasks as quickly as she could: there were half a dozen stalls and shops selling simple clothes, made for sailors and servants, and she hastened there to select two suits of clothes, remarking that her younger brother would have need of them—in case any of the vendors recognized her as the sword-smith had done. Before Enrico had returned, she had acquired long hose, upper hose, and two simple giaquettas and a pair of rope-soled shoes, all of which she put into one large sack; then she purchased two silken shawls to put atop them so that Enrico would not see all she had bought.

"Here," said Enrico, showing her the parcel she had deliberately left behind. "You did leave it." He glanced about swiftly.

"No, Enrico," she said with exaggerated patience. "I have not met either of my suitors, or any other lover while I waited for you. I have spent my time"—she lifted her sack—"doing the last of my shopping. Now I have only two more items and I will be finished."

"Where do you go for the final gifts?" he inquired as he took her sack from her.

"There is a wonderful shop in the Merceria, near San Luca. We can leave these packages at our house before going there; it is only a few steps out of the way." She favored him with another smile. "And then you may rest from your labors."

"They are your labors, Dona Fenice," he pointed out, but added, "It would be sensible not to carry so many things. Thieves watch for laden servants."

"So they do," Fenice agreed, secretly wishing she could fend off an attack. "But we have a dagger and a stiletto," she reminded him.

"Do not jest about such things," he said, following her toward the bridge of San Stefano.

"I am not jesting," she said, but so quietly that he did not hear her.

Three days later Fenice joined her mother in a gondola bound for San Giacomo del' Orio, where Tomasina degli Urbanesei lived with her simple-minded nephew in the family's oldest house. It was raining but the wind had not come up, so the short journey was pleasant except for a single instant when they passed a funeral barge bound for San Pietro di Castello.

"We should pray for the repose of that soul," said Rosamonda as the procession behind the barge went by them in silence.

"I will," said Fenice, fighting a sudden impulse to follow the barge as if she herself had died.

They ordered the gondoliere to wait for them, and paid him enough to ensure he would. As they climbed the stairs to the campo, Rosamonda repeated her instructions one last time. "Be sure you say nothing about the rumors. You do not want to make her think you have listened to any lies. She is said to be religious, so maintain your dignity. And let me set the tone. You are such an impulsive creature, Fenice, that I despair of you."

"I know how to behave, Madre Mia," Fenice said, wishing the day were over and this visit behind her.

"Yes, yes. But that doesn't mean you will behave." She cast a knowing glance at her daughter. "We will have to learn all that we can but without prying. Let me deal with her."

"I've already said I would," said Fenice as they approached the gloomy front of the old house.

"Be patient," said her mother as she reached the door and reached for the bellpull that would summon the servants. She rang once, decisively. "Don't ask too many questions."

"I won't," Fenice promised. She drew the hood of her cloak more closely around her face. "There," she said. "Is this demure enough?"

Rosamonda was about to say something when the door opened and a manservant of middle years opened the door. Recovering herself, Rosamonda said, "I am Rosamonda Zucchar, here with my daughter Fenice to call upon Tomasina degli Urbanesei. We are expected."

"Come in," the manservant told them, holding the door and standing aside to admit them to the dimly lit vestibule of the house.

The rooms beyond were as ill-lit as the entrance. After surrendering their cloaks to the manservant, Rosamonda and Fenice prepared to accompany him to whatever reception area might be the one chosen for this meeting. The long corridor toward the withdrawing rooms toward the rear of the house was lined with old portraits of degli Urbanesei of generations past, interspersed with tall mirrors dark and cracked with age. The manservant finally indicated a room, saying, "Dona Tomasina degli Urbanesei," before he turned away.

"God keep you in His favor," said the woman who had risen from the chair near the window; she was dressed in the elegance of a generation ago, in a gonella designed for a fuller figure than she now had. Her neat gray hair was braided in an elaborate coronet and covered with a silver filigree chaplet more suited to someone Fenice's age. Although she stood very straight, her hands were gnarled, and when she gestured to the chairs for her guests, the fingers were crabbed half-shut. "I am pleased to meet you, Rosamonda Zucchar, and your daughter, in this most blessed season. My son has told me a great deal about you."

"I am sorry we have not called sooner," said Rosamonda as she chose the taller of the two guest chairs.

"Nonsense. You were very correctly waiting for me to send an invitation. I can only tell you that my health has been such that I do not usually entertain. I am relieved that God has permitted me some respite in the troubles this body has suffered, so that I might honor the Nativity as a good Catholic should." She sat down so that Rosamonda and Fenice would not have to remain standing for her. "Does this mean your daughter has decided to accept Rocco's offer?"

It was an effort for Fenice not to answer the question herself; she bit down on the insides of her cheeks to keep from speaking.

"Alas, no," said Rosamonda with a heavy sigh. She cocked her head. "It is my hope that meeting you might help my child to know her heart."

"Heart!" said Tomasina with a snort of contempt. "In my day, girls left such decisions to the wisdom of their parents. I am old-fashioned in saying so, I am sure, but I cannot believe that any child can know what is best for her more than her parents do. I was pleased to abide by my father's choice, as I am certain you were, Dona Rosamonda, and never had cause to complain of what my lot was in life. But there! I am not as certain as many are that the heart is any wiser than the love of parents." She looked from Rosamonda to Fenice. "You are a very pretty young woman."

"You are kind to say so," Fenice responded. She had the strange impression that Tomasina was evaluating her as she might reckon the worth of a piece of art.

"You should age well, which is all to the good." Tomasina directed her attention to Rosamonda again. "There are so many beauties who are faded before they are twenty, don't you think? You are fortunate to have a daughter who is not likely to become aged too quickly." She gave a wintery smile to Rosamonda. "Not that the world should value beauty, but men are the slaves of their eyes, and we forget that at our peril." She touched the edge of her chaplet with her knotted fingers. "My son is very much of that character, as you must have seen. Anything lovely holds his attention, but he cannot endure ugliness."

Rosamonda strove to find some remark to make that would not offend their hostess. "Your son has always shown himself to be a great admirer of beauty."

"And therefore he is devoted to your daughter, though he tells me her youngest sister may yet outstrip this girl in beauty." She leaned back in her chair. "I do not require him to wait upon me as so many mothers do. I have means of my own and need not hang on his sleeve for my food and shelter."

"You have lived retired from the world for . . . many years," said Rosamonda, glancing at Fenice, worried that her daughter might say something out of hand.

"The world lost its attractions for me many years ago," she concurred. "But as I have no vocation, I elected to remain with my own; I am not suited to the rigors of the convent, not with such disease as makes my life hard." Her smile came and went again. "I may be indolent in my habits, but it is forced upon me; my son understands that I have no wish to partake of the gaieties of life as he does and therefore makes no complaint at my choice of habitation."

"Commendable, I am sure," said Rosamonda, not meaning it. "You must be grateful to him, Dona Tomasina."

"I do not wish to compel him to devote his time to me. He has far better things to do than care for an old woman. And here at least I can provide a home for Fortunato; his affliction makes it impossible to permit him to be without some supervision, which it is my honor to provide. Others may account for my decision as they wish; I know that charity is a most laudable virtue and one I aspire to attain. Providing a home for one of childlike mind can only be seen as charity." This casual reference to the simple-minded cousin whose presence always embarrassed Rocco made Rosamonda cough with alarm; Fenice glanced toward her mother.

"Are you well, Madre Mia?" she asked, and saw Tomasina nod her approval.

"Very prettily said. You are an ornament to your family. I can understand why my son is so captivated with you." It was meant as approval but it set Fenice's teeth on edge. "You are not so self-sure as many girls are these days."

"You are . . . kind to say so," Fenice said, knowing some response was expected.

"And when you marry my son, I give my word I will not interfere in anything you do. I will remain in this house, never fear, and I will not require you to be in attendance any oftener than custom recommends. I will be glad to see my grandchildren when my health permits, but I will not be able to come to your aid. For that, you will have to depend upon your mother, who must surely be the wiser guide." Tomasina inclined her head to Fenice. "You will not want to disdain any advice I may tender from time to time, I know, but I will be sparing of it."

Fenice was ready to say something outrageous, but she could not bring herself to embarrass her mother, so she murmured thanks and tried to find something in the room to hold her attention. If she had to listen to much more of Dona Tomasina, she realized she would be goaded into speaking unwisely. There was a map of the Greek islands in a gold-trimmed frame on the far wall; she rose, saying, "I hope you will not mind, but I have been tutored in geography. I would like to—" She went to the map without waiting for permission.

"Oh, yes; you are one of the educated girls. My son has mentioned it. In my time, few girls were taught anything but prayers and sewing, and I am not sure we were not the better for it. To fill a girl's head with useless knowledge would seem to be planting seeds for the Devil to sprout. But there is a fashion for learning, and I know few would agree with me in these times." She made a gesture to show she was not concerned with such matters. "I never impose my will on others."

"How wise of you," said Rosamonda. "No doubt Rocco approves."

"He knows that the thoughts of women are light and of little consequence for anything but jewels and children," said his mother fondly; she turned toward Fenice. "You need not fear he will busy himself with your life. As a husband he will not impose upon you in any way but what a husband may rightly do."

Fenice, who was tracing the route of the Galley of Romania, from Corfu into the Black Sea and on to Tana and Trebizond, was flustered at being addressed. "You must know him better than I," she said, so she would not have to admit she had been only half listening.

"You comport yourself with humility," Tomasina approved. "That will stand you in good stead over the years. It would not suit Rocco to have a proud wife who cannot bend herself to his will. I know that children make demands on their mothers that are the true glory of womanhood, but it is never prudent for a wife to put herself ahead of her husband in anything but their children."

Rosamonda almost bristled. "My daughters know their duty, Dona Tomasina, and need no instruction from anyone."

"No doubt," said Tomasina. "But it is well for girls to know that the world can be more stringent than their family. You have a gently raised child in Fenice, and it is good to remind such girls that the strictures of the world will be with them all their lives long, well beyond the time their parents guide them." She looked at Rosamonda with a critical eye. "You do not disagree with me, I think."

"No," said Rosamonda grudgingly.

Fenice returned to her study of the map and let her attention drift along the ports whose names she had memorized before she was six. Reciting them as she traced the coast, she let her mother deal with Dona Tomasina. "Paxos, Strophandes, Cythrera, Paros, Naxos, Chios, Lemnos, the Dardanelles, Chalcedon, Constantinople, Varna, Kaffa—" Her whispered recitation was interrupted by a question from Rocco's mother. "You must pardon me, I was . . ." She indicated the map.

"Why would you want to study it?" demanded Tomasina, disapproval in every line of her posture.

"Well, my brothers trade on the Galleys of Alexandria and Romania," she said, tailoring her answer to the company. "I have often heard them recount stories of their voyages, and I—"

"She has been an apt pupil of geography," said Rosamonda in defense of her wayward daughter. "Indeed, my husband says she has a fine grasp of the lay of the world."

"High praise, if true," said Tomasina, and then added without other remarks. "I must ask you to excuse me; my hands are troubling me and it is my habit to rub them with wool-fat and oil of camphor." She rose to her feet. "I am grateful you called upon me. I look forward to seeing you once again when our families are joined." With that, she walked unsteadily from the room, leaving her callers alone in the dreary room to wait for the manservant to return.

When they were once again outside the house, their cloaks wrapped about them, Rosamonda said to her daughter. "I begin to understand Rocco better than I did."

"And I," said Fenice with feeling. Holding her mother's arm she went to the edge of the canal to get into the gondola; she remained thoughtfully silent for most of the ride back to the Campo Sant' Angelo. As they turned from the Grand Canal into the Rio Sant' Angelo, she said, "I would rather die than become what she is."

"You could not," said Rosamonda with strong feeling. "And I thank God for it. For all your tempestuousness, I would rather you were ten times the minx you are than have you become . . ." She did not finish; the gondola pulled to the steps and the two women got out, paid the gondoliere and made the rest of their way home.

Fenice pulled her treasures out of the bottom of her chest where they lay hidden under clothes and Epiphany gifts. She had almost enough to try her plan: she still had to acquire a leather wallet and a short cloak, and she would be ready to attempt her escape. Taking care to pack her supplies safely once again, she prepared to go down to receive Rocco for an afternoon visit, the first he had made since Fenice and Rosamonda called on his mother. Fenice was dreading the encounter and hoped she would be able to speak with Rocco without recalling his mother's unwelcome approval. She paused before the mirror to adjust the chaplet on her hair and to twitch her elaborate skirts into a more becoming drape over her hip-roll.

Rocco was dressed in splendid brocades with puffed-and-slashed sleeves lined in shiny sand-colored satin to set off the deep green of the brocade. His ruff was small, of Belgian point-lace, and his long hose were green-black worked in a pattern of leaves. He bowed to Fenice as she came up to him; she could smell the sandalwood perfume in his hair from ten paces away. "I hope I find you well, carina," he said as he led her to the afternoon sitting room which had been left conveniently empty today.

"I am well," said Fenice. "And you?" She had the uncomfortable sensation of talking to a stranger, though she had known Rocco degli Urbanesei for more than ten years.

"Only the maladies of the season—a rushed life and too much rich food." He chuckled fulsomely, escorting her to the upholstered bench in the alcove at the window. "I trust you have not been exhausting yourself these last weeks." He leaned toward her, his lips pursed.

"No, Rocco, I have not," she said, realizing he was very much like his mother, a recognition that did nothing to improve her frame of mind.

"I have often thought that fatigue is as much the enemy of beauty as age is." He remained standing beside her, as if to demonstrate a proprietary relationship. "It is fitting that I should venture some observations on such matters, so you will know my fascination is not fleeting or based on frivolity. I know the loveliness I so admire now will not remain with you forever, much as we may desire it. Your vivacity and your warmth of character should sustain you through your middle years, and I pray that age will touch you lightly."

"How . . . kind," said Fenice, thinking that she would have preferred another word. How could she ever have considered this man a suitor? she asked herself, and answered her inner question with the recollection that he had been a guest in their house since she was six and his attentions had become something of a habit over time. Everyone—including Fenice herself—had taken his gallantry as a matter of course. How could she have thought she could endure him, even for a week, let alone a lifetime?

"A man must consider these things or he will lose his respect for his wife, and for no greater fault than obeying the strictures of nature. I will not prove as fickle as the years will be, you may rest assured, for I understand that time takes its toll of us all, and I, unlike so many others, am prepared to make allowances and not rail against the years." He gave her his best tolerant smile. "We have seen this happen more often than anyone would wish, for men do not often stop to think about what time will bring, that the freshness and beauty we so adore will not last forever." He touched her cheek lightly with one finger. "I am captivated by what I see, but I accept you will not always be thus."

"That's true," said Fenice without inflection.

"I have been most relieved to see your mother, who has remained handsome. I have noticed how often one may see the future of the daughter in the mother." He regarded her in silence for a short while, then said, "My mother tells me that you are too learned to suit her, but that she can comprehend the reason for my attachment."

"How generous," said Fenice, unable to think of anything that could adequately express her indignation.

"Yes, she is," said Rocco, unaware of her sarcasm. "I was relieved that she was willing to receive you. She does not go into the world, as you know, and she is not often willing to let the world come to her. It is her affection for me that moved her to accept your visit."

Listening to Rocco blather on, Fenice realized that her plan was essential, and that as soon as she could, she must act.

At the Bascino di San Marco four ships were being loaded, their holds gaping open like the mouths of baby birds. Bales, barrels, and crates of merchandise were lifted from the quays into the holds, as the ships made ready to set out on the morning tide. The crewmen sang as they worked, and while the music was far from beautiful, Fenice heard it as the song of the sirens, seductive and infinitely promising; the lure of adventure took urgent hold of her imagination. She made herself stay awake to hear the sailors, trying to believe that she was one of them, that she, too, was making ready to go out on the broad sea toward the distant lands her brothers spoke of. Her soul quivered like the sails of the ships, yearning to fly beyond Venezia.

Drifting off to sleep, Fenice envisioned the spires and minarets and cupolas of the ports of call, and she swore to herself that somehow, someday, she would see them for herself. Nothing would stop her. It was a promise she made often but with increasing fervor. "I will go there. Not husband, not family, not anything will stop me. On my life, I will go there." These words served as litany and lullaby as sleep claimed her, carrying her off into the distant realms of her dreams.

As white flowers spring up in the meadow
So fairest hope is reborn in my heart . . .
—Lodovico Ariosto

— IV —

It was the dark of the year, the longest night before the promise of God's Son would light the earth again. The Zucchar family had dined simply at noon and were now preparing to go to hear evening Mass at Sant' Angelo in preparation for the holy observations of the Eve of Christ's Birth. Shortly before they were to walk across the campo to the church, word came from the shipbuilding Arsenal requiring Ercole's presence. With many excuses, he departed, leaving Gaetano to await his return while the rest of the household went to the church.

Twilight, thick and nebulous at once, held Venice in its embrace, obscuring the buildings on the other side of the canal and promising a night of danger to anyone on the water; Gaetano and Ercole, newly returned from his inspection of their new ship *Impresa*, were involved in reassessing their plans for the next year.

"We can have the *Impresa* at sea in two months," Ercole repeated. "A new ship, bigger than the others, and better designed. If we do not hurry the repairs on my ship, then I could captain the *Impresa* instead." His face lit with excitement. "I could follow the Galley of Romania, where I have prospered so well before. The Zucchar ships are known in those ports and when a fine, new one arrives, it will announce to all the world that Zucchar prospers. The *Impresa* will attract notice wherever we sail. In a superior ship, our profits must increase, and the *Signor Tiziano* may be saved for shorter voyages: the Galley of Alexandria, for example. Your brother's son Maurizio is ready for something more than escorting barges—you have said so yourself; why not let him have the *Signor Tiziano* for the Dalmatian coast and the Greek islands?"

"You want the *Impresa*, Ercole," said his father with a touch of amusement. "You would not care if Maurizio had commanded at Lepanto if you did not want our new ship."

"I cannot deny it," said Ercole. "Think. I could depart before Lent. We would have the advantage of being underway before most of the rest of the merchants on those Galleys, who will wait until Easter before setting out." He paced his father's study, his gestures abrupt with impatience. "I cannot promise finding another such prize as pepper, but there is red amber to be had in Varna, brought from the Carpathians. That is not often seen in the markets here. If I am there first this year, we will not have to contend with any of our rivals."

"And you will have the chance to show the world how Zucchar is prospering," said Gaetano. "I felt the same way when I was going to sea. In time I realized that I found more joy here in Venice than I did in those foreign ports." He sighed and leaned back. "But as you have not yet discovered this for yourself, I can think of no reason to deny this thing you want so much." He saw victory in Ercole's face.

"Oh, Padre Mio, do you mean it?" Ercole asked, hardly daring to believe what he heard.

"Yes, yes, I mean it. What good would it do to put you back on the *Signor Tiziano* if your heart is bent on the *Impresa?*" He shrugged. "And Febo will not be back for a few more months, so he will not be here in time to take command of her. Lionello has not had enough experience to handle such a ship. In any case, you are the oldest and so the choice should be yours."

"I hope you are not saying this in jest," Ercole said, unwilling to believe his good fortune.

"Why would I jest with you about something you want so ardently?" Gaetano asked his son. "You will have to ready your crew and find four or five new sailors; the courts will provide the men for the oars." He rose and clapped his son on the shoulder. "We will show them that reducing the cargo capacity but increasing speed is no detriment to trade."

"And if we must outrun any other ship, we shall," said Ercole. "The Doge may have driven the Turks back, but not all of them will stay away from merchant ships simply because their navy lost a battle." He grinned. "And we have shown that oars speed the passage through the Dardanelles and across the Black Sea. With the *Impresa* we shall demonstrate our point beyond all question." He grinned as he stood. "Padre Mio, I am the happiest of men."

"Well, well," said Gaetano, pleased in spite of himself. "Then you will want to inspect the progress on her after the Nativity, I suppose."

"And every day thereafter," said Ercole, doing his best to keep his excitement in rein. "When will you tell the rest of the family?"

"Tomorrow after morning prayers, I should think," Gaetano said. He cocked his head toward the shuttered window as a reminder of the hour and the devotions for the rest of the evening. "This will set the tone for the Feast of the Mass of Christ."

"For me, most certainly," said Ercole. He touched cheeks with his father, declaring, "I will make you proud of what you have done for me."

"You have already, Ercole," Gaetano told him.

"But you will be gone before Lionello or Febo returns," said Fenice the next morning when Ercole's glad announcement was made. "The *Impresa* will be ready to put to sea by Carnival."

"And we will come to put flowers aboard her," Eloisa exclaimed, glancing once at Bianca, who sat with her head bowed. "You can pray for the ship, if you'd rather," she said audaciously.

"Eloisa, for the sake of your Saint," Rosamonda chided her. "Bianca's prayers are always welcome."

Bianca, who was spending most of the Nativity celebration in church, merely smiled, keeping her head turned so that her birthmark could not easily be seen. "Each has a part to play."

"And the prayers of a holy nun are pleasing to God," said Artemesia in her oldest sister's defense. "I know the *Impresa* will sail more safely with your prayers to protect her, Bianca."

"So she will," said Rosamonda.

Fenice went up to Ercole. "Will you let us come aboard her before she puts to sea? I would love to see her. I have been on the *Bonaventura* once, when it was being unloaded."

"Febo should not have done that," said Rosamonda, then realized how downcast Fenice looked. "But I suppose we might all go aboard her. Husband? What do you say?"

Gaetano did not need long to decide. "I think your notion has much to recommend it," he said, smiling at his daughters. "Not long before she is launched, Ercole will show you the ship."

"That should convince you, Fenice, that your dreams of adventure are more dreams than reality," said Bianca, wanting to make sure her sisters remembered who was the most senior among them.

"You forget I have already seen the *Bonaventura*," Fenice reminded her. "If that ship could not change my mind, why should this one?"

Hoping to forestall an argument among his daughters, Gaetano said, "In any case, you will all see the ship and you will better understand what it is your brothers do on the sea lanes." He smiled at Ercole. "You are a man of good heart, my son, and you have done much to make all of us proud of you. It will be a pleasure to see your fine new ship."

This assertion quieted the budding conflict; Artemesia and Bianca withdrew to a corner of the room to whisper, and Eloisa hurried away to attend to various errands before she went with her mother to begin planning her clothes for the evening.

Only Fenice lingered with her oldest brother. "I can find it in my heart to wish I were you," she confessed. "You have such a wonderful ship, and you will be going to such fascinating places."

"You have heard tales of them before. They are not going to change." He studied her face, trying to see what thoughts had possessed her.

"Varna, Tana, Trebizond. What wonderful places those must be." She stared into the distance as if the walls of their house had vanished and in their place were the Black Sea ports.

"They can be, but they are also filled with Islamites, and they can be harsh for those who have no means to survive. The markets are fine, but only if you have something of value to trade. Otherwise you would do well to stay away from those cities." His eyes showed real concern. "You think you can simply enter one of those ports and your fortune is made, don't you? And Febo has probably encouraged you to think so." He folded his arms in a show of authority. "He has done you a disservice, Fenice. There are taxes to pay and officials to bribe before you can haggle for a single piece of cargo. I have seen men from Genoa trying to purchase dyes in Tyre who were taken in charge by the Sultan's Guards, for it is not legal for the merchants of Tyre to sell dyes to Christians. You would find similar strictures in other ports, and you would be treated with the same severity the Genovese were—you would be branded on the forehead and never allowed to land in that place again. You may think that you would not be singled out because you are a woman, but the Islamites keep their women as confined as prisoners; if you sailed on a ship, you would not be allowed to come ashore unless you were completely covered but for your eyes. Foreign women are all thought to be whores because they show their faces."

Fenice did her best to look calm. "I would not be foolish enough to draw attention to my being a woman. Don't you think Febo told me these things?" He had made light of them, as if they were nothing more than an inconvenience; Fenice thought she had been wise to plan as she had done.

"I think Febo told you that you would be able to disguise yourself in some way and go about unhindered." His statement was so near the truth that Fenice could not conceal her shock.

She did her best to account for her expression in some other way. "Hardly," she said, feeling herself blush. "He told me that the women of the Islamites might as well go about in tents and that any woman showing her face risks rape." That was the truth, and she knew Ercole would recognize it as such.

"Well, at least he had sense enough to tell you that," said Ercole grudgingly.

"And I listened to him, you may be sure of it." That was why she had been purchasing boy's clothes and sailor's shoes for the last month.

"You relieve me," said Ercole, which he would not have done had he known her thoughts. "I have believed that you had no regard for your own safety, and that you have let your dreams run away with you. That would be a pity. Discontent with real things is hard enough to bear: when dreams are the issue, discontent can be tragic." He bent down and kissed her forehead. "You are a good girl, for all that you are lively. You will do nothing to bring disgrace on your family."

"Not disgrace, no," she said, convinced that her plans would never reflect badly on her family.

"Just as well you remember this, sorella mia." He shook his finger at her, feeling very old as he did. "Do not allow yourself to be seduced by your own desires."

"How could that be?" Fenice asked, certain that she would never allow anything like that to happen to her.

"You do not want me to begin to enumerate them," said Ercole, abandoning his position of elder advisor.

She decided to take advantage of the moment, saying, "I think Rocco degli Urbanesei may be prey to his own desires. Don't you?"

"He is a man of . . . acquisitive tastes," said Ercole very carefully. "That does not mean that his desires seduce him."

"Do you think not?" she asked gently. "You are a man, and you may comprehend these things better than I do. It seems to me that the only reason he has chosen me to pursue above my sisters is that he thinks I am the most . . . ornamental of us all, and he wants to have the pleasuring of displaying me among his other treasures."

"Surely he cannot be—" He broke off. "He is proud of what he has bought, that is true enough. But Zucchar has no need for his ducats and all the world knows it." He patted her shoulder. "You will know how to choose, Fenice, when you must."

"I pray you are right," she said.

On the day after the Nativity, while the household prepared boxes of donations to be given to the poor of the city, Fenice was able to secure a second pair of long hose from among those items of clothing Febo had outgrown years before. It made her feel more confident to have something of his among the things she had claimed for herself, to know that in some way he would be part of her adventure. She dutifully put two more sottanas in her donation box to make up for her theft before she carried the box down to join the others from the household.

Bianca had brought hers down first. It contained almost every festive garment she had worn during the past two years; she would have no finery in her convent, and donating the clothing showed her readiness to renounce the world. She stayed long enough to greet her sisters and then went off to her apartment for her extended morning prayers.

"You are not keeping that lace ruff?" Eloisa asked as she poked through Fenice's box.

"No, I don't think so," she said, taking the item from the box and holding it up for her youngest sister to see. "You would not like it. It is sadly worn along the bands. Someone can take it off and use it on a cap or a veil." She had liked that ruff, but knew she would have no use of it in the next several months and would just as soon be rid of it.

"You are being generous with the poor," said Artemesia, but whether in praise or not was not apparent.

"Not that I can tell," said Fenice, her head coming up sharply. "I have things I have not worn in more than a year. Surely it is good practice to give such things to those who have need of them, when I do not."

Eloisa sighed. "It's such a pretty bit of lace. It seems sad to give it away."

"If you like it so well, keep it for yourself," Fenice recommended, doing her best not to let her temper flare. "It is all one to me."

"I don't like it that well," said Eloisa, putting the ruff back in the box. "I like the way the lace is made, is all."

"So do I," Fenice admitted, thinking that when she set out she would have to give up all these pretty things; it would be hard to do, but it would be harder still to be without adventure in her life. She had toyed with the idea of setting aside one of her simpler dresses to take with her, but had decided against it, thinking it would be unwise to bring such clothing into Islamite countries. Reluctantly she had decided it would be best to take only boy's clothes. By the time Febo returned, she would be ready, and he would help her achieve her dream.

"You seem preoccupied, Fenice," Rosamonda remarked as she noted the distant look in Fenice's eyes.

Fenice shook her head. "I was trying to recall what we are doing this evening."

"There is that masque tonight at the Gritti house," said Rosamonda as she brought her box of donations further into the entryway where the rest were waiting. "I have yet to decide what to wear, and going through my things was no help at all."

"You have that ropa with the high rolls at the top of the sleeves," said Artemesia. "You haven't worn that since Easter."

"No, I haven't," said Rosamonda, "which is why it is in my donation box. I am tired to death of it—the color is insipid. I have not thought it becoming since I wore it for the grand festival of San Giovanni. I will make up my mind before we leave, but—" She broke off. "What are you going to wear, Fenice?"

She had given the matter little thought. "Oh, the sottana with the pattern of birds in sea-blue. I don't know what I'll put over it: probably something darker. That is the fashion."

"Not the deep red, I pray you," Rosamonda exclaimed.

"Of course not," said Fenice, who knew better than to make such a combination of colors. "Either the deep brown with the gold thread or the bottle-green with the double sleeves. It is too soon to wear the bronze again, much as I like it. And the deep red, as you said, will not do. The deep brown brings out my hair and makes my eyes look very dark." She smiled at her mother. "Which would you prefer?"

"Good Heaven, you are giving me a choice?" marveled Rosamonda. "You haven't done that in more than two years." She glanced at Fenice as if doubting her offer. "Well," she said at last, "since you allow me to choose, I would recommend the dark brown. You are right that it shows your hair to advantage. And be sure your chaplet is the gold one."

"Certainly," said Fenice, glad she was doing something her mother would remember with kindness when she learned of Fenice's exploits. She thought of the plans to have her married by summer; she could surely be back by then, and she would accept what her parents wanted for her without feeling she had been thwarted. They would be upset with her—she expected that, but they would not disown her. At least she hoped they would not.

"Oh, and wear the gold drops in your ears, the ones with the amber. They will make the whole," Rosamonda advised.

"That was my plan," said Fenice, once again pleased to be able to do something that would make her mother happy with her. "At what time should I be ready?"

"We should begin to dress at midafternoon," Rosamonda announced to all her daughters. "And when you resume work with your tutor, Fenice," she added, "you will have to spend an extra hour on Greek. Your father wants you to be more proficient."

"Very well," she said, thinking she would not have many Greek lessons before she would have to speak the language in earnest; the prospect of more tutoring was not unwelcome.

"Then I will meet you all later in the day. There will be cheese, bread, and broiled scallops served at noon. We will eat lavishly tonight and you will not want to be full." With that, she left her donation box and turned away from her daughters, leaving them to plan for the masque.

"I wish we could go in real disguises," said Fenice as she anticipated the evening's entertainment.

"You mean as we do at Carnival?" asked Eloisa, her face brightening.

"No—not costumes, disguises," Fenice said. "So we could be mistaken for someone we are not." She sighed, thinking she wanted to give her disguise a trial before it was put to the test; that would be impossible and she accepted it, but it was tempting.

"Why would we want to do that?" Artemesia inquired as if she found the notion distasteful.

Fenice could not give them her real reason, and so she improvised. "Oh, you could find out things. You could find out if Umberto is really devoted to you, or if he might like another lady better. You could pretend to be older and more worldly, or foreign—"

"Why?" Artemesia looked shocked. "That is very close to lying."

"It isn't," Fenice insisted. "Because the deception would be . . . understood." She felt confusion come over her and she turned away, her face rosy.

"An understood deception," said Eloisa with an impish smile. "Yes. I can see it could be amusing." Her smile vanished. "It could also be embarrassing."

"Only if it weren't understood," Fenice insisted but without conviction.

Artemesia made a gesture of aggravation and Eloisa shook her head, observing, "You want to find out if Rocco degli Urbanesei is more interested in finding a beauty than in courting you. That is why you would like him to think you are someone else?"

Fenice was able to smile. "Yes. I cannot believe that Rocco is as committed to me as he claims. A disguise would reveal his sentiments. It would be useless with Aurelio," she added. "For you know Aurelio would never notice a disguise." Her laughter was forced, but her sisters joined it readily enough, and the awkward moment passed.

* * *

Two days before Epiphany, Gaetano called Fenice to his study in the middle of the afternoon. "I must have a word with you, figlia mia."

Fenice recognized his tone of voice and steeled herself for what was to come. "Yes, Padre Mio?" she asked, her hands folded in front of her. She knew it was best to appear meek when Gaetano spoke in that tone of voice.

Gaetano frowned at the top of his desk. "I have spoken with Niccolo Dandin, and he is urging the wedding of his son and Artemesia for midsummer. He has very good reasons to do this, and I cannot refuse his request without creating bad feelings between us, which it is not prudent to do." He coughed to show he was upset with what he was saying. "You know we have many dealings with Dandin. He came to talk to me not out of caprice but for the benefit of his son and your sister."

"What are you trying to say to me, Padre Mio?" Fenice came a step nearer the desk; she felt as if she were made of wood.

"I am trying to tell you that while I realize I said I would not require an answer from you in regard to your choice of husbands at once, I must now make plans to have your wedding before Lent. A fine wedding at the beginning of Carnival would be the most fortuitous—" He broke off as he looked at Fenice. "What is the matter?"

"So soon? Before Febo returns?" The words came out unevenly and she felt slightly dizzy, as if she were standing on the edge of a precipice

"It would be best," said Gaetano, then tried his best to bolster his daughter's state of mind. "Come, now, Fenice. You must have been thinking about this. You knew you would have to make up your mind soon, and this only serves to resolve your doubts more quickly."

"How can you . . . You said I . . . Padre Mio . . ." To her intense chagrin she burst into tears.

Gaetano got up and came around the desk to embrace Fenice. "Hush, hush," he said as he patted her shoulder. "You must not weep, figlia mia. You must not. You will break my heart."

"But . . ." She sniffed, trying to stem the flow of tears. "I thought . . . I would have . . . the spring to decide."

"Fenice, don't," he pleaded.

"I thought . . . I would have . . . more time." She pulled one arm free and wiped her tears away. "How can you?"

"Niccolo Dandin has a partnership he is offering us on a voyage on the Galley of Flanders. That would open those markets to us with less than half the risk we would have to take otherwise. His *Luna d'Autunn* is to depart in July, and by then the *Impresa* will be back and can set out with Dandin's ship for Antwerp, Bruges, and London. Think what this will mean: there will be Zucchar ships on every Galley of Venice." He gave her a gentle shake. "Is it so terrible, to ask you to marry a few months sooner than you would have done?"

She wanted to scream *yes*, to rail at him for what he was doing. All she said was, "I suppose not," in a subdued voice.

"Well, then," he said heartily. "You have a few more days before I will need an answer from you." He released her and stepped back. "You will not have to do anything until . . . shall we say the beginning of February?"

Fenice nodded numbly. She wanted to run to her room and sob; she made herself ask, "Padre Mio, when does Ercole sail?"

"Do not worry. He will not leave until just before Carnival." Gaetano made an impatient gesture directed at himself. "I had promised you and your sisters could see the *Impresa* before she sails, didn't I?"

"Yes," said Fenice, and realized this was now more important than ever. "If I cannot go with my brothers, I want to see their ships."

Relieved that he could offer her something in exchange for her agreement to marry before he had said she would have to, Gaetano said, "Then three days after Epiphany we will go to see the *Impresa*. I will have Ercole come with us and show you over the whole ship. Will that make you a little less downcast?"

"I do want to see it," said Fenice, knowing she had to be careful or she would reveal far too much. "And I know Ercole would like to show her off."

"That he would. He is as proud as the father of twins. I would have felt the same way, if I had been given such a ship at his age." Gaetano's last words were wistful.

"Do you miss the sea, Padre Mio?" Fenice asked, for once feeling an intense sympathy with her father.

"Sometimes," he confessed. "When I see the ships standing out from the Bacino di San Marco, I remember how it felt, how proud it made me to command my own vessel and see Venice at my back, the most beautiful city in the world. And I miss that first glimpse of San Giorgio Maggiore on the return. But I do *not* miss battling corsairs, or trying to run before storms with a following sea about to swamp the ship, or fever among the crew, or foreign tax collectors claiming half my profits, or rotted food, or the rats—" He stopped abruptly. "You do not think of these things when you wish to go along with your brothers. You think only of the mystery of foreign cities and the lure of . . . Well, figlia mia, for every hour you spend in port, there are four or five days on the sea. And those days are either boring or terrifying." He decided he had told her too much; he sat down again and pretended to read an account sheet.

"Padre Mio," said Fenice very quietly, "I am not afraid of the sea."

He looked squarely at her. "Then you are a fool. No sailor, no matter how much he may love the sea, is not afraid of her. The sea is enormous and indifferent, Fenice."

Taken aback, Fenice lowered her eyes so he would not see the excitement that lurked in their depths "Yes, Padre Mio," she said.

He continued his mendacious perusal of the sheet. "Do not make me regret that I have not demanded a decision from you before now," he said. "I have given you more license than most fathers would; do not force me to impose my will on you out of hand."

"I will try not to, Padre Mio," she assured him.

"Consider your suitors carefully. Each has much to recommend him. Rocco is the better established, but Aurelio may have the brighter future."

"I will keep these things in mind," Fenice said. She backed toward the door, as if leaving the presence of the Doge himself.

"You will want to talk to your mother. She can advise you on . . . womanly things." His large face went scarlet. "I will wait for your answer."

"So!" Rosamonda cried when Fenice came to her room that evening, "Have you made up your mind?"

"I am trying, Madre Mia. Truly I am. I am weighing the possibilities. But I will need a little more time." She did not say what she would need the time for, knowing it would serve only to ruin her plans.

"I know you wanted Febo to attend your wedding, but he will understand," Rosamonda said by way of comforting her daughter. "Your father is very pleased that you were willing to agree. When I was a girl, a daughter as reluctant as you have been would have been—"

"—beaten," Fenice finished for her. "Yes, I know. You have told me, and so has Ercole. I know my father is being lenient, and I am grateful . . ." Her words trailed off.

"But you still do not want to marry," said Rosamonda, bewildered by her child. "What do you think marriage will do?" Before Fenice could answer, she held up her hand. "No. Do not tell me. I would probably only find it distressing. You have tried before, and I could not grasp it." She sighed. "There are those who would say you are not a dutiful child, putting yourself against the hopes of your family. But I do not think this of you."

Fenice did her best to smile her appreciation. "*Grazie*, Madre Mia."

"I am only sorry that you have taken marriage in such . . . aversion. I confess I am puzzled how you came to. . . . You are a sensible girl, in general. Your mind is as keen as a boy's. You do not deplore your place in the world but for this one consideration." Rosamonda indicated the upholstered bench next to her chair. "I have wondered of late whether you are uneasy as to a woman's duties in marriage."

Fenice smiled. "I know all about that, how men have to do with women. I know about their parts, and how they fit with women's." She saw the confusion in Rosamonda's face.

"How on earth . . . ?" Rosamonda began.

"Your sister, Cassandra, told me these things. I must have been ten." She was able to chuckle. "I noticed she was increasing, and I asked her how it happened."

"That was most improper of her," said Rosamonda, doing her best to look stern. "There is no reason that a girl should know such things until she is betrothed. Still, as you do know, I have little more to tell you. But I will say one thing." She leaned forward, lowering her voice as if she was afraid they might be overheard. "You will have to consider who you would like to . . .

do . . . with more: Aurelio or Rocco. Whichever man you decide upon will have the right to your body. I was fortunate in your father, for he has always treated me with respect and affection. You will want those things for yourself."

"And you think one man will be more likely to give it to me than the other?" Fenice asked, her interest feigned but expected of her.

"I think each of your suitors has his merits. Rocco is the more . . . practiced, I would suppose, but he may be more . . . demanding. Aurelio would be very . . . grateful. At least that is how they seem to me." She said this last more briskly. "You will have to make up your own mind on that point. No one else can do it. Your husband will be the father of your children. You will have to think of them, as well."

"My husband?" Fenice asked, having difficulty following what she was being told.

"No, your children," said Rosamonda, her cheeks coloring. "As a mother, you will have the well-being of your children uppermost in your mind."

"Oh." Fenice had not let herself think about this, for it was surely the end of all hope of adventure. She shied away from asking anything more.

But Rosamonda had not finished. "Women find their glory in motherhood. This is known everywhere in the world. Even the Islamites know it. It is the purpose for which God has intended us from the first day in Eden. Men may conquer the world, but they cannot pass it on to their sons without a woman to give them. It is our strength, the children we have." She shook her head once. "I do not despise daughters as some mothers do, for a world of sons only would quickly come to an end. Daughters are to be valued, too."

"I have always thought you valued yours, Madre Mia," said Fenice sincerely.

"That is because you are a good girl at heart, figlia mia." Rosamonda reached out and patted Fenice's hand. "You have too much good sense to . . ." She did not go on.

"To do what?" Fenice asked, afraid that Rosamonda had sensed something in her that gave her away.

"Oh, anything your husband would not like," said Rosamonda in some confusion. "You are a reasonable child, and although your imagination is lively, you have never forgotten what is due your family. I don't think you ever could." There was a hint of a question in her statement, as if she needed to be reassured.

"No, Madre Mia, I cannot forget my family. I wouldn't want to." She kissed her mother's hand. "Nor would I want the family to forget me."

. . . Lovers, stop and hear me;
How truly cursed I am . . .
—Agnolo Poliziano

— V —

Half a dozen sailors were loitering about the dock where the *Impresa* was tied up; they were looking her over, comparing opinions on her design. As Ercole arrived in a gondola with his sisters, he told the sailors to leave. He did not want Fenice, Artemesia, and Eloisa to hear any of the rough language that was typical of sailors, and he had no wish to have his judgment questioned by men who had been to sea and had seen innovative designs come to grief before.

The day was cold and windy with high, thready clouds overhead and whitecaps in the lagoon, promising heavy weather. Even tied to the dock, the *Impresa* bounced with the waves, making Artemesia cling to the hempen railing of the gangplank, swearing she was going to be sick.

"Craven!" Fenice called to her merrily as she made her way onto the deck without mishap; she grinned back at her sisters. "It's easy."

"So you say," Artemesia shouted to her. "If it is this bad at the dock, how can you stand it at sea?"

Ercole could not help but share Fenice's poor estimation of Artemesia's response, but he only encouraged her to stand upright and climb the last few steps. "It is easier on the deck," he said.

Eloisa brought up the rear, and she was managing rather well, treating the outing like some kind of game. "Does it always pitch this way?" she asked as she came onto the deck.

"Not always," said Ercole, and pointed to the stern of the ship where the deck rose another level. "My cabin is back there. The afterdeck is where the helmsman steers." He indicated the open hatch. "The oarsmen sit on the level immediately below us. There are twenty oars, ten on a side, six in the front and four in the rear. That's many fewer than the war galleys, but it makes us faster than the round ships most merchants sail." He pointed up at the masts where the huge lateen sails would hang. "In two weeks we will have our sails finished, and then this ship will be something to see."

"Will you bring us back?" Fenice asked, shading her eyes as she peered up into the hazy glare of the morning. "When she is all finished?"

"You want another tour?" Ercole wanted to chide her but could not bring himself to utter any condemnation. "Be content with this, sorella mia. It is more than most girls ever see." He motioned them toward the door leading to his cabin. "Follow me. I'll show you where I will live while we sail."

From his quarters he took them belowdecks to where the sailors had their bunks, and then to the after-hold where the convict slaves who manned the oars would live while not sitting at their posts. "You see where the hold is, beneath? And how there is a kind of tunnel leading from the deck to the cargo holds? This is to discourage theft and to make it easier to secure the cargo in bad weather. Come along, and I'll take you below, if you want to go."

"What is that?" Fenice asked, pointing to a small room between the crew's and the oarsmen's quarters.

"That is the dining hall, and that alcove beyond it the kitchen." Ercole pointed to the steep stairs between the kitchen and the dining hall leading to the deck. "That is for the cook, in case the kitchen catches fire. The cook can get out of the kitchen, and so can anyone eating, and water can be poured down the stairs. We pray nothing of the sort ever happens, but we are prepared if it does."

"Have you ever been on a ship when there was such a fire?" Fenice asked, making an effort to keep the exhilaration out of her voice.

"Only once, thank God. I pray I will never see another such again. Nothing is more terrifying than a fire at sea." He crossed himself, then sought to reassure his sisters. "You need not worry about this ship. We have a good cook for this ship and that will make us safer. Good cooks do not make idiotic mistakes."

"What kind of mistakes are those?" Fenice asked, going into the dining hall, which was nothing more than a medium-sized room with a low ceiling, as far as she could reckon.

"Leaving embers in the stove. That may work well enough on land, but on a ship, which rocks on the sea, such neglect can lead to a blaze. Aboard ship, you only have a fire when it can be constantly tended." As Ercole explained, he knew that Fenice understood, and he thought again that she was wasted as a female. He could almost agree with Febo's indulgence of her; he was tempted to indulge her himself.

"That could be dangerous, I can see," she said.

"And the companionway can be used as another way into the hold, for it goes down below as well as up to the deck. If the loads we carry shift, then the sailors have an alternate way to reach the trouble, which speeds their tasks and reduces the chance of damaging either the hull or the cargo. That improvement was one of Aurelio's innovations," he added slyly.

"The Doge thinks well of his work, too," said Fenice, trying not to be smug on her suitor's behalf, and not quite succeeding.

"With excellent cause," said Ercole, and glanced at Fenice to see her reaction.

"As you have better reason to know than I," Fenice remarked. She started up the stairs to the deck when something occurred to her. "Is there more than one hold?"

"There are two ballast holds, fore and aft; they're quite small. Then there are three divisions of the main hold, and six smaller holds, designed to carry bales and barrels. Most of the cargo room is in the main hold, in the three divisions. That is so we may evenly distribute the weight of what we carry and if it shifts, it will not put us on our beam-ends."

"Does that mean over on your side?" Fenice asked; she had heard the expression many times and knew it boded ill for anyone aboard.

"That is what it means," Ercole confirmed. He decided he might be able to use this to discourage her infatuation with voyaging. "When that happens, you pray for a ship, even an enemy ship, to find you. Otherwise you will die of thirst or drown. Sometimes sailors deliberately drown themselves because dying of thirst is so hideous."

Fenice heard him out. "A ship like this will not go on her beam-ends, will she?"

"Not if she is properly loaded and the seas are not so high that she is—" He broke off, seeing the horror in Artemesia's face.

"It would be a paltry thing, to drown if it wasn't necessary," said Eloisa; she had gone to the edge of the deck and was standing on the devil-plank while holding onto the glossy wooden railing.

"I doubt the sailors who've done it saw it that way," said Fenice before Ercole could think of a response. "They had to be desperate, very desperate."

"That is true enough," said Ercole, aware that Artemesia was looking a bit sick. "I think it may be time that we leave the ship. The only thing you have not seen is the quarters for the oarsmen, and since they are convict slaves, there can be nothing you would want to see." He shot a quick look at Fenice, thinking she might protest; when she did not, he led them to the gangplank and down to the dock once again. "So. That is the *Impresa*. You should be proud of her, for she is going to increase our wealth beyond anything you can imagine."

"Our father must be delighted," said Artemesia, wanting to make up for her queasiness on board. "I hope she will sail the world over."

"I will be content if we can sail all the Galleys. I have no desire to cross the ocean to the New World, not when it is such a savage place as I have heard it is." He gave his sister an indulgent smile. "You may long for such places, but I do not."

Artemesia tossed her head. "Not I. Fenice is the one who wants to leave Venice. I can't think why she would want to, but she does."

Fenice studied Artemesia silently for a short while, then said, "I can't explain it if you do not understand."

"Then I will have to remain baffled," said Artemesia, walking somewhat ahead of Fenice and Ercole. She looked about her, then signaled to Eloisa to walk beside her so that no one would suppose she was on the street alone.

"I probably shouldn't ask you," Ercole began in a low voice to Fenice, "but have you made up your mind yet? About your suitors?"

"You're right; you shouldn't ask," Fenice snapped, then said, "Almost."

"Father will be eager for your answer," he said.

"He's given me a while longer to decide," Fenice reminded him. "When I know which man I will accept, I will tell our father, and our mother."

"Good," Ercole approved with a trace too much enthusiasm. "It will not be as bad as you fear, sorella mia. You will find out that marriage is very much an adventure in its own right."

"Which is why you are still single," said Fenice.

Ercole regarded her with renewed respect. "Yes. I recall how our mother would pine while our father was at sea, and all the fears that distressed her. I decided I would not ask my wife to endure all our mother endured. When I have sailed my last, then I will marry. And who knows?" he added playfully, "I may find my bride in a foreign land, and bring her back to Venice."

"Do you go to the women in those distant ports?" Fenice asked as artlessly as she could.

"What a thing to ask your brother!" he burst out. "You know I mustn't answer that."

"Well, I think you probably do," said Fenice with a pragmatic gesture at the sailors waiting at the docks. "There are women in Venice—I know we are not supposed to see them, but how can anyone avoid it—I also know that the reason we must always walk with others and have a man with us is that so we will not be mistaken for women of that sort—and I am certain that other harbors are not so unlike Venice as that." She saw she had upset him and did her best to nullify his dismay. "You said that sailors are men, and our mother tells me that men have . . . desires that can overtake them."

"Since Adam, if the priests are to be believed," Ercole said, and cleared his throat.

"Oh, don't lecture me," Fenice pleaded. "It has been such a fine day. I do not want you to make me forget how much I have learned, and how enjoyable this has been."

"All right, no lecture. But do not say anything about women of that sort where our parents can hear you, I beg you," he told her. "They would not be pleased."

"No, I know they would not," she admitted. "But that doesn't mean I am blind or stupid or so naive that I cannot see what men are."

Ercole continued to stare at her. "Did Febo tell you this?"

"No; he confirmed my guesses, and he wasn't nearly as priggish about it as you are, Ercole," she said, making a face at him. "You are almost like Artemesia's Umberto."

He held up his hands in surrender. "Anything but that, please." He lengthened his stride; she had to trot to keep up with him, for her skirts hampered her walking.

They were in the Piazzetta di San Marco when Ercole said suddenly, "I think you would make a good seafarer if you were a man."

This high praise stopped Fenice in her tracks; she turned and stared at Ercole, many emotions roiling within her. Finally she trusted herself to say, "Thank you, fratello mio. I am grateful to know that."

"I'm surprised Febo hasn't said the same thing," he added as they began to walk again, half a dozen paces behind Eloisa and Artemesia.

"Oh, he has," she said, "but it means something different, coming from you."

He gave her a half-bow and put the incident out of his mind.

The silence between Fenice and Aurelio lengthened; he stared out across the canal, his eyes unblinking. It was late afternoon on a clear, cold winter day, and the reflections in the water seemed preternaturally brilliant. Behind them the Zucchar house shone where the angled sun struck its windows; in contrast the shadows were stygian.

"Did you hear me?" Fenice asked him after she could not stand it any longer.

"I heard you," he said, and turned to her, his face flushed; he was as well-dressed as she had ever seen him, and had made a real effort at conversation when he and his family arrived. Now he was his usual awkward self, out of place in his puff-and-slashed-sleeved giaquetta of pearl-colored silk with silver-edged slashings. "I just didn't think you could possibly mean it." He fiddled with the lace at his sleeve; it was coming loose from his camisa and his tugging at it only made it worse.

"You mean you don't want to marry me?" she asked, incredulity making her voice rise.

"No, no, nothing like that," he said hastily, a nervous smile quirking at the corners of his mouth. "No. Of course not. But I thought you would choose Rocco instead of me." His lace was coming apart under his nervous fingers. "He's so rich, and so . . . fine."

"And no one thinks so more than he," said Fenice, laughing a little. "I would rather have someone who will not make me part of a collection to be admired for his satisfaction." She had also surmised that Aurelio would suffer less when she left on her travels, and would be far more likely than Rocco to welcome her upon her return. He might, she told herself, even understand why she found the strictures of Venetian society so stifling. She said nothing of these thoughts; Aurelio was oddly touching in his inept attempt at gallantry; he was bowing to her.

"I am very much honored." Aurelio tugged the lace off his cuff and threw it into the Rio Sant' Angelo, watching it float on the shiny water. "I don't know what else to say."

"Well," Fenice ventured, "you could kiss me. Since I have accepted you, it would be permissible." Her smile showed her dimples admirably, and well she knew it.

"As you say," he muttered, more confused than before.

"Don't you *want* to kiss me?" she asked provocatively.

"Yes," he admitted. "Naturally." He turned toward her stiffly, fumbled his hands around her waist and pulled her abruptly up against him. "Do you . . . is it all right?"

"It's fine," she said, and pressed her lips to his. She was somewhat disappointed when his mouth felt like other mouths; she had no overwhelming urge to cling to him, or to faint with joy, or to do any of the things she had been told lovers were driven to do. She took this as a sign that her decision to have her adventure was the right one for her. When she came back, she would be able to accept Aurelio's lack of fire without feeling she had compromised herself forever.

He broke their kiss first. Panting a little, he continued to hold her. "I . . . Never in all my life. I haven't . . ." Then he kissed her again, this time more successfully.

She realized that he might awaken something in her, after all, if he were given enough time and encouragement. She moved back, amazed that she could have that kind of response to Aurelio Pirenetto. But something had stirred within her, and it might become more than it was if she sought to make it more. "Aurelio," she said as she took a step back. "Perhaps we should speak to our fathers?"

"Oh. Yes. That would be . . ." His clumsiness overwhelmed him again; his torn cuff caught on the brooch holding her sleeve to the body of her simarra, and tore loose a section of damask fabric along with the pearl-and-garnet brooch. He cringed at the sound of ripping, and jerked his hand away, making the tear worse.

"Hold still," Fenice said, being as practical as she could. "It will take—"

But he wrenched his cuff free and pulled loose a length of her outer sleeve, exposing the sottana beneath in a way the dressmaker had never intended. His expression was stricken as he realized what he had done. "I'm sorry," he whispered.

"Oh, dear," said Fenice, and began to giggle. "Oh, dear. They will think we were fighting."

"Or worse," he whispered. "They might think I tried . . . to . . . to . . ."

"No," she said, her giggling increasing. The whole situation was so silly, she thought. But it was unkind to laugh at Aurelio; he was so abashed. She put her hand on his arm. "No one could think that of you, Aurelio. I give you my word." Again she was seized with giggles, which served only to cast doubt on what she had said.

"It's all very well for you," he said sulkily. "No one will cry shame."

"They will not do so for you, either," Fenice promised him, trying to look contrite; she pressed her lips tightly together and pursed her lips in an effort to keep from laughing.

He shot her an annoyed glance, saw her face, and began to chuckle. "You look ridiculous," he told her as his chuckles turned to laughter.

In a moment they were clinging to each other, not in passion but in mirth.

Their laughter rang over the fretwork shine of the canal and echoed on the fronts of San Stefano and the close-built houses.

"Stop!" Fenice protested, struggling to get a deep breath of air.

"I . . . can't," Aurelio answered, and succumbed to a new wave of hilarity. They had reached out to grab each other in an effort to maintain their stability there on the steps to the canal. He was holding onto her arms, trying to keep his balance and laugh all at once. He began to list toward the edge of the steps down to the Rio Sant' Angelo. His hands tightened on her, upsetting her precarious footing. They rocked back and forth, and then fell onto the steps, still laughing.

"Are you hurt?" Fenice asked when she had sat up. The palms of her hands were scraped and she felt breathless. The hem of her sottana was wet, and one of her felt shoes, but there was no harm done.

"No," he said, though there was a bump on his forehead. He chuckled, but this time it was an uneasy sound. "You're all right?"

"I'm fine," she said, thinking that she could not say the same for her simarra with its torn sleeve, and her sottana. She got up and held out her hand to him, which he took reluctantly. "We should go in," she said, looking at the smear of green on his pearl-colored silk. "But perhaps not through the front of the house."

He rubbed at the stain, spreading it. "Yes. I . . . don't want anyone to see. . . ."

"We can go through the servants' door, behind the kitchen," she assured him. "I will send for my . . . mother." She knew that either parent would have a thousand questions to ask, but she was sure that Rosamonda would be more compassionate than Gaetano. "Come on; I'll show you the way."

He staggered to his feet, one hand to the lump on his forehead. "How will we explain?"

"Leave that to me," she said. "Just come along," she said, ducking down the narrow alley that ran the length of the house to the bakehouse behind the kitchen. Her wet foot squished as she walked, and her damp hem slapped at her ankles. She told herself that this was only inconvenient, not as distressing as Aurelio thought it was.

The heat from the bakehouse reminded her that she was cold. Motioning Aurelio to follow, she went into the hall that led past the pantry to the kitchen. She did her best to ignore the stares of the cooks and their scullions. With her most nonchalant manner, she told the wine steward to please ask her mother to come to the kitchen, and waved Aurelio to one of the tall stools that stood, unused, next to the dough bowl. "There is nothing wrong, but, as you see, we have . . . had a mishap."

The wine steward, a white-haired man of forty who had served the Zucchar family since youth, regarded Fenice with suspicion. "What happened?"

Fenice had been thinking as she made her way here, and her answer was ready. "We were walking by the canal, paying no attention, and we tripped." She swallowed hard and added, "Aurelio Pirenetto hurt himself to keep us from falling in."

"Your sleeve is torn," he said critically.

"Aurelio grabbed hold of whatever he could; that he tore only my sleeve is fortunate. And, as you see, he has smirched his giaquetta and struck his head in the process." How he managed all those things, Fenice had not worked out; by the time her mother got to the kitchen, she would have.

Aurelio was holding his head and looking a bit more shaken than he had admitted to being. "I . . . wouldn't . . ."

"Signor Pirenetto needs a cloth for his head," said Fenice, and pointed to one of the scullions. "You. Get it."

The boy rushed off to do as Fenice commanded. The rest of the staff in the kitchen suddenly got back to work.

"I will summon Signora Zucchar," said the wine steward grandly, and went off at a dignified pace, unwilling to rush for anyone.

Now that she had set everything in motion, Fenice felt her knees weaken. She was convinced that she had done all she could to make the best of this situation, but now that she could do no more, a kind of emptiness took hold of her and she began to anticipate all sorts of difficulties. Would Rosamonda agree to help Aurelio? Would there be a way to make her decision known without bringing any immediate gossip on Aurelio? She was mildly surprised that she wanted to protect him—after all, she reasoned, she would not be in Venice much longer: why should she bother with his feelings, which would certainly be much more affronted by her departure than this aftermath of her supposed acceptance of his hand? The only thing that made any sense to her was that she hoped to spare him as much distress as possible.

"Here is the cloth," said the scullion, handing it to Fenice.

"Well, wrap it around his brow," Fenice recommended. "You can do it as well as I can." She folded her arms and sighed, thinking those few moments of laughter beside the Rio Sant' Angelo had almost been enough to persuade her to change her mind about her adventure.

"That's very good," said Aurelio, and handed the boy a scudo for his efforts; the lad took the coin, his eyes as large as his reward.

They were spared any effusive thanks; the wine steward returned with Rosamonda bustling behind him, her handsome face creased by a frown. She stopped beside the dough bowl and looked inquiringly at her daughter.

"I'm afraid I tripped," said Fenice without preamble. "I was not paying attention to where I was; Aurelio tried to keep me from falling. He grabbed my sleeve and—"

"I can see that," said Rosamonda. Her trouble gaze fell on Aurelio. "How did he hit his head?"

"He slipped on the moss; he fell and struck his head. But he thrust me away from him so I would not be knocked into the water." Given what everyone knew about Aurelio, her account was believable.

Rosamonda shook her head in an attempt to look severe and ended up smiling. "You have made up your mind, and you were too distracted." She turned to Aurelio, her expression concerned. "You were not hurt, were you?"

"I have a knot on my head. It's nothing. But look at my clothes—" He gestured to the green smear.

Rosamonda was solicitous; she went to him and scowled at the stain. "It isn't quite proper, but if you will take off the giaquetta, I will have my laundress do what she can to get it out. What possessed you to wear so light a color? Everything shows against pearl."

He accepted her scolding with good humor. "I wanted to look . . . splendid." His face was rosy as he admitted this. "When Fenice sent me word that she wanted time with me, I let myself hope it was for something other than consoling me." He glanced at Fenice. "Not that I really thought she would consent, but I wanted to be prepared for whatever she told me."

"And you were so surprised that this is the result," said Rosamonda, her smile taking any sting from her observation. She rounded on Fenice. "What can have possessed you to tell him anything of the sort near the canal? You must have known how he would react."

"I . . . I didn't think it would result in this," said Fenice, turning away from Aurelio so he could get out of his giaquetta.

"Almidoro," Rosamonda called out, summoning the understeward; now that she had made her remarks, she was all business. "Take Signor Pirenetto's giaquetta to Anamaria and tell her to do what she can to get rid of the stain. At once. And then fetch Ercole. He must have something Aurelio can wear while his giaquetta is being cleaned." She all but shoved Almidoro toward Aurelio. "Hurry, man; you have no reason to tarry."

Almidoro grabbed the giaquetta and made his way toward the servants' stairs at the rear of the house, muttering as he went about feckless youngsters.

"Now, then," said Rosamonda, regarding Fenice. "The sottana will dry, but that simarra—" She shook her head in condemnation. "Go up the backstairs and change. The dark red will do; you can change your shoes, too. The brocade ones will go well enough." She all but shooed her daughter out of the room so she could turn all her attention to Aurelio.

When Fenice came downstairs, she found Gaetano waiting for her at the foot of the stairs, his face one vast smile. "Your mother told me you have chosen at last. I will send word to Marin Pirenetto, so that we may set a day to celebrate your betrothal. And choose a day for the wedding." He took her hand and kissed it. "I knew you would not forget your duty to the family."

Aurelio had donned one of Ercole's giaquettas; it was over-large on him and the color was not entirely flattering, but he was as presentable as he usually was, so no one minded that he was in borrowed clothing.

There was an awkward moment a short while later when Rocco degli Urbanesei came up to Fenice and bowed to her. "I have been told that I must surrender you to another man. Your brother's servant told my man. . . ."

Fenice stiffened at his choice of words. "I hope I have not injured your feelings."

"I will recover," said Rocco philosophically. "And I will not give up all aspiration to be a part of this family. Your youngest sister has not yet reached an age for courtship, but no doubt she will not be adverse to receiving a family friend." He bowed again. "Permit me to tell you that she is likely to surpass you in loveliness."

"I shouldn't be surprised," said Fenice, amazed at what he said. "And she is fair, which I am not."

"We will not know that will be the case always until she is a little older," said Rocco, as if speculating on the possible value of an unpolished jewel. "And she will certainly have a more womanly shape."

At another time Fenice would have been offended by Rocco's remark, but she made allowances for him; she had disappointed him and he was entitled to a moment of spite. She nodded. "Very likely. Our mother has said she expects Eloisa to have an ample figure."

"Mothers always know these things," said Rocco. "My own mother said she did not think you would suit me as I . . . But I will not scold you. You have my wishes that you will never regret the course you have chosen."

"You are very . . . kind." The last word almost stuck in her teeth.

Rocco left her alone then, and a moment later Ercole came toward her, filled with good wishes and beaming his approval; Fenice fixed a smile on her mouth and prepared to endure the rest of the evening.

"So the wedding will be the first night of Carnival," exclaimed Marin Pirenetto. "That will make for a fine display."

Gaetano Zucchar was still reading over the wedding contract the two fathers had agreed upon; he wanted to be certain all the provisos were spelled out precisely as they had negotiated them. Finally he put the parchment down and grinned. "Our children have every reason to rejoice."

"And we along with them," said Marin. He had been looking over Gaetano's study with a knowing eye. "You have some fine volumes here."

"Thank you," said Gaetano, holding up the contract. "I will summon the notary for tomorrow night, if that is satisfactory."

"Oh, we will be here, Aurelio and I, make no doubt of it." He rocked back on his heels. "Not that I had any doubt of him, but he seems quite astonished that your daughter preferred him to degli Urbanesei. I was not as surprised as he. But then, that is Aurelio—he was ever a modest fellow, even as a boy. Arrigo was always the one who was determined to shine."

"Every family has such children," said Gaetano. "I know my daughter will be a happy woman with your son. He has a generosity of spirit that she will—"

"Oh, yes; your Fenice is a wild one, hankering to live like a boy," said Marin. "I think that is one of the reasons Aurelio was so intrigued by her: she is like the boy we hoped he would be."

"Instead he is someone whose designs will make the Venetian navy the most powerful force afloat." Gaetano could not share Marin's apparent indifference to his son.

"And I thank God for it, every morning," said Marin, belatedly showing pride in his second son. "Since he designed that round ship when he was eleven, I have known he would be more use ashore than at sea." He laughed.

"Leave the sea to Arrigo," Gaetano recommended. "And to Andrea, who should be getting his own ship one day soon."

"So he should. I am thinking about giving him a year on the *Cittadella* before putting him on his command. He has much to learn yet, and a year on the *Cittadella* would be good preparation for him. The Galley of Barbary should teach him much, too."

Gaetano's reminiscent smile was eloquent. "The men who know that Galley have stories unmatched by anyone else." He indicated the other chair. "Do you want to read this over?"

"No," said Marin Pirenetto, waving the proffered document away. "I have reviewed it twice; the words will not change on the page. I am content with the terms. Our children and their children can rest assured that they will not suffer from the demands of their siblings."

"All the provisions are fair," agreed Gaetano, and rolled up the parchment to put it in one of the pigeonholes of his desk. "And tomorrow evening we will have it signed, witnessed, and notarized so that we may present it to the priest when we arrange for the wedding."

"It's a shame that not one of your sons will be here," said Marin, as much for form's sake than out of any genuine concern.

"If Ercole is going to get the advantage of his ship, he will have to leave the day before Carnival. Otherwise his crew will refuse to leave until Carnival is over, and that would lose him precious time. I have said we will have one grand celebration before he goes so that he will not miss the whole celebration." Gaetano went and touched cheeks with Marin; their beards scraped together as they observed this courtesy. "Your family and mine must dine together very soon, to make our plans and to—"

"Yes, yes," said Marin impatiently. "Not that Aurelio will notice if we do nothing." He sighed once, as if his talented son perplexed him. "I assume your daughter knows that he will never be one to keep to social form."

"Yes, I am sure she does. She is not one to keep to social form, herself," Gaetano said.

"Then perhaps they will make a good match, after all," Marin Pirenetto said, as if relieved of a great burden.

Gaetano could not be rid of a sense of apprehension, which he did his best to discount. "It is what I would want for my daughter. She has always been a girl of great spirit and I have worried that her husband would seek to stifle that in her." This admission was made in a rush, as if he feared that if he slowed down, he would stop entirely.

"She has nothing to fear about that with Aurelio. I doubt he would notice if she took to negotiating the canals in her own gondola." His single laugh was eloquent. "I am thankful that your girl has so much enterprise; she will need it with a husband like Aurelio."

Gaetano did his best smile for Marin. "Then we may be certain of their happiness."

I tremble now but with one desire:
To please the lover whose image haunts me.
—Giovanni Boccaccio

— VI —

"You do not seem pleased, figlia mia," said Rosamonda to Fenice as they worked on the embroidery for her wedding dress. "I would have thought you would now be serene, with your choice made and your life set."

Fenice wanted to say that she dreaded the thought of a set life; she curbed this impulse and told her mother and sisters, all of whom had spent the afternoon at needlework, "I suppose that I must relinquish the perfect suitor."

"You mean there was someone else?" Eloisa asked, her eyes shining with intrigue.

"Not a real suitor," Fenice confessed. "But someone I . . . imagined. I have longed for a man who—" She stopped abruptly. "It isn't fitting."

"Go on," urged Rosamonda. "We will say nothing of it to Aurelio," and added with a note of amusement, "Not that I think he would mind."

"You mean notice," said Artemesia, doing her best not to smile.

"Everyone should be kinder to Aurelio," Bianca declared as she pushed her needle for emphasis. In the next instant she was sucking the end of her finger.

"I would agree if I thought it mattered to him," Fenice said, her expression thoughtful. "I think he uses his eccentricity as a way to buffer himself against the world. He would much rather spend an evening working on the design of ships than attending any of the festivities that the merchants of Venice rejoice in."

"You may have hit upon the very heart of the matter," said Rosamonda approvingly.

"You still haven't said the kind of suitor you wanted to have," said Eloisa, mischief in her voice. "We know you will marry Aurelio, but what would you truly want your suitor to be?"

"Eloisa," her mother reprimanded her, then seconded her request. "Since you know that the suitor is a dream, you might as well tell us what he is."

"Yes," Artemesia urged. "You have chosen Aurelio, so this won't matter."

She grinned. "I am very pleased with Umberto, but I confess I am not immune to the charm of Ernan Tedesco."

"No one is immune to Ernan Tedesco," said Rosamonda in what should have been condemning accents but were tinged with interest.

"Who is your dream-suitor?" Eloisa insisted, leaning toward Fenice in a conspiratorial way.

Fenice did her best to avoid the question. "If Bianca says I should tell, I will," she promised, relying on her religious sister to spare her the revelation.

Bianca considered and said, "I would like to hear of whom you dream."

"You will think it very . . . odd of me," Fenice began reluctantly as she secured her needle in the fabric; she knew she would not be able to work and speak at the same time. Her expression became distant, as if she were looking at faraway places. "He would be foreign," she said at last.

"And a great lord," interjected Eloisa.

Fenice frowned at her. "Yes, a man of standing. Someone with enough power that he would not have to rule over me, but would encourage me to expand my horizons, and not just with studying Greek and geography; he would take me traveling, offering me adventures, going to places to show me sights I have never before been, places I have only read about and seen marked on maps, and he would delight in my longing for excitement instead of condemning it. He would make me like him, giving me strength of my own, and he would admire what I could accomplish with his . . ." Her words faltered. "He's not real. But I wish he were, and that he had found me in time."

"Gracious," said Rosamonda in the silence that followed this revelation. "Where did you suppose you would find such a man in Venice?"

"I said I know he's not real," Fenice said, making no apology for her wistful tone of voice. "You asked what I dreamed of."

"You would have to search the world, I think, to find such a man," said Artemesia.

This was so much a part of Fenice's private intentions that she started at Artemesia's observation, and said in some confusion, "Even if I did, I would have no certainty of finding him. He is a dream. Just a dream."

"But a strange one," said Bianca, staring at the tip of her finger to see if she had stopped bleeding. "What would make you want such a man?"

"I said he was a dream," Fenice said with asperity. "A dream is not real."

"Still," said Eloisa, "who would not like to be courted by a powerful, mysterious foreigner? He would have to be mysterious," she went on with great practicality, "or there would be no point in his foreignness."

"Yes," Artemesia said, joining in the fun. "Not an Islamite, of course, because they keep their women sequestered from the world, and no Islamite lord would encourage such an enterprising spirit as yours." She cocked her head. "He might be . . . oh, Russian perhaps. Or Hungarian. Hungarians are all mad, aren't they? Very well, a Hungarian lord would be the likely one to embody your suitor, Fenice." She laughed aloud.

Stung, Fenice said, "All right, I have told you the suitor of my dreams, in spite of my choice of husband. What is your dream, Artemesia?" She looked directly at her sister, challenging her.

Eloisa was enjoying herself tremendously. "Yes. Who do you dream of in secret, Artemesia? And if you say Umberto, I won't believe you."

"Goodness," said Rosamonda, trying to restore the tone of their conversation. "You would think all of you have longed for unknown men."

"They're only dreams, Madre Mia," said Fenice. "Let Artemesia tell us about her dreams. I told you about mine."

Rosamonda considered her answer. "Very well. But what we say does not leave this room. There will be no mention of dream-suitors where the men might hear of it."

"All right," Artemesia agreed, and tossed her head. "If I dream of anyone other than Umberto," she said with a defiant glance at Fenice, "I would dream of Lorenzo Loredan. There was never a Doge as handsome as he, or so I think."

The cries of disagreement that greeted her confession made Fenice smile.

"Why not Doge Lorenzo Loredan?" asked Rosamonda, coming to Artemesia's aid. "To be sure, his austerity is not to my taste, but I can see what Artemesia would find to admire in him." She made a gesture with her free hand. "Look at you. You would think that no woman ever dreamed of men."

Bianca crossed herself. "Dreams may lead to sins," she warned.

"Then you had better be careful, since dreams are all you will have of men," said Eloisa boldly.

This was more than Rosamonda would countenance. "You are much too pert, child. You will have to learn to curb your tongue."

Eloisa tried to look demure and failed. "There are so many dreams, how can I answer for all of them?"

"Dreams are less than shadows, and shadows do not sin," said Artemesia, her head coming up defiantly. "I don't expect a dead Doge to court me, I only mean that occasionally he is the man I find in my dreams. I would not trade my Umberto for my dream."

"You are a wise daughter," Rosamonda approved.

"Dagger, stiletto, two giaquettas, sailor's shoes, upper and lower hose, a wallet, and a large cloth sack," Fenice murmured as she went through her hidden trove. "Two maps, an oil lamp, a jar of oil, flint-and-steel, nine ducats and thirteen scudi, a cap, scissors, oiled paper"—this would wrap the bread she would take from the kitchen on her way to the docks—"a fork, a spoon, a pewter cup." She had almost everything she thought she would need for her escape, for she thought of it in no other terms. She was still wondering if she should take a sottana, but was not yet convinced she would have any occasion to need it. Besides, she told herself, if she was leaving behind her life in Venice, she would accomplish it more successfully if she had nothing female with her. "Once you cut your hair," she said to her reflection in the mirror, "you will have to be a boy in all things. Or almost all," she added as she thought of her monthly courses. On a ship they would prove inconvenient;

she would have to bring rags for those times. She carefully hid her supplies and went to finish dressing for the grand dinner that her family was giving in honor of the Pirenettos that evening.

Aurelio was as well-dressed as Fenice had ever seen him; she felt a pang knowing that he would be disappointed by her flight. He came to her and held out his hand, bowing over hers with something that was almost grace. His delight was apparent in his smile, making Fenice feel more the traitor than ever. "I am proud to be with you tonight," he murmured as he pressed her hand.

"And I am glad you have shown me such favor," said Fenice, because it was expected of her. She did her best to look at ease as she laid her hand on his arm and allowed him to escort her to the dining room, his father and brothers falling in behind them.

"How have you spent your day, cara mia?" Aurelio asked.

"In the morning I was with my tutor. I translated some Greek discourses, and then we took up geography," she said, trying not to sound bored. "In the afternoon, I played my chittarrone." She realized as she spoke that she would miss the instrument more than any other single item she would leave behind. She banished that unhappy thought from her mind as she took her place at the women's table opposite where Aurelio would sit with the men of her family, facing his father and brothers. She felt Artemesia tweak her sleeve.

"Aurelio is very grand tonight, isn't he?" she whispered, teasing Fenice.

"I think he looks splendid," said Fenice quietly.

"Not as handsome as Arrigo," said Artemesia, considering the backs of the Pirenetto men.

"It would be difficult for anyone to be as handsome as Arrigo," said Fenice drily. "If you doubt me, ask Arrigo."

Artemesia stifled her laughter. "At least Aurelio isn't such a peacock as his brother. I wonder who dressed him tonight? His lower hose match and his camisa is spotless."

"Don't be spiteful," Rosamonda admonished her daughters, keeping her voice low enough so that only Fenice and Artemesia heard her. She sighed. "I am sorry Bianca's devotions keep her from dining with us, but she—"

At the men's table Gaetano clapped loudly, summoning the servants with the first course of their meal. "In Florence," he said to begin the evening, "I would be expected to serve the meal; here in Venice, we are more practical."

The Pirenettos all laughed appreciatively as was expected of them, and Marin said, "Florentines are an indulgent lot."

"They have got used to wealth, that is their problem," said Arrigo as if he had lost money to them.

"Wealth and art," said Aurelio. "They cannot be faulted for that."

"I suppose not," said Ercole, adding, "But we Venetians have the greater place in the world."

At this all the men expressed their agreement, and Marin said, "I hear your *Impresa* will soon take to the sea. You must be impatient for that day."

"Of course," said Ercole with an attempt to seem nonchalant.

Fenice listened to them, wishing she could move nearer to the men's table. She was distracted from her eavesdropping by Rosamonda's nudge of her arm. "Natale has to put your soup down," she said, indicating the servant who stood behind her.

"Oh. Yes." Fenice moved so Natale could place the bowl in front of her; the pungent smell of crab and mushroom rose in the steam.

Gaetano had risen to say the blessing on the meal as the party fell silent. "Gracious God, we thank Thee and praise Thee for Thy bounty; we bless Thy Name and all Thy works; we adore Thee in Thy majesty and mightiness. For Thy Mercy, we extoll Thee, for Thy Grace we are forever indebted to Thee and Thy Son. For family, friends, health, and success we esteem Thee and Thy manifest Kindness. For the joy of this night we are grateful to Thee, as in all things. Amen." He crossed himself as the rest of the company did the same.

Enrico was pouring the wine, and he took care to see that every gold-stemmed glass was full as he made his rounds. He had a second carafe with him, which he left on the men's table.

"The soup is excellent," said Marin as he took the first sip.

Everyone else prepared to eat. Bread was placed before each diner and the meal began in earnest.

From his place beside Gaetano, Aurelio stared across to the women's table; Fenice could feel his gaze as if it were summer sunlight. She lifted her wineglass in a toast to him and saw him blush, grinning, at her tribute.

"I think you have chosen well," Rosamonda approved. "He will strive to please you as Rocco never would."

"Yes; I think so, too," said Fenice, lowering her eyes. The soup was superb, but to Fenice it had all the savor of gruel.

By the end of the meal, most of the party was quite merry; Gaetano was generous with his wine. Marin had pronounced the end of meal blessing with haste and a few slurred words, which earned him some chuckles and the comment that "Since God has given us wine, we thank Him by our enjoyment of it." This was not as witty as everyone told Ercole it was.

They went into the reception hall where a consort of musicians was waiting to play for them: two crumhorns, an alto recorder, a psaltery, a tenor viola da gamba, and a tambor. It was an extravagant display for such a small group, and Marin Pirenetto remarked upon it to Gaetano.

"Well, she is my first daughter to marry. The least I can do is celebrate," he said, and nodded to the musicians, who struck up an almande to start the dancing.

Aurelio accompanied Fenice onto the floor as her sisters served as partners for his brothers. "I do not dance very well," he reminded her.

"The almande isn't hard," she said in the hope that he would not refuse to dance. "And it's slow."

"But they'll be playing bransles soon, and gagliardas," he protested.

"We'll get them to play pavanes and rondes," she said, winking at him. "And you can do the Tourdion, can't you?"

"Not very well," he confessed as they began the first steps.

She had to admit he was doing his best, but that was not very good. He tended to get lost in the sequence of steps, and rather than pick up where the dance had gone, he hurried through all his missed steps to catch up, making it impossible to be a good partner for him. At least, she told herself, there were only four movements in the Tourdion. That would be less of an ordeal for all of them. She glanced toward Artemesia dancing with Andrea, both moving gracefully and at tempo. If only Aurelio would do half as well as his brothers.

Arrigo danced with Rosamonda, as courtesy demanded. He was gallant, adding a flourish to his movements that attracted much attention; in other company he might have been admired, but here his flamboyance was met with nothing more than mild exasperation.

"I'm sorry," said Aurelio as he missed another step. "You had far better dance with Arrigo or Ercole."

"I am pleased to be where I am," said Fenice, and almost meant it.

The almande came to an end, and the musicians paused, waiting for instructions.

"Let's have a gagliarda," Arrigo called out.

Beside Fenice, Aurelio sighed.

"So soon after eating?" Fenice responded. "Why not a pavane or a spagnoletta?" Neither dance would tax Aurelio, and she would be able to dance with Ercole when the second dance was over. She reminded herself that Aurelio would be as grateful as she to surrender her to her brother.

"The spagnoletta," Artemesia seconded. "I like the pace."

The musicians saw Gaetano nod, and began the spagnoletta. The formal steps were not so fast or complex that Aurelio got lost more than twice.

"How do you manage to keep it all straight?" he asked Fenice as they fumbled their way to the end. "I can never remember."

Fenice was well aware of this, but she gave him the only answer she could. "I follow the music and the steps come with it," she said as she saw Ercole approaching. She did her best not to look too pleased to be able to dance with her brother.

"You may want a different partner by the time we are through. It's going to be a basse." He smiled wickedly at her. "You and Febo always do it so well."

"But Febo isn't here," she pointed out, feeling an intense pang of missing him. "You know how to do it well enough."

"High praise," said Ercole as the musicians launched into the brisk rhythms of the basse.

Fenice danced all evening, and discovered she was glad of the chance to do it, though it made her tired. She would have few occasions to please her family between now and the day Ercole left; she vowed to make the most of them.

At the end of the party Aurelio took her aside. "I just want you to know when we are married I will not force you to be my partner all the time. Dance with your brothers or mine, or your cousins. I will not deny you the pleasure, and I will not lessen it by foisting myself on you."

"Aurelio," said Fenice, doing her best to be kind, for he was being more generous than many men would be, "I think if you would practice a little more you would dance as well as anyone in your family."

He shook his head a little. "I am not as certain as you are. But when we are married, you will have the opportunity to teach me I am wrong." His smile was shy but eager. "You have already made my family think better of me because I have you."

Fenice nodded, her throat too tight for her to speak; she hoped his newly found approval would not vanish when she did. "I chose the better man," she said sincerely.

"It is hard for me to think so," Aurelio confessed. "But I thank God you believe it."

She allowed him to kiss her cheek and reminded herself as she did that Judas, too, had betrayed with a kiss.

During the next two weeks storms rushed in one after the other; rain and wind lashed at Venice and the hills beyond the lagoon as if bent on paying the Venetian Republic back for defeating the Turks at Lepanto.

"I don't know if I will be able to put to sea as we planned if this keeps up," Ercole remarked to his family one morning after prayers. He had been indoors for four days and was growing restless and discontented.

"Oh, the weather will clear," said Gaetano. "In fact, the storms should blow themselves out early this year." He came and clapped his son on the shoulder.

"I could still be here when Fenice marries," Ercole grumbled.

His complaint filled Fenice with dread; she could feel the color drain from her face. "Don't say that, Ercole," she whispered.

"Why not?" he inquired, and gave the tippet on her ropa a playful tug. "Don't you want me here for the wedding?"

She realized her mistake at once. "It's not that," she said with a nervous titter. "I only meant that it would be terrible if you had to battle storms all through the spring."

"That it would," said Ercole, his smile indulgent. "But I'm surprised you don't want to go out this very day and battle the waves."

"If I knew how to captain a ship, I probably would," said Fenice, her head coming up. She had a short while before she would meet with her tutor and she had hoped to go out to the shops to see if she could find a rain cloak, for this weather reminded her that she would need one aboard ship. But going out in such stormy weather would draw attention to her errand, so she remained where she was, hoping that there would be clearing before she had to sneak onto the *Impresa*.

"I think you might, at that," said Ercole, and paced the length of the room. "I am getting bored."

"So is everyone else," said Fenice. "Except Bianca. She's been at prayers since before dawn. I don't know how she stands it. How many times can you say a prayer before it becomes nonsense?" She regarded Ercole for a short while longer. "Do you never get bored at sea? I don't think I would."

"Then you do not know as much about sailing as you think you do. Sometimes the routine is so boring it takes all my concentration to attend to the most necessary tasks. Although I prefer it to be boring than to be fighting weather like this." He indicated the rain pelting the shutters.

"But this would be exciting to sail in," Fenice protested.

"You will soon learn that excitement is not always desirable," Ercole told her; he had picked up a small agate-colored bottle and tossed it from hand to hand as he walked. "Excitement is generally hazardous, and no sailor wants any more of it than absolutely necessary."

Fenice considered what he said and nodded once. "You are probably right; I have no way of knowing." Inwardly she added *yet*.

Ercole paused and looked at her in mild surprise. "You admit so much? I'm astonished. Are you feeling well?"

"I am fine," she said curtly. She rose and prepared to leave the room. "My tutor will arrive shortly. I should prepare for my lessons."

"Study diligently," Ercole recommended, waving a negligent hand to her.

Fenice returned his courtesy with a salute, as neatly done as any lancer. She went off to the library where her lessons were conducted, and occupied the time before her tutor's arrival in going over charts of the waters around Cyprus and Rhodes.

Walking toward the Rialto Bridge with Aurelio, Fenice had to resist the panic that threatened to take hold of her. She had been with him since morning and they had spent most of the day choosing things for their apartments in the Pirenetto house. She had done her best to seem interested and enthusiastic, but now she was having trouble remembering that she intended to leave Venice before their marriage took place and that all this selecting and buying was a sham.

Aurelio pointed to the Rialto Bridge and said, "I could design one better than that." It was not a boast, only an admission of the truth. "Most of the bridges in Venice could be improved, but that one most of all."

"Are you going to do it?" Fenice asked, aware of how important this was to him.

"If I were allowed to, I would. I can offer a recommendation and an improved design, but then the Doge must make the decision." He stepped onto the bridge and became thoughtfully silent.

"What is it?" She did not expect much of an answer, which was just as well.

"Many people would like to keep the bridge as it is." He became silent once more.

Fenice continued to walk beside him, her mind on what lay ahead; she had so little time to complete her arrangements, and she was certain that she would leave something important undone. She glanced at Aurelio and wondered if she could go through with the wedding in eleven days. Could she give up her bid for adventure and be content to look after Aurelio for years and years? Aurelio was a decent man, one who regarded her highly and would be at pains to treat her well. But if she remained in Venice, her hunger for faraway places would increase as time went on; eventually she would find a way to venture out on the sea, and she was convinced it would be kinder to go now, before Aurelio had grown used to having her about, than wait for the marriage—and the possibility of a pregnancy—to go out into the world. She had not thought it would be so difficult to leave: after all, she would be coming back when the *Impresa* returned from the Galley of Romania. She would work out her explanation for her actions while she was gone.

"What are you thinking about?" Aurelio's question cut into her thoughts with the keenness of steel. "You look so . . . fierce."

"Oh, I was thinking of all the things I have to do in the next week," she said, and favored him with a wide smile. "Sometimes I think I will not get it all done in time."

"You may not," said Aurelio, and laughed self-consciously. "I won't notice."

She could think of nothing to say, so she leaned on the side of the bridge and pointed out the boats coming from the inner lagoon. "Look. The first flowers, and all those vegetables!"

"Mushrooms, too," said Aurelio, glancing at the boats. "The cooks will be glad to buy. Though I am becoming very tired of cabbages. It seems to be all we eat from November to April."

Fenice laughed because she knew he wanted her to. "My mother is planning to have candied violets for the wedding feast, as a sweet."

"Good," said Aurelio as they walked off the bridge. He started toward a shop that sold chairs, but turned back to her, saying in a diffident manner, "Someday I hope you will tell me what has really been on your mind."

"There is nothing, Aurelio; daydreaming." She cocked her head and offered a fetching smile. "You may wish someday that I would keep more to myself than I do."

"Actually," he responded with a self-effacing glance away from her, "I wish you would tell me more; I feel you are a mystery I will never understand."

"Aren't women supposed to be mysterious?" Fenice countered, hoping she was provocative enough to make him change the subject.

"You are not a mystery, not that way," Aurelio said. "But you *are* keeping a secret from me; I wish you would not."

Fenice went scarlet, not knowing what to say to him; apparently this did not bother him, for he motioned to her to come into the shop with him, and began to explain about the design of chairs.

"Only six more days," Rosamonda exclaimed as she inspected the wedding gown Fenice would wear. "If I can find another thirty seed pearls, the neckline will be just as I envisioned it."

Fenice studied the lovely simarra with its pearl-embroidered damask with double-bell sleeves, the slashings edged in pearls. The neckline was modest, with a soft lace ruff to set off her face. The sottana of fine satin was not quite finished, and Rosamonda despaired of seeing it done in time. Following tradition, Fenice's mother was sewing the dress herself. As Fenice touched the simarra, she noticed that there was a spot of blood on the rosy fabric, right next to a cluster of pearls. She hoped no one would notice it; at least, she thought, it was below the waist, where it was not as obvious as it would be on another part of the garment. Which, she reminded herself, she was not going to wear, so it hardly mattered. She felt a pang of regret, and wondered if she could persuade Rosamonda to let her wear it upon her return. Assuming Aurelio still wanted to marry her. She hated all the complications that were piling up, making her more confused than she had ever been in her life.

"It is not unusual for brides to become forgetful and flustered as their weddings draw near," said Rosamonda, noticing the abstracted expression in her daughter's eyes.

"I have been, haven't I?" Fenice agreed, and made herself sit down and speak directly with her mother. "I can't really believe it is going to happen. It seems impossible."

"Do you think your hoped-for suitor might still appear and sweep you away?" Rosamonda suggested. "If you think about what such a man would have to be like, you must realize that you are very fortunate in Aurelio Pirenetto. He will not subject you to anything worse than occasional absentmindedness."

"No doubt," said Fenice. "And do you like Rocco degli Urbanesei paying so much attention to Eloisa?"

"No, not entirely," Rosamonda admitted. "And I am going to advise her to put little stock in anything he says to her. Men of his stripe are not to be encouraged."

"And what do you think she will say?" Fenice wanted to keep her mother from questioning her too closely about her state of mind; she did not want to give herself away, and she had a high regard for Rosamonda's powers of observation.

"She is young enough that it hardly matters. I will talk to your father as well, so that any pretensions Rocco may have may be ended before Eloisa comes to think of him as a suitor." She frowned as she threaded her needle. "He should not have sought your hand if he wants Eloisa's."

"Goodness, what will his mother say?" Fenice asked in mock distress. "She will think this family is beyond everything."

"No doubt," Rosamonda answered tartly. "But we will have to struggle along as best we may with the burden of her poor opinion." She went to the window to examine the simarra more closely, frowning with concentration.

"Would it really be such a horrid thing?" Fenice wondered aloud, her voice hushed. "To have the poor opinion of a great many people?"

"It would depend upon why you had it, or so I think," said Rosamonda. "If you had done something truly despicable, then it would be most unpleasant to have people hold you in contempt."

"How despicable would it have to be?" Fenice pursued.

Rosamonda laughed softly. "Why? Are you planning something that would appall me? Just planning this wedding is appalling enough. If only Aurelio's mother were still alive. His stepmother cannot fill her duties." She shook her head as if this were an oversight.

Her mother's guess was close enough to the mark that Fenice winced. "No . . . nothing like that," she lied. "But I was remembering all the whispers when Orsola Gritti was kidnaped. Everyone said the most terrible things about her brothers for all they did." As she spoke, a notion was forming in her mind, a way to make her flight less dreadful for her family.

"I will want to try this on you tomorrow. We have a little time to finish the changes, and I pray that Santa Catarina will look favorably on us." She sighed once. "And in a few months we will have to do this all again, when Artemesia gets married."

"Oh, yes," said Fenice. "Artemesia will not want to be sent off with less style than I."

"And it would matter to Umberto in a way that means nothing to your Aurelio." She came away from the window, the simarra clutched in her hands. "I daresay Aurelio would not mind if you were married in a gondola and went home without fuss."

"He would probably prefer it," Fenice said, and giggled.

"Figlia mia." Rosamonda did her best to make this a reprimand, but her efforts failed when she smiled. "You are probably right. Not that I would disapprove in any way," she went on hastily, "but there are certain things expected of Venetian merchants if gossip is to be avoided."

"And we must do that, mustn't we, Madre Mia?" Fenice asked her, unable to keep the wistfulness from her voice.

"Well, it is easier on all of us if we do," said Rosamonda. "And having a fine wedding provides pleasure for so many." She sat down and reached for her needle and thread. "If you are going to help me, draw up that stool. If you are not, leave me to do this."

Fenice bobbed a curtsy, and went from the room; she needed time to herself to think. It would take a while to order these new plans, and she did not have very much time left.

The next afternoon as she strolled the front of the Doge's Palace, watching the ships being provisioned and loaded, she said to Aurelio, "Did you see that man? The one with the squint?" She pointed back into the crowd.

"What man?" Aurelio peered into the human throng.

"The one with the squint, in the Greek clothes," she said, pretending to search for him. "Oh, dear. He's gone again."

Aurelio shrugged and went back to studying the ships.

"I've seen him several times in the last few days," she went on when Aurelio did not question her about the man. "I thought he might be following me."

"One always sees people many times in Venice. It comes from being on islands." He showed no more interest in her remarks than in what he had for supper.

"That is what I thought, too, but . . ." She shrugged. "You're probably right. I am anticipating trouble because we are so close to our wedding. I cannot believe it will happen without—" She stopped. "I will not bring bad cess upon us by speaking my worries."

"Good," said Aurelio. "Do you see how they are using that crane?" he went on with more enthusiasm. "This is going to be very interesting. They're about to have trouble if they keep on as they're going."

Fenice let him explain the problem to her, and thanked him for showing her. They continued their stroll a bit later, and when they did, she said with surprise, "Why, there's the man with the squint again. Right over there." She pointed to a dense part of the crowd at the Bacino di San Marco.

"I don't see him," said Aurelio, making a bit more effort to pick this figure out of the mass of people.

Fenice pointed. "He's just there." She shook her head. "Now he's turned away."

"Probably found what he was looking for," said Aurelio and patted Fenice's shoulder affectionately. "Not that I am astonished that any man would want to look at you." His cheeks went rosy and not from the wind. "You are the loveliest woman in Venice, in *all* Venice—the empire as well as the city."

"Are you sure of that?" She made a gesture to the south and east. "There is so much out there you have never seen. How can you be so certain?"

"I need not travel the world to know I have a treasure," he said, his eyes filled with adoration.

Fenice raised her head, fighting down the impulse to abandon her plans to keep from hurting this devoted, sweet man. She did not like telling him this fable, but she had convinced herself that it was a greater kindness for him to think she had been kidnaped than to believe she had run away from him. She wanted him to know that she did not intend to abandon him, that she had not preferred adventure to him, but that she wanted to have adventures and then come back to him and all his befuddled goodness. She hoped he would forgive her.

"What are you thinking?" Aurelio asked when Fenice had been silent for some little time.

"I was just wondering where my brothers are. What ports they have reached." She was deliberately vague.

"You worry for their safety," he said. "That shows your kindness and your understanding."

For a moment she wanted to shout at him that it showed her desire to be with them, to be walking the streets of the ports they had seen. She wanted him to know that she was not the soft-tempered girl he thought she was. But she saw the concern in his eyes, and could not bring herself to refute his sympathetic compliment. "Anyone in La Serenissima must worry for those who go out on the broad sea, be they father or brother or stranger."

Aurelio smiled. "You see? This is what I most like in you—your compassionate nature."

"I am not so compassionate as you think me," she said, wanting to get away from him before she betrayed herself with an ill-considered remark.

"That shows your greatness of mind, to know that you have not attained your full capacity for virtue." He blushed as he spoke. "I am thankful that you are willing to entrust your goodness to my care."

If he had not been so utterly sincere she might have yelled at him. As it was she mumbled something about needing to speak to her mother, and fled, leaving him to stare after her, an expression that was almost adoration on his face, and an ache in his chest that was bliss.

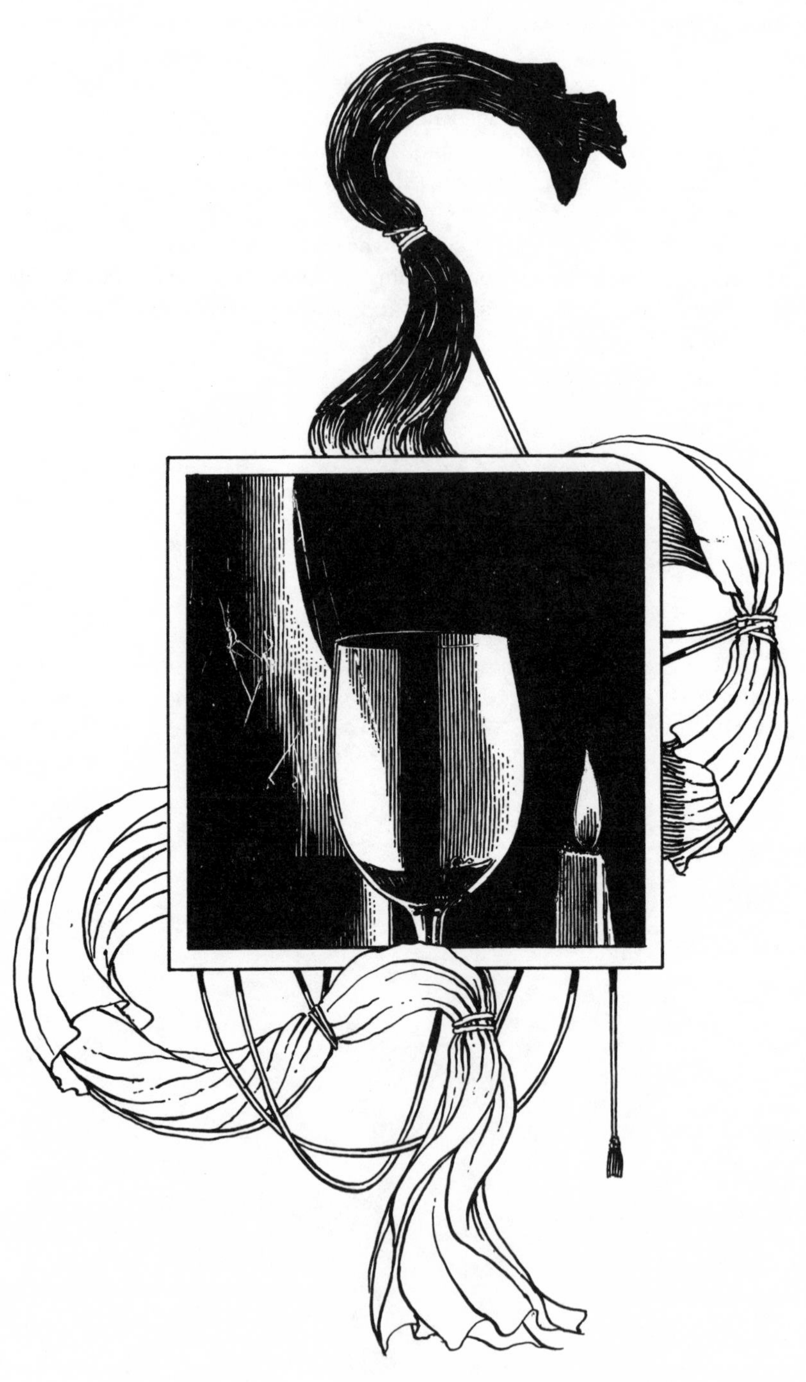

But I can find no way so wild and remote
That Love will not come there . . .
—Francesco Petrarca

— VII —

"I think someone has been following me," said Fenice to Artemesia that evening after prayers.

"Aurelio?" Artemesia suggested. "When he notices you he is like a puppy."

"No," Fenice said, keeping her voice low. "I don't know this man. He wears Greek clothes and he has a squint." She had chosen Artemesia to tell her tale to because her younger sister was not particularly observant and was inclined to view all foreigners with distrust: Eloisa would want to go looking for the fellow and Bianca would recommend confining Fenice to the house, and neither of those options were what Fenice wanted.

"Are you sure?" Artemesia asked just above a whisper.

"No. But I have seen him for several days, and when I notice him, he turns away or . . ." She finished with a hitch of her shoulder. "I do not like to think he is watching me, but what else can I assume? If it had happened only once I would think nothing of it, but it has happened several times, and that worries me."

"More than once? But this is . . . is terrible," Artemesia said in an undervoice. "Have you told our father?"

"Not yet. I'm not certain of his intentions—if indeed he has any—and I do not want to cause our father alarm without reason. And the man may mean nothing by it, if he is following me. It may be a sailor who has been on our ships, or someone who has taken a fancy to a Venetian girl while he is in port." She shook her head once. "I will say nothing until I know more. How can I accuse a stranger without reason?"

Artemesia nodded. "Be very careful," she recommended. "And if you think there is any likelihood of his hurting you, speak to our father or Ercole at once."

"Ercole is leaving shortly," Fenice reminded her. "In a few days he will be gone."

"And Lionello and Febo will not yet be back," Artemesia agreed. "Have you said anything to Aurelio? Perhaps you should."

"I have mentioned it. I doubt he has been much alarmed by it," said Fenice, managing a slight smile. "But you know what Aurelio is."

"A dear, good man," Artemesia said staunchly.

"Yes, he is," Fenice agreed. "And I know he would keep me from any harm that he knew of, but think! He does not know what day of the week it is except Sunday. I do not think it would be wise to burden him with this."

"But you *have* told him," Artemesia persisted. "He knows about it?"

"Yes, I said I have. I have pointed the man out to him." She made a sign for silence. "I don't want to alarm the family with what may be nothing at all. But it does trouble me. I cannot determine what he wants, and that bothers me the most. If I knew what he wanted . . ."

"Are you sure he wants something?" Artemesia asked.

"No. But if he does, what can it be?" Fenice let the question hang. "I will see you in the morning."

"Yes; goodnight," said Artemesia, looking mildly worried. She touched cheeks with Fenice and went into her room.

Satisfied that she had done well, Fenice closed the door of her room and began the process of undressing without the help of a servant. She would have to fend for herself on the ship, she knew, and she wanted to become accustomed to managing without help. The ropa she wore was not difficult to loosen and slip off her shoulders; its lack of sleeves made it easy. The sottana, more elaborate to set off the ropa, was another matter, the lacing up the back requiring extensive twisting and stretching to get the laces between her shoulder-blades slack enough to make it possible for her to wrestle the garment over her head. The undergarments were easy to remove. Her night rail was soft cotton and she tugged it on with ease, then set about combing and braiding her hair for the night. As she let the silky tresses run through her fingers, she thought this was one of the few things she would miss—her long, shining hair. But, she reminded herself, it was a small price to pay for the adventure she sought; and it would grow back, which was the reason for including scissors in her supplies. She pulled back the hangings around the bed and got into it, listening to the sounds of bells and water, the two she most associated with Venice.

The separation of sleep and wakefulness came so imperceptively that Fenice had the odd sensation that she was still awake when her dreams began: *She stood on the deck of a ship in rough seas, the spray in her face, a darkening sky overhead. Wind made the sails thrum and the oarsmen had shipped their oars to keep them from damage in the heavy swells. As the ship broached a wave, Fenice felt its surge within her. She grabbed the hilt of the dagger thrust through her belt as if she would attack the weather with it.*

There was someone else on the deck with her—not the helmsman, who kept stoically to his post, but another figure, a tall, powerful man who praised her for her courage and inspired her to embrace the storm. He held her attention as much as the tempest did, and she knew it was important to show no sign of cowardice to him. She turned to face the wind and set her sights on a distant speck of land, ordering the helmsman to hold them on course. Beside her the stranger nodded; she saw the fierce smile he gave her and her heart soared with the wild wind.

The morning found her exhausted, as if she had truly spent the night in a tempest-tossed ship and not in her bed. Her muscles ached in that insidious way that often presaged illness. She rose slowly and dressed automatically; as she went down the stairs, she walked with care as if she expected the stairs to pitch and roll under her feet.

"You look tired," said Rosamonda as the family gathered for morning prayers. "I hope you are not making yourself ill with all our plans." She studied Fenice's face. "Should I have you bled, do you think?"

"I'm not ill," said Fenice. "I didn't sleep very well." She was able to smile her reassurance. "I will rest in the afternoon. That will restore me."

"We are supposed to meet with the—" Rosamonda interrupted herself. "I can attend to it on my own. It would be better if you were rested for this evening."

"This evening is Cousin Valerio's banquet, isn't it?" Fenice remembered the engagement as she spoke; her dream seemed to have driven such things from her mind. She tried to look enthusiastic about the coming event.

"Yes; you and Aurelio will be honored by him." Rosamonda approved; Valerio was on her side of the family and one of the most successful of a wealthy merchant clan that was now connected with half the major trading families in Venice. "Let the Bellin family show its pleasure for a change. Zucchar and Pirenetto have had their chances already."

"At least this will not continue much longer," said Fenice.

"What will not continue much longer?" asked Ercole as he came into the morning room. He would spend most of the day with his ship and would probably arrive at the banquet late.

"All this fuss," said Fenice impatiently. "Not that I am unmindful of the compliment we are being paid—I am, but there is so much of it."

"That there is," said Rosamonda. "And it is a good thing you will be married soon, so that we may all recuperate from your wedding before we prepare for Artemesia's." She patted Fenice's hand. "You rest in the afternoon. It will do you good."

"I suppose you're right," Fenice said, and readied herself for prayers, all the while recalling the passion that had coursed in her veins while the stranger in her dream had urged her on.

By the time Ercole arrived at Cousin Valerio's house, the banquet was half over. He apologized and his apologies were laughed off by his host, who had spent twenty years at sea before turning that part of the business over to his sons. He welcomed Ercole and wished him a profitable voyage.

Fenice was not so forgiving. "You promised you would be here," she scolded him when he found her cutting slices of capon at the serving table.

"And so I am, but not on time." He permitted her to serve him.

"You are here for Febo and Lionello, not just for you. It makes a poor show when my only brother in Venice cannot bring himself to attend this banquet." Her smile belied the severity of her words. "What will our families say?"

"That I am going to sail shortly and I have many things to attend to, the *Impresa* being a new ship, and they would be right." He added some small onions in gravy to his plate. "You would do the same as I have done, if you were in my place."

She lifted her chin defiantly. "Tell me, fratello mio, would I ever be in your place?"

"Of course not; I thought you were through with such fancies," he answered quickly. "No matter what Febo may have told you, you will not go to sea unless your husband is so uncaring as to take you there." He poured wine for himself and for her. "Where is your Aurelio?"

"With the Doge's nephew. They are discussing some plans Aurelio has submitted to the Doge. It would not be proper to disturb them," she replied.

"Good for Aurelio," Ercole approved.

"The Doge has asked him to present himself tomorrow to discuss . . . something about the designs, for the Console." She had listened to Aurelio talk about this honor and had been happy for him, but she had not been able to follow the sketchy description he offered her. She wanted Ercole to think she was as happy for this show of the Doge's support as Aurelio was, but could not think of a way to do it. She drank some wine instead of trying to discuss this with him.

"He will be a very important man one day," Ercole approved. "The family will be fortunate to be part of him."

"So I think," said Fenice, doing her best not to choke on the wine. "Come. I want to find a place to sit and finish eating. Join me, and tell me how things are with the *Impresa*."

This he was glad to do, and began without any polite disclaiming. "She is a fine vessel. I wish I could describe her to you so you would understand what I mean when I say it. She is probably the best of her sort in all Venice, and I say that without bias. I know we will have many successes with her, and that she will sail for many years." He carried his plate in one hand and his glass in the other; he led her to a small table near the windows overlooking the Rio Santa Maria Formosa. "Cousin Valerio has been lavish tonight," he said as they sat down.

"And he has been lapping up the praise it has brought him as readily as a cat laps cream," she said. "I don't mean to sound spiteful, but this is all so grand it is oppressive. I realize it is supposed to be in honor of my wedding, but it strikes me as more intended to glorify Valerio."

"I understand you," said Ercole. "He always seeks to be at the forefront of society, and he is lucky that he can afford to do so."

"Yes," said Fenice. She was beginning to hate the display and the pomp she encountered everywhere she went. It would be easier, she thought, if much less attention was paid to her forthcoming marriage, for then she would not have to bother so much about her disappearance.

"Don't worry. Marriage isn't so bad," said Ercole. "You and Aurelio will learn to make each other good partners."

Fenice nodded, and thought of the sheet of old vellum she had found that was now hidden with her other treasures; she had written a threatening note in Greek, using her left hand so it would appear done by an unlettered hand. She would leave this behind when she left and it would provide an explanation for her absence, and the chance to return to Venice with little scandal attached to her name. She looked at Ercole. "Are you getting anxious to be gone? I know I would be."

"I admit I am," he said, and grinned. "The two of us will be undertaking new ventures at very nearly the same time."

"It must seem so to you," said Fenice. She ate more of the capon and had a long sip of wine. "You might not say so if you were the one getting married."

He was about to give her a glib response, then changed his mind. "I know you think what I do is more exciting, and it may seem so to many, but you would not like the way the excitement is made. I've said this before, and it bears repeating: on the sea excitement comes from fear. In marriage it comes from other emotions." He smiled heartily. "Febo and you might have made children's games out of going to sea, but the voyages are not like that; the sea is huge and ships are tiny, and the fate of mariners is always in the hands of God. Wherever we go, we are always one wave away from disaster. I wish I could convince you."

"If I had been to sea, I might be convinced." She frowned down at her plate. "Let's say nothing more, my brother. I don't want to feel disappointed."

"And you shouldn't," he informed her a bit grandly, adding, "I am sorry I will not be here for your wedding. But—" He made a gesture to show how much was out of his hands.

She glanced at Aurelio. "But you must sail when you must sail."

"The sea is a most demanding mistress," Ercole proclaimed.

Fenice decided her brother had had too much wine. "May you prosper." It was the safest thing to say.

"May God hear you and be gracious," he replied, certain he had done his utmost to make her willing to relinquish the dreams of her youth.

A bit later Aurelio came to the table and drew up a chair to join them. He gave her the same besotted stare he had been showing the last few days. She had no idea how to respond to it, but when she tried to make him smile, he only sighed.

Some time later, Aurelio worked up the courage to kiss her cheek. "You are so splendid," he murmured to her.

"And you are brilliant—a perfect combination," she said lightly, ashamed of herself for disdaining his affection so callously. She vowed she would make it up to him upon her return, and did her best to be content with that.

* * *

Toward the end of the evening Aurelio hurried up to Fenice, beaming and restless, full of apologies for not spending more of the banquet in her company. "But the Doge was determined to find out all of my thoughts about the new ships—you know the designs I have prepared for him?—and he insisted that I answer his questions. What could I do?"

"What you did—put yourself at the disposal of the Doge, of course," said Fenice, slightly amused.

"I would have brought you over to him, but our talk was such that I knew you would not be interested," he went on ingenuously. "And it is not fitting for a woman to hear such talk, for it is intended for the defense of the republic."

Fenice's laughter concealed her annoyance. "What would I know of such plans, after all?" she asked lightly.

"Yes," Aurelio concurred. "Yes, that is it exactly. You are not taught such things, are you?"

"No," she said. "I am not."

"There, you see?" he exclaimed. "You would not want me to subject you to all the things we must go over. You would be bored, and that would not please me." He took her hand. "When we are married I will not impose my work upon you. I promise you."

"I would not mind," Fenice said, feeling sad that he knew her so little that he thought she would not be interested in the designs of ships. "My family often talks of such things."

"You will have other concerns to occupy your thoughts, if God is gracious." His cheeks grew ruddy. "I hope we will have many sons."

Because it was expected of her, Fenice said, "And I."

Aurelio went silent for a moment. "I should not speak of such things, should I? Not yet. When we are married, then we will talk about children."

It was tempting to upbraid him, to tell him that she already knew everything she needed to know about babies. But such an admission would shock Aurelio, so she only remarked, "The day is approaching quickly."

"Yes. It is," he said, his awkwardness returning. "I have no reason to be afraid of so joyous an occasion, and yet I tremble whenever I think of it."

"Do you?" She felt a surge of sympathy for him, and was about to offer him a few words of comfort when he cut into her thoughts.

"Your father has made a very favorable settlement on you—did you know? My father is quite pleased." He managed an uneasy smile.

"I am glad to hear it," she said automatically, thinking that she was being bargained like any cargo would be. She might have said more, but Ercole came up to them, grinning.

"There you are! I am bidden to bring you to our host, who is going to make a presentation to you in anticipation of your wedding." He met Fenice's gaze without any sign of noticing her state of mind. "Come along. Cousin Valerio is not going to wait for you much longer, and that would not make either of you very happy."

Fenice thought that in fact she would be delighted to be able to put all this behind her, but she merely nodded and took her brother's offered hand and said to her affianced husband, "It would be what our families expect us to do."

"They have many things they expect of us," said Aurelio, frowning as he walked slightly behind Ercole. "My family has never paid so much attention to me as they have since we became engaged. You have transformed me in their eyes."

"I . . . do not know what to say," Fenice responded, suddenly feeling subdued again; what would her departure mean to Aurelio? she wondered. With the approval of his family at last within his grasp, would her departure consign him again to obscurity, being always in Arrigo's shadow? She could not let this influence what she did, but she could not keep from a pang of an emotion that was not quite guilt.

"You have changed my life," said Aurelio quietly.

Ercole listened to this with less turbulent feelings than Fenice did. "It is well you think highly of my sister," he said. "It would not be a worthy thing for you to marry her without regard for her. Such marriages never prosper, no matter what good the families may obtain from the match. See that you don't forget this."

"I could not," said Aurelio, trying to sound sincere and only managing a kind of ill-defined earnestness.

Fenice wanted to make both of them stop talking about her, and she declared, "You are not going to embarrass me, are you?"

"What?" Ercole asked archly. "Are you so modest that your brother cannot speak well of you to your fiancé?"

"I am not modest," Fenice said. "Or not modest that way." They were back in the reception hall now, surrounded by their families and other guests, and Fenice had to raise her voice to be heard. "I do not welcome praise that is only given because it is expected."

"Do you mean you think you are not valued? How could we not value you—the prettiest young woman in Venice and a scholar to boot?" Ercole chuckled as he was leading the way through the press of well-wishers.

Her answer was lost in the general noise of the festivities: she said, "To value me you would have to know me."

"A great day for our families," Cousin Valerio boomed out as Fenice was handed to him by Ercole, and Aurelio tagged after her. "And one that deserves to be recognized."

Gaetano made his way through the crowd, followed by Marin Pirenetto. Both men took up places flanking their children, with Cousin Valerio standing in front of them, two cups of Murano glass ornamented with gold in his raised hands.

"We are here to show our joy at the coming marriage of Fenice Zucchar and Aurelio Pirenetto, so that their families may know how much fortune has favored them in this union." He beamed as he signaled his servants to bring wine. "We pledge these two young people our approval and endorsement in the world. It is a fine thing when two great houses can be so fortuitously joined." As the servants filled the glasses, Valerio went on, "All Venice must look favorably on this wedding, and anticipate the clever sons these two will give la Serenissima."

This was met with general cheers and the raising of glasses throughout the reception hall. Gaetano and Marin were handed filled glasses as Valerio gave his two glasses to Aurelio and Fenice. "As you two drink to your years together, we will drink to them as well." He watched as the couple did as he told them. "Now. All the rest."

The company complied at once. When the glasses were lowered, Artemesia noticed that Ercole had not been given a glass. She pulled at Eloisa's sleeve. "Did you notice? Ercole—"

"Did not drink. Yes," Eloisa answered. "I hope no one else did."

"It is a bad omen," said Artemesia, her voice hushed.

"I know," said Eloisa impatiently. "If the rest saw it, well, it will not . . ." She did not finish her thoughts.

Artemesia shook her head. "Did our mother notice?"

"I don't know," said Eloisa, starting to move away from her sister as if their continued closeness would add to the power of the unfortunate omen.

A moment later, a servant handed a filled glass to Ercole, and the whole room became hushed as the guests realized the significance of this act.

Valerio was determined to keep this from being a blight on the evening. "The servant will answer for his laxness. He has always been lazy. The glass was ready, but the servant shirked his duty." He stood a bit nearer to Gaetano. "It means nothing."

Everyone tried to agree with him, a bit too hastily.

Aurelio glanced uneasily at Fenice. "It was nothing," he insisted. "I would easily make such an error myself." His self-conscious laughter made Fenice wince.

"I will not attend the wedding, since I will sail before it happens," Ercole said, doing his best to salvage the situation. "My drinking to them need not be with the rest of you since I will not be in Venice." He downed all the wine in his glass. "There. It is done."

The sound of conversation surged like a swarm of angry wasps as the assembled guests did their best to make the omen less ominous with assurances that they did not believe it.

Fenice listened with elation and dismay. She could not have asked for a better incident than this, for it would make her disappearance less questionable; but at the same time it would cast doubts on Aurelio that might make it difficult to marry him upon her return. She did not like to think that Aurelio would be more critically regarded than he was already. But she supposed that it could not be helped; she would straighten it out later, when her adventure was over. Belatedly she turned and kissed Ercole's cheek to show she put no stock in the omen.

"That's a brave girl," approved Cousin Valerio. He motioned to another group of servants. "Bring the final dish!"

Relieved to be past the dreadful moment, the guests surged forward, going toward the banqueting table where the servants were putting out crab shells stuffed with crab, scallops, clams, oysters, and braised calves' sweetbreads in a white-wine-and-cream sauce with garlic and tarragon. This was a dish for which Cousin Valerio's chef was famous, and this spectacular finale was greeted with a cheer.

"Do you want more than one crabshell?" Aurelio asked Fenice as he prepared to brave the crowd to get food for them both.

"No, I am quite full already," she said, doing her best to smile at him. "Thank you for fetching it for me."

His cheeks went rosy. "Of course. It is what I ought to do, isn't it?" He left before she could say anything more.

"I am heartily sorry, sorella mia," said Ercole as Aurelio went away from them. "I hope it does not bring you any ill will."

"Those who want to think badly will do it no matter what the omens are," she said, and smiled at him. "I do not think a glass of wine will change my life one way or another."

He returned her smile. "You are all pluck, Fenice, and that's the truth." His eyes were not as merry as his expression. "I wish I could undo what I have done."

"Well, you can't," she said with such pragmatism that he could find nothing to say to continue his excuses. "So let it be forgotten."

"I hope the rest are as willing to forget as you are," said Ercole. "If Febo were here, he would have thought of something to make the world ignore it."

"He is *not* here," Fenice pointed out. "So it doesn't matter what he might or might not have done."

"You're right," said Ercole, shaking his head. "I am being foolish. But I am so ashamed . . . I should not have—"

"Ercole," Fenice warned him, "if you are going to dwell on this, you will only fix it in my mind and in the minds of those who are listening, and any good your gesture might have done will be lost."

"Yes." Ercole nodded. "Yes. I am more rattled than I thought." He wiped his brow with the ruffled cuff of his camisa. "I will leave you now, sorella mia, so I cannot make a greater hash of it."

"Probably wise," she said, and noticed that Aurelio had succeeded in preparing two plates for them. "I will leave you, that will make it easier."

"I wish everyone were not watching," Ercole muttered.

"So do I, but that will not change anything," she told him as she went through the crowd toward Aurelio, who was standing beside one of the small tables; he looked slightly lost, Fenice thought, and slightly perplexed. She came as close to loving him in that instant as she ever had.

As she reached him one of the oil lamps suspended above their table sputtered, flared, and went out.

Conversation in the reception hall ceased; then someone coughed uneasily and everyone began to talk at once.

"Another omen," said Aurelio anxiously as he held the chair for Fenice. "This celebration will be talked about for some time to come, I fear."

"No doubt," said Fenice, beginning to wonder if her decision to run away had somehow become known to forces she did not understand, and those forces had begun to communicate her intent to Venice. The implications of that made her shiver.

"Are you cold?" Aurelio asked; he was just sitting down opposite her, but stopped.

"A draught," she said with a shrug. "There must be a window open."

"Or the door," said Aurelio, calming down and settling into his chair at last.

"Yes." She picked up her fork and began to eat; she made herself be calm and disinterested in omens and the speculations of the other guests.

"Fenice?" Aurelio ventured a short while later.

"Yes?" she replied.

"Are you happy? I'm very happy." His eyes beseeched her to agree. "Are you?"

She smiled at him. "Yes, Aurelio. I am happy."

He nodded. "It's all right, then."

"Yes," she said, vexed at herself for lying so easily.

When he had almost finished his first stuffed crab shell, Aurelio spoke again. "I am counting the days. Aren't you?"

This time she could answer him without mendacity. "Oh, yes, Aurelio. I am counting the days."

Fenice burned the sheets of vellum she had used to practice writing her note on: now that she had the words right and she knew she could make the message legible—barely—with her left hand, she took out the inkpad she had filched from the customs officer's desk at the Bacino di San Marco and picked up a quill. Although it was after midnight, she could not keep from looking about uneasily as she spread the Greek vellum on the library table and began to scrawl the note; she deliberately misused Greek words so that it would seem an uneducated person was the author:

> *Zucchar Family,* it read, *We have took your girl Fenice to hold for ransom. Do not look for her or she will be harm. What money we want we will tell you later. If you do all we say she will be safe.*
>
> *A Brother of the Scimitar.*

She studied the message, thinking the signature was a nice touch; it sounded sinister and foreign, and she decided that she was satisfied with the way it read—just threatening enough to make her family believe it. She hoped Artemesia would remember what she had said about being followed by a man in Greek sailor's clothes, for that would set the seal on her disappearance and save Aurelio from humiliation. While the ink dried she carefully took the inkpad and the quill and went to the window, where she eased the shutter open enough to drop them into the canal. Closing the window, she sighed once as she reached to roll up the vellum. This would be her last night to sleep in her own bed for some time. She hoped she would not be so nervous she would not rest well.

She let herself out of the library, the note tucked in her sleeve feeling as if it were on fire. She lowered her eyes as she made her way down the corridor toward her own room. It would be awkward to explain what she was doing up at this hour. She made it back to her chamber without detection. She closed the latch once she was inside, and leaned back against the door as if to assure herself it was shut. Then she went to her bed and climbed into it, stretching out in an effort to relax.

For some while sleep eluded her; when it came it was sudden, like a candle being extinguished, and she found herself in the realm of her dreams again.

The port was unknown to her, filled with spires and onion-domed buildings as fantastical as anything in Ariosto's fables. The people in the streets were equally astonishing, arrayed in brilliant colors that swirled around their bodies without shape; they gathered in market-squares as large as the island of Murano, where goods unlike anything Fenice had ever seen were offered under stalls and shop awnings as vivid as the clothes the people wore. Fenice's dream-self ambled through the market, stopping to examine some of the articles for sale, and to haggle in a language she did not recognize.

He was there, the foreigner from the ship—a proud figure in the gaudy chaos. He was cloaked in black, his hawklike features arresting, his manner imposing. Fenice found herself drawn to him through the market as if she were a lodestone and he were the north. More than anything she wanted him to notice her, to applaud her enterprise.

But the man paid no attention to her, and continued to search the crowd as if looking for someone or something other than Fenice. As the day gave way to night, he spread his cloak and rose in the air, flying far overhead, like a tremendous bird of prey; he circled the city and then headed toward the distant line of mountains away from the port. Fenice stood in rapt fascination, thrilled to the very core of her being and wishing she, too, could fly through the air and make her way to distant lands where the sea could not carry her.

Let the angry clouds rise up, the fatal tempest,
The hissing waves, all in confusion . . .
—Lodovico Ariosto

— VIII —

The day took forever to pass, moving from hour to hour as ponderously as the Doge in the Bucintoro going out toward the Adriatic Sea; when it finally ended, it seemed to have vanished in a moment, the separation of morning and evening nothing more than a breath or a blink. Fenice sat with her family through their farewell supper for Ercole, but she felt as if she were made of clockworks, controlled by a distant awareness that only grew more remote as she tried to bring herself back to herself. She said all the things that were expected of her, and she accepted Ercole's good wishes and apologies with what grace she could. When family prayers were over and everyone but Ercole prepared to retire for the night, Fenice began at last to feel she was master of her fate.

"Sail well, Ercole, and in safety," Fenice called to her brother from the stairs as he left the house bound for the docks to attend to the final loading and provisioning of the *Impresa*. She saw him wave and she did her best to smile.

"The tide turns the hour before dawn," he called back to her. "By the time you rise for morning prayers, I will be away from Venice."

"The hopes of the family go with you," she told him, repeating what had already been said earlier in the evening. Now it had more meaning for her than he knew.

"The *Impresa* will be worthy of your faith," Ercole promised as he opened the door to leave; he handed a scudo to the servant who waited to secure the house for the night. A heartbeat later he was gone.

In her room Fenice pulled her hidden treasures from their hiding place for the last time. She got out of her clothes and left them strewn about the floor, wholly unlike herself. After a brief reflection she turned her chest on its side and let the contents spill out, to help the impression that her room had been ransacked. She then dressed in her sailor's clothes, finding their strangeness exciting. The texture of the hose on her skin was rough enough to be at the edge of discomfort, and she tugged at them as she secured them around her waist before donning her upper hose. These were not stiff and so did not seem too uncomfortable, although Fenice wondered how men could stride about in them as they did. The giaquetta was long enough to make the shape of her body uncertain; she was once again grateful that she had small, high breasts which were easily disguised. She attached her wallet to the belt and buckled it around her waist, taking care not to fasten it too tightly so that her figure would not be revealed. She took out the rope-soled shoes and put them on; they were stiff and clumsy compared to the felt slippers she wore around the house, and she suspected they would give her blisters in time, but that was of small concern to her now.

She saved the most final for last: she unbraided her hair, letting the dark strands cascade over her shoulders one last time. This, she realized, would be more difficult to do than she had thought it would be. Giving up her hair had not seemed like much when she made up her mind to run away, but now that she faced the task, she hesitated. "Come, are you such a coward that you cannot cut your hair? Novice nuns do it—so can you." Her exhortation seemed forced, but she made herself answer. "I am able to do this. Watch," she said, and pulled a section of it toward her, and chopped it off at the level of her ear. She caught the hair before it fell and put it into a small cotton sack so that her family would not know what she had done. By the time she had cut it all to roughly the same length, she was crying, but continued steadfast in her plan. When she was done she pulled out one of her two caps and jammed it down over her head to conceal the ruin of her hair. Looking in the mirror she decided she was a passable boy, but for the lack of a beard. She would find a way to deal with that later.

Putting the sack of hair aside, she readied the larger bag with the things she would be taking with her—stiletto, scissors, flint-and-steel, changes of clothes, a wooden comb, and all the rest of the items she had gathered so carefully—testing its weight from time to time so that she would be able to carry it without being too much encumbered. That done, she set about rumpling her bed and disarranging her room. It was nerve-wracking to tip and overturn furniture in slow silence. Finally she took out the note she had scribbled in Greek and set it on her dressing table. Satisfied with her efforts, she began the wait for the servants to go to bed.

She was too excited to be sleepy, but a treacherous doze nearly overtook her while she waited, as if her dreams wanted to participate in her escape. She sternly told herself to remain awake, and concentrated on the shutters on her window to keep herself from becoming distracted.

The last sounds of the night were over and the Zucchar house had been silent for some little while when Fenice crept out of her room, taking care not to run into the jumbled furnishings, and made her way toward the servants' stairs in the rear of the house. Alert as a prowling cat, she went from shadow to shadow as silently as she could, pausing often to listen before making her next move. Her pulse sounded so loudly in her ears that she was surprised she did not wake the whole house.

In the kitchen she took four rounds of bread, a slab of smoked ham, and three whole cheeses, as well as a small crock of preserved fruit and a jug of olive oil. This would last her at least five days, and by then she was certain she could find her way around the ship well enough to get food. She hesitated, and then took a good-sized goatskin of water, for she remembered everything Febo had told her about the danger of drinking salt water, a second wick for her oil lamp, and she was ready to go.

The back door was at the end of a short corridor: a massive, thick thing, banded with iron. As she pushed back the bolt that served as a lock, the wood shuddered and groaned. Fenice froze, listening with such intensity that she thought she could hear the footsteps of mice in the pantry. When nothing happened, she continued her work, moving much more slowly and making every effort to keep the bolt from touching anything that might give the alarm. She thought of the man sleeping behind the pantry to prevent theft by servants or rats, and prayed that he was a sound sleeper. She held her breath, waiting, and then completed her work. When the bolt was free of the large iron staples, she eased the door open enough to slip out; she pulled the door closed and felt slightly guilty that she could not set the bolt back in place from the outside. She hurried to the edge of the canal where the cook kept a small boat tied up for market trips. Fenice loosened its line as she tossed her sack of hair and bag of supplies into it, then she climbed into it, shoving back from the steps at the same time. She used the oars clumsily, but was able to maneuver toward the docks without mishap.

Now that she was away from the house, Fenice began to feel excitement deep within her. She had to admit to herself that she had not believed she could get as far as she had; her dream of adventure had been as much a dream as a plan until this moment. She would have liked to cheer her accomplishment, but she knew that was folly; she continued her steady, inexpert rowing toward the docks at the edge of the Bacino di San Marco.

Approaching the docks, Fenice recognized the *Impresa* at once: the ship was at the second pier, a crane swinging wrapped bales from the dock, over the deck to the hold. In the torchlight the shadows were huge and unsteady as the flames wavered in the southwesterly wind. The water was a pattern of firelight and darkness as Fenice pulled into the shadow of the dock and eased the boat toward the place where the *Impresa* waited. Working carefully, she eased the boat up to the steps at the edge of the Bacino, and then she secured the boat to a piling while she took her things and climbed out. This was the last part of her escape, and surely it was the riskiest. She loosened the line around the piling and set the boat adrift, then crept up to the wharfside. The smell of the docks had never struck her before, but now it did—that combination of salt, brine, tar, and wet wood that she had not thought of any importance was a symbol of her home, the home she would leave before first light. The finality of it was staggering.

She reminded herself she would be back before the year was over, but it did not lessen the impact of her realization. She put her head down until she was certain she had control of her emotions at last, and then she started toward the loading area, doing her best to look like she belonged here. If she were discovered now, she would be disgraced and her family with her, and that was more than she could bear; she had been watching sailors, and now she did her best to emulate all she had seen. It took all her concentration to keep from staring at the activity around her, but she made herself behave as if she had seen all this many times before; she even spat as she had seen the sailors do, pleased that she had hit upon such an authentic act.

Approaching the men working the crane, Fenice slipped into the shadow of the ship and stood there, wondering how she would get aboard. She had not imagined she would have any trouble if she got this far, as if she had only to reach the ship to be aboard it. But she clearly could not go up the gangplank with the rest of the crew, and she could not join the convicts at the oars, for they were carefully counted and delivered to the ship in the care of a prison official. She gave a soft snort of frustration as she contemplated the difficulty of her situation. Turning back now was unthinkable; she would be too humiliated to do anything more than hide in her room, assuming she found a way back into the Zucchar house. There had to be some way onto the ship. She could not come this far only to be thwarted in boarding. She squinted up at the hull, realizing she could not get up it, and the heavy lines holding the ship to the pier would be watched for rats.

The crane swung over the dock again, and the loading pallet lowered for the next part of the cargo. Fenice watched it carefully, her mind working furiously. It would be chancy but she knew it would be her best—perhaps her only—opportunity. Quickly she studied the cargo waiting to be loaded. One of the corded bales caught her eye: a pallet of Milano wool standing on end. There were spaces between the bales—not very large, but enough for her to fit into one if she stuffed her bag into another of the spaces. She could remain there for a while after the pallet was stowed, and that would diminish the likelihood of her being found. The trick would be to get into the bales without being noticed.

As if in response to her wish, a short while later a small cannon being loaded aboard the next ship down the docks slipped in its lines and began to roll toward the water. Shouts for help went up at once, and the men working all rushed to save the cannon.

Fenice moved quickly. She glanced about to be certain no one watched from the deck of the *Impresa,* and then rushed toward the bales. She scrambled atop them using the heavy ropes that bound them for footholds. The cloth was not a very stable footing and she nearly fell as she made her way to the first opening between the great rolls of cloth. She shoved her bag down the nearest hole and slipped into the largest one. The bales held her upright and kept her from taking a deep breath, but they also concealed her completely.

A short while later the loading resumed, and Fenice waited for the moment when the pallet of wool bales would be swung aloft in its journey into the hold. She listened to the sounds, but the cloth muffled so much of it that she gave up trying to make sense of what she heard. It was enough, she told herself, to be about to be off on her adventure; these last moments of discomfort and uncertainty meant little to her, for in a very short while she would be bound for all the ports on the Galley of Romania. She remembered her geography lessons and smiled as she recounted the ports to herself: Corfu, Coron, Negroponte, Constantinople, Varna, Kaffa, Tana, Trebizond, Sinop, Constantinople again, and back to Corfu and Venice. They might stop at Serres or Salonika on the way back if trading had gone very well. Not as far as the Galleys of Barbary-and-Aigues-Mortes or Flanders, perhaps, but much more exciting because of the foreignness of the places. She smiled in anticipation. All her studies had told her much about these places but she knew that the cities themselves were much more than she had learned about in her studies.

Her thoughts were interrupted by a jolting as the first lines were secured to the pallet. She felt the bales shift, pressing in on her more tightly than before. She resigned herself to the impossibility of taking a deep breath until she was secure in the hold.

The pallet lurched upward, swinging in a way that made Fenice wonder if she would be seasick. Up the cloth went, hovered, swaying, then swung over and began to be lowered. It was so thrilling that Fenice had to bite her lower lip to keep from crying out in triumph. The pallet swung precariously, and there were shouts from the men on the ship as they struggled to keep it from slamming into the side of the hold or being upset on the deck; in her hiding place Fenice tried to hang onto the wool in the bale in order to keep from sliding between the bales where she might be crushed. Steadying hands seized the cables and guided the pallet with its load of baled wool into the hold where other hands wrestled it into position.

"Thank God and my good Angel," whispered Fenice as the pallet was lashed in place in the hold. She waited where she was until the men left the cargo hold and the hatch was battened into place; it would be some little time before the last inspection was made of the hold prior to getting underway, and for that time the hold would be left alone. She listened to be sure all the sailors had left: only then did she try to get out of her hiding place; it turned out to be more difficult than she had expected. When she had got into it she had had the ropes securing the load for purchase, but now she had only the wool, which resisted being pulled or bunched to give her hand- and footholds. By the time she reached the top of the bale she was exhausted; the bales were within four handsbreadths of the ceiling of the hold, which meant she had to lie on her stomach to move about. Slowly she pulled her bag from its place between the bales and then slithered over to the edge. There was no light in the hold and she did not trust herself to feel her way, since she had so little knowledge of what else had been loaded here. She could hear the convict oarsmen being brought aboard as the smaller holds were filled and closed, and she realized they would soon be underway.

The palpitation she had expected to have at this realization was lessened by fatigue. Now that she was actually on the ship and the ship was preparing to sail, her hours of work and anxiety took their toll on her. The rocking of the ship proved too much, and she began to drift off.

* * *

At the Zucchar house, Enrico, who was sleeping in the alcove beside the pantry, was dreaming of cheeses and buttered crab—no doubt due to the odors from the kitchen—when he became dimly aware of the sound of scampering feet. He roused himself enough to contemplate the stone ceiling over his head, trying to determine what had interrupted his slumber. The two blankets he had were hardly enough to keep off the chill, but that was true all winter long, so it was not the cold that had brought him out of sleep. Groggy, and with his dream still lingering, he rubbed his eyes and sat up, peering into the darkness.

Gradually he became aware of movement, skittering near the door to the pantry, and he realized that rats had got into the house again. Cursing quietly, he sat up and reached for the wooden club he kept near to his bed. The rats would regret disturbing him, he vowed to the air. His feet were cold as soon as they landed on the flagstone floor, and he added this to his indignities the rats would answer for.

Club in hand, he began to move about in the dark, listening to the rats scrabble across the stones, hearing their high, chittering cries. "Too late," he told them, his voice soft with menace. With that he brought his club down where the noise was the loudest and was rewarded with high, shrill shrieks; he had struck at least one of the interlopers. Feeling disgusted and pleased at once, he listened intently to determine where his quarry was; a single squeak alerted him: he swung the club again and his club found its mark a second time. More squeals of outrage and a sound of scattering activity. Very slowly Enrico lowered the club and went into the kitchen for the night-lantern; its light was feeble, flickering sporadically, possibly from low fuel, possibly from a draft: he did not know which and was in no state of mind to find out. Before he worried about the lanternlight, he had another duty to attend to go; if he allowed himself to be distracted, he would never remove the dead rat or rats, and the cook would be furious.

When he brought the lantern to the corridor where the rats had been, he found the bodies of four with a fifth still twitching feebly, its hindquarters broken. He brought the club down one last time to end the rat's misery; it was only vermin, but Enrico did not like to see it suffer, for he knew it was not Christian to make a dumb creature die in agony, even if it was a rat. He went back to the kitchen for the garbage bucket, feeling slightly nauseated at the prospect of handling the rats; they were so disgusting that the very sight of them made him squeamish—dead ones were as bad as ones alive. He scowled in anticipation of getting rid of them.

As he picked up each rat in turn by its tail and dropped it in with the chicken skins and fish heads, he tasted bile at the back of his throat. Damn the rats, he thought, always getting in and ruining his sleep; eating food and stealing rags to put in their nests. If there was one thing he disliked about Venice it was the rats which swarmed from ships to the lagoon islands in hoards that were unthinkable in their numbers and voracity. He put the bucket and the lantern back in the kitchen where the cook would expect them to be, and then helped himself to a large cup of wine to steady his nerves and make him get back to sleep; he would be rising soon enough, and he did not want to be so worn out from his activities that he could not work well during the day.

When he was back on his narrow bed, a thought occurred to him—how had the rats got in this time? He had tried to block every entrance they might use, and still they had gotten in.

Sailors were inspecting the hold, checking the lashings on all the cargo before their departure. Fenice watched them muzzily from her place atop the bales of wool, and she pondered her situation; she would have to find a place in the hold where she would not be noticed. She had not counted on the hold being so dark, but she would find a way to deal with it, she was certain of it. Her vantage point was protected enough that she was confident she could remain hidden until they were past Constantinople, when Ercole would have to welcome her to his voyage. Their lanterns brought a welcome brightness to her place in the shadows and she began to understand how much darkness she would have to endure on the voyage. Watching the crewmen go about their work she felt invisible, and this amused her: how she and Febo would laugh when she told him about it. She was not certain that Ercole would be as amused as Febo would be, but she suspected he would come to share her satisfaction in what she had done. She had to cling to the selvage of the rolled fabric as two of the sailors shoved the pallet more firmly into place. Between the motion of the bales and the rocking of the ship, she had to clamp her teeth shut to keep from vomiting. She had not expected the movement of the ship would distress her so much. Telling herself that she would become accustomed to it, she did the best she could to maintain her self-control.

Then the sailors were gone and the hold was dark again. Trying not to feel too wretched, Fenice reminded herself sternly that she had wanted to do this for years.

Lying in the dark, she became aware of the low growl of the ship's cat. It was too much, she thought, for the cat to be angry with her. She was about to shoo it away when she heard it land on something—she assumed with a shudder that it must have been a rat—and begin to devour its prey. At least, she thought, the cat would not give her away. It was little enough comfort for her on what she was starting to think would be an experience quite unlike the adventure she had always imagined. Feeling suddenly very sorry for herself, she began to drift into sleep once again.

This time she saw the man on the ramparts of a castle, high, forbidding crags behind him. The place seemed as remote as the moon, and the man the master of the wilderness and desolation. He stretched out his hands and beckoned to her, saying something she could not hear or understand, something that made her think of her own dissatisfaction as petty. She would have to be able to endure far more to be capable of him; she understood this with an intensity that shocked her.

A second figure entered the dream, and with the logic of dreams, the ship's cat did not seem out of place, although it was now the size of a bullock and the mouse that dangled from its jaws had Fenice's face. The cat leaped away and she saw the man again, commanding, austere, majestic; she wanted to call out to him, to promise she was coming as quickly as she could. But as she watched he rose into the air again and was soon a black place in the night sky and she was alone on the imposing battlements facing a phalanx of crags and peaks.

The activity on the deck above intensified. The calls of men took on an urgency they had not had a moment before. Ercole stood beside the helmsman, his eyes squinted toward the east. "The tide is turning," he announced, although all the crew knew it. "Make ready the ship!"

His boatswain repeated the order and signaled to the men in charge of the convicts at the oars; they would pull the ship away from the dock and out past the islands of Venice into the Adriatic, where the sails would be set to carry them south to Corfu.

The cook, a wizened man of mixed parentage who had grown up in a brothel in Palermo and had gone to sea at age nine, hurried to Ercole's side. "I have two more crates of chickens to be brought aboard," he said, mixing deference with authority.

"Aren't they loaded yet?" Ercole asked in some annoyance. He had wanted everything to go perfectly, and this was one of four disruptions he had endured that night.

"No, sir, and they will be more costly in Corfu." He knew that this mention of price would get Ercole's attention.

It did. "Manfredo!" he shouted. "Get those crates of chicken aboard. Now."

The tall sailor near the gangplank shrugged and did as he was ordered.

The ship rocked heavily, the weight of her cargo holding her well into the water, and Ercole wondered how it would feel to have her out on the sea at last. He thought of his mistresses and chuckled as he realized that of all the women he had ever known, none had held the fascination for him that this ship did. He thought of himself as her lover as well as her master, and the understanding made him have a moment of pity for Fenice.

Manfredo trudged up the gangplank, the crates of clucking, flustered chickens balanced on his shoulders. "For the kitchen?" he asked as he stepped onto the deck once more.

"Niccola will know what to do with them," Ercole confirmed. "See that he has them where he wants them. He has two barrels of salt beef and enough smoked hams to make a raft." This recitation was precariously close to boasting, but he made no apology for it; the men had every reason to be proud to be on this ship and in the employ of Zucchar.

The helmsman pointed down toward the pier. "The priest is here to bless our sailing," he announced.

"Summon the crew on deck and order the oarsmen to kneel," said Ercole, so pleased that he could hardly get the words out calmly. This would be a voyage he would remember all his life; it would change the House of Zucchar forever.

The boatswain bawled out orders, and in a very little while all the hands were on deck facing the pier where the vested priest stood in the predawn gloom, an aspergilium clasped in one hand, a pyx in the other. At his order all the men knelt.

Ercole made his way down the gangplank and knelt before the priest, who put the pyx in his hands, saying, "To keep you from the toils of Satan and the danger of the sea, with the Saints and Angels to guard and guide you." He made the sign of the cross over Ercole's head and bent to kiss his forehead; then he began his sonorous recitation in Latin while Ercole and his men spoke their responses.

"May God bless and keep the good ship *Impresa*, the family Zucchar, and all who sail on their ships," the priest intoned at the end of his prayers. "May no harm come to her, and may her name be held in high respect wherever she sails."

"Amen," said Ercole, getting to his feet with the pyx still in his hands. "Thank you, Padre, for coming to see us off."

"Do not forget you are forever in our prayers, my son," he said, and prepared to leave the pier. "I look forward to welcoming you home."

"As I look forward to returning," said Ercole, and continued on up the gangplank. Carrying the pyx to the helm and putting it in the little compartment at the base of the lantern above the tiller, he signaled the boatswain to hold up the image of Maria Regina Celeste as he knelt again.

The helmsman crossed himself and said to Ercole, "This will be a voyage unlike any other, I think."

Ercole grinned. "I think so, too," he said as he got to his feet. He ordered the men in charge of the convict oarsmen to set them at their benches: unlike in the war galleys, the oarsmen would not be permanently chained in place on the *Impresa* but would be allowed to retire to the narrow bunks or the small chamber where they would be fed when they were not needed to row. He paced while he waited for word that all was ready.

"Your brothers will be jealous, I think," said the helmsman; he had sailed on Zucchar ships for almost twenty years and was reputed to be one of the five best helmsmen in all la Serenissima. "I know I would be if I were not on this ship."

"They might be at that," said Ercole, doing his best not to appear as smug as he felt. "I hope they will have ships as fine as this one."

"But not yet," said the canny helmsman.

"Exactly," Ercole agreed. He was secretly pleased that one of his men understood his satisfaction: a ship named *Impresa* would surely be worthy of so well-omened an identity. He could not help himself—he knew this was his voyage of triumph, and he vowed he would make himself worthy of the trust his House put in him.

A short while later word was sent up from the oar-deck that all was ready. Ercole folded his arms to keep his chest from bursting with pride, and began to give the series of orders for castoff. His one regret was that the tide was turning too early for his family to be here to see him leave. That would have made the moment perfect.

The *Impresa* pulled away from the pier as the oarsmen began their work to bring the ship around in the Bacino di San Marco. The first glint of light was shining in the east when the *Impresa* swung around to face the southeast and the channel that led around the Lido to the open sea; below in the hold, Fenice slept on, lulled by the rhythm of the oars and the dark splendor of her dreams.

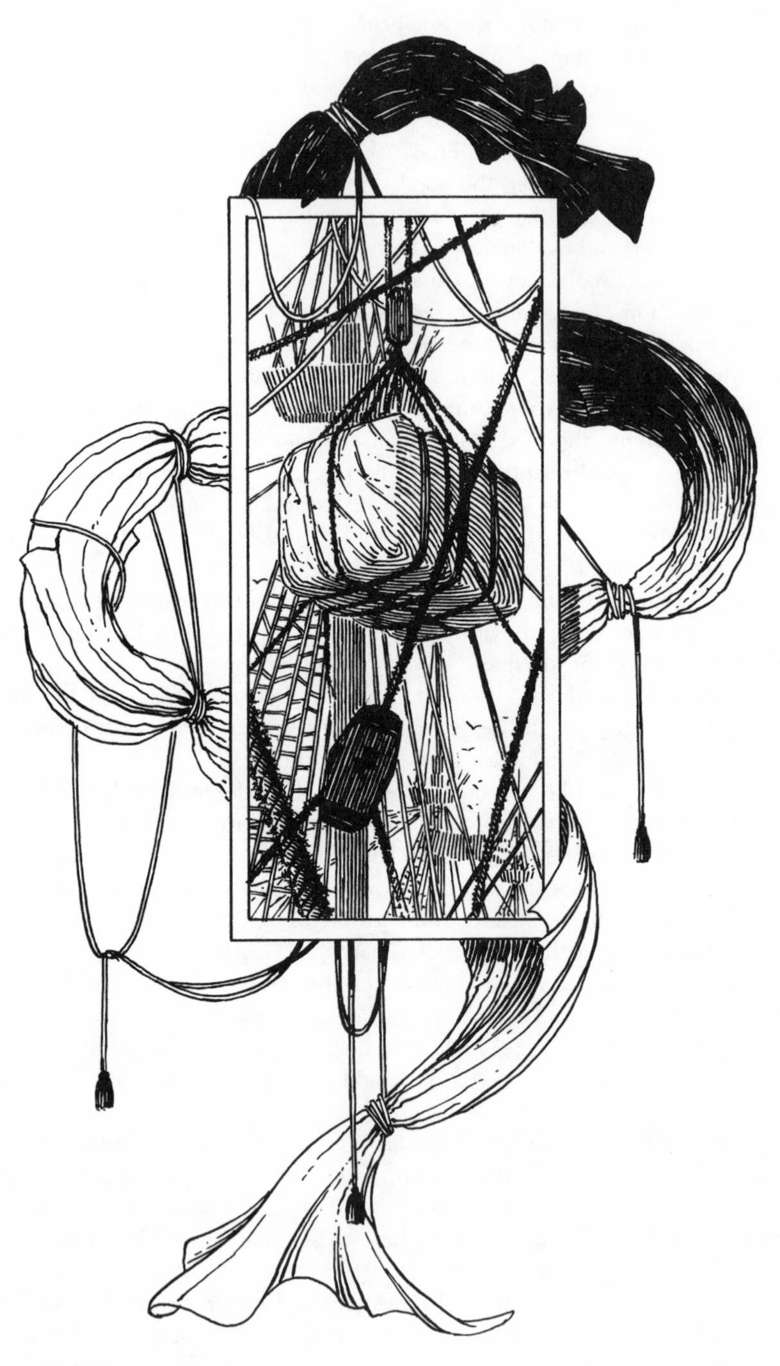

Beware that no one discovers you,
No gentle enemy apprehends . . .
—Guido Cavalcanti

— IX —

As the *Impresa* pulled away from the pier, Enrico woke for a second time. This time he did not bother to curse, for the light in the window warned him it was nearly time to be up. The cook would come soon and the household would gather for prayers and a meal; the few minutes of sleep he lost were of no importance. He rubbed his face and got out of his night-smock and into his clothes as quickly as possible, for the morning was damp and chilly. Rubbing his hands together, he went into the kitchen and was startled to see one of the scullions returning from the back of the house, the bucket that had held the dead rats in his hands. Enrico was surprised that the scullion had been able to get the bolt drawn, but said nothing about it so that he would not discourage the youngster from showing such responsibility.

"Who went out?" the scullion asked, cocking his head in the direction of the back door.

"You did," said Enrico, not yet awake enough to enjoy such games.

"No," said the scullion. "Before me."

"What do you mean, before you?" Enrico wanted a cup of wine and his bread-and-cheese; until he had them he wanted no disturbances.

"When I got here, the jigger was off the door," said the scullion, his back-alley jargon reminding Enrico that there were thieves about, and that the house of a rich merchant might be one that would be hard to resist. He straightened up, and although still not completely awake, gave the scullion his whole attention. "Tell me."

The boy coughed nervously. "Well, if you don't mind, I think I'd rather wait until the majordomo is down, if you take my meaning."

"You mean you do not want to be blamed for the back door being unbolted. I will vouch for you," Enrico said, and thought he might have been too hasty, for if the scullion was an accomplice of thieves, Enrico could be left accountable for any misfortune the Zucchar family suffered through his lack of vigilance.

The scullion shrugged his apology. "You can see my worry, can't you?"

"Of course, of course," said Enrico quickly. "But if mischief has been done, the sooner it can be identified and made known, the better, don't you think?"

"If it's been done, it's too late," said the scullion; his dirty face had a crafty look to it, as if he were trying to judge how he could use this to his advantage.

"I'll just go see," said Enrico, belatedly thinking this could be the scullion's idea of a joke. He stepped into the corridor and felt the draft that was testament to the door being open; he went and looked anyway, and noticed how carefully the bolt had been stood against the wall, as if the person who removed it might have planned on returning. He studied the open door with some perplexity, but no answers suggested themselves, and he abandoned his efforts with the uneasy sensation that he was overlooking something obvious. As he went back to the kitchen, he said, "It was like that when you discovered it? You changed nothing?"

"My word, I didn't," said the youngster with feeling. "I'm not loopy."

"When the cook comes, I will go and find the majordomo," said Enrico, anticipating what that formidable man would have to say at having his morning disrupted.

"Good on you," the scullion responded impertinently. He was beginning to enjoy himself; he had been expecting a scolding for the rear door, but now it looked as if he would not have to endure it, and that he might get some favorable recognition for a change.

"The sooner we report this, the better it will look," said Enrico, making another attempt at persuasion.

"Maybe," said the scullion, his face closed; he would not welcome any more prying. "If you don't got work to do, I have."

"Truly." So Enrico set to getting the kitchen ready for the cook. As he went about his chores, he made an attempt at conversation, thinking he might be able to learn more if the lad could be moved to reveal what he knew before the cook and the major domo arrived. "Do you think Captain Enrico's ship has left the Bacino yet?"

"Not yet," said the scullion, scoffing at the notion. "She has to come around and go out past San Giorgio Maggiore. Then she'll steer for the northeast end of the Lido before she's in the sea for proper."

"You sound as if you're interested in seafaring," said Enrico, recalling how often he had longed to go out on the ships when he was younger.

"Aren't I," said the scullion.

"Then why do you not find a ship's master who will take you as an assistant to his cook? You could advance to a higher position if you wanted to make yourself useful." He hoped this might shake the boy's resolve to remain silent.

"What ship would have me?" the scullion asked.

"One of Zucchars', perhaps, if you help them now," said Enrico. "If you do them a service now, you might have the reward you seek."

The youngster's face was a study in conflict: ambition and hope warring with suspicion and cynicism. He moved away from Enrico as if to conceal his state of mind. Finally he wiped his face with his sleeve and rounded on Enrico. "You will say that I didn't open the door."

"I will say that you said you did not, and that you spoke willingly," Enrico replied. "And I will tell the majordomo you have come forward out of concern for the household."

For a short while the scullion considered this; then he nodded. "All right. You get the majordomo now and I will tell him what I know. But," he added sharply, "you tell him that I was the one who found it out. I won't have you getting favor because of my telling."

"Certainly," said Enrico promptly, and took one of the oil lamps as he went to present the majordomo with the troubling news about the rear door. As he made his way to the ground-floor apartments of the majordomo, he began to rehearse what he would say, for the very presence of the majordomo rattled him and left him stammering as if he were a youth like the scullion. At the door, he hesitated, then knocked with more force than he had intended. "Signor Bruscanti," he called before he knocked again.

"I am awake," came the grumbling response a moment later. "What is the matter?"

"It is Enrico, sir, from the pantry? The scullion has alerted me to a . . . problem." He had chosen the least serious word he could find. He was conscientious about giving credit to the scullion, for he relied on the lad to be cooperative.

"A problem, is it?" Bruscanti coughed on the other side of the door. "Has there been pilfering?"

"There may have been," said Enrico cautiously. "You see, the back door was not bolted when the scullion came to the kitchen this morning."

"And the cook?" Bruscanti asked, his question measured, which in this man was a sure sign of concern. "What does he say?"

"He has not yet come to the kitchen, so he knows nothing of this. He will not be in the kitchen for a while yet," said Enrico, thinking it was too early for him to be waking the majordomo. He should have waited for the cook, he told himself inwardly.

"Then he could not have removed the bolt," said Bruscanti, making up his mind and opening his door at the same time. "Do you know how long the bolt was off the door?"

"No," Enrico said, faltering. "It was put in place last night, as it always is."

"Yes, yes," said Bruscanti impatiently. "And you were in the pantry anteroom, weren't you? Did you hear anything?" He was in his sleeping smock, his graying, normally clubbed hair in disarray around his shoulders, his eyes bleary with missed sleep.

"Only rats," said Enrico, apologizing with the admission. "I killed a few and the rest scattered."

"When was that?" Bruscanti demanded.

Enrico shrugged helplessly. "I heard nothing, not from Sant' Angelo, or

San Stefano. It would have been after midnight, but how much after . . ." He ended on a shrug.

"Had you any reason to think the door was unbolted then?" Bruscanti asked, the muzziness of early morning fading rapidly.

"There was no reason to think it was unbolted this morning until the scullion pointed it out to me." He was becoming very uncomfortable. "The cook should be in the kitchen shortly. Shall I go back? To go talk to him?"

Bruscanti was frowning thoughtfully. "What? Oh, yes. I will dress and be with you then." He was about to close his door when he gave one more order. "Post the scullion at the door."

"The rear door?" Enrico asked, to be certain he understood.

"Of course the rear door—what other door did you think? The pantry?" He shook his head. "Go. I will be along shortly."

Enrico was glad to comply.

Seabirds flocked around the masts of the *Impresa* as she passed San Giorgio Maggiore and turned north by northeast, keeping to the channel. The bell at San Lazzaro degli Armeni sounded its one dismal note to herald the dawn, making its greeting a dirge; aboard ship the activity was increasing as the men readied to unfurl the huge lateen sails; this being the first voyage, the yards were already hoisted and the sails were furled to them. They would be let down and tackled in this time; after this the yards would be raised with sails ready. It was light enough to make out shapes instead of shadows, so that the sailors were more than anonymous figures, and in a short while the sunrise would make the sea glow with its brilliance.

Coming down the channel, a Flemish brevarum was taking in sail for the approach to the Bacino; half a dozen of her crew came to the rail and stared as the *Impresa* continued on her way. Their excited shouts carried across the water.

Ercole strode about the deck, watching the crew with a sharp eye; he was not willing to allow any of them to interfere with his day of satisfaction. His ship was going to bring glory to his House, he was determined on that, and every aspect of this voyage would have to be near perfection. He squinted toward the eastern horizon, a bit disappointed that they would not be in position to hoist sail until shortly after sunrise, for he would have loved to see the sails spread at the first touch of the shining rays; that would have been a sight to boast of for years to come. But that was a minor consideration. There were fishing boats coming in from their night's work, and the fishermen stood in awe as the *Impresa* went regally on her way; with the Flemish ship, Ercole decided they had had witnesses enough, given the hour of the morning. There were four more ships moving into position in the Bacino, and they, too, would remember the *Impresa*.

The helmsman called for a sounding and was answered almost at once with a depth reading that was satisfactory; the Venetian lagoon was notorious for the shifting sandbars that were part of the waterways, and although the channel was dredged often, all ships took soundings as a routine precaution. "Three fathoms under the hull," he called out.

"Steady on, helmsman," Ercole shouted, hoping all the fishermen would hear the ring of his voice.

The first effulgence shot across the water, glowing and wonderful. The *Impresa*, new and unblemished, shone as if made of gold. This Ercole took as another good omen, and he saw some of his crew nodding in approval; he walked to the fo'c'sle, and across it to the bow, and looked at the sailors tugging the spritsail. He smiled as the spray stung his face and congratulated himself once more.

The Lido was just ahead, and the Adriatic lay beyond, beckoning.

"Spread sails!" he ordered, and heard the boatswain repeat it at a bellow; the great trapezoidal sails were released from the lateen yardarms as the sailors on the deck tugged at the shroudlines to trim the expanses of canvas.

The oarsmen slowed their rowing as the sails began to catch the wind.

"Ship oars!" Ercole called, and the chief of the oars roared it to his men.

The wind tugged at the ship, and she began to lean, shoulder to the swell.

In the rigging, the sailors cheered.

Signor Bruscanti showed no sign of his earlier disorder as he came into the kitchen. The cook, a burly man, stood indecisively with Enrico; Bruscanti regarded them dubiously. "Nothing is missing here?"

"A little bread and some cheese, perhaps one or two other things," said the cook.

"Bread and cheese," said Bruscanti thoughtfully. "Not meat, not spices?"

"Perhaps some meat," the cook conceded. "But not very much."

Bruscanti scowled. "The scullion—do you trust him?" The question was an accusation.

"In matters of the kitchen I do," the cook replied.

"Then you do not think he helped himself and conjured up this tale to cover his theft?" It was a very serious matter, and the cook replied carefully.

"I have sometimes given him small portions of food we have not used, at the end of the day. He has no reason to steal from this house and every reason to defend it. I would never think he would steal so capriciously and leave the household at risk."

"If that is what he did," said Bruscanti, unconvinced.

"If it was his intention to steal," the cook persisted, "he should have been intelligent enough to take more than a few meals' worth. Why should he risk losing his hands for a few rounds of cheese?"

"Perhaps he thought it would not be noticed?" Enrico suggested, doubting it himself.

"He knows the kitchen is inventoried daily; where would be the sense in theft? There is so little to be gained and so much to be lost, judging by what appears to be gone. If he were going to take something, he would do better to take spices, if he wanted to conceal his prizes." He jerked his thumb in the direction of the passage where the scullion waited. "He could have escaped, if he had done anything so reprehensible. But he has not."

"It may be he is clever enough to know he could not escape this city," said Bruscanti, then held up his index finger to show he wanted no comment from the cook. "Still, as you say, he cannot be clever and foolish at once about the same thing." He sighed. "Bring the lad here. I suppose I will have to talk to him."

Enrico hastened to obey; he found the scullion by the back door, staring bleakly at the wet stones outside, though where the first rays of the sun struck they shone like fire. "Signor Bruscanti wants to talk to you," Enrico told him. "You have nothing to fear," he added, and knew it was a lie.

The scullion shrugged in a failed attempt at indifference to his fate. "He'll have questions, won't he? He thinks I done it."

"I've told him you did not," Enrico said, hoping to reassure the boy.

Two more scullions had arrived in the kitchen and they worked steadily so that it would not be too obvious that they were listening to what the majordomo had to say to one of their numbers.

"Now then," said Bruscanti. "What is your name, boy?"

The scullion looked slightly puzzled that he should be asked such a question, but answered quickly enough: "I'm Simone," he answered, ducking his head to show respect. "And I did not open the door. It was open when I got here."

"So Enrico has told me," Bruscanti remarked. "And I am inclined to believe him unless you give me cause not to." He shot a penetrating glance at Simone. "Well?"

"I found it open," Simone said hastily. "On my mother's grave I did."

"And there was no sign of damage beyond the door being open?" Bruscanti asked.

"If you mean it didn't look broke into, no, it didn't." Simone had a stubborn cast to his chin, and he was prepared to stand his ground as long as necessary. "The door's untouched and the bolt hasn't a mark on it. Go have a look at it yourself if you don't think I know what I saw." If he knew that making such a suggestion to a superior servant was audacious, he did not show it.

"And only a little food is missing," Bruscanti mused. "That is the most puzzling."

The cook stared at the pans hanging over the iron range, and he said, "The family will be down shortly and they will be hungry. I should be making their breakfasts."

"Yes—you shall directly," said Bruscanti, his manner distant while he thought. "Were any clothes missing from the servants' room?"

"I didn't look," said the cook, who rarely left his domain. "Enrico said nothing about it."

"If you like—" Enrico offered.

"Yes," said Bruscanti, continuing to muse over the baffling problem of the open door. He watched Enrico hurry off toward the servants' room, and remarked, "What can the purpose be? Could someone have wanted to watch the *Impresa* sail? Why not make a request to go? Signor Zucchar would not refuse to permit a servant to watch. Surely that would account for—" It was the most optimistic possibility, and the cook knew it.

"You would not think anyone would leave the house unprotected," the cook said, making this observation as calmly as he could. "No matter what their purpose was in leaving the house this way." He shook his head. "The master should be informed."

Bruscanti nodded, dreading his interview with Gaetano Zucchar; it was always risky to bear what might be bad news to the head of the house. "I will do so, when I understand a bit more."

"Is there anything to understand beyond what we know? What more is there to know?" The cook was starting to think about breakfast, and he stared at the bowl of eggs waiting at the end of the cutting table. "I should not delay, Signor Bruscanti. It is nearly time for prayers. The family expects—"

"Yes, yes," Bruscanti said with a fussy motion of dismissal, "go ahead." He paid no attention as the cook began to make his first preparations, dicing ham and crab with scallions and putting them to sauté with butter in a large iron pan; he stirred the contents occasionally with a long-handled metal spatula while he cut bread-rounds in half and hollowed out the center of each half; he soon had a dozen bread-shells waiting for their filling. The two scullions had built up the fire in the iron range and they now began to cut thick slices of cheese and put them on wide metal sheets to toast.

"Strange, that the door should be . . ." the cook ventured as he worked.

The scullions exchanged glances and tried to look busy.

"Do you think Simone will get into trouble?" one of them finally asked the cook, not daring to look at Simone himself.

"I think Simone has done a good thing in alerting Enrico to what he found," said the cook in a tone that did not encourage more questions.

Simone had sunk down on the stool by the open hearth and was looking woebegone. "I should have come later," he muttered. "I should've let one of you lot find it."

"You did well, Simone," said the cook, continuing his preparations so that the most wonderful aroma filled the kitchen, making them all hungry.

A moment later Enrico came back, his frown deeper than when he left. "Nothing is missing that I can tell," he said. "I don't like this, Signor Bruscanti. I am beginning to hope it was a thief and not someone . . . worse." He crossed himself for protection.

"What do you mean?" Bruscanti asked, suddenly paying close attention.

Enrico retreated a step. "Nothing," he said unconvincingly.

"If you know something, you had best tell me now." Bruscanti made this clearly a threat. "You should keep nothing back."

"I . . . I thought only that it could be that someone came into the house to harm . . ." He could not go on.

"You mean an assassin?" Bruscanti demanded, his own level of apprehension rising with each word.

"Well, it has happened in the past," said Enrico. "Not among merchants, but it could be that there are some who are jealous of the success our master has had, what with the *Impresa* sailing and all." He coughed delicately. "Not that I think anyone would do such a thing."

"Of course not," said the cook, who was adding pepper and ginger to the sauté.

"It is impossible," Bruscanti stated flatly, but there was a shine in his eyes that said otherwise.

"All the sons are away," said the cook as if this were a dire development. "The family will not easily put more ships on the sea."

Bruscanti went to Simone, who remained beside the hearth. "Did you see no one when you found the door had been opened?"

"No," said Simone, without apology for rudeness.

"You're certain of that?" Bruscanti pursued.

"Yes." He folded his skinny arms and looked up at the major domo. "If I had seen anyone, I'd've said so by now."

"Of course," said Bruscanti. He made up his mind. "I am going to tell the master. He will have to decide how this is to be dealt with."

Simone sighed deeply. "Trouble."

"Let us pray not," said Enrico devoutly.

Bruscanti turned crisply and went out of the kitchen toward the main part of the house, his stride long and purposeful. But once he was beyond the servants' rooms, his walk slowed and some of his determination faded. He made his way to the main stairs and went up them at a faltering pace. He was trying to decide what to tell his master when he reached the door to Gaetano's apartments; he knocked twice and waited.

Gaetano was almost dressed as he let Bruscanti into the room. "Have we heard from the docks? Has the *Impresa* sailed?" His smile bordered on smug.

"No," said Bruscanti, then said, "That is, I do not know. No one has brought word."

"Then why are you here?" Gaetano Zucchar's face showed no sign of alarm, only bafflement. "Is something the matter? Is one of the servants ill?"

"Nothing like that," said Bruscanti, his eyes lowered respectfully. "The scullion reported that he found the rear door unbolted this morning."

"Unbolted?" Gaetano repeated. "How is that possible?"

"I have been trying to determine just that, sir." He made a sign of deference. "It seemed best to tell you."

"Yes, you're right about that." He went to put his ruff on, adjusting it in a tall mirror of the best Venetian glass—flawless and thick with beveled edges in a handsome frame. "What an odd thing, having the door unbolted. Was anything taken?"

"A little food. Not much," said Bruscanti, glad that he had something encouraging to tell his master. "The scullion says he saw no one. And Enrico was sleeping in the pantry antechamber, and he saw and heard nothing."

"Um," said Gaetano; he was too happy with his family's newest success to be vexed by such a strange event. "Perhaps someone went out early," he suggested.

"We will know when the household gathers for morning prayers," said Bruscanti. "If anyone is missing—"

"Unless the culprit had been out and returned," said Gaetano, chuckling.

"Then why leave the bolt off the door?" asked Bruscanti, troubled that his master was not taking this news more seriously.

"Someone wanted to see the *Impresa* leave the Bacino; that will be the answer. The fellow will be back shortly, now that the sun's up and the ship underway. I'll scold him, certainly, but I can't blame him for wanting to see her go." Gaetano stood back and admired his ruff. He was dressed very finely, to show everyone in Venice how proud he was.

"If that is the reason the door was left open," said Bruscanti glumly. "It could mean something less . . . less flattering, sir."

"So it might, so it might," Gaetano agreed. "But let's not think of such things until we must, Bruscanti." He clapped his hands. "It is almost time for prayers. Come along."

Bruscanti fell in behind his master, closing the door for them both as they stepped into the corridor; Gaetano was already at the top of the stairs, moving briskly, smiling with satisfaction in anticipation of the news of Ercole's departure.

Rosamonda emerged from her chamber and went to touch cheeks with her husband, wishing him the joy of the day. She, too, had dressed well, looking forward to promenading at the Piazzetta di San Marco later that morning.

Eloisa followed them down the stairs, all but frisking, and a moment later Bianca joined her, her clothes as chaste as a nun's habit; they provided a striking contrast, the one young and flirtatious, the other older and restrained. The two sisters smiled at one another.

At the foot of the stairs, Gaetano looked back up them. "Where are Artemesia and Fenice? I thought they would be the first ones down this morning."

"Artemesia is finishing dressing," said Eloisa. "I heard her singing."

"And Fenice?" asked Rosamonda. "She is probably nervous with her wedding so near. This is a very exciting time for her."

"She must have stayed up late," said Bianca. "I heard her moving about at a late hour." She blushed, as if admission of so much was a fault in her.

"She was reading maps," said Eloisa derisively. "To know where Ercole is going."

"She may have been," said Bianca, unwilling to say anything that seemed uncharitable. "I think it is very kind of her to care so deeply about the travels of our brothers."

"It is," Gaetano seconded, his face brightening as Artemesia rushed out of her room, her neat ropa over a satin sottana showing that she, too, looked forward to showing the world how well the House of Zucchar was doing. "Now if your sister will only join us, we can have prayers."

"Master," said Bruscanti in a low voice. "This other matter?"

"Yes, we will tend to that, Bruscanti," said Gaetano. "Artemesia, go knock on Fenice's door and remind her she is late."

Artemesia, who had come down only four steps, retraced them and went toward Fenice's room, her steps sounding lightly as she went to knock on the door. She rapped twice. "Fenice? Are you up? We're about to begin prayers." She waited, expecting a reply. When none came she knocked again. "Don't tell me you're still asleep," she teased. "I will come in and rock you out of bed."

"What is she saying?" Rosamonda called up from below.

"Nothing," Artemesia answered. "She probably overslept." She laughed. "And all this shouting should shake the dreams from her head."

"Then go in and wake her at once," said Rosamonda. "It is time she was dressed, let alone awake."

Knocking again, Artemesia called merrily, "You do not want Aurelio to think you lazy, do you? I am coming in." With that she lifted the latch and swung the door open. The disarray shocked her so much that she did not move as she stared at it; she thought she had somehow got into the wrong room, a place where such confusion was expected. She put her hands to her face, realizing that some great catastrophe had overtaken her family, but she could not yet comprehend what it was. Then she dropped to her knees and wailed.

"Artemesia?" Rosamonda called out sharply. "What on earth? Is she ill?"

"No," Artemesia answered just above a whisper, then repeated the word loudly enough to be heard. "Come up. You must come up."

The distress in her voice brought her family as rapidly as gunfire would; they stood in the door dumbfounded at what they saw. Only Bruscanti, standing behind Eloisa and Bianca, realized the significance of the state of the room, and that left him speechless.

"Oh, Dio Mio," Rosamonda exclaimed as she came to Artemesia's side. "Where is Fenice?"

"Not here," Artemesia said, and began to sob. "Look, Madre Mia, look."

Gaetano wandered about the strewn clothes and bedding, the overturned furniture. He noticed the sheet of vellum, and stared at it as if he had no idea what it was. With his wife watching him in horror, he picked it up and read it. Then he read it a second time. "I . . . I can't . . ." He held it out to Bianca. "What does this say?"

Bianca took the note and read it through, her pale features turning ashen as she read. "It means," she said very quietly, "that someone has taken her."

Gaetano nodded once. "That is what I thought, too." His face was dazed.

Rosamonda hurried to his side and took the letter from Bianca, staring down at it in disbelief. She looked blankly at the poorly written words. "What is it?"

"Greek, Madre Mia," said Bianca. "Very ill-framed Greek." She crossed herself and began to pray.

Eloisa had not moved from her place in the door. "What are you saying?"

Now Rosamonda began to cry. "She is gone." The anguish of her cry brought Gaetano out of his stupor.

He turned decisively to Bruscanti. "You. I want you to summon all the servants. Ask if any of them heard anything in the night. If you find out anything, inform me at once." He strode about the room with so much contained force that the air all but crackled around him. "We will have prayers when that is done. Well, go on, Bruscanti. Now."

Bruscanti bowed and hurried off to do as he was told. He was already thinking about the rumors that would be flying in a matter of hours.

Bianca stopped her prayer long enough to ask, "Do you think they will hurt her?"

"I pray not," said Gaetano. "It is bad enough that she has been taken. We must hope that her captors will leave her unharmed."

"Oh, they must, surely they must. If they intend to ask a ransom, they would not do anything that would . . ." Bianca fumbled for the best words.

"You mean she will not be raped," said Artemesia, and heard her mother shriek. "Well, that is what you mean, isn't it?"

"Yes," said Gaetano for Bianca, his heart heavy. "I must send word to the Guard."

"Yes. At once," said Rosamonda, trying to control her weeping. "Find out what ships have sailed other than ours."

"You do not think she has been carried away, do you?" Bianca asked, more appalled than before.

"They would be foolish to keep her here," said Gaetano heavily. "They will have to take her away from Venice."

"She wants to . . ." Eloisa began, then thrust her fist against her mouth.

"Oh, Madre Maria!" Artemesia exclaimed. "She told me someone had been following her. She said it was a man in Greek clothing. I thought she was being playful, but if that letter is in Greek—" She swallowed hard.

"What are you saying?" Gaetano demanded, coming and taking Artemesia by the arms.

"Padre!" Artemesia protested. "She said a man had been following her. She pointed him out to me."

"Then you saw him?" Gaetano asked with a ferocious glance toward his wife.

"N . . . No," Artemesia admitted. "I didn't think it mattered," she added. "I thought it was some kind of . . . mistake. Oh, Padre Mio, I am sorry. If I had thought there was anything *wrong,* I would have said something. But it seemed so . . . trivial."

Rosamonda looked stricken. "A man followed her and we were told nothing?"

"She told Aurelio," Artemesia said, offering it as an excuse.

In the door, Eloisa stood shaking her head, large tears sliding down her face unnoticed.

"Aurelio!" Rosamonda moaned. "Oh, poor, poor man."

Now Gaetano's shoulders sagged as if the weight of this disaster had become too heavy. "I must send him word."

"Yes," said Rosamonda automatically. "He must not hear it from anyone but us." She wiped her face with the sleeve of her sottana, the grandeur of her clothes forgotten.

"Then I will have to tend to it now," said Gaetano dully as he released Artemesia. "I will want to know more from you, figlia mia."

Artemesia ducked her head to show compliance. "Do you think we will find her?" she asked in a small voice.

"If God is good," said Gaetano as he took the note in his hand again. "Dear God, what am I to say to Aurelio?"

PART II

THE GALLEY OF ROMANIA AND THE PORT OF VARNA

1573

Therefore I only call him wise
Whose actions rise from reason's ordered thought . . .
—Enzo Re

— X —

Cheers from the sailors and the squeal of rats woke Fenice; she felt the ship heel on the wind, and she had to fight down a sudden fright; the ship was not sinking. She had seen how ships tilted in the water as the wind carried them along, but she had never felt it for herself. Morning bells from San Nicolo carried across the water from the Lido; she recognized them and realized they must have entered the Adriatic for the sound to be on her right. She hung onto the wool with such tenacity that her hands shook with the effort. She could not keep that up all day long, she told herself as she listened to the oarsmen on the deck above her move about, preparing to retire to their cramped bunks for some sleep. How could they? She was so consumed with the joy of her adventure that she could not have slept again if she had been awake for three days. She strove to make herself more comfortable atop the bales and discovered she shared her perch with rats. At another time she might have screamed; now she hissed and struck out, using her cap for a weapon. She could not let them find her, not yet, not before they were well beyond Corfu and into the Greek islands, for her brother might decide to put her ashore at Corfu—they had cousins who would keep her until either Lionello or Febo should stop there on the way home. That would disgrace her completely, and her ruse of a kidnaping would be revealed for what it was.

"Stop it," she whispered vehemently to herself. "You cannot keep on this way." She would dishearten herself before she was out of sight of land—not that she could see anything here in the hold, which was a problem she had not counted on—and her adventure would be over before she had seen anything of the world. She frowned at herself, knowing she would need to be more stalwart than this if she was to have the fun she had planned. She tugged her bag of supplies toward her protectively and pulled out some of the bread she had taken; immediately the rats were back, crowding near her. Fenice had not considered the rats when she prepared for her voyage, and she had an uneasy moment when she wondered what else she might have overlooked in her planning. As she gnawed at the bread, she realized she would not be able to eat much of it. How she had laughed at tales of seasickness, and how unamusing it was now! She put her head down and did her best to ignore the rats. It would serve them right, she thought, if she threw up all over them. She tasted bile at the back of her throat and had to clamp her mouth closed against it. She shoved her bread underneath her, to keep the rats from eating it as she tried to regain a smidgen of appetite, while the *Impresa* stood out to sea, magnificent in the full light of morning.

The sounds on the deck were changing: immediately above her the convicts were being given their food; from the smell that came down to Fenice, it was some kind of gruel, made of boiled grain and suet. With her stomach already feeling uncertain, this odor banished her appetite but not her hunger. She could not imagine eating anything so disgusting. Above her the convicts' activity steadied. From time to time Fenice could hear Ercole call out something, which occasionally the boatswain would repeat in stentorian tones; each time she heard his voice, she felt less lonely. Then there would be a scramble and the trim of the ship would alter a bit. Fenice tried to use this to determine the passage of time, but was not familiar enough with the ship traveling for her to find it reliable. She let her thoughts drift as she braced herself again, picturing in her mind what she assumed had to be taking place on the *Impresa,* and decided she would have as much enjoyment this way as she would have at Ercole's side.

Pointing to a spire on the distant shore, Ercole said, "We are making good time. We will be out of sight of land shortly." The morning breeze was brisk and chilly, but the sky was clear winter blue, portending a day of fine sailing. "The oarsmen made our departure very fast. Not like a war galley, but faster than our carracks." He made no attempt to hide his deep confidence in his new ship, even though she was untried.

The boatswain nodded. "This is a fast girl; well, we knew that, didn't we? She'll make all the merchants jealous, the Sultan's as well as the Doge's."

"It would please me to find you are right." It was just what Ercole expected to happen. With the defeat of the Turks at Lepanto, he thought that the Sultan's merchants would want to find every opportunity to best the Venetians in trading, for they had failed to do so in arms. Few things would delight him so much as seeing a copy of his ship under the Ottoman flag next year.

"Your cousins at Corfu will be overjoyed to see this ship," the boatswain said, his leathery face coming as close to a smile as it ever did.

"So I think," agreed Ercole. "And for an early sailing, God has been kind to us. May He show us such favor the rest of our journey."

"It is the ship. *Impresa*, the daughter of Fortune." The boatswain nodded a strict approval. "She will look after us."

"May it always be so," Ercole said, narrowing his eyes at the receding land. "Bring me the Dutch glass," he ordered. The brass-cased spyglass was another of Ercole's treasures, one he used with great self-satisfaction, for it was known that the Dutch were the finest opticians in the world.

"Tell me, Captain," said the boatswain, "has the Doge asked you to do any . . . favors for him on our Galley?"

"Favors?" Ercole echoed. "What do you mean, favors?"

"Oh, you know what sort of favors the Doge requests—a note delivered here, a chest of ducats there, a word of warning at another place, a gift somewhere else." The boatswain winked. "With such a fast ship, and so much cargo, it would not be noticed if one or two of the cases loaded aboard carried the Doge's Seal."

"Why should I undertake such a mission on this first voyage, and on an unproven vessel?" Ercole's question rang false even to him.

"Why?" The boatswain pretended to consider his question. "You have left port earlier than most merchants; you carry a full cargo; the ship is expected to be fast; and the oarsmen are convicts of the Venetian state."

"We have paid for their labor," said Ercole quickly. "What else would honest merchants do?"

"They might agree to do something unofficial for the Doge, just to oblige him." The boatswain gestured a dismissal.

"Thank you, Rainardo," said Ercole. "If it seems necessary, I will speak to you."

"*Sta bene,*" said the boatswain, standing aside to allow the cabin boy to hand the spyglass to Ercole; Ercole reached out and tousled the lad's hair before lifting the spyglass to his eye and directing it toward the dark line along the western horizon. "There. San Procopio. And we are here in excellent time."

"You're not surprised, are you?" Rainardo inquired.

"Not really," Ercole said, though he was startled by the swiftness of their passage. The narrower hull—though not so narrow as a war galley—and the heavier keel had given the ship more speed than he had anticipated. "We will be in Corfu twelve hours ahead of schedule if we can keep up this pace."

"That should make your cousins glad," said Rainardo. "I will inform the crew, if you like, that we are—"

"Not yet," said Ercole. "We do not know what weather we may face ahead, and if we must battle the winds, we may yet lose some of the headway we have gained." He scanned the horizon all around the ship for any signs of clouds. "Clear, and clear, and clear." Lowering the spyglass he added before Rainardo could speak, "Yes, we might still have winds. If they are behind us, so much the better. We'll set the sails goosewing and give the oarsmen a rest for a while."

"Goosewing it is," said Rainardo, "when the wind is at our back. We are on a broad reach now, a few more points to the southeast and we should have it."

"It is not the swiftest sail we have," Ercole said, "but it is the steadiest, and I am curious to see how much progress we can make without making this a race."

"Do you still think we would arrive in Corfu early if we do this?"

"I think we will." Ercole spoke as if of a beloved mistress. "She is the finest ship on the Adriatic." He held up his spyglass again and satisfied himself that they were now completely out of sight of land. "When we stop at Zara, we will have the opportunity to set the first of our times." He grinned. "And the Doge will hear of it."

"The harbormaster will be astonished." Rainardo rubbed his beard. "And we may well be in Corfu before word is back in Venice." He decided to make one other observation. "The Galley of Romania is usually begun in the summer. Do you have no fear that we may pay for our early departure with storms?"

"We may, but we will return in more clement weather than is usual, which will be splendid. We will bring amber and furs from Tana, silk from Trebizond, and jewels and spices from Constantinople." He made a gesture of enthusiasm. "My father may have ordered me to depart early for other reasons, but he will yet say that he has made the most audacious use of good fortune ever known in our family."

"You are missing your sister's wedding," said Rainardo. "That must make you sad."

"Two sisters' weddings, I think," said Ercole. "What better gift can I bring them than their share of the wealth we will have on our return?"

"As you say," was Rainardo's neutral response.

"Do not fret, boatswain. We will triumph on every point."

"Of course we will," said Rainardo with a lack of conviction that annoyed Ercole.

"Why are you so . . . so determined to anticipate the worst?" he demanded.

"Because you will not consider it," said Rainardo. "You are telling yourself that we can have nothing to contend with but how to spend our fortunes; I know the sea too well for that, and so should you." He walked a few paces away. "You are a fine captain, and in the past you have been prudent. But now that you have the *Impresa,* you are as reckless as a youth on his first voyage. It is unlike you to assume that nothing will go wrong."

Ercole shook his head. "You have a right to say this, I suppose. And I hope you will remind me of it if you worry. But I am too happy to be brought down by your foreboding." He looked up into the boundless blue of the sky. "What better sign is there than a clear day and the wind at our backs?"

Fenice was sure she would never get used to the motion of the ship. Why did her brothers think it was pleasant? Perhaps if she were on deck and could see the movement of the water she would not feel so much at a disadvantage in her current situation. She had found a way to sit leaning against the inside of the hull using the bales of cloth to brace her and provide her a little protection from the rats. She was beginning to be sleepy again, and the grogginess she felt made her afraid she would not see the rats before they were on her. She wished the ship's cat would come back: she could offer him a feast. She loathed the sound the rats made; it was malign and furious.

The oarsmen above her exchanged occasional remarks, one or two of them growling insults only to be overruled by the others who were trying to sleep.

"You mark my words, we'll all feed fishes before we reach Constantinople," one of the oarsmen warned the rest.

"Shut your teeth!" another complained. "We'll be bending our backs again before noon."

Fenice wondered how she would feel chained to an oar and a bench; she suspected she would have more to decry than any of these men, though they earned almost thirty-two ducats for the voyage by order of the state, better pay for less work than oarsmen had aboard war galleys. She lay back, trying to stay alert, hearing the shifting of the cargo and the rush of the water on the other side of the hull.

A bit later in the morning, as the sun reached into the hold, she saw the ship's cat wander into the hold; it was gray with black stripes, with a big head, with notches out of the side of one ear. He was larger than most of the cats Fenice had seen, and he gave no sign of being aware of her as he dropped down low on his belly and took after the rats. There was a short, intense scuffle behind some barrels filled with Florentine slippers, and then the cat emerged with a rat drooping in his jaws.

"Good boy, good boy," Fenice whispered, only to be glared at. "I don't want your rat," Fenice assured him, smiling a little at the ludicrousness of the possibility. She was pleased when the cat hunkered down at the foot of the bales and began to consume the rat; the sound of breaking bones and other things was disquieting, but his presence kept the rats away and she was able to sleep. She had not appreciated how exhausted she was, for when she fell asleep, she was swept away into a dreamless limbo that was only interrupted by the sound of the oarsmen being summoned back to their oars.

A bit later a wedge of light shone down from above; the angle of it suggested that it was now about midday, and the ship had changed course enough for the sails to be set goosewing. The shadows of the sails cut into the light; it took a short while for Fenice to determine the reason. She did her best to stretch in the cramped hiding place, and felt a knot in her shoulder from lying so awkwardly against the wood. She was less queasy than she had been, and she told herself she was becoming used to the roll of the ship. She tried eating again and was relieved when the bread did not disagree with her. She decided she would take a chance and have a bite or two of cheese. This turned out to be better than she hoped. She was becoming truly hungry, which she took as an indication that her voyage would not be so bad, after all. She had been afraid that sailing would prove unbearable, in which case she would have had to find a way to sneak ashore at Zara and command a place on a ship bound back to Venice.

Her tale of escape from kidnapers could be made plausible so long as she did not fall into her brother's hands. She had the uneasy conviction that getting about on the *Impresa* without being noticed would be more difficult than she had supposed. She had known that there was always a man aloft in the crow's nest and a man at the helm, but with so many oarsmen and the activity the ship required, she reckoned there would be few times when she could go onto the deck or even peer out of the hold when she would not be risking discovery. So much for her plans of standing on the foredeck with the spray in her face, as she had heard her brothers describe. For her the sea would be a presence, a sound rather than a sight.

Toward afternoon she remembered something Valerio had told her in one of his tales that was almost as long as the voyage it recounted. He had been troubled with rats, and he had told his men to urinate around their beds and around the tables where they ate because the smell of urine would keep the rats away. The idea had seemed disgusting when he revealed it, but now Fenice wondered if it might not work for her. Surely no one would notice the smell of urine in the hold, except, she hoped, the rats. She had brought a small chamber pot along with her other supplies and now was glad of it. When she had enough, she poured it out around the edge of the pallet, making sure that there was an unbroken ring of it. Then she got back into her hiding place, thinking as she did that if she had done this in error, it would not be the worst thing she could do. She looked into her bag for the lamp she had brought, and debated with herself if she ought to bring it out and light it. She decided that she would have to wait until much later, for she did not have much lamp oil and she would have to ration it carefully. She asked herself if she had enough food, because her assumption that she would be able to find scraps from the kitchen were fading quickly. Life aboard ship, Fenice was learning, was not so carefree as she had assumed it would be; her brothers, in describing their travels, had not mentioned the discipline or the strict attention to such things as supplies that was necessary on ships. She shoved her sack behind her, using it as a lumpy support and at the same time protecting it with her body.

The oarsmen suddenly went to work, a steady drumming keeping them working together. Only the oars at the front of the *Impresa* were in use; the rear banks were still shipped. The noise of the drum and the regular pull of the oars through the water made Fenice uncomfortably aware of the distance they had to cover before she would be safe from return.

Gradually the oars became a monotonous presence. Fenice was no longer troubled by the sound they made as the oarsmen augmented the speed of their sails, so that the ship continued across the water with the wind behind her as she would have done with the wind crossing her. The sailors continued to keep the sails trimmed, tolerating no luffing.

Fenice had never realized how much noise a ship made as it went through the water: the sails thrummed, the wood creaked in the body, the oars moaned in their locks, the water gurgled and pounded past the hull, the yards scraped on the masts, and the sea made a constant, restless sighing. She wondered how sailors ever managed to rest during such a constant barrage of sound. She was astonished that she had been able to sleep when they left port, for surely the whirr and clatter of the rigging must have been enough to waken her, although clearly it had not.

At midday there was a call to prayer, and the sailors came down onto the deck for prayers as the men at their oars recited petitions to Heaven in time to their labors. During this time only the helmsman remained at his post, and he prayed along with the rest. It was as if the voyage had been suspended for a short moment in time. Then a horn blew and all the crew resumed their work.

Fenice tried to pray along with the others, but she could not follow the prayers, and so she made up her own, hoping as she did that God would not be offended by her improvisation. She crossed herself and dug out some of the cheese to nibble on, aware as she did that she would have to move about at night when much of the crew was sleeping, or she would end up cramped in one limited posture for the whole of the voyage. She made herself move out to the edge of the bales again and stare about for rats; she was curious to see if her urine was keeping them away. If it was, she would use more to broaden her protected area so that she would not have to be constantly on the watch for the loathsome animals.

Some while later the smell of cooking came down to Fenice again, and this time she was glad she had eaten a bit of cheese. The grain concoction was starting to smell appetizing to her, much to her dismay. She sat crosslegged in her hiding place and pictured the convicts above her, one crew at the oars, one sitting at plank tables to eat, and she longed for the camaraderie these men shared. She would have liked to go on deck and surprise her brother, just to have a chance to share the companionship of the men of the ship, but she knew Ercole well enough to know he would insist on putting her ashore at Zara. She would have to remain hidden, no matter how seductive the lure of community seemed. If only Febo were captain, she thought again, feeling more ill-used than before, she would not have to hide in this paltry way. She would be able to go into the sunlight instead of hiding like some damned soul in the pit.

"Stop it," she ordered herself. "You decided to come on this voyage. You knew what the travel would demand of you. You have no reason to complain." Her whisper was a hiss. "It wouldn't do any good if you . . ." She could not make herself go on.

One of the rats came to the foot of the pallet where the bales of wool were lashed. It sniffed and chittered, then scampered off; Fenice began to hope that she might be protected after all. And it made it easier for her to think about the need for a chamber pot. She frowned. Somehow she would have to get onto the deck or to the part of the rear of the ship where the oarsmen had a simple latrine, so she could empty the pot from time to time.

She remained where she was well into the afternoon; she became used to the sound of the water and the regular dip of the oars. The rocking of the ship in calm seas ceased to make her uneasy and her hunger increased. She had to remind herself she would have to make her food last at least past Corfu, for she would not dare to sneak ashore and then try to get back aboard before then; the chance of being apprehended was too great. "So," she said, "the bread will get hard and so will the cheese. But I must not eat all of it at once." She patted her sack. "And I must have only a little meat every day."

This prospect was a glum one, but she cheered herself up with the reminder that it would not last long. What was two weeks when she had months of adventure ahead of her?

No one knew what to say to Aurelio after he came to the Zucchar house. He looked so downcast and miserable that even Rosamonda was roused from her despondency to try to comfort him as she invited him into her part of the house. Gaetano was at the Doge's Palace. His wife and three daughters were the ones to receive Fenice's promised bridegroom.

"They will not want to hurt her," Rosamonda said, more to convince herself than him. "If they intend to ask for a ransom, they will have to keep her well and . . . safe."

"I don't care about that," said Aurelio, shocking the entire family. "I want her back again, and if they have raped her, I know she will have fought them; what more can any man ask? Her virginity is a small thing, compared to her life."

Bianca's expression was appalled. "When a woman loses her chastity, no matter how she loses it, she is disgraced in the world, and nothing can restore her."

"Don't say that!" Eloisa burst out. "Don't!" She began to cry, making no apology for her tears or the emotion that brought them. "She will not be . . . raped. They will preserve her."

"If they kidnaped her, they could do anything," said Bianca with a certainty that made Aurelio glare at her.

"Why do you have such a poor opinion of your sister?" He spoke more emphatically than any of the Zucchars had ever heard him speak. "You make it sound as if she was to blame for her kidnaping." He put his hand to the front of his giaquetta. "I should have listened to her. She told me about being followed, but I thought nothing of it. I should have had more sense, for if I had, she would still be here. If anyone is to blame for what has happened, it is I. I was so willing to doubt her, to dismiss her fears, that she is now gone from Venice."

"Or so we suppose," said Artemesia, striving to remain calm.

"What do you mean?" Rosamonda asked sharply.

"Well, I have been thinking: if I wanted to kidnap someone and get away without trouble, I would not announce myself. I would be disguised—say, as a Greek sailor—and I would do everything to send pursuers in the wrong direction. I would leave my ransom note in Greek, to confirm my disguise, and I would do the kidnaping on a day when at least two ships bound for Greece left the harbor, so that I would make everyone think I had gone to sea, to the south, and then I would cross the lagoon and go north, or west." She nodded to show her conviction. "Yes. We have more rivals in Genoa than we do in Greece. Our House has enemies in Europe that might want to curtail our trading, and what better way than this? Our ships will be pressed into looking for Fenice, and we will not make the profits we have expected. This would be of more use to our rivals in Europe than any Greeks I can imagine. Remember how few ships set out this early in the year, and how many merchants come from Milano and France as soon as the worst of the snows are over. It is safer on the road to Genoa than on the sea. And we all know it, including Ercole." She went silent as she continued to think.

"You know, there may be something in what she says," remarked Aurelio, his dejection less apparent than when he arrived. "Think of the merchants from Genoa and France, as well as those from the Lowlands and the German States." He took a long stride down the withdrawing room, his thoughts racing. "Artemesia, you are a clever girl. You may have hit upon the answer we're all looking for."

Artemesia gave a quick smile. "It seems worth considering."

"Yes it does," said Rosamonda, doing her best to sound encouraged. "You have the right of it, figlia mia."

"But what if she has been taken to Greece, after all?" Eloisa asked, her sobbing now becoming hiccups.

"Our ships go to Greek harbors," said Bianca. "Inquiries can be made."

"In two months or more," said Artemesia. "Febo and Lionello will not be home for several weeks at least, and Ercole will not be back until autumn." She folded her hands. "By then, she will be very hard to find."

"So she might be," said Aurelio. "But we cannot overlook the possibility that Artemesia is right, and the kidnapers are not going by sea, but by land." He stopped pacing and regarded Artemesia with narrowed eyes. "We cannot ignore either possibility."

Rosamonda, impressed with his decisiveness, said, "I will speak to my cousins. They trade with the north; they will know how to make inquiries."

"And I will talk to my father tonight," Aurelio decided aloud. "I want her back, and my father will not refuse his help."

Privately Rosamonda thought Marin Pirenetto might do just that, as he might demand the engagement be canceled, but she had no wish to discourage Aurelio. "Your help is very welcome. And I am pleased to see your devotion is so strong."

Aurelio studied her a moment, then said, "I may not be much for courtesy and fashion, but I know someone of value when I encounter one. Fenice is a jewel."

This simple declaration rendered Rosamonda speechless; Artemesia had to daub her eyes with her lace handkerchief, her mouth quivering; Bianca returned to her prayers; and Eloisa let out a howl of distress that was heard all the way to the kitchen.

But the greatest cure of all
Comes from the lakes, streams, and sea . . .
—Fologore da San Gimignano

— XI —

On the third night of the voyage there was rain, and Fenice managed to catch some of the fresh water in her drinking cup and add it to her depleted water-skin. She was on the verge of feeling sorry for herself, having had to remain in her hiding place in the hold while the *Impresa* docked briefly at Zara to report the sailing time and to take on eight barrels of fresh water and a load of flour for bread. It had taken all her prudence to keep from going on deck. Zara was a Venetian city, but it was the first port of call for the *Impresa*, and Fenice longed to have a look at it. She promised herself she would see it on her way back, as the last leg of her travels.

To her annoyance she had discovered there were small, biting insects in the hold, and tiny puckers marked her legs and back. She wished she had some of the aromatic boughs that were under her bed at home, for that would protect her from these minute intruders. She had to make herself resist the urge to scratch the bites, but when she slept her will faded, and now she had patches of little scabs to remind her of the things that bit. She had scraped her hands on the rough ropes holding the bales in place and now they hurt whenever she closed them. "You will *not* give way," she told herself sternly. "You are not a craven child. You came on this ship to experience new things. You were foolish to believe all those things would be pleasant."

The ship rocked as it battled the storm, one of the lateen sails partially rigged, the other furled; the oarsmen were all sleeping, most of them so exhausted that they could not snore. Fenice had heard Ercole order two men to hold the helm when he himself went to his cabin for the night. The watch in the crow's nest was lashed into place.

Daring to risk discovery, Fenice began to climb out of her protected place in the hold. She did not mind the wild weather; she wanted to prove to herself that she could face any weather without giving in to fear. But getting out of the hold of a pitching ship was more difficult than she thought it would be.

Her nightly forays to the oarsmen's deck to add her slops to theirs had not prepared her for keeping her balance in such weather as this.

Making her way into the hold behind the one in which she hid, she found the aft companionway, which was little more than a rope ladder leading up past the kitchen. She remembered Ercole showing this to her while the ship was being finished, but she did not find any of it familiar in this tossing darkness. The noise was so tremendous that it seemed to be everywhere—including inside herself. She tried to listen for voices, but none could be heard over the raging of the storm and the moaning of the ship. The oarsmen were praying, most of them muttering but one or two braying out their petitions to God. Fenice said amen with them. At last she decided to move up the ladder and past the kitchen. The stairs to the deck here were wider and less steep. She clung, her hands aching, to the rope bannister as she made her way up to the deck.

There the rain, nearly horizontal in the wind, struck her with icy wet needles. She squinted, trying to see what was only an arm's length ahead of her while she continued to clutch the last loop of the bannister. In spite of the ferocity of the storm, she could not keep from grinning at her success. She was on the deck, undetected! She had succeeded!

Two large buckets were hanging from the raised part of the deck, swinging wildly; they had been put out to catch the rain water, but the pitching of the ship had left very little in either bucket. Fenice made up her mind quickly; taking down one bucket, she held it, determined to catch as much water as possible. Although they had reached Zara in record time, the voyage to Corfu could take longer; this storm would slow them down. And she would not be able to count on a second storm to provide her with more fresh water.

Her intention to stroll about the deck was given up when she saw a wave crash across the bow; the deck was awash in frothing seawater. She realized that she could be swept away without anyone being aware of it; she might be seeking adventure, she told herself, but that did not include drowning. She found a place on the deck near the water barrels that had been brought aboard at Zara. She noticed that one of the ropes holding the barrels in place was loose, and ignoring the pain in her hands, she set about securing the rope so that none of the barrels would be lost in the storm. During the time she struggled with the rope, she lost hold of the bucket; it was washed over the side before she could retrieve it.

This reminded her forcefully that she was wholly at the mercy of the sea. She now fully understood what Febo meant when he described the sea as jealous; wind and water were in contention with this ship for a trophy. Fenice recalled the storms she had seen in Venice, a few strong enough to flood the Piazetta di San Marco; she had thought then that she knew what it was to have the sea running amok, but what she had seen at home was a distant echo of the fury she experienced here.

The rigging strained and moaned as the wind turned it into a demented harp; Fenice listened to the malign singing of the lines and began to compre-

hend how sailors could believe in spirits in the sea. She crossed herself, just in case, and then retraced her steps to her place in the hold. As she took up her old position there, she knew the cold she felt would not end quickly, not in her wet clothes. She began to wriggle out of the soaked garments she wore, pulling the slightly damp spares from her bag. Her skin prickled with cold as she did her best to wipe herself at least partially dry, using the bag itself as her towel.

"The next time I can, I must get a drying cloth," she whispered as she did her best to dress while standing doubled over in her hiding place in a ship being flung about in stormy seas. Aware that she was not completely without supplies, she rummaged through her sack, pulling out everything but her dwindling supply of food. She looked at the rags she had put in the bag to use when her courses were on her, and knew she could use them if she had to, but she decided she would rather not. There was something about those rags, and the blood, that made her shy away from any use of them but the intended one. She was shivering intensely by the time she had contorted herself into her change of clothes, as much from muscle tension as from cold.

As she tried to make herself comfortable in her hiding place once again, she thought ahead. What if they had to be repaired and were forced to lay over at Corfu—what then? How would she manage to keep from being discovered? She was not at all certain that they would reach Corfu, given the relentlessness of the storm, but she had to plan ahead in case she had to contend with such trouble. She put her head into her arms and reminded herself that at least she was no longer seasick, which was as much consolation as she could summon up for herself at this time. She supposed she ought to pray, but given what she had done in running away, she was not convinced that God had not sent the storm to punish her, and if that were the case, she would be unwise to remind Him of her existence; she hoped God would not punish the whole ship for something she alone had done, without the help of anyone aboard. On these jumbled and unhappy thoughts she drifted into sleep.

She dreamed she rode on the storm like some fantastic bird, borne up by a huge cloak that was more like wings than a cloak; she hovered over the ship and knew it to be safe before she sailed off toward the distant, eastern shore, riding on the tempest as waterbirds ride on the surging waves. The first outline of the land was soon behind her, and rather than remaining at the coast, she went eastward, bearing slightly to the north, across a huge, high plain and into tall mountains like the broken teeth of giants. She felt she knew the way and was returning rather than venturing anew. She let her mind anticipate what was to come: an isolated castle-fortress, ancient and imposing, on the edge of a crag, with a river beneath it in a narrow canyon; she saw the battlements ahead, snow surrounding the place like a mantle of ermine. She settled onto the battlements as if returning to her nest. A moment later, the hawk-faced foreigner of her previous dreams landed beside her, his face shining with ferocious pleasure. She laughed aloud to see him so taken with her.

And if in the dream the stone walls of the castle lurched with the ship, what of it? It was all a dream, after all.

* * *

"I hate to think of what they are enduring; three storms in as many days, as if the winter were never going to end," said Gaetano to Aurelio as he looked out into the night at the approaching storm; the waves were already frothing at the Bacino, and boats tied up along the canals rocked and jostled. "If we feel it tomorrow—and barring a miracle, we will—they are in the thick of it."

"You mean the *Impresa*," said Aurelio.

"What else should I mean?" Gaetano said sharply, daring his guest to remind him of their shared sorrow. "The men we seek will be near the mountains by now, and snow will keep them from going into Austria, or beyond the plains of Milano." He frowned. "We knew it was a risk, leaving so early in the year. I hope we have not tempted the gods too much with our audacity. The storms might continue until May. It has happened before."

"The *Impresa* is a powerful ship," said Aurelio. He was dressed in black and deep blue as if in mourning, and he seemed much less foolish than he often did at celebrations; his thoughtful eyes dwelled on the maps hanging over Gaetano's desk. "If you worry for your fine new ship in this season, I think we must put more credence in Artemesia's theory—that Fenice was taken away from the sea and into the mountains."

Gaetano sighed. "I suppose it is prudent. I would not want to escape into that weather," he answered after a brief pause. "I have paid for three Masses daily at Sant' Angelo until she has been found. God willing, she will have the protection of His Angels." He put his hands flat on the surface of his desk. "I have permission to offer a reward."

"How generous a reward?" asked Aurelio, looking doubtful.

"One hundred ducats," said Gaetano, revealing that considerable sum with feigned nonchalance. "The Doge has said he will authorize it."

Aurelio shook his head. "Not the whole amount at first, Signor Zucchar. Think what would happen if you were to do that. Consider this instead: half on being given worthwhile information and half upon Fenice's return, at the very least. Reserve as much of the total as you can," he said. "Otherwise every rascal from here to Spain will be claiming he knows where she is, and you will lose a fortune to no purpose."

Gaetano regarded Aurelio with increasing respect. "You know, I didn't understand at first why my daughter preferred you, but I am beginning to think that she had a greater appreciation of you than anyone else. You are a canny fellow underneath it all." He stared down at his hands. "Your advice is well taken. I will offer ten ducats for genuine information, another forty if it is determined to be correct, and fifty more when Fenice is returned to us."

"You may want to make some adjustment in what is paid . . . more if she is alive." He said the last in muffled tones.

"I see what you mean," Gaetano said at last. "And again, you are right: another twenty-five ducats if she is not living, fifty if she is."

"That should keep any of the miscreants who might have helped in the kidnaping from claiming the reward and the ransom, and returning only her body to you." Aurelio coughed. "Think what that would mean to the family."

"And to you," said Gaetano. "Yes, yes, Aurelio. It is true, all the things you say." He looked out into the night again.

"I am sorry to bring you more trouble than you have already, but—" Aurelio's diffidence was as genuine as his distress. "You would not want any of your misfortunes compounded, would you?"

"No, I would not," said Gaetano. "It would make us look gullible, which would be of no help to Fenice, and it would make those whose aid we seek laugh at our attempts." He stood up suddenly, facing Aurelio to make himself feel more confident. "I will adjust the manner in which the money is paid, and I will see to it that the word is put about in the most useful places what could become of anyone seeking to take advantage of this family at this time."

"It affects me, as well," said Aurelio. "I would not like to think that these criminals would try to make you pay more than twice for Fenice's return."

Gaetano coughed diplomatically, and forced himself to speak. "You understand, do you not, that we would not fault you for abjuring your promise to Fenice. Under the circumstances, we cannot think poorly of you for rescinding the marriage contract."

At that Aurelio shook his head. "No. There is no reason for me to break my pledge. It is not Fenice's fault that she is gone. I will not add to her disgrace by saying that she has been defiled." He went to close the shutter against the night and the rising storm. "Besides, Signor Zucchar, I *want* to marry Fenice. I have never met another girl who was half so pleasing to me, or half so clever. She has been a friend to me since we were children. How could I repay her kindness with condemnation?"

"Fenice is such a madcap, there must be those who think that she brought this . . . misery upon herself; I have heard the whispers," Gaetano said with difficulty. "She has always been high-spirited and full of imagination, but even she could not so completely forget herself to put herself in danger only to defy . . ." He could not go on.

"She is your daughter, Signor Zucchar," Aurelio reminded him. "You know she has a generous heart and a clever mind. As much as she might yearn for the fables her brothers tell, her good sense would keep her from doing anything so ruinous to her reputation and her family's well-being." His indignation faded. "You are too upset to think what you are accusing her of doing. You let yourself hear calumnies you would not tolerate under other circumstances. And as Fenice's affianced husband, I will defend her honor."

"You may decide to relinquish your claim. Oh," he went on, his hands raised to silence Aurelio, "you say now you will not, and I am in your debt for this loyalty. But if at any time you change your mind, you must tell me. I will not hold you accountable."

"No; that is of no concern to me. I want Fenice to be safe. If she can be safe and come back to me, I will be grateful to God for His Mercy." He swung around to face Gaetano. "But I consider my promise binding until God Himself releases me."

"I am . . . overwhelmed. You . . . you shame me, Aurelio. Many another would be glad of the opportunity to—" Gaetano began, but Aurelio would not permit it. "No one would think the less of you, not even I."

"*I* would," said Aurelio, ending the matter.

It took Fenice nearly an hour to wake up on the morning after the storm had passed. She could hear the men on deck, and the oarsmen keeping to their steady beat, but by now she was accustomed to this, and she was so exhausted that she could not bring herself to stir merely because the sun had risen on calm seas.

"Corfu by tomorrow evening!" The boatswain announced to the crew. "God saving us from harm."

There were shouts and cheers of agreement, and someone recommended they lay on more sail.

"In a while," Ercole shouted. "After the hull has been inspected, so that we will know if we have sustained any real damage. If we have not, both lateens!"

Fenice was suddenly and unpleasantly awake. "Inspect the hull?" she whispered, repeating the order. That could mean men in the hold, where they might discover her hiding place, and then they would find her. Looking about the dim interior of the hold, she began to get the beginning of an idea: she had used the bales of wool to get into the ship, and she could use them to remain hidden—if she did not allow herself to become so frightened that she could not keep her nerves from giving her away. She moved out of her hiding place cautiously, as if expecting to find herself apprehended at each step; she gathered up her things and shoved them into the bag, noticing as she did that she was down to the very last of her cheese: food had become very important to her in the last several days, the attention she gave to it increasing as the amount she had in reserve diminished. She stuffed the bag into the middle of the bales, where it was fully concealed. Only by untying and separating the bales could the bag be found. The sailors, she was certain, would not do anything of the sort. The wine cup was harder to dispose of; she finally added it to the bilge.

She rocked back on her heels, deciding that she could be safe, after all. She knew this hold better than anyone on the ship, and she would be safe in it. And once the hull was inspected—she already knew that the sailors would find nothing leaking in this hold, for she had inspected it herself as soon as the seas had calmed enough—she knew they would go on to Corfu without further incident.

Longingly, Fenice thought of the next hold, where some of the foodstuffs were stored. She had been trying to work up the courage to get into the hold and take out something to eat—nothing so big or important that the cook would notice, but sufficient to keep her from going hungry for a day or two. She decided that she would make a cursory foray this evening, while the oarsmen were eating and there was enough noise and confusion to cover any sound she might make. It pleased her to think that she knew the patterns of the ship well enough to dare to do this. With so many to feed, she decided the cook would not notice one or two rounds of bread gone missing. If she could get that and a lemon or two, she would do well enough until Corfu, and she would use the time between now and their reaching that port to prepare to get more food for herself. She wanted to be sure of her hiding place until they were beyond Constantinople, and that was at least three weeks away. How short that time had seemed when she had learned her geography lessons, and how long a time it seemed now! She had wanted to mark the time staring at the horizon for mountains and the foreign cities she had heard tales of all her life, but that, she accepted now, was not to be. She would have to wait in the dark hold until she knew she was beyond return. Well, she told herself, she had managed almost a week: she could do three more without distress.

She was not completely convinced by her own argument, but she was well enough aware of the reality of her situation that she did not want to expose herself any more than absolutely necessary. So, she told herself, she would take a very little food and would retire to her hiding place inside the bales of wool. She would do her best to keep the rats at bay, and she would learn everything she could about the ship so that she would not risk discovery any more often than absolutely essential. Certain that she was being circumspect, she wriggled down into the woolen bales and waited for the sailors to arrive to inspect the hold.

"The hull is sound aforeships," said the boatswain, nodding as if to punctuate his report. "No seam so much as dribbled."

"Excellent," Ercole approved. He had total confidence in his ship, but he was relieved to know his confidence was justified. "Make sure the men have spirits of wine tonight, if the aftership is equally sound."

"They will appreciate your kindness, Captain Zucchar," said the boatswain. He pointed down toward the regular dipping of the oars. "And them? Spirits of wine for them as well?"

Ercole thought about it. "Make it beer. We will take more aboard in Corfu, and it will keep them from being resentful. If we were a military ship it would not matter, but in this case, we must suppose that the oarsmen will expect some occasional encouragement."

"I will inform the cook," the boatswain offered. "I will make sure the sailors are diligent in their work."

"Good. But have a care going into the hold. Make sure you have lamps enough." He folded his arms, wanting the world to see how pleased he was with the *Impresa*. Few ships would come through such weather as they had without damage, yet so far it appeared that the *Impresa* had not been harmed in any way. He looked forward to boasting of her valor when he returned to Venice.

"I will report to you directly," said the boatswain, and signaled to the five sailors who would help him in his work.

Ercole gave a gesture of approval. He would write a report for his father while they were in port at Corfu, with instructions to have it carried back to Venice on the next returning Zucchar ship. He thought about Gaetano, and realized that the family had much to be proud of.

There was a shout from the crow's nest, and the announcement that another ship had been spotted, on a north-by-northwest course.

"What ship?" Ercole shouted up.

"Can't see yet!" The sailor shouted down. "Looks like a Spanish hull!"

"Merchant ship, then?" Ercole called.

"By the look of it," came the reply.

Ercole kept himself from sighing in relief: as high as his opinion was of the *Impresa*, he knew she could not take on a war galley and win; she lacked the speed, maneuverability, and arms of a true fighting ship, and although she could give a corsair an equal fight, she was no match for a true warship. He glanced back at the stern where the lantern stood, and the standard of the Winged Lion of San Marco flew, the badge of the Venetian Republic. "Hold her on course, helmsman!"

"Holding steady!" the helmsman replied.

Again the sense of confidence that had burgeoned in Ercole's heart was restored. He would not protest putting his ship to any test so long as it was one she was designed to meet.

"You sure you want to give the oarsmen beer?" The question, coming from the ship's cook standing behind him, took Ercole unaware; he was startled and turned a bit too quickly to face the small, walnut-faced man who waited patiently for his answer.

"Yes," said Ercole as he collected his thoughts.

"It's early in the voyage; you don't want them getting used to it," said Niccola; he scratched his grizzled chin. "Storms are part of sailing."

"So they are, but that was a severe one, and our first as well." Ercole indicated the sky. "For now the gods are showing us favor. I thought I would do the same for the crew."

Niccola nodded. "Yes. The spirits of wine. Very sensible. But the oarsmen are not sailors; they are criminals, and they might assume a privilege was more of a reward than you suppose it is. They may come to think you will give them beer any time you ask them to do what any sailor ought to do." He spat and glowered. "They would not be worth much if they began to think they could expect you to give them beer for bending their backs with vigor."

Ercole heard him out. "I understand why you have the concerns you do, and if this were not our first voyage, I would agree with you. But it is our first, and there are many things we are discovering about this ship that we will need to know in future. So it is not just that they have made the effort, but that they have done it for the first time. I will make sure this is explained to them."

"Very well," Niccola said, shrugging. "You know what you want for your ship."

"Yes; yes I do," said Ercole; he smiled as he looked out at the sea again. "You have sailed on Zucchar ships for many years, haven't you?"

"Since I first stowed aboard your father's *Dona Volante,* the most misnamed ship in all the ports of Venice. It was a miracle that we ever made land in that ancient tub. She wallowed every moment of the voyage, and she moved like a pregnant goat, but she brought back more wealth than any other ship before her, and restored your family's riches." He rubbed his hands together. "That was before you were born, Captain Ercole," he added, to make sure the tale was not lost on this Zucchar.

"You were the lucky stowaway," said Ercole.

"Truly; thank San Iago and Santa Lucia for their aid." He crossed himself, and looked at Ercole narrowly. "Do you want me to make new bread tomorrow? We will be at Corfu that day or the day after and the men will have food ashore then."

"Are you certain we will be at Corfu in two days?" Ercole could not keep himself from asking.

"I have been up and down this sea for twenty-six years, and I know where I am. By evening we will have sight of land, and by tomorrow we will be on vision course for Corfu, barring fog. We should be at the dock before sunset if we continue as we have been going. Even without the oarsmen, we would reach port tomorrow in the evening." He clapped his hands together. "The ship is fast enough that we may reach the harbor before the night chain is raised."

"May God show you aright," said Ercole.

"What I mean is there is enough old bread to serve us until we reach port, if you would like me to save the rest until we are underway again. You will be taking flour and other food aboard at Corfu, so you may not want me to save what I have now." He looked disgruntled as he realized that very little of this mattered to Ercole. "If you would like me to decide, Captain Zucchar, you have only to tell me. But as these provisions are your concern as much as the trim of the sails . . ."

"Make long loaves for all," Ercole said abruptly, and used the boatswain's return as reason to ignore the cook. "Well? What did you find?"

"Well," Rainardo announced, "the hull of this ship is remarkable. We found one plank on the oarsmen's deck not quite secure. All the rest is in fine condition." He cocked his head in the direction of the cook. "Two of your barrels were overset—the one with pickles and the one with cheeses in oil. They're in place once more, and secure in their restraints."

"Very good," said Niccola, who had been aware of those mishaps. "There was also a basket of hard flat breads that was askew, but I've taken care of it."

"Excellent," said Ercole so that the two men would not find an excuse to argue; men at sea often became angry over trifles. "My father will rejoice when he learns of this. I will send him my account of our beginning—"

"From Corfu," Niccola finished for him. "All Zucchar ships do the same."

He smiled at this parting shot and made his way toward the kitchen companionway.

The boatswain looked after the cook. "He's getting to be an old man," he said as if he had only just noticed Niccola's graying hair.

"Yes," said Ercole, "and it is making him wise." He was not interested in having a feud erupt between his boatswain and his cook, and was determined to keep it from getting more heated than it already was. He did his best to seem unaware of the rivalry.

"One day he will have to leave the sea." Rainardo sounded pleased at the prospect.

"We will lose an important member of our crew when that happens." Ercole pointed toward the bow. "Dolphins. Our journey is going to be fortunate."

Rainardo scowled. "If we are, it will not be the dolphins' doing."

"Don't let the others hear you say that," Ercole recommended. "Most Venetians would not permit any such blasphemy to be spoken aloud, and well you know it."

"And you permit it only to keep me from giving you my opinion of the cook." The boatswain nodded once. "I know you too well, Captain. Very well," he said in a slightly bored tone. "I will watch the dolphins."

From her hiding place Fenice heard some mention of dolphins; she cursed silently, for she wanted to see these cheerful creatures for herself. She had seen them at a distance a few times in her life, and some years ago a dead one had washed ashore near San Giorgio Maggiore, but that only saddened her. Now she might see them if she dared to go on deck: if the men were given beer and spirits to drink tonight, it could be safe to come out.

Three men were making their way through her hold and the hatch was open, bringing a shaft of brilliant light down upon the close-packed cargo. The men were looking for signs of water in the hold, aside from the wash of brine in the bottom of the hold, above the massive, sand-filled keel. The men were not concerned with the crates, barrels, cases, and bales, but with the hull and the ribs of the ship.

One of the men let out a stream of profanity as he kicked one of the rats. "Bugger bit me!" he exclaimed, holding up a bleeding hand to prove it was true.

"Have Niccola take care of it," one of the others suggested as he prodded at the edge of a barrel. "More of them."

"We should kill them all," complained the sailor who had been bitten.

"Possibly," said the third man. "But who would sail the ship then?"

"Not the convicts," said the second, and the three sailors laughed.

"Did you hear—?" The first man silenced the others.

"A noise on deck," said the third. "Nothing to bother about."

There was the crinkle of chains; immediately men began to trudge down the rowing deck above them.

"They're putting on the aft oarsmen. We'll move now." The second man patted the high roll of Milanese wool. "Get these to market before the month is out."

"We'll be in Corfu before this time tomorrow; that's the wager," said the first man. "I'll have one of those Greeks put unguents on the bite."

Fenice held her breath and wanted to close her eyes, but did not dare; she hardly breathed as the sailors finished up their inspection of the hold.

"Should we pull these away from the wall? There could be trouble behind," the third man said.

"The wool would be wet if there were," said the first man. "Is it?"

"No." The second man leaned against the wool. "We'll be able to boast that we were on this ship on her maiden Galley."

"We have to get back to Venice to do that,"

The second man was near enough to Fenice that she could have reached out and touched him had she made the effort. Listening to him, she realized she was getting lonely, something she never thought would trouble her while she was on her family's ship. But she had not reckoned on spending the whole of the voyage hiding in the hold. She would not let herself cry, she decided sternly. She had other things to concern her: she had to keep from being discovered. There might come a time when she was ready to join the crew properly, when Ercole would not be able to send her back, but that was a long way ahead.

A short while later the three sailors closed the hatch and left the hold. The darkness seemed vaster and blacker than it had been before the hatch had been opened. Fenice sagged against the tall bales and began to shiver. She had been afraid, more afraid than she had known. Now that the men were gone, her bones felt like wet straw. She had not liked the dryness of her mouth or the chill that had hold of her; she made up her mind that she would have to change her clothes again. She had been able to keep them fairly neat, but everything was in need of a washing: being soaked in a storm would not be a substitute for soap. She recalled the maids at home who kept all her things fresh, mended, and clean; they would be appalled to see how she had been living—Fenice herself was appalled when she allowed herself to think of it.

At last she made up her mind not to venture onto the deck again until they were beyond Corfu. Disappointed in herself for lacking the gumption to brave all while the crew and oarsmen were enjoying their drink, she forced herself to sneak into the hold where the food was stored in order to take enough to feed her for the next four days, when, God willing, they would be past Corfu and into the Greek islands.

There was a barrel of small cheeses in oil: she took two, thinking that she had never seen anything so delicious-looking in her whole life. Then she pulled down the hard flat-bread from the racks where they were stored. Three of these would have to suffice. And there was a wedge of salt beef, hardly enough to make more than a couple of bites of. She took it, promising herself that she would not waste a scrap of it. Then she went back to the bales in the hold and carefully rationed out the food she had stolen.

In all ways you continue to oppose me
And why? for I am in your hands . . .
—Guittone d' Arezzo

— XII —

By midafternoon the following day, the *Impresa* was on the approach to the harbor at Corfu. Along the eastern horizon the hills of the Dalmatian Coast marked their progress. Most of the crew had come on deck and were standing to order as the swift, graceful vessel made for the Venetian docks. Sharp orders to furl the sails left her moving on oars alone; then the order was given to turn her, shipping the starboard oars as they finished their approach, the port oars aiding the helm to turn and brake the unorthodox craft as she came neatly to rest.

The crew cheered, and the people gathered at the dock stared and pointed and marveled. It was a most satisfying welcome for the *Impresa*.

"She's a fine craft, no doubt about it," said the boatswain to Ercole.

"True enough." He wanted to say more but knew that such immodesty would not sit well with Rainardo. "She has done very well, well enough for me to think we will have cause to celebrate when we stop here again. We are maintaining excellent speed, and I cannot think we will not continue to do so. If we are not three weeks ahead of our expected arrival, I will be disappointed in her and in all of us. She can easily make such speed. And as speed is of the essence, since we have cargo to unload here, let's have the men about it at once." He rapped out a few terse instructions and stood by while the hatches were opened. "Have the martial magistrate of the city come and take the convicts to his dockside prison. They will have to be inspected for illness and injury."

"Does it bother you to have dangerous men on your ship?" asked the customs officer who had just come aboard.

"It would bother me a great deal more to have this ship taken by pirates," Ercole announced, and offered the invoices the official required.

"Your brother Lionello is expected here in a week or two," the customs official remarked as he reviewed the invoices. "If you lay over, you and he might well—"

"If I lay over more than a day, I give up much of the advantage I have gained coming here," said Ercole, knowing he sounded haughty and not minding it; he had the finest ship in all Venice and knew he deserved deference.

"Will you want to leave a letter for him?" The official sounded slightly disapproving.

"Certainly, and one for him to carry back to our father in Venice, who caused this swift ship to be built." He made no attempt to conceal his pride. "Our speed is the tribute I make to him."

"Is it?" said the official, and glowered at the invoices. "All seems in order."

"Zucchar is always careful to keep our records properly." Ercole whistled loudly for his boatswain. "Rainardo, when all is secure, you may release the crew for the night. They are to report back after noon Mass tomorrow. See each of them has an extra scudo for the speed of our journey."

Rainardo pursed his lips. "If this voyage continues so swiftly, they will expect many more scudi. Will you disappoint them later, when we are far beyond the might of Venice?"

"I planned for all of this," said Ercole. "The men will not question the bounty, for we will be first to many ports and our profits will be high. Isn't it prudent to share such fortune with the crew who makes it possible?"

"And the convicts, what of them?" asked the customs official who had been openly listening.

"They will have their pay at the end of the voyage and a bonus if we have profit to spare for them. The amounts are recorded with the Doge's remembrancer." Ercole knew that such a passing reference to the Doge would impress the customs official.

"Very good. We will review your records on your return; I will want a full accounting of all you have done and everywhere you have been. Do not think you can fool me. I have done this work for twenty years and I have seen every ruse on the sea. You will not find one to gull me."

"Nor will I try," said Ercole. "My men are eager to unload the goods you have recorded from our invoices. If you will stamp our—"

Grudgingly the official complied. Huffing with blighted self-importance he went off down the gangplank.

"You know your work, Boatswain," said Ercole. "I will be in my cabin; I have to prepare my report for my father and a letter to my brother Lionello." He did not wait to hear Rainardo answer but strode away across the deck, making for his cabin.

Two crates were taken out of the hold where Fenice was hiding. The sunlight poured down from the open hatch, and she shaded her eyes to look at it; she had grown accustomed to the dimness, and this glorious brilliance hurt her when she stared directly at it. She had crept back into the bales once more and was keeping still while the sailors secured and raised the two crates, one of which contained fine Murano glass, each piece wrapped in shredded rags and straw; the other of which was filled with Bolognese crockery, not so lovingly wrapped. Once the crates were gone, Fenice expected the hatch to be closed again, but to her surprise it was left open to air out.

"Not as bad as a war galley," one of the crew remarked with a cock of his head to the oarsmen's quarters. "These men aren't chained to the oars forever. But they're still . . . ripe."

"Sun'll help, and air," said his companion so automatically that it was apparent he was not thinking about what he was saying.

Fenice listened to them as if they were poets or great singers; just the sound of their voices was welcome—their promise of light and air were paradise. She wanted to lie in the sun, to let it warm her, but she remained where she was. If the hatch was not closed again, she might risk being seen once most of the crew had left.

The martial magistrate came with an armed escort; the oarsmen were taken away to the prison maintained for them and men like them. They would be examined before they returned the next day and Ercole would be given a certificate of soundness for the men. If any were ill or hurt, one of the other convicts at the prison would take his place.

Finally Ercole emerged from his cabin, his cabin boy at his heels. "I will not be gone very long, Rainardo. I'm going to hear Mass and present my report to my cousin, and then I will return. I will not hurry my evening. No doubt my cousin will feed me, so tell Niccola that he need not bother. He can take the time to find a few more sides of lamb or pork in salt. We can't have this ship run on nothing more than cheese and bread." He chuckled at his own humor.

"He will be pleased," said Rainardo dryly.

"And so will you, when we have been three weeks at sea," remarked Ercole; he signaled to the cabin boy to remain on the ship. "See the lad has something to pass the time."

"That I will," said Rainardo.

Ercole made the sign of the cross to keep the ship in God's care while he was away from her, and then hurried to the gangplank, whistling merrily.

From her place in the hold, Fenice listened, feeling sorry for herself and upset that she felt so. She had not planned for this journey as well as she had thought: that had been apparent from the first, but the disadvantages had not seemed dreadful for the first few days. That was no longer the case. The life of a stowaway was nothing like what she had assumed it would be—although she could no longer quite remember what she had thought it would be like—and the prospects for the next several weeks were dismal. Her early hope that Ercole might understand and endorse her adventure was vanishing. Unlike Febo, Ercole had no grasp of the wildness in her soul. When she was discovered, for eventually she would be, she might trade one sequestration for another. She no longer thought she would be able to persuade him to allow her to venture out into the distant cities the ship would visit. He would never allow her to leave the ship—if he even permitted her on deck. She wished again that she had been able to sail with Febo. She was beginning to think she would have to spend the whole voyage hidden away from Ercole, and this increased her bleakness of spirit. Mulling over her dwindling options, Fenice waited for evening to come, when she could sneak on deck, at least for a short while.

Rosamonda had been praying in the little chapel under the main stairs; she had been trying to picture Fenice, hoping God would give her some sense of her missing daughter. She blessed herself and looked with intense concentration at the small statue of the Virgin; today Our Lady had a kindly smile, or so Rosamonda thought, and she took heart at the sight.

Bianca was waiting for her in the corridor. "Still no word," she said as her mother closed the chapel door.

"No. Your father tells me he is going to engage men to search for her." Rosamonda frowned as she said this, clearly not as certain of this plan as her husband was. "I hope he chooses well."

"He must. God will not guide him amiss." Bianca crossed herself. "We have been told that Aurelio wants to help."

"Certainly he does," said Rosamonda, as if this were not remarkable.

"Do you think he will be able to? Help?" Bianca asked nervously. "He is so inept."

"He hasn't been so lately," said Rosamonda, nodding in the direction of the stairs. "We should be going up: our morning sweetmeats are about to be served."

Bianca made a motion to show her disgust. "How can anyone eat sweetmeats at such a time as this?"

"We had all better, or the servants will say we have lost hope and are mourning Fenice as dead." She said this quietly, but there was no accommodation in her tone, or in her intent. "You will do nothing that implies we have given up finding her. Do you understand me?"

"Ye . . . yes," said Bianca unsteadily. She was distressed at what she was hearing: her long hours of prayers had not been offered to make the household fear the worst, but to help them maintain the conviction that Fenice would come back to them in safety.

"Whatever you believe has happened to her, you will say nothing about it. You will tell everyone, including your sisters, that you expect to have Fenice restored to our family. You will make your prayers those of thanks for her preservation, or you will say them in silence. I will not have word spreading through the household and the city that we know our search is in vain." Rosamonda shook her head once. "You are a good woman, Bianca, and so devout that you do not always see how your devotion appears to others. Most of the time this would mean little, but given what we encounter here in this difficult time, we cannot indulge ourselves as we might like. Artemesia weeps in her room alone at night, so that she may not appear to grieve where the world would see and assume things to the detriment of our House. Eloisa asks questions only when she and I are alone. Even Aurelio has become prudent in his conduct, for which I am deeply thankful to him." She went up the stairs, not waiting to discover if Bianca was coming with her. "You have only a few more months before you begin your novitiate. I would like to think you will use the time to come to terms with the world, not only so that you may leave it more . . . consciously, knowing what you have put behind you, but so that you will not have your last service to this House be an unkind one."

"Madre Mia, I meant nothing harmful, to the family or to Fenice. I seek only to bring about the return of my unfortunate sister. I know that many things are being done to help her, and I pray they will succeed. But where only God can help, I will prostrate myself and beg Him for His Mercy. If unfaithful souls think this is surrender, it is their lack—"

"Exactly," said Rosamonda. "And you will give full cognizance to how such deprived souls see the world, for it is their good report we must have now." This brusque determination left Bianca standing halfway up the stairs, feeling as if her whole worth had vanished.

A short while later Bianca went back down to the ground level of the house and into the chapel where she began to pray at the feet of the Virgin; but to please her mother she addressed God's Mother in whispers so that her despair would not be overheard and reported.

At dusk lanterns were hung on the rigging of the *Impresa,* imparting their pools of light and swaying shadows to the deck; customs guards strolled the dock where the ship was tied up, their weapons displayed in warning: with most of the crew gone, and all the convicts taken off to their port prison, the ship was vulnerable to intruders of many kinds, and all reasonable precautions were made to preserve the vessel and its cargo. The guards had stared at the *Impresa* at first, but now they paid more attention to the docks and the lanterns hung to illuminate them. On the ship, the helmsman had been replaced by a youngster who whiled the time away by playing tunes inexpertly on a shawm; his unsteady but enthusiastic efforts threaded through the gathering darkness as if summoning some mystical creature of unpredictable temperament.

Fenice listened to the shawm, waiting for the young musician to falter, revealing his flagging attention. She had decided that she would have a short time before Ercole returned that would make it possible for her to have a brief look at the harbor—or as much as the lanterns revealed. She also wanted to move freely for a few moments, if only to prove to herself that she had not made herself a complete prisoner.

Finally the shawm bleated a last few discordant notes and fell silent. One of the customs guards on the dock laughed, and the young sailor yelled down a mild insult. This was the most fortuitous time Fenice was likely to find, and she steeled herself against discovery as she went into the kitchen hold and up the rope ladder.

There were smells coming from the kitchen that made her belly knot with hunger and reminded her that the cook was still aboard. From the odor that was coming from the kitchen, Fenice supposed that Niccola would be busy for some time to come, which meant she would be able to make her way around the ship without worrying about her return.

Far in the west there was a low line of glowing gold, the last token of daylight until dawn came. Fenice stood up, making sure she was away from the puddles of light cast by the lamps; she knew her shadow could give her away as readily as the sight of her face, so she kept away from the light. She stretched and tried not to yawn for fear of making a sound that might catch the attention of the others waiting on the dock or those few of the crew still aboard the ship. She went to the railing and looked over cautiously, noticing the five customs guards on their rounds. That was another thing she had never imagined—that the ship would be guarded so constantly. As a bell sounded a short distance away the guards crossed themselves; after a moment so did Fenice, reciting the *Angelus* prayers so automatically that they meant nothing more than a series of comforting sounds to her.

The crates and cases lashed to the deck gave Fenice some protection as she made her way toward the mast. She marveled at the shroud lines and was again amazed at how easily the sailors worked this complex of rope which to her was more bewildering than a tangled skein of silk. She wished now she could watch them rig and set the sails, for that seemed to be the most exciting thing these men did. She had come to recognize how the sails pulled on the ship and how their disposition moved the *Impresa* through the water: she wanted now to see it as it happened, to watch the lateen sails bend on the wind. The luff and trim was still a mystery to her, one she wanted to comprehend as more than an angle of lean and a level of noise.

Making her way nearer the helm, she saw the young sailor; he leaned on the edge of the lantern that lit the Venetian Lion, gazing at the lights along the waterfront. As Fenice studied him, he licked his lips and murmured something about foreign women and Venetian men.

Knowing it was not wise to linger, Fenice went back through the cargo on deck, picking her way for protection and silence more than any interest she had in what they carried. She did notice that one large crate was labeled *German Silver*, and she was mildly surprised to find such valuable cargo on deck. She wondered where it was going; then she could not keep from wondering where she was going, for at least the cargo had destinations and she was increasingly aware that she did not.

She found herself a small barrel to sit on, one that was just high enough to give her a chance to look out to the northwest side of the harbor. She could make out lights on the hill and supposed they must be from the villas of the merchants who lived there, like her cousins. What was their life like, and would she be content to remain in this place, if she had been born here? She considered the question and knew she would not have settled down in Corfu any more readily than she would have done in Venice. This was hardly consoling, but it did make it easier for her to accept her current predicament; she could not deceive herself on that account: she would have longed to travel had she been born in fabled India or the New World.

A short while later a commotion on the dock claimed the attention of the customs guards and the few aboard the *Impresa*: three sailors with strong Sicilian accents slurred from wine arrived to demand a look at this new design of ship that was going to drive all the other merchants from the seas. The sailors were rowdy, but drunk enough not to be dangerous.

The customs officers, with a few encouraging shouts from the boatswain—who had come on deck at the first commotion—and the helm-watch soon had the Sicilians going back toward the land, one of them vowing eternal friendship for the officer who had hold of his elbow.

Fenice let herself laugh once, and realized this was the first actual sound she had produced since she climbed out of the hold. That took her aback, reminding her of the danger she still could be in if she were imprudent. She put her hands to her mouth to keep any treacherous noise from escaping as she hunkered down behind two barrels of books, one barrel of Latin volumes, the other of Greek. She had an intense longing for something to read—it had been so long since she had been able to spend an hour or two reading that she now missed it as much as she missed her bed at home. To her dismay she felt a tear on her cheek. How could she be crying at a moment like this? She had just had a glimpse of Corfu and tomorrow or the next day they would be underway again for Constantinople: just that name conjured up minarets and palaces, strange people and exotic goods such as Febo spoke of. If the promise of Constantinople could not banish her gloom, she castigated herself silently, then perhaps she should go ashore here and be sent back to Venice when Lionello came through on his way home. She would tell her family she escaped from the kidnapers, and that would make it possible for her to resume her old life.

"But it wouldn't," she said just loudly enough to hear herself speak. "I would have to marry Aurelio. If he will still have me." That prospect was more daunting than anything she had troubled herself with so far that she whispered, "You will not give way like some paltry fool of a seamstress. This is what you sought." She wanted to argue with herself that her plans had not included being compelled to hide in the hold for days on end, but she would not accept such an excuse. "You were ready to do anything you had to in order to travel," she muttered ferociously. "Well, it turns out that you must hide in the hold. That is the condition of your wish. Accept it."

Aurelio Pirenetto had lost the bewildered look he had worn for most of his life. He fairly bristled with purpose as he faced the scarred miscreant across a table in the back of the inn near San Ambrogio. The chants of the monks came as odd counterpoint to the roistering around the hearth, nearer the front of the inn. This taproom served as a tavern for the innkeeper, and it catered to men whose work was not always honest, and whose names were often long-forgotten: that was the case with the man Aurelio faced across the plank table.

"I have done all that I can," said the scarred man, his mouth pursed by greed as much as by the puckered tissue along his lip. His accent was faintly Spanish though the weapons he carried were German: Aurelio assumed he had been a mercenary soldier who had taken to crime when his company broke up. "I have asked everywhere I can dare to ask, and I have learned nothing of value."

"Tell me; let me decide," said Aurelio, tapping his finger on the table.

The man coughed. "Well, the soldiers were French and they said there was not even a whisper about an abducted Venetian woman being held for ransom anywhere in France."

"They have scoured the whole of it, so they are certain," Aurelio said sarcastically. "No doubt you are right."

"They hear things," the man said resentfully. In that light, with that expression, it was easy to see why he was called Il Talpa, the mole.

"But not everything," Aurelio said. "There must be others who—"

"And if she was taken into Austria, what then? The French would know nothing of it." He folded his arms to show his resolve, and he tried not to be put off by the doubt he saw in Aurelio's face. "I can ask my . . . associates in Udine to make some inquiries."

"Then do so," Aurelio snapped. "Every day she is gone they can take her farther away from us, and the greater the risk to her safety."

"You . . . would still . . . want her back?" Il Talpa asked, mildly surprised; he had long decided that men with money did all manner of imponderable things; taking back a compromised woman was not the most absurd thing he had ever encountered in the rich.

"Of course. She is promised to me, and I know she would never dishonor our pledge." The light in his eyes dared Il Talpa to contradict him.

"Certainly not," said Il Talpa staunchly, willing to humor anyone who was paying him as well as Aurelio was.

"Have your men start off at once. If there is any hint of a clue, send word to my house at once. My servant's name is Giuseppe; give your message to him and only to him. He will reward you for your work, and I will make your efforts worth your while." He held up a small purse and shook it once so that it jingled. "Ducats, Talpa."

One of the men drinking at the table across from them slumped forward, shoving the unoccupied stool forward into Il Talpa's thigh; at another time Il Talpa would have stabbed him for such impertinence, but not when it would lose him ducats—Il Talpa could not hide the greed he felt. "Do not let the others see it," he warned in a whisper. "This is no place to display money."

"I have two men with me. They are in the front of the room, but they are watching us; if you look toward the hearth you will see them: one is quite tall and fair-haired, the other is wearing a leather giaquetta and striped lower hose, and both are armed," said Aurelio, who had protested the need for a guard but was now convinced he had been well advised. He leaned forward on the table which rocked on uneven legs. "You will report to me in two days, even if you have no news. If you learn anything before then, you will send me word at once. If you fail in any of these missions, you will find yourself chained to an oar on a war galley. This I promise you."

"So you say," grumbled Il Talpa. "But you—" He stopped, aware it was useless to object to anything this young man required of him; he paid well and he had the ear of the Doge.

"You know who I am, Signor Talpa"—his tone made the honorific an insult—"and you know what I can do if I decide it is necessary. I advise you to give me no reason to doubt your reliability. Do I make myself clear?"

"Yes. Clear," said Il Talpa. He thought back to the man who had brought Aurelio to him, and had assured him that Aurelio was an absentminded scholarly sort who could be easily led. He would have a bone to pick with that fellow when next they met.

Aurelio took hold of Il Talpa's wrist—it was a gesture that would earn most men a dagger-thrust—and said in a calm, conversational voice, "If you should try to hoodwink me, Talpa, recall that I have brothers, and the lady has brothers, and your treachery would not be excused. I am paying you well, but I demand value for my money. You will bring me worthwhile news or you will admit you have none, but you will not lead me on with false clues."

"I would never!" Il Talpa exclaimed, who had been planning to do just that. "What sort of man do you think you're dealing with?"

"A man who knows criminals," said Aurelio. "I have no illusions about you."

"Only about the girl," said Il Talpa bitterly.

In the next instant Aurelio was on his feet and leaning over Il Talpa. "If anyone even hints that, I shall know who to come to for an answer," he said, and there was such deadly intent in his words that Il Talpa, who had faced Turks in battle, quailed.

"Sorry," he said finally. "Soldiers are cynics. It's a hazard of the trade."

Aurelio sat down again. "But you are soldier no more."

"As you say." Il Talpa rubbed at his sleeve and shot a sidelong glance at Aurelio's two guards. "I will tell you everything I learn in two days, or as soon as word reaches me."

"Very good," Aurelio approved. He remained on his feet, straightening up. "Then our business is concluded for today, it would appear." He gave the pouch of money to Il Talpa. "There. This should be sufficient for you and your men. Find me real news and worthwhile information and the sum will be doubled. Deceive me or attempt to be paid for no effort and you will regret it."

Il Talpa nodded. "I have your instructions."

"Very good," said Aurelio, and left the scarred man at the unsteady table; he made his way out of the inn to the side of the canal, his guards falling in behind him. "Watch him," he told the shorter man.

On the second night out from Corfu, Fenice became careless. She had climbed to the deck about midnight to have a look at the Greek islands, for the moon gave enough light to mark where the shining sea ended and the black land began. She had found a place among the barrels on deck where she could sit concealed; she took advantage of this to stay there for some time, listening to the sails and the creak of the rigging as the small night crew held the ship on course. This was not what she had hoped for, but it was better than staying in the hold for three weeks, and she had made up her mind to do what she could to enjoy her travels.

There was something about the distant, dark shapes looming in the shining night that was magical to Fenice; she could imagine fabulous things on the unknown slopes, far more fascinating than olive groves and flocks of sheep. In the dark she could summon up palaces grander than anything the Sultan knew, and cities domed in jewels with ships that made the *Impresa* seem old-fashioned, or wild expanses where the beasts that hid in the tangle of the trees were fey and demonic by turns. She remembered the songs she had heard as a child about dragons and wyverns and gryphons as well as the monsters of the sea; all of them inhabited the night-shrouded slopes in her mind's vision, and the dark, imperious man she had dreamed of more recently held sway at the top of the crags that stood against the sky like blackened, broken teeth.

It was shortly before the change of watch before dawn that she finally made her way back down the narrow stairs toward the rope ladder leading to her hiding place. She was very tired and happy, her mind fixed on how she would be able to contrive to get on deck for some time every night, and she did not pay attention to the dark kitchen.

"There you are, you scallywag," a voice said softly as a gnarled hand shot out and grabbed the back of Fenice's giaquetta.

Fenice remained utterly still as her captor came into the faint light cast by a single lantern. She had to keep her jaw clamped closed to stop her teeth from chattering. She could say nothing; words had fled as soon as she felt the hand on her.

Niccola the cook gave her a shake. "You thought no one knew you were aboard, didn't you?" he asked, waiting for Fenice to fight him. "I was aware of you soon after you sneaked aboard at Zara." He nodded once, pleased to see the stowaway look shocked. "You thought you were so careful—and you were—but you see, I was a stowaway once myself, and I know all the tricks." He gave Fenice an appraising look. "Still, I will say this about you: you have been more successful than the rest I have met through the years. Most stowaways are trying to steal half the kitchen within a day of coming aboard. Either you planned well, or you can fast like a monk."

"I planned well," said Fenice, keeping her voice low. She wondered what Niccola was going to do, for surely if he intended to have her taken in hand, he would have summoned the boatswain by now.

"So you do talk," said Niccola, releasing his hold on Fenice's clothes. "Well, then, let's get down to it, young fellow. Don't try to get away. You have nowhere you can hide on this ship that you will not be found."

"They didn't find me once," she said, made bold by his lack of threat to her. "And they searched the ship then."

"But they were not looking for you," said Niccola. He put his hands on his hips. "What am I going to do about you?—that is what I have to decide now."

"What do you mean?" she asked.

"I mean I have to decide how to deal with you," said Niccola thoughtfully.

"But—I thought—" She kept stopping herself.

"Stowaways can be useful," said Niccola. "And not just as a boy-whore for the sailors. I have been planning to ask for a lad to—" Now he fell silent.

This reminder of her immediate peril only served to sharpen her wits; she lowered her head as if ashamed. "What can I do? If you have no use for me . . . You'll tell the captain? He'll put me ashore, and . . . and I will never become a sailor."

"You should apprentice yourself," said Niccola sternly but with little conviction. He gave a single hard sigh. "I could use a hand in the kitchen. Cooking for the crew keeps me busy enough, but taking care of the oarsmen is a real imposition." He glowered at Fenice. "If you will work for me—and I will keep you busy, you need not doubt that—then I will take care of you. I will arrange something with the captain: he's not such a bad fellow, though he has a good opinion of himself."

Fenice had to bite back her agreement with this assessment of Ercole. Instead she said, "Won't he want to question me himself?" She could not keep the dread out of her voice: Ercole would be outraged to discover her, she knew that now beyond all doubt.

"Probably not," said Niccola. "The kitchen is my realm. It isn't as if you'll be in the crow's nest or at the helm. You let me deal with Captain Zucchar." He patted Fenice on the shoulder. "What's your name, lad? And how old are you?"

"I'm . . . thirteen," she lied, knowing she had to account for her voice and lack of beard. "And I am Aeneo."

Niccola's chuckle expressed his disbelief. "Twelve, more like, by the look at you," he said. "And Aeneo—a Greek hero's name."

Fenice wanted to point out that the Captain's name was Ercole, who was as much a hero as Aeneo was, but she held her tongue. "I am Aeneo," she insisted.

"All right," said Niccola, accepting this fiction without any reservation greater than a raised eyebrow. He slapped her shoulder. "Go get your things and come back to the kitchen. I'll see you have a place to sleep behind the stove. That will keep you out of sight and it will be an extra guard against fire." He laughed softly. "You must prove your worth, Aeneo, one way or the other. If you cannot stir soup, you will watch the stove all night."

"Yes, Signor," said Fenice.

"Niccola. You must call me Niccola. No one calls a cook Signor." He grinned at this courtesy. "Now hurry. I must have you stowed before the next watch is rung, and it is very near."

Taking his pat as impetus to move, Fenice went down the rope ladder, her thoughts in disarray: she was jubilant to have found a way to leave the hold in safety, but at the same time she was filled with anxiety, for she was now much closer to being recognized. If Ercole saw her, she knew she would be humiliated. But until she was identified as Ercole's sister, she had a chance to enjoy herself that had eluded her since she came aboard the *Impresa:* she would make the most of it for as long as it lasted.

Alas! am I then so truly base
That you despise me as an unworthy foe?
—Cino da Pistoia

— XIII —

Ercole studied his cook's visage, looking for any trickery in the deep seams fretting his features. "You say the lad came aboard at Zara? And he managed to keep hidden until just before dawn?"

"Just before dawn, yes," said Niccola. "I tried to find him once, but he was well hidden. And he didn't take many chances. He kept himself out of sight." He shifted his stance. "He's a clever lad, Captain—quick, you know?—thin as a pikestaff, but presents himself well; seems to have some education. I think he might know how to read and write, which tells you something right there. You'd be surprised how he kept his head when I finally came upon him."

"What do you think? Is he a thief, trying to escape the law, or . . ."

"He's probably just what he says he is—a boy who wants to go to sea. I know how he feels—I was one such. Probably an only son, or pledged to the Church, or something of the sort. That would explain the reading. He has the look of breeding about him; he could be the child of an impoverished nobleman: there's plenty of them about, or he could be some nobleman's bastard who wants to make something of himself, and knows he'll never do it at home. If you want to talk to him—?" Niccola started toward the door of the captain's cabin.

Ercole stopped him. "No. No, don't bother. Just as well you keep him out of sight. I'd have to enter him in my log if I see him, and if he is a runaway, his family could make a claim against me for helping him, and frankly, I can do without that. This voyage is going too well." He tapped his fingertips together. "I'll tell you what: you keep him in the kitchen, and report to me from time to time on his progress. Find out if he has any talent for the sea. If he seems to have promise, I will put him among the crew when we reach Tana. Any need to answer to his family should be over by then, and the Church would not want him back after such an absence. Teach him what you know. That should do well enough, don't you think." He held up a single finger in warning. "If he turns out not to be as useful as you hoped, let me know and we will put him ashore—unofficially—before Tana."

"Very good," said Niccola, delighted by the decision Ercole had made. "I'll do just that. He'll do fine, you'll see. He's made for this life: I can smell it."

"May you be right," said Ercole. "But remember that not all stowaways are like you, Niccola. If he is not able to be a good sailor, then it would be best if you told him so as soon as possible so he may do what he can to make a more fitting life for himself." He frowned. "What is he calling himself?"

"Aeneo," said Niccola, and laughed. "Sounds like he could be one of your brothers. Ercole, Febo . . . why not an Aeneo?" He stopped, aware that he had gone too far. "I'm sorry, Captain Zucchar. I overstepped myself."

"So you did," said Ercole, "not that there isn't some truth in what you say. I can imagine my parents giving a son such a name. But it would be best to keep such thoughts to yourself." His warning was cordial.

"Of course." Niccola ducked his head. "I will tell the boy to keep himself out of sight, and I will have work enough for him that he will not long be idle. He has shown himself willing to work, and I will make full use of him." He started toward the cabin door when he caught sight of the cabin boy. "A pity, to have two youngsters aboard and have to keep them apart."

"Yes. A pity, but a necessity as well," said Ercole without turning.

Niccola went to tell Aeneo of the bargain he had struck with Captain Zucchar. He was pleased with his accomplishment and gave thanks to a God—in Whom he vaguely believed—for allowing him to extend to Aeneo the same opportunity he had been given all those years ago. He whistled as he began to think of chores he could assign to the boy.

The space behind the stove was cramped, but not nearly so uncomfortable as the place she had made for herself between the woollen bales and the hull; she was permitted to bathe twice a week and wash her clothes once a week, which she welcomed with more emotion than she would have thought such commonplace things deserved before she came aboard the *Impresa*. The kitchen had two small portholes, allowing her to look out at the sea while she tended to the work Niccola gave her.

"You have to cut up the rest of the onions for tomorrow; I will bake them with hard cheese, and the men can have them with the lentil stew; that will lend a savor," Niccola told her at the end of the day; she had been working for him for nearly three weeks and Constantinople was not far ahead, for the *Impresa* continued to make good speed through the Greek islands and through the Dardanelles. "We will bring more aboard when we dock, along with soft cheeses packed in oil; we've been out of them for more than a week. I've been told we will have two days in port, and I will spend most of that time in the markets, buying grain and legumes. There will be onions in the markets and I will purchase them fresh, and lemons."

"And I will have to remain aboard, won't I?" Fenice asked.

"Yes, lad, you will," said Niccola, his deep-set eyes sympathetic. "Wait another few weeks and perhaps Captain Zucchar will permit you greater freedom. I am going to ask if you can be allowed on deck during the day as well as after the night watch has been set." He smiled his encouragement. "On the way back, you will have the chance to visit Constantinople."

"I hope so," said Fenice, no longer as convinced as she had been at the start of the voyage that it would be the escapade she had imagined. She indicated the flour she had ground. "Do you want me to make the bread?"

"After you chop the onions. Use the last of the soft cheese—bake it in the breads. The crew will like it and it will make our need for more apparent." Niccola chuckled. "It is an old trick, but still worthwhile: you use all of the supplies you wish most to replace and then protest that if you cannot purchase fresh, you will have none at all. It is difficult for any captain to refuse when nothing is left." He winked. "The captain knows I do this—all cooks do it—but he likes his food tasty, and he allows me to do as I think best."

Over the last several days, Fenice had come to think of Ercole as Captain Zucchar instead of her brother. "He does not mind?"

"With the progress we have made, I doubt he would mind if I wanted to buy a dozen suckling pigs." Niccola nodded in emphasis. "Get to the onions, Aeneo. We have meals to serve before we arrive at Constantinople."

"All right," she said, and hurried to comply.

"When I am ashore, you will have to keep watch on the kitchen. Mind you keep the door closed. No one is to see you." He forestalled her objection at once. "Oh, they know you are aboard. Secrets cannot be kept on a ship. But we must not force the captain or the boatswain to notice you, for then you will have to be entered on the ship's rolls, and you will answer to them instead of me." He pointed to the wide baking board. "Make sure that is cleaned before you start to knead on it."

"Yes, I will," said Fenice. She reached into the bin for the onions and noticed that three of them had sprouted.

"Be sure you chop up the sprouts," said Niccola. "We cannot throw such things away." He indicated the large crockery bowls used for baking. "When you mix the onions with the hard cheese, grate the cheese first, and use a little flour to hold it together." He went about cleaning his knives, testing the edges and honing those in need. "I will buy some crates of chickens—we will have eggs and meat from them, and all fresh." He smiled. "You're a good lad. You work willingly and you do not make the same mistake more than once."

Fenice flushed with this praise; she wished her brother could hear it, although she knew he would not be as pleased as she was with such flattery. "I want to stay aboard," she said with feeling.

"And so you shall, if my opinion has any weight," Niccola promised her. "I've come to depend on your help."

As she felt her face flush with pride, Fenice said, "I am only carrying out your orders, Niccola. If I do well, it is because you teach me well."

Niccola grinned at her, showing a fair number of teeth still in place. "You're a good lad. When we're a little beyond Constantinople, I will see that

Captain Zucchar enters you on the rolls of the ship. There is no reason to treat you like human contraband any longer than that. Now," he went on more firmly, "you know what has to be done: set to work, lad."

"Yes, Signor Niccola," said Fenice; she did as he ordered, her mind only half engaged in the work: the rest of her thoughts drifted to the distant shore and the mysterious lands beyond the shores, lands where the hawk-faced man of her reveries held sway in a stone castle high on a mountain-crag. She rocked with the ship and imagined herself on those remote battlements, all the world at her feet; she told herself the tears were from the onions.

Although he looked weary, Gaetano Zucchar responded with energy as he sat down with his son Lionello and Aurelio Pirenetto; the reception hall was empty but for these three, for the women of the Zucchar household were at Mass to pray for Fenice's safe return. "We have not been lax in our efforts, and I have spared no cost to find her," Gaetano said as Lionello strove to comprehend what had happened in his absence. "Aurelio, here, has done more than any man could be expected to do to recover his promised bride."

"Aurelio has?" Lionello said, unaware of the change Fenice's disappearance had wrought in her accepted suitor.

"Yes," said Gaetano, and added, "No one in this family has been as diligent as he, and no one has accomplished so much." He reached across the table and put his hand on Aurelio's shoulder. "He has been a son to me without the marriage vows that would have made him one."

Lionello shook his head. "And yet there has been no word?"

"No," said Aurelio. "No demands for ransom, no threats." He rubbed at his neat, short beard. "I have men looking as far away as Paris and Krakow for her. As their reports come in, we will know more." Lionello stared at him. "I have sent dispatches to Corfu as well, although I doubt she was taken that way for reasons your father can tell you later. When your brothers visit your cousin there, they will have a full account of these events waiting for them."

"You see?" Gaetano said, indicating Aurelio with pride. "He has been diligent; he has taken much of the burden upon himself."

"I am sorry," Aurelio said to Lionello, "that my account of all that has transpired had not reached Corfu when you did. You would not have had all this to contemplate without any preparation. My brother's ship must have passed yours between Zara and Corfu."

"So it would seem," said Lionello, sounding bemused. "You say the note left was in Greek?" He waited for his father to answer.

"Very poor Greek, and in an uneducated hand," said Gaetano, as if reciting a phrase whose only meaning was in the ritual of speaking it.

"You would think that our cousins in Corfu would—" Lionello began, then stopped. "But word must have got out."

"Yes. It is known that Fenice was abducted the very day that the *Impresa* put to sea," said Gaetano.

"The *Impresa!*" Lionello exclaimed. "Have you considered that she might have tried to get aboard her?" He faltered. "Not that Ercole would allow it; he isn't Febo, after all." He looked from his father to Aurelio. "She did want to go to sea. She might do something so reckless."

"But she did not have herself abducted for the chance," said Gaetano firmly.

"Think, Lionello," said Aurelio, confronting Fenice's youngest brother with purpose. "What would she have to do to get aboard a ship—any ship—on her own. She is a female of ingenuity, but her experience is, naturally, limited, and she would not know how to bring off any such venture as you suggest. In time she would realize the futility of her efforts."

"And she would have to have help," said Gaetano heavily. "No, I fear that the kidnapers used the departure of the *Impresa* to misdirect us, but luckily that ruse failed." He put his hands on his knees. "If Fenice had wanted anyone to help her, she would have asked Aurelio. With Febo gone, what man could she turn to but him?"

Lionello nodded slowly. "Febo will be—" He could find no word sufficiently overwhelming to describe how his brother would feel.

"We must ready ourselves to comfort him," said Aurelio. "He can be of help in searching for her."

"And you already know what is to be done," said Lionello, still astonished at the purpose Aurelio displayed.

"I have a few recommendations," said Aurelio in a tone that made it clear his mind was made up. "No doubt Febo will want to consider them."

"He has a ship to sail," said Lionello. "We cannot sacrifice our business to a search that may lead to nothing." He studied Aurelio with resentment, as if this focused young man was an interloper in his family.

"Lionello!" Gaetano admonished him. "You cannot think what you are saying."

"I can," said Lionello. "From what I can see, Aurelio is leading us all around by the nose, saying where we will and will not search, and intruding on what should be our burden." His face was mottled with anger. When he shouted, his voice broke.

Gaetano stared at his son helplessly. "What is the matter with you, boy?" he demanded. "Aurelio has done nothing to deserve these calumnies. You have not been here, so you do not know what a stanch support he has been through these trying times."

"No, I do not know," said Lionello angrily. "But I am all consternation to see how you have been hoodwinked by him."

"Hoodwinked?" Gaetano repeated incredulously. "How can we be hoodwinked by anything Aurelio does? He has been our stay at a time when we might have been in disorder. Without him we could have lost precious time in beginning our search, and I will not hear you speak against him."

It was Aurelio who forestalled further dispute by saying, "Do not blame him, Signor Zucchar; he already blames himself so much that it is a keen pain within him. He is afraid that he has failed his sister by being away when she is in danger." He looked directly at Lionello. "I give you my word that I have never wanted anything but the safe return of Fenice, and I will go to the ends of the earth to find her."

"The ends of the earth," said Lionello sarcastically. "You have not left Venice."

"I will when I know in which direction to go; then nothing will stop me." He bowed to Gaetano. "You will do better if I am gone," he said, and left father and son alone.

"What in the name of the Prophets is the matter with you?" Gaetano demanded of his youngest boy. "Aurelio Pirenetto has been more help than anyone ever could have thought. He has been generous with his time and his money, he has been unstinting in his devotion, and you—you make me ashamed to be your father!"

Lionello glared in recalcitrant hostility at a place on the far wall. "You . . . you have let him take over."

"I have welcomed his help," said Gaetano. "You ought to, as well, unless you were planning to remain here and supervise the search for Fenice." He shook his head. "What do you mean, suggesting she ran away? She is a gently reared girl with a vivid imagination, but she would never do anything so disgraceful as you suggest. There was a note and her room was in disarray. What a poor opinion you have of your sister!"

"She is full of mischief," Lionello muttered.

"She may well be," said Gaetano, "but this is not mischief that you are suggesting, it is something wicked. Why would she do anything so . . . unspeakable? She was about to be married. She had everything any girl could want waiting for her. You think she would be willing to give it all up in order to disgrace herself and her family?"

Lionello shrugged. "No," he said at last. "Not really."

"No," Gaetano said. "So we must continue to search for her and pray that she is not dead or debauched." His indignation evaporated. "At least the note mentioned ransom. If she had been taken away to be sold to the Turks, there would have been no—" He broke off and put his hand to his eyes.

"Then you have thought she might have gone—" Lionello broke off. "They don't usually take well-to-do girls, not as old as Fenice." He shook his head. "She is not one to be seduced, least of all by a Turk or a Greek. She knows too much about them."

"I've thought about that. But could you imagine Fenice in a harem?" His laughter was forced and a bit wild, but he made himself stop before it became something worse.

"I refuse to think of that," said Lionello, who had thought of little else since he had learned of Fenice's disappearance.

Gaetano caught his meaning and lowered his eyes. "Just so."

From Constantinople the *Impresa* went north along the coast of the Black Sea toward Varna. It was as if every advantage they had enjoyed to this point was being balanced now by mishaps and difficulties; the ship was facing the last of the winter winds, and their speed was reduced. Squalls sprang up out of nothing and bedeviled the vessel as it plowed northward.

"Make sure you put pepper in the porridge," said Niccola as the *Impresa* slogged onward. "The oarsmen will need it to steady their stomachs."

"Of course," said Fenice, who was feeling a trifle woozy herself.

"And make sure you have your bedroll strapped in place: the night is going to be rough." Niccola continued to work at preparing a thick soup of beans and pork haunch. He swore as the ship canted to starboard, slopping a bit of the soup out of the large pot in which it cooked. "Aeneo, clean this up. At once."

"Yes," said Fenice. She no longer found inclement weather as exciting as when she first came aboard. She found rags and used them to wipe away the soup on the hot stove. She could not bring herself to feel hungry; the ship's antics robbed her of appetite.

"Keep at your work," said Niccola, his frown becoming a glower. "The men will be famished when they come to eat. They will want good portions."

"But—" Fenice protested, the ship's plunging making her certain she would never want to eat anything again.

"You will discover that you will wolf your food when you come to eat," said Niccola knowingly. "You think now that you could not put so much as a morsel of bread in your mouth, but you will, and you will be voracious." He wagged a ladle at her. "This is your first time at sea, Aeneo, and for all that you think you have accustomed yourself, you have much to learn. You are doing well for a lad on his first journey," he conceded as the ship rolled and more of his soup sloshed out of the pot.

This time Fenice did not have to be told. She used the rag at once, and was pleased by the smile of approval Niccola gave her. She did her best to look confident and secure as the ship rolled heavily in an unruly buffet of wind, and almost succeeded. "I will get the bowls," she offered, used to putting them out well in advance of serving.

"Not in this weather," said Niccola. "We'll have half of them on the floor and broken if we put them out a moment before they are needed." He knew he had snapped without cause, and added, "You will learn, boy, but it's better to find out from a warning than from losing crockery."

"Yes, it is," said Fenice, feeling absurdly grateful to him. She did her best to concentrate on her tasks, doing all she could to stand without swaying in the confines of the kitchen.

Niccola watched her, approving of the spirit she showed. "You'll do. In another two hundred leagues of sailing you'll wonder how you ever felt out of place."

"I am counting on it," she said, although she knew it would be increasingly difficult to avoid being recognized once she officially joined the *Impresa*'s crew.

"When you finish there, get me a head of garlic," Niccola ordered a little later. "The men will want to have something against worms."

"Yes," said Fenice, trying her best not to look disgusted.

"You will cut it up and put it in this soup," said Niccola. "I put some in at the start, but it was not enough." He grabbed the edge of a cupboard as the ship lurched sharply.

There was a chorus of oaths and a single harsh cry from the deck above.

"Someone's hurt," said Niccola as a flurry of activity erupted. "Bring the rags and follow me."

"But the food—" Fenice protested, suddenly frightened of what might await her.

"There is a man hurt!" Niccola shouted. "We must hurry." He had already grabbed a box of special supplies, including sail-mending needles and heavy thread. "Rags, boy!"

Fenice nodded, feeling as if her head were loosely joined to her neck. "Yes. Rags." She reached for the sack that contained them; the shouts overhead were becoming sharper and more specific: someone in the rigging had fallen to the deck and was lying unconscious. The crew was torn between wanting to help him and tending to the ship. As Fenice emerged from the companionway behind Niccola, she was terribly aware that this was the first time most of the crew had seen her. Suddenly her disguise seemed woefully inadequate.

The men gathered around the fallen sailor were grave, their oaths almost prayers. One of them looked pale and shaken; he kept repeating, "I saw him fall, I saw him fall, I saw him fall," as if repetition would make it untrue.

"Move aside," said Niccola, shoving his way through the men. "Stay with me, Aeneo."

At another time the men would have joked about a personable youngster in the company of the grizzled old cook, but not now. They parted willingly and stood silently as Niccola went to the limp figure of the man.

Fenice could see blood coming from the unconscious sailor's ears. The sailor's face was waxen and his breathing sounded strange; Fenice shivered at the sound as she knelt beside the sailor where Niccola ordered her to. She no longer felt the ship move—all her attention was on the injured man.

"Wipe his face, Aeneo," said Niccola so quietly that it was astonishing that she heard him over the wind and the pounding of the sea.

Fenice did as she was told, being as gentle as she could. She could not shake the feeling that she was preparing him for burial, and the notion chilled her as the wind-driven spume could not. She could hear the breath shudder in him and she looked at Niccola, trying to discern what she ought to do.

"He's done for," said one of the sailors, and a few of the others muttered their agreement.

It took an effort of will for Fenice to continue to touch the sailor; she had the terrible conviction that he would somehow blame her in the next world for allowing him to die in this one. She wanted to call for a priest to tend to him, but of course there was no priest on the *Impresa*; any rites performed over the sailor would be done by the captain. She was so caught up in the trouble the sailor had that she did not realize what that might mean to her. When she gradually became aware of what she might have to confront, she decided that she would not be allowed near the captain. All she had to do was remain with Niccola and she would be safe from discovery; with something so grave as this sailor's death to deal with, it was unlikely that anyone would pay any attention to her, an assistant to the cook.

"He's slipping," said one of the men.

Fenice had reached to steady the sailor before she realized that the speaker had meant something else. She hastily tried to cover her error by wiping the man's face once more; she was fairly certain that no one had noticed, or that if they had, they had not minded what she had done.

"How long?" Rainardo had come through the group around the unconscious man.

"No more than an hour," said Niccola, getting slowly to his feet. "Might as well make him comfortable. He won't wake up."

"So the captain won't have to hear his Confession," said the boatswain. He became very businesslike.

"Go get the cabin ready, Aeneo," said Niccola. "Someone has to stay with him, and we can spare few of these men." He regarded her sympathetically. "It is a duty all Christians must do sometime in their lives: this is your turn."

She paled. "But—" How could she explain it was the captain who troubled her and not the dying man?

"Tend to this and I will make sure you are thanked for your charity," said Niccola, motioning her along to the captain's cabin. "It will not be long, and I will see you have spirits of wine tonight."

Reluctantly she nodded. "All right."

"Good lad," said Niccola. He took the sack of rags from her and indicated Rainardo's back. "He is the boatswain: follow his instruction as if it were mine."

"Yes, yes," said Fenice, and made her way through the crew toward the door that gaped like a maw. She would have to be careful; perhaps Ercole would not want to see the dying man until he was dead. She could be back in the kitchen before he visited the sailor.

The cabin was small, every space put to fullest use. The bed was atop two large chests with drawers, making access to them easy. The injured sailor would be carried here.

"Shall I pray for him?" she asked, uncertain what was expected of her.

"If you think God will care," said one of the sailors from outside the door. "He has probably made up His mind about Giancarlo already." Looking out into the storm, she saw he was still bleeding from his ears.

A foot entered the corner of her vision and she heard, "So you're Niccola's stowaway, are you?"

Terrified, she bobbed her head, trying to keep her face averted; she could not escape no matter how devoutly she wanted to. It was useless: fingers fixed on her shoulder and she turned to face the dawning outrage in her brother's eyes.

. . . But I will not depart
Though you hate me; my heart is afire.
—Cielo d'Alcamo

— XIV —

Ercole's face showed first disbelief, then astonishment, then rage, in quick and intensifying succession. He dragged Fenice to her feet, shaking her as he did. "How dare you? How *dare* you?

"How dare you!" he thundered at her. He stood in the cabin, filling it up.

"No, no," said Niccola, rushing in behind him and trying to pull at Ercole's sleeve. "No. He was helping."

Filled with shock and unexpected shame, Fenice could say nothing; as often as she had anticipated this moment, she had never assumed the experience would be anything like this. She felt the force of his fingers on her arms and his strength in her helplessness. She could not make herself speak, for fear she would betray herself more than she had already.

"He? Help? He?" Ercole burst out. He pointed to Niccola; he held onto Fenice as if he expected her to fly away. "You must explain."

Niccola looked baffled. "But you knew about Aeneo. I told you about him," he protested.

"Aeneo? This is Aeneo? This?"

"I told you the boy was young," said Niccola hurriedly. "And he has the look of someone well born. I told you that, too." He was very nearly whining.

The first of his anger was gone and now Ercole was more aware of the risks they all ran. "You," he said sharply to Fenice. "Don't talk to him."

Fenice was relieved not to be disgraced before all the crew. She ducked her head and shot an apologetic look to Niccola. When she started to speak, Ercole cuffed her ear. Fenice stifled a cry of protest; she knew no sailor would do anything of the sort, and she clung to her disguise in the hope that Ercole might allow her to continue it. Her head rung and she felt slightly dizzy as she made her way aft in the ship; she could feel the curious stares of the sailors follow her as she went.

The ship rolled heavily and a large wave sloshed over the deck, running into the corridor and the open cabin, soaking Fenice to the waist and nearly knocking her off her feet. Fenice watched in horror as the water carried the unconscious man from beyond the entrance to the corridor over the side of the ship and into the turbulent water.

There were shouts of alarm; half a dozen of the crew rushed to the rail and leaned out, straining to catch sight of Giancarlo in the sea in the vain hope of pulling him aboard. But it was impossible; one of the men began to intone prayers for the lost sailor and several of the men braved other waves to kneel on the deck.

Chilled and shocked, Fenice stood alone and suddenly ignored in the corridor entrance, shaken by what she had just seen. Her face paled and she slowly crossed herself as she moved deeper into the shadows. She did not want to be seen—her long days in the hold had taught her to equate visibility with danger, and that impression was never stronger than now. The cold of her wet clothes bit more deeply into her.

The cabin boy, his face impassive, emerged from the shadows behind her, looked Fenice over and snorted. "He'll be tired of you in a week."

Fenice blinked. "What?" she asked, feeling very stupid.

"He'll want me back," said the cabin boy with calm certainty.

She stared at him, her thoughts jumbled. "I . . . I don't know . . ."

"Don't know? You're in for a surprise, then," said the cabin boy, and laughed unpleasantly as he started toward the door of the cabin. "I watched the whole thing."

"The whole thing?" Fenice repeated, her mind refusing to work.

"On the deck." He laughed again, the sound nastier than before. "You will not know what he wants; I have a talent for such things. I can see you don't." His scorn was apparent in the way he bowed Fenice into her brother's cabin. "I'd use a knife on you if I thought he had any real interest in you. But you aren't worth the flogging. You are only a diversion."

Suddenly Fenice understood what the cabin boy was saying. Fever-heat mounted in her face as she studied the boy: he was somewhat smaller than she, his face like one of the angels over the altar at Sant' Angelo, lovely and equivocal. Only the resentment in the cabin boy's eyes belied his angelic looks. Fenice shook her head. "I don't think you have anything to worry about. The captain—"

"—will not want you very long," the cabin boy insisted.

"Probably not," she said, feeling forlorn. She looked about the cabin. "I'm all wet," she said, trying to determine how she was to get dry.

"How sad," said the cabin boy. "Get out of the clothes and into the bed. Your things will be dry when you wake."

Fenice shook her head. "He won't want . . . that. Not from me."

The cabin boy barked a single, cynical chuckle. "What else would he have you here for?" With that he turned and left Fenice alone in the cabin, her courage running out of her as surely as if it were blood. She grabbed her elbows, hugging her arms tightly across her chest. She saw again in her mind

Giancarlo washing over the side of the ship, and the aghast expressions among the crew as he vanished from sight. She had been told of the cruelty of the sea but had not grasped it wholly until now, for no cat with a mouse was as cruel as the sea had been with Giancarlo.

Il Talpa peered over his tankard of wine at Aurelio, his ugly features distorted with apprehension. "I . . . have not heard anything."

"Then continue your search. Have you explored every possibility?" Aurelio's questions were crisp and authoritative. "You said your men would do the work. You have yet to prove it to me." He put his hands on the table, palms down. "You are not trying to milk more money from me, are you? You would not be so dishonorable."

"Of course not," said Il Talpa, a shade too hastily. "I have nothing to report: that is the truth. My men have been searching. That is also the truth." He looked around the tavern as if he expected the patrons to speak in his support. "Everyone knows I have been busy on your behalf, Signor Pirenetto." He drank a larger gulp of wine than he had intended and coughed after swallowing it.

"Perhaps everyone does," said Aurelio, clearly unconvinced. "But until I have results beyond the excuses you offer, I must reserve judgment." His smile was unpleasant.

"You are being . . . too harsh." Il Talpa gave a furtive look toward the door.

"I may be. But it is my bride who is missing, and the longer she is gone, the greater my fear for her safety becomes. You must make allowances for this." Again he smiled, so coldly that Il Talpa shivered.

"Naturally," said Il Talpa. He studied the tabletop with such intensity that he might have been reading coded messages hidden in the grain of the wood. "We might try another approach," he suggested after a moment. "We could see if any of the Greek sailors have heard stories of an abducted girl. They may know something."

"The girl's father and uncles have attended to that, and have had no word." Aurelio studied the criminal on the other side of the table. "Do not think to impose on them. They have also had many promises which have resulted in nothing. They are becoming discouraged, and would close the door on you. I am becoming more determined. You would do well to keep that in mind while dealing with me." He slapped his palms down once; Il Talpa jumped. "I will speak to you again in a week. If you still can tell me nothing, I will have to find another deputy to take your place; I am unwilling to continue to support your foolishness, if it is nothing more than fantasy."

Il Talpa bristled. "My men have worked hard to help you."

"No doubt they have," said Aurelio flatly as he got to his feet. "And so you will not doubt my conviction that the young woman can be found, I am prepared to pay an additional reward, beyond the one offered by her family . . . but only for results. I will pay nothing for vague rumors. Nor will I bargain in order to secure any news you may hear. My gold is ready for knowledge of value. Otherwise, I have no inclination to listen to the fables you might spin." He turned and went out of the tavern into the wispy fog of early spring. His cloak quickly spangled with moisture. He summoned his family's gondola to the landing and got into it. "The Doge's Palace," he said as he sat back and allowed the gondoliere to do his business.

The Doge's servants escorted Aurelio to the private withdrawing room where the Doge held his private meetings; their demeanor was courteous but without flair, for this meeting was a clandestine one.

Alvise Mocenigo was in fully dogal regalia; he was a handsome man, with regular, mobile features; his red-blond beard was brushed and burnished, his gaze penetrating. He waited while Aurelio went down on one knee to him, then motioned the young man to take a seat opposite him. "I have heard you are still looking for Fenice Zucchar."

This blunt beginning surprised Aurelio. "Yes," he said. "And I intend to continue to do so. Pray do not ask me to stop."

Mocenigo shook his head; his left brow raised eloquently. "Why should I do that? No, Pirenetto, nothing of the sort. In fact," he went on very smoothly, "I was hoping that while you are conducting your inquiries for the young woman, you might also make one or two on my behalf." He did not give Aurelio a chance to reply. "Yes, I have my own means of getting information, but there are times I question the quality of the information I obtain, and so I have decided to ask you to help me in verifying what I have learned thus far. It is nothing dangerous, only . . . shall we say careful?"

Aurelio had barely taken this in and was still trying to determine what it was that Mocenigo wanted to know; he faltered as he answered. "I . . . I am willing . . . to serve La Serenissima in any way I can, as any Venetian would do." He regarded the Doge a moment. "What sort of things do you want to know?"

If this question relieved Mocenigo, it did not show in his face. "There is a question of Genoa and the Corsican pirates. Are they really the danger the Genoese claim, or is this nothing more than a ploy to excuse them from continuing to assist in monitoring the movements of the Turks?" He asked this so easily it was apparent he had framed the question some time before and rehearsed it.

"The Corsican pirates are real enough," said Aurelio. "As are the Sardinian ones, the Sicilian ones, and the Maltese, for that matter. You wonder how much of a danger they are, not if they are real. You are more concerned about the Genoese than the pirates." He felt confident in speaking to Mocenigo this way, for his long association with the shipbuilders of the Arsenal had taught him that the Doge did not like obfuscation or elaborate civility.

"Precisely," said Mocenigo as he stroked his beard.

Aurelio hesitated. "Are you telling me that the pirates may have information about Fenice Zucchar?"

"I have no reason to think so, but it is always possible. Such men hear things and occasionally they will trade what they know, or think they know," said Mocenigo. "I cannot offer you false hope, my friend. You have it in your power to help me. If it will bring the lady back to you, so much the better, but I am not asking your help for that reason. In searching for her, you have come to know those I cannot approach. I would like you to do it for me, if you are willing to." He put the tips of his fingers together. "You have been valuable to Venice, and I hope you will continue to be. This is one way you can help—in finding out through your . . . associates, how great a danger those pirates are. Then I will know how to deal with the Genoese." He looked directly at Aurelio, waiting for an answer.

Aurelio considered and shrugged. "So long as I am searching for one thing, I might as well search for another," he said, and changed the course of his life.

"Niccola explained his part to me," Ercole said without greeting as he came into his cabin some time later. "You convinced him well enough that you are a boy, and for that I must be grateful." He came to where Fenice lay huddled on her side next to Ercole's bed. "What made you do such a mad thing?"

"It isn't mad," she said, wanting not to sulk.

"But look where you are. Look what you've done," Ercole accused her.

Fenice looked at her brother as if she could not understand what he said. "But you know the reason: I want adventures. I've always wanted adventure. I've said so for as long as I can remember. You didn't believe me, but I meant it." She pushed herself up on her elbow; in spite of everything, sleep tugged at her; she wanted to have her dreams now, not this increasingly unpleasant predicament. "I just wanted a chance to see what you see, Ercole."

"So you disgrace your family and bring shame on us?" Ercole demanded. "You have lost your mind, Fenice. You have let yourself forget everything you have ever been told of good conduct. No woman can hold her—"

"I made it look as if I had been abducted," she said, interrupting his vituperative flow. "I know enough not to simply vanish. There was a note and my room was in disarray." She glared at her brother. "A fine opinion you have of me, to think I would ruin us."

Ercole rocked back on his heels. "You must admit you have given me more than sufficient reason to think so." He glared at her. "At least you made the effort to seem a boy. You haven't completely lost your wits."

"I told you I had not," she replied, trying not to sulk. She frowned at him. "You will not undo everything I've done, will you?"

His face was set in shock. "How do you mean?"

She got onto her knees, readying herself to stand; the roll of the ship made her timing crucial. "I mean that I have been at pains to keep the family from embarrassment. I have left the impression that I was kidnaped, so that the family would not have to be ashamed; I have maintained my disguise as a boy; I have kept away from the crew, except for Niccola, so that little or nothing is known about me. You do not think I have been circumspect, but I have. If you insist on crying aloud to the world that I am your sister, all my precautions will be for nothing." She shoved herself to her feet and glared at him. "Think before you answer. Little as you may condone what I have done, consider what will happen if you let everyone know who I am." She would not beg him; that would be fatal. She would have to persuade him or capitulate: her determination gave her patience and a fixity of purpose that would not be swayed by bullying or sullenness.

"At least Niccola is certain you're a boy. He thinks you were intended for the Church and ran away to sea to avoid the cloister." His tone was resentful and he refused to face her. "If he had guessed the truth, I would not have any choice in the matter."

"But you do," she insisted. "You can decide what is to be done, and how it is to be done. You may think that this is unimportant, now that you have found me out, but it is."

"You would like me to believe so, wouldn't you?" he challenged. "You, Fenice, are in no position to make demands of me. You have behaved so disgracefully that you have no right to ask anything of me. You lost that right when you got aboard at Zara."

Fenice blinked; so Ercole was going to continue that fiction about her, that she had not stowed away in Venice but had got onto the ship at the first port of call. "Yes. I know why you think this is so. I know you think I have done something very wrong and I . . . I can understand why," she said uncertainly. It would take care on her part to ensure his continuing desire to support the tale; she watched him narrowly. "I thought this out with great diligence, Ercole. I made sure that none of you could be blamed for my . . . departure. You know how little I want our family to suffer because of what I have done. And Aurelio. I do not want anyone to think that I left to avoid marrying him."

"And you didn't?" Ercole asked incredulously.

"Of course not," she said at once. "I like Aurelio very much. I . . . I hope he will not refuse me when I return."

Ercole laughed angrily. "Aurelio may be foolish, but he is not as foolish as that, my girl." He folded his arms. "I would like to think you are not mad, or not so mad that you have no grasp of the world. You have gone away from Venice, Fenice," he said, making an effort to be patient with her. "You have made yourself unacceptable to any man. Even the Church might not take you in, since you brought this on yourself."

Fenice did what she could to conceal her emotions. "I tried to make it—"

"Your ploy may spare the family some disgrace, but you . . . you are another matter entirely." He scowled at her; it was apparent he was making an effort to control his temper, but not as successfully as he hoped. "Listen to me. You have done something that cannot be erased or overlooked. You have thrown over all constraints put in place to protect you. It makes no difference that you gave your adventure the appearance of a kidnaping—you have shamed yourself forever by your long absence. Everyone will have no doubt that you have been compromised."

"But I'm not," Fenice protested. "I can prove no man touched me . . . not that way."

Ercole's expression did not soften. "That's not important; your total lack of regard for good conduct is."

"It isn't so wrong," Fenice said, knowing it was.

"You may try to convince yourself of that if you like, girl; you know as well as I do that you will be dishonored when you go back to Venice. Which you must surely do." He fell silent a moment, then added, "You have made this very difficult for me."

"Difficult for *you?*" she echoed him, aghast that he should put himself first in this predicament. "I am the one who must live with what I have done."

"When did you decide this? If you had thought about it at all before you sneaked aboard, you would never have done anything so . . . so brazen." He had made his hands into fists; he relaxed them slowly, as if to keep from striking her.

"I told you I did everything I could to spare the family," she said, her chin coming up.

"And I suppose I should thank you for taking such care to hide as long as you did," said Ercole sarcastically. "Your presence aboard was not noticed until after Zara. That, at least, was well-done of you."

"I had to be sure you could not send me back," said Fenice candidly. "I never thought you would be so . . . so unyielding. I thought you would see that it would be folly to make it known that your sister had contrived to get aboard." She looked directly at him. "You have always been a strict man, much more than Febo. But I thought you would see the advantage in going along with my disguise."

"Your disguise is repugnant," said Ercole. "And as to the rest, you are right on one point: I do not want it known that my sister has contrived to get aboard. That would be lunacy." He paced the length of his cabin. "But Niccola thinks you are running away from the Church, so I will keep you confined until I can put you in the hands of the Church."

Fenice went pale. "The Church?" She felt tears in her eyes; of all the ends she had imagined for her escapade, being held in a monk's cell was not one she had anticipated. "You can't do that, Ercole."

"I not only can, I begin to think it is the wisest thing I can do," said Ercole, fingering his short-trimmed beard. "You cannot remain on board any longer than necessary. The men will want you off. I will be able to put you ashore in the hands of the Church without any questioning from the crew."

"What would the crew care?" she asked, suspicious about his motives now.

"The sailors on this ship, like all sailors, look to signs and portents to keep them safe on the sea." He bowed slightly to her. "Had you been a sailor signed on with the rest, I could not keep you aboard after Giancarlo's death. So it is out of my hands." He chuckled at her dismay. "I will say you are being kept in my cabin because you are a runaway monk, and the sailors will be more determined than ever to get you off this ship."

"But—what will you do?" Fenice asked; she felt her courage lessening as she spoke.

"You will be put into the hands of the Church. It will probably have to be Orthodox, but we cannot have it another way. You will remain there until you can be picked up by one of our other ships; the crew would not tolerate having you aboard the *Impresa* again." He continued to stroke his beard. "You will have months to think over what you have done. Oh, don't worry," he added. "I will maintain your fiction of abduction, and I will let the family believe that I came upon you by good fortune, not your willfulness. I will let them be consoled in their conviction that you did not do anything so reprehensible as you have done. I will keep that between us."

"And you will never let me forget," said Fenice with bitter certainty.

"You should not be allowed to forget," said Ercole with determination. "We will reach Varna in three or four days. You might use the time you have here to accustom yourself to penitence and prayer." He started toward the door.

"And you have nothing to repent?" she charged him as she saw she was about to be locked in. "What of that cabin boy? Do you repent him?"

Ercole put back his head and laughed. "He is no sin; every seagoing man has such a boy if he is fortunate. No one thinks anything about it."

"The priests would not agree," said Fenice darkly.

"The priests are worse than any sailor ever was," said Ercole as he prepared to close the door. "I will have a guard put on this door; you will have nothing to fear."

Had she not been so despondent, Fenice would have laughed; as it was she ended up huddled on the bed doing her best not to cry.

As she began to dream, she saw the massive crags of mountains above her, and the battlements she had walked in her dreams formed around her. The hawk-faced man was at her side, saying, "You have no reason to honor your brother if he will not honor you. This is the place you should find, for there is freedom here." Fenice heard him out, her thoughts in disorder, for she did not like to think what would happen if she were to put herself beyond her family so utterly as this man suggested.

She woke suddenly, panting a little, as if she had been running hard.

Varna was a busy place, its docks like docks everywhere, and yet with a foreignness about them that was not entirely caused by the sailors in unfamiliar garments or the number of ships of designs Fenice had never seen. The *Impresa* was greeted with cries of astonishment and curious stares as her crew secured her lines to the stanchions on the dock. From his cabin, Ercole pointed out places that might interest Fenice; she stood beside him drinking it all in, aware she was being taunted.

"There is a convent—it is Orthodox. It is not far from the main market, and that is the most sensible place to take you. The nuns will look after you and will not ask too many questions." He put his hand on her shoulder. "I am sorry it has come to this, but you brought it on yourself. You must pay the price of your folly, Fenice."

"So you have been telling me," she responded, wishing he would be quiet so that she could take in the splendor of Varna: it would have to make up for so much, this single look at one foreign port. She wanted to have an hour or so to explore, to make the most of this single chance, but she was certain that Ercole would not allow her even so minor an adventure as that. She had to fight down the longing that filled her; there were so many things she had desired to do that would be unattainable once she set foot inside the convent. She would have to resign herself to the rigors of nuns' rituals and the order of the cloister, which she thought unbearable. Leave such disciplines to Bianca, she thought, and permit her to be about the world.

"You will stay with the nuns until we can contrive some way to bring you home. And when we do, you will accept a penitent's life. Resign yourself to that, Fenice; you will not be able to remain in the world after this. The Church will want a high bride-price to take you in, but the family will pay it, to ensure our honor is not compromised. You cannot think how your mad—" He saw her expression. "At least Artemesia is promised. I don't know what will happen to Eloisa, not once it is known you have been found alive."

"Would it be better if I were dead?" Fenice asked sharply.

"It would be less embarrassing," said Ercole. "Your death would be a tragedy, but it would spare the family chagrin. If you were dead, we would have much less to explain." He looked around as a knock sounded on his door. "Is it time?"

Rainardo answered. "We are readying the gangplank for lowering. You must give the order."

"In a moment," said Ercole. He stared hard at his sister. "Have everything you want to take with you ready. I will come back for you shortly. When I do, I will not want to wait for you to make up your mind about what you must have with you."

Fenice, still stung by his callous remark about her death, could only nod. She put her hands on her hips. "I will take everything I brought aboard. You need not fear you will be contaminated by me."

"You have no right to sulk," Ercole admonished her. "If you have misfortune, it is of your own making."

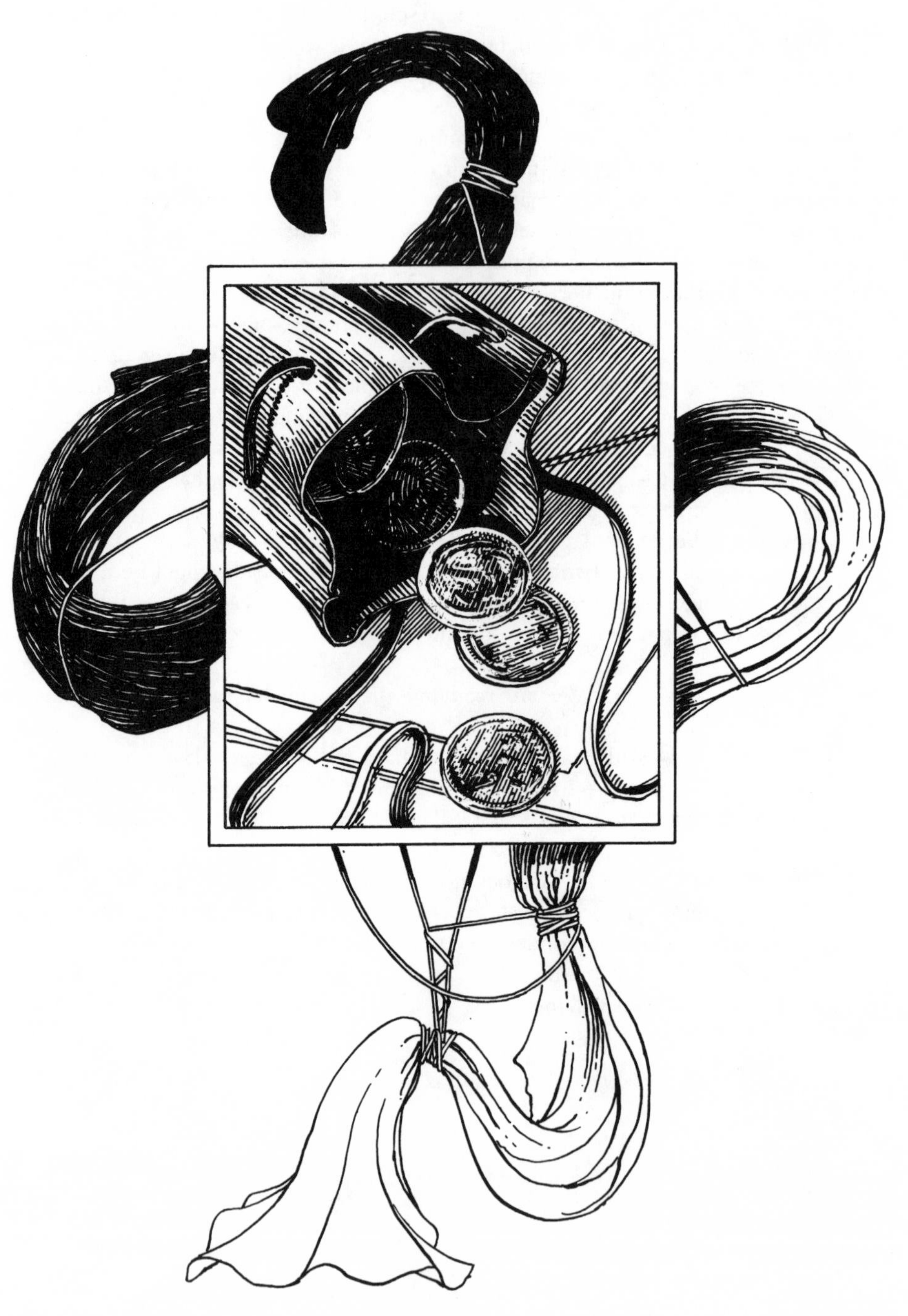

. . . omens of terrible misfortune—
I compare all these disasters to love . . .
—Giacomo da Lentino

— XV —

Ercole held Fenice by the arm as he guided her along the narrow, busy streets of Varna toward the thin towers marking the central mosque. The largest market in the city was only two streets away from the mosque, so the traffic between those two places was constant and intense. The air smelled of animals, sweat, and cooking, at once attractive and repellent. A babel of languages spilled around them: Bulgar, Greek, Russian, Turkish, and many that were unfamiliar to Fenice.

"I will have to make a donation to the convent," Ercole reminded her as he all but dragged her in the direction of Hagia Charis. "You will have to be supported while you are in their hands."

"I am willing to work," said Fenice, craning her neck to see a pair of Bactrian camels being led toward the market; their humps were limp, with shaggy hair, so that they looked as if two very scruffy dogs were tied to the animals' backs. Fenice had only heard about Bactrian camels and she wanted to make the most of this opportunity. For an instant she thought about her sack slung over her shoulder and decided it was not unlike the camels' humps, though more unwieldy.

"Oh, and you shall, never fear," Ercole promised her grimly as he tugged her around a wagon laden with sacks of grain. "You will have calluses on your hands and knees before you see Venice again. *If* you see Venice again."

Fenice looked at him sharply. "What do you mean? You said you would bring me back, or one of the family would."

"You may decide you would rather stay here, so that your family will not have to endure the condemnation and the pity of their friends. There is less disgrace in your absence than in your presence, no matter how guarded and repentant your presence might be. If you should decide to remain in this convent, the family will have less to answer for than if you come back to Venice." He said this so easily that Fenice realized he had been thinking about it for some time. "The convent here is no worse than many another would be. And it would keep you from having to add to your lies, since you could not readily be questioned here."

Fenice was looking about, trying to fix buildings in her mind, so she would be able to find her way again; she hoped she would have the chance to put her memory to the test, for convent life had no attractions for her: only Bianca could think that hours on her knees to pray and to clean floors would bring about joy. She was not listening to Ercole very closely; she was afraid that if she gave him her full attention she would not be able to contain her anger. She had not railed at Ercole once in the three days she was confined to his cabin, though she filled the long, empty hours rehearsing all she wanted to say to him while she pored over the maps and charts Ercole kept in his high-fronted desk. She knew better than to appear too inquisitive, for that would put Ercole on the alert.

"At least you know Greek," Ercole said, plainly coming to the end of an exhortation.

"Well enough," said Fenice, concealing her lack of attention with a bravado that she hoped would convince Ercole more than it did her. She wriggled in his grasp and was rewarded with a slap that made her face sting.

"You will do nothing to disgrace yourself further," he said, making it a threat. "You have nothing to gain by defying me now."

"Not much, perhaps," she allowed, wincing as his grip tightened. "But I do not like being dragged along like a new slave or a criminal. You may treat the oarsmen this way, but you will not treat me—"

Ercole halted and swung her around to face him. "You are a criminal, Fenice. You have broken the laws of Venice and the Church. You do not yet comprehend how greatly you have wronged your family by such ill-considered actions as you have taken. I would be doing right to clap you in chains. But you are my sister and I cannot bring myself to treat you so . . . harshly, much as you deserve it. If I brought you to the nuns as the criminal you are, they would want you sent to the harlot's prison, and though it would be right to confine you there, I cannot let it happen to you. I will have to Confess my leniency when I reach Corfu." He shook her, giving no notice to the throng around them.

"You want the nuns to punish me, don't you?" she demanded, her fear subsumed in her growing fury.

"I hope they will teach you to know the gravity of your errors, Fenice," said Ercole. "Since no one in the family has done so, I must pray they will succeed where we have failed."

Fenice spat over her shoulder to show her contempt. "Don't worry," she told Ercole scornfully. "They all think I'm a boy."

"Then we must be thankful for that mercy," said Ercole as he resumed his progress toward the convent.

The streets became narrower, the buildings less grand, many of them showing signs of neglect and age. Here the sounds of Greek were everywhere, and unlike the streets nearer the market, the women covered only their hair and not their faces. A few ragged beggars lingered in the doorways of inns, the hands lifted in perpetual appeal for alms; those who stopped to give them money were blessed extravagantly. Ercole dropped two scudi into the hands of one who began to proclaim the might of Venice in Bulgar-accented Greek that Fenice found difficult to comprehend.

"Why did you do that?" she asked when they were out of range of the beggar.

"Because they are a guild; if one of them does not receive some money, the rest follow a foreigner—like you and me—and waylay them. Foolish travelers have been killed by the Beggars' Guild."

"Oh," said Fenice, who remembered the beggars she had seen in Venice; they did not seem to be as dangerous as these men were.

"It would be bad for you, Fenice. Once they found out you are a girl, they would do worse than rob or beat you." He shoved her ahead of him into a narrow alley with a high wall on one side and the flank of a house on the other. "The gate is on the left."

"Is this the convent?" It looked more like an undersized fortress, too small to hold a fighting force, but built to withstand the onslaught of whole companies of armed men.

"Hagia Charis," Ercole confirmed. "The nuns are considered very holy women, even by the Ottomites." He finally released his hold on her. "You may bolt if you like. There is only one access to this alley."

"What a splendid opinion you have of me," she snapped.

"Do you mean to say I have no reason for it?" His inquiry was more insulting for the polite manner in which he offered it.

You are not going to show the nuns an ill-mannered and disrespectful demeanor, she thought, stifling her anger. It was possible her brother had wanted to goad her into an outburst in order to make her appear obstreperous. She reached the gate and looked for the bell to summon the warden.

"You will have to knock. The mallet will serve," said Ercole, indicating a small iron mallet hanging on a short chain. "Rap the door three times, for the Trinity."

Fenice did as he told her, making each blow distinct and separate. "Do we wait long?" she asked, as if they were about to be entertained.

"Not very long," said Ercole. "They do not like to leave good Christians waiting in this Ottomite city." He made an attempt at a smile. "You will find these women set an excellent example."

"No doubt; Bianca certainly does." As she said this, she recalled her sister would now be a novice in the convent in Venice; if only she could summon up some vestige of her sister's piety! She had never before envied Bianca, but here, waiting for the convent door to open, she did.

After a short while the door opened and a woman in a gray habit looked out. "Yes?" She spoke in Greek.

"May God bless you, good Sister, and reward your faith in Heaven," said Ercole, also in Greek. "We beg admittance and a little of your Superior's time."

The nun stared, then stepped back. "In the Name of God Father, Son, and Holy Spirit, enter," she recited as she stepped aside.

Fenice stifled the urge to run; she knew she could not escape Ercole, and such a desperate act would put the nuns on the alert to her emerging plans; she would have to keep everything secret, even in Confession, and hope that God would not hold her reticence against her. She crossed herself Roman fashion and went meekly into the courtyard, noticing as she did that it was small and cramped, with chicken coops and rabbit hutches at one end and what appeared to be the chapel at the other end. "Thank you."

The timbre of her voice struck the nun, who stared at her in surprised recognition. "Lord send us Grace," she whispered, crossing herself in the Orthodox manner, right to left shoulder.

"Amen to that," Fenice said in Greek, continuing to look around the courtyard. "You are well-protected here, I see."

"It is to serve God more freely," the nun replied, her expression once again serene to the point of blankness. "I will summon the Superior," she said, ducked her head, and hurried away.

"Ercole, what Order is this?" Fenice asked; she saw nothing that would tell her which of the various Rules these nuns followed.

"The Orthodox Church has no Orders. There is just one Rule for all," said Ercole. "It prevents squabbling."

"I suppose so," said Fenice, beginning to think her stay here would be more intolerable than anything she had anticipated. If these nuns were unlike the ones she knew, living by their Rule could prove intolerable almost at once; she resolved to keep her sack of possessions close to hand in case she had to leave quickly; she was fairly certain she could not stand to wait for her family to bring her home: judging from what Ercole said, she could not expect that to happen in any brief time, and she would not wait for someone—probably Ercole—to decide she had been punished enough. She became aware that Ercole was speaking to her and did her best to listen.

"—in case you have to pay for your maintenance. You are not to give the whole sum to the nuns, but since I may not be back for months, it would be wise for you to have a few ducats so that they will not have to turn you out into the streets to beg your living. Or worse." With that he handed her four golden coins. "This will keep the nuns well-disposed to you, if you are sensible how you spend them."

Surprised, Fenice took the coins and slipped them inside the quilting on her giaquetta; there was a small, concealed pocket to hold money and small weapons so that they could not readily be seen. "Thank you, fratello mio."

"You may have been foolhardy, but you have come this far unscathed, and so I must do what I can to see you are not reduced to complete humiliation." He nodded toward one of the imposing doors in the main building; this was just beginning to open and three nuns were emerging: the one in the middle carried a massive key-chain bound around her waist, but otherwise was indistinguishable from the other two. Ercole nodded to her. "Superior."

The nun raised her head, showing worn features of uncompromising middle-age. "My son," she said. "I am told you have come here for our help." She held up one hand. "I cannot give shelter to any girl who has been whored. If you are tired of her . . ." She indicated the gate. "There are those who will pay well for a European woman."

"No, no," said Ercole as Fenice stared in shock. "It is nothing of the sort."

"He's my *brother,*" Fenice exclaimed in disgust.

Ercole nodded heavily. "Fenice is my sister, my too-wild sister." He saw that the Superior was waiting for a more extensive explanation. "Our family are merchants, and she wanted to do what all the sons and male cousins do. So she made a disguise for herself, and without regard to her reputation or the position of the family, she found a way aboard my ship. She hid herself very well and took care to remain out of sight for several days. Her disguise stood her in good stead, for it was only after a tragedy aboard that I realized what she had done."

"Ah?" said the Superior. "And what then?"

"I confined her to my cabin. I let the rest of the crew think she was a runaway monk so that she would not be exposed to anything . . . compromising to the family honor." He folded his arms. "She has not yet understood the enormity of what she has done."

"And you brought her here with what purpose?" The Superior watched Ercole narrowly as he considered his answer.

"I would like her kept safe, of course. And if she can be made cognizant of the extent of her errors and transgressions, that would be most . . . charitable of you." He took Fenice by the wrist, but did not pull her any nearer to him than she already was. "She is an obstinate girl, with more desires than is fitting for women to possess; she has never been schooled in the disciplines it is fitting that she possess. If she learns to hold herself in check and to comport herself as a virtuous woman ought, then our family will be forever in your debt and I will promise you will have a generous donation from us every year my sister lives, though we are Catholic and not Orthodox. Your Christian goodness will transcend the arguments of our Churches."

"You are being most generous with these assurances," said the Superior with a degree of skepticism that neither Ercole nor Fenice missed. "Promises are made easily when you are in need of help, but as easily forgotten when the travail is past."

"Yes," said Ercole. "But we are not among those who are so base as to make a vow to God and then relent when it suits our purpose to do so." He glared at Fenice. "If you can improve the character of my sister, you will have done what no one else has managed, and her gratitude will exceed ours, I am convinced of it."

"If you are willing to sign a pledge to that end, I will consider taking the child in." She inclined her head. "I am Mother Sophronia."

"Mother Sophronia," said Ercole. "This is my sister, Fenice. I am Ercole Zucchar of Venice."

"Venice was apparent," said Mother Sophronia, and turned to Fenice. "You have many grave trespasses laid against you, child. How do you defend yourself?"

Fenice made a gesture to show she had no answer. "I have done nothing I did not say I would do since I was in leading-strings," she said. "My brother—Febo, not this one—has said I have a wild soul; I suppose I may have. If I do, God gave it to me."

Mother Sophronia slapped her sharply. "We will have none of that, young woman. You put yourself above the wisdom of Christians. Your wildness is an error: God does not lead us to err. It is our capacity for sin that makes us do what is not pleasing to God." She came and stared directly into Fenice's face. "You take pride in a wild soul, but you do not know what that wildness has done to keep God from bestowing Grace on you; it is always thus with pride, which leads all other sins in its malignance, and which is the most blinding to those who have succumbed to its lures, and most destructive to a Christian life." She slapped Fenice again. "You must learn to turn away from your pride not pridefully, which you may wish to do, but in humility, which we will do what we can to instill in you, along with gratitude to God for leading you to this place where you could find your salvation and the end of your obduracy."

"That's splendid," said Ercole. He let go of Fenice's wrist. "I have here twelve gold ducats to keep my sister for a year—"

"A year?" Fenice cried out in dismay.

"At least that," Ercole said, giving her a determined glance. "You will need that long in the nun's care, and I will need the time to make the appropriate arrangements with the family. You may think a year is a long time—"

"It is eternity," said Fenice; she felt wetness in her eyes and hated her lack of courage.

"You will need every day if you are to be rid of your faults," said Ercole before Mother Sophronia could speak.

"I am not Bianca, Ercole," Fenice protested. "She is made for this life—I am not."

"You will be, in time," said Ercole, then added to Mother Sophronia, "In a year I, or one of my brothers, will speak with you. If you are convinced she has truly repented her . . . madness, then we will take her back to Venice. If you are still uncertain that she understands what she has done, then we will pay you as many ducats as you require to keep her until she has fully realized—"

"Ercole! No!" Fenice protested. "You cannot do this."

"Oh, yes I can, sorella mia." He handed the ducats to Mother Sophronia, who bit them before she accepted them. "I will be in port for a day more. You may leave a message for me at my ship, the *Impresa*; it is a merchantman with a partial deck of oars. There is no other ship like her in the harbor."

"The *Impresa*," said Mother Sophronia. "I will remember." She motioned to the two nuns accompanying her. "Take this young woman to a cell and see she is given a modest habit to wear, but without the veil. She has no vocation that would entitle her to it." Then she addressed Ercole. "I will expect to see you in a year. The women here do not read, so any message will be sent with the priest who hears our Confessions."

"Very good," said Ercole, looking uncomfortable now that this unpleasant task was discharged. "God will show you favor for your goodness, Mother Sophronia. And in time, my sister will be thankful for the care you will give her."

"May God spare you on the sea," said the Superior as the door was opened to allow him to leave.

Fenice watched him go, missing him ferociously even as she wanted to curse him for leaving her in this place. She lifted her sack and faced the nuns. "I am ready," she said.

One of the nuns reached for her sack; Fenice clung to it. "You must give it up," said the nun firmly.

"She is not a novice, Sister Euphemia. If she decides to become one, she will give it to us then," said Mother Sophronia. "But she must surrender those clothes. You, young woman, will dress humbly as we do, and you will learn to beg your bread on your knees, and to lower your eyes as you walk; you will not raise your voice but to thank God for delivering you from your headstrong independence." She signaled the third nun to open the door for them. "You will fast tonight and tomorrow, and you will pray."

"One of my sisters is preparing to be a nun," said Fenice as she managed to slip the four ducats out of her giaquetta and secret them in her sack; she was sure that if she gave them up with her giaquetta she would never see them again.

"You should have followed her example," said Mother Sophronia. "Give me the coins you have hidden. Now. You would not be in disgrace now had you conducted yourself properly. As it is, your brother is ready to disown you." The room they entered was austere as any convent in Venice. The walls were whitewashed and a screen covered in images of saints and angels stood to one side. "This is the iconostasis," the Superior went on. "You will bless yourself and its icons every time you pass it. Fail to do this and you will earn yourself a beating."

Fenice nodded, and remembered to cross herself Orthodox fashion as she went past the screen.

Six nights later, her back aching from the thrashing she had been given for not staying awake all night in the chapel, Fenice pulled her sack from under the simple cot that served as her bed. For the last five days she had been forced to work at menial tasks from dawn until dusk all the while being exhorted to repent her failings and accept the stern demands of her family and her faith; then to spend the nights in prayerful vigils. She had no chance to solace herself with dreams, and she was now so exhausted that she was jittery; this would be her last opportunity to escape, she knew, for she would soon be too enervated by the demanding routine the nuns had imposed on her.

The moon was nearing full and riding halfway up the sky; most of the nuns were in their cells, asleep or praying, and the novices were busy in the bakery and creamery. This slack time of the evening provided a short opportunity, and Fenice was resolved to take advantage of it. Very carefully she pulled her habit over her head, wincing as the rough-woven fabric brushed the bruises on her shoulders. She rolled the habit into a long shape which she put in the bed, arranging it as if it were a human figure; it would not fool anyone for very long, but it would probably give her until morning to be missed, by which time she would be in another part of the city. Her already short hair had been chopped even shorter, to keep her from the sin of vanity. She did not want the nuns to know she was grateful for this, for fear of making them more suspicious of her than they already were. She reached into her sack and pulled out her second giaquetta and underhose as well as short-hose. They all looked shabby to her, which suited her purposes admirably; the only thing she wished for in her old giaquetta was the four gold ducats Ercole had given her; those would have come in useful. Still, she decided, four ducats was a small price to pay for freedom. She dressed quickly, keeping only the simple sandals the nuns had provided.

When she was dressed, she put her short knife through her belt at the small of her back, slung her sack over her shoulder and, listening closely, let herself out of her cell; in another hour it would be bolted shut for the night, but until the kitchen chores were done, the cells remained unsecured. She closed the door with the caution she had learned hiding in the hold of her brother's ship. She went along in the general direction of the latrines, where her passage would not be noticed. Beyond the walls was an Ottomite city, she reminded herself, and so she would have to be doubly circumspect once she was out of the convent: there were stringent laws pertaining to women, so Fenice would have to convince the world she was truly Aeneo or face consequences she did not want to contemplate. This realization of danger gave her a moment's pause, for surely the convent was safer than the world. "Come to that," she murmured, "the grave is safer than the world, too, but I don't want to lie in mine." Hearing her own voice made her more decisive, and she made her way out past the midden into the small vegetable garden. She had considered climbing the chicken coops, but the birds were unpredictable and noisy and might give her away with squawking. So she went to the garden shed and pulled her way onto its roof. Her shoulders were so sore she felt slightly sick as she moved, but she would not relent. The outer wall rose above her, two handsbreadths higher than her head. This would be her test: if she were caught, she knew she would be confined to the penitant's cell in the cellar, which was a prison in everything but name.

Straining to pull herself onto the top of the wall, Fenice suddenly stopped as she heard one of the novices start to sing as she came out into the garden. There was enough moonlight for the darkness to be milky; Fenice lay down full length on the roof and hoped—for she dared not pray—that the novice would not look up. Breathing fast through her open mouth, Fenice waited, prepared to make a leap and run if she had to.

While she waited for the novice to go back inside, Fenice tried to recall everything she had seen on her single, swift progress through the streets. She had no idea of what lay to the north or west of her, for she had come to the convent from the southeast; she would have to start in streets she knew and learn the others over time. With mild amazement, she realized she was preparing to remain in Varna, to throw herself on the world. This flight from the convent would surely place her beyond her family forever; she grasped this with a pang, for she did not want to be lost to the House of Zucchar. In the previous nights' vigils she had begun to think that it was Ercole's intention to leave her at Hagia Charis forever, paying the nuns to be her jailers in order to keep Fenice from embarrassing the family. Once that possibility entered her contemplations, she had been unable to eradicate it, and it had served to spur her to action when nothing else could.

The garden was empty once more: Fenice pushed herself up to a sitting position and began to peer into the street below. She hefted her sack over her shoulder, thinking as she did that it was lighter than when she came, and that she would need to replace the boy's clothes they had taken from her when she arrived. With her back as sore as it was, she was grateful that she did not have to deal with anything truly heavy. But her shoulders would heal and her giaquetta and hose were already frayed. She hoped her Greek would enable her to make her way in the city, for she dared not speak Venetian Italian and expose herself to recapture.

Finally she found what she decided was the lowest place in the wall. She lowered herself with care over the edge, letting herself down to the full length of her aching arms. Then she dropped, landing awkwardly; she fell to the side, knocking her elbow but doing no greater damage. After a brief assessment, she decided it was safe to get up; she got to her feet, picked up her sack, dusted herself off, and put her mind on finding a place to sleep.

Febo hurried from the Bacino di San Marco to the Zucchar house on Campo Sant' Angelo; he had heard the news in Zara and was overcome with anxiety: his sister kidnaped. The words made no sense when he had first heard them; they made very little more now, five days later. Unwilling to summon a gondola, Febo walked the distance. The sights and sounds of Venice, usually a balm to his senses, were now nothing more than intrusions on his worry. As he reached the house, he saw Aurelio getting out of a gondola just ahead of him.

"Pirenetto!" Febo cried out; he had been told of Aurelio's devotion to Fenice, which touched him deeply. "Wait!"

Aurelio stopped and turned. "Febo," he said as Fenice's brother came up to him; they brushed cheeks and faced one another. "You've just returned." It was not a question. "Your father has been expecting you."

Febo nodded. "I left my boatswain in charge of unloading and came at once. I had to find out all I could—" He took Aurelio by the shoulders. "Do you know anything more?"

"I don't know what you have been told," said Aurelio with calmness of purpose. "But we have learned where she is *not,* and that helps us to learn where she is." He started toward the house, leaving Febo to come after him. "Your parents will be glad to have you home."

"And in other circumstances, I would rejoice to be here." Febo caught up with Aurelio at the door. "It must be painful for you to have to do these things, to hunt for the woman who should have been your bride."

"When she is found, she will be my bride," he told Febo, his eyes bright and hard as light on steel. "Nothing will change that."

Febo looked mildly surprised at this response. He remembered Aurelio as intelligent but bumbling, a man who would forget to tie his underhose to his giaquetta likely as not, and who would not be able to eat soup without getting some of it on his sleeve. "Your devotion is—"

Aurelio stopped on the steps up to the door and said, "My devotion shapes my life, Febo. I was a lump before I had the good fortune to love your sister. For the first time I have purpose beyond curiosity to fire me." His face shone with the same light Febo had seen in the visages of certain very devout men.

Knowing he had to say something, Febo remarked, "Fenice does not know how good God has been to her, sending you to her." He saw that the door was opening; he directed his gaze to the face he saw there. "Artemesia," he exclaimed as his sister flung the door open.

"Thank God you are home safe!" She held out her arms to embrace Febo as Aurelio walked past them into the house. Then she began to weep, making no apology for her tears. "You know?" she asked between sobs.

"Yes," said Febo, holding Artemesia so tightly that he knew he must be hurting her; he was unable to let go.

A moment later Rosamonda appeared at the top of the central staircase; she called out Febo's name, then came rushing down to him. "Oh, I have been longing to see you."

He noticed she had lost flesh and that there were many more threads of silver in her hair than he recalled being there. He released Artemesia in order to embrace his mother. "I was . . . horrified by what I have been told."

"At least," said Artemesia with a quick glance at her mother. "At least it was Fenice. She, of all of us, would be able to deal with her travail."

This dispute was not a new one, Febo realized, as Rosamonda sighed heavily. "No one should have to—" she said, then stopped as Artemesia glared at her.

"Umberto will be coming shortly," said Artemesia, giving herself an excuse to abandon the useless dispute.

"Umberto will be welcome," said Rosamonda, her voice low and soft. "Come, Febo. Your father will be happy to see you, and you will want him to tell you everything that has happened." She put her hand on his arm. "Without Aurelio, we would have been lost."

"So I gather," said Febo, trying to take his tone from her. "I am . . . startled. Who would have thought that he would become so . . . so . . ." He could not find a word that described the transformation in Aurelio Pirenetto. "I hope you will tell me all about it."

"Aurelio will do that." Rosamonda looked around. "I want him to talk to Eloisa. She has been keeping to her room and the library since Bianca entered the convent. She is frightened, I think."

"Who can blame her?" Febo asked, startled that his mother would think of asking such a favor of Aurelio. "Is it true that Fenice was taken from her own chamber?"

"Yes," said Rosamonda. "There was a note, a dreadful note, in bad Greek." She faltered, then looked at her son. "But things will be better now that you are home."

He thanked her for her kindness, and said, "I will do my part," all the while wondering what he would be expected to do that Aurelio had not already done.

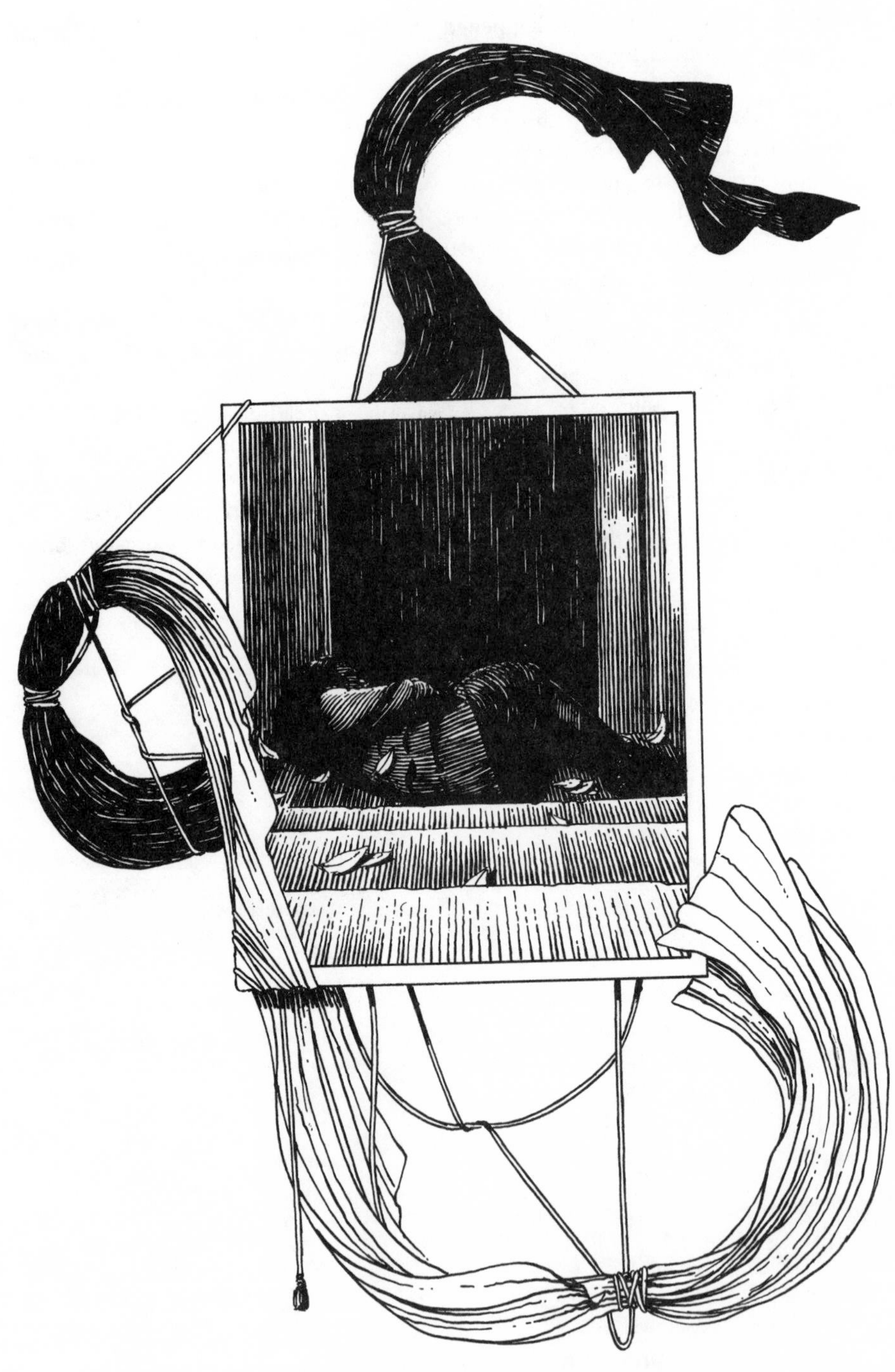

I am told your hands are clever
And if they are, you will do very well.
—Forese Donati

— XVI —

Shouts in the marketplace awoke her shortly before dawn; she had finally settled behind a stack of barrels where a discarded mat had provided her a bed and a fitful night's rest. Fenice attempted to stretch and felt her shoulders balk at the movement; her sack had proven to be a poor pillow during the night. Gingerly she got to her feet, trying to ease her back and shoulders while keeping an eye out for the early arrivals in the market. After a short while, she realized she was grinning. Emerging from her hiding place, she caught sight of four young men, lean and gray as wolves, patrolling the edge of the stalls as the vendors set them up; she watched them carefully, remembering how Ercole had dealt with the beggars. She knew she would have to deal with men who had already found places for themselves in the streets and markets of Varna, and they would not welcome an interloper.

As she became aware of hunger, she lost some of her pleasure at seeing the marketplace made ready for a busy day; now she missed her four ducats more than she had assumed was possible. She thought of fruit and the sweet pastries she could smell being baked in small, portable ovens. The food's aroma was even stronger than the marketplace's pervasive odor of sweat and dung. Many of the vendors and merchants had stopped their labors to buy pastries, holding the treats in sticky fingers while exchanging news with those who had made similar decisions.

Fenice bent down and rubbed her hands in the dust; she then wiped her hands on her jaw in the hope of concealing her unbearded skin: satisfied, she ventured out of her hiding place, starting toward the front of the market where the foreign vendors were to be found under the watchful eyes of the customs officials. She was hopeful that her knowledge of Greek and Italian could stand her in good stead; she was keenly aware that she had learned only a few words of the local tongue, and those she had gleaned from the nuns. Now she would discover if she could deal with the world as she hoped she would be able to.

"You wanted an adventure," she growled to herself under her breath so that her courage would not fail her. "Well, you have it."

The merchants paid no attention to Fenice as she began to walk around the edge of the square, heading in the general direction of the foreign merchants, hoping as she did that her goal was not too obvious. She had no wish to become an object of curiosity. But after a short while she realized that she was one among many and that nothing about her was so remarkable that anyone paid her any attention. She discovered this lack of attention served to give her courage, and she became bold enough to approach the Greek olive merchant who stood near the customs table. "Pardon, worthy merchant," she said in Greek, and was pleased that he did not order her to depart at once.

"What is it?" he asked sharply.

"I speak Italian, especially the Venetian dialect," she said. "I could not help but see that you have not approached the Genoese and Venetian merchants, and I thought perhaps I could be of help."

The olive merchant spat. "I have no reason to trade with Catholics. Why should I want your help? Be off with you." He made a halfhearted attempt to kick Fenice, then turned away as if she was nothing more than a minor pest.

Fenice took the rebuke as well as she could; she had not supposed she would be welcomed the first time she tried to make herself useful. But she had to confess—if only to herself—that the comprehensive rebuff had been worse than she had anticipated. She stepped into the small alley leading away from the customs table, and let herself take a little longer to assess what she saw in the market-square: the Greeks were at the southeast corner of the market, so that they could easily reach their ships at the docks. The Italians were to the west of them, still in the south of the square: she would concentrate her efforts in this quarter and trust she would not go hungry all day.

The fourth merchant she approached—a tall, big-bellied man with rough features and a Salonikan accent—regarded her with curiosity. "You speak like a scholar," he remarked.

"I have . . . studied," she said cautiously.

"Do you also read and write?" the merchant asked. "My own clerk took a fever at sea and died on me. The customs officers will lend me one of their men, but I want no part of them. For the clerks here will cheat you as readily as any vendor. They tell me one thing and write down another. Are you any different from them?"

"I can read and write, and I have no reason to cheat you," said Fenice carefully. "I know that merchants must guard against theft of all kinds."

He folded his arms. "And would you say you will not do the same?"

"I will say I have no reason to cheat you and every reason to be honest in my dealings with you or any merchant." She smiled, trying to ingratiate herself to him.

The merchant considered her for a short while. "You are a brave youngster," he said, and laughed. "Very well, I will give you a try—say for three days? If you keep my records correctly, I will pay you four silver martyrs for your service. I am Dorus, from Salonika. I deal in brasses and pottery. And you are?"

"Aeneo. From Zara." She did her best to give him a more eager smile than before, and hoped he would not think the less of her for her eagerness.

"Aeneo," said Dorus. "A fine name." He chuckled. "Did they call you that in the monastery?" He patted Fenice on the shoulder. "Don't be shocked. Your secret is safe with me. Not all of us are cut out for the cloisters, are we?"

What, she wondered, had convinced him she had been a monk? She straightened up, saying, "When do you want me to start?" Her voice quivered with anticipation. "I am ready to begin whenever you—"

"As soon as you have had your breakfast," said Dorus. "And here are three coppers to buy it for you." He tossed them to her negligently; she snatched them out of the air with ease, a boy's trick of which she was especially proud: she hoped Dorus noticed. "I can't have you dozing over my records, can I?"

"No," said Fenice, flushing as if she had been caught in a lie.

"Well, then," said Dorus indulgently, "get to it, Aeneo." He gave Fenice a gentle shove in the direction of the stall where fried sweet pastries were being sold. "And hot tea, as well," he recommended.

Fenice bowed her acknowledgment; she knew she would have to eat quickly and perform her tasks with a strict attention to detail in order to keep her job; she went to the stall where the pastries were being sold and purchased two with one copper. She took these carefully, letting the grease drip on the paving stones and not her clothes. She then found a tea-vendor, and purchasing a cup from him, she had it filled with steaming mint tea.

She was on her way back to Dorus when she noticed a beggar-boy, no more than eight, with a withered leg and a hump on his back. She paused, aware now that he had been watching her. "God send you good morning," she said in very formal Greek, not at all certain he would understand.

"God has nothing to do with it," the lad answered, his Greek nearly as good as her own. "You're new in the market; off one of the ships, I suppose."

"Yes. The *Impresa,*" said Fenice, adding with unexpected difficulty, "she sailed . . . a few days ago." She broke off half of her second pastry and gave it to the beggar.

"Everyone was talking about her," the crippled boy declared, then bit into the pastry, smiling as he did. "She will do very well if she doesn't turn turtle in heavy weather."

"She managed well enough coming from . . . Zara, and there were storms and heavy seas," said Fenice, remembering she had claimed to come from there, and she did not want marketplace gossip to raise questions about her. She held out her hand, Italian fashion. "I am Aeneo."

"I am Libu," he replied, grasping her wrist as she took his. He glanced around the market. "The gangs have not yet noticed you. But they will. You had better be ready to bargain with them."

"If I must. I doubt they will bother with me," she said, and recalled at the same time the bribes her brother had offered the beggars on his way to the convent.

"If you have anything they want, they will notice you," said Libu, shaking his head. "You cannot know what they will assume they must have." He finished the pastry and grinned. "They beat me from time to time, but for the most part I am ignored. They do not know what to make of me, and so they usually leave me alone. You probably will not be so fortunate."

"Why should it be that way?" Fenice shrugged in spite of the chill she felt. "Why should they bother with me?"

"Because you have made yourself important to the merchants," said Libu. "That Greek has paid you, and as soon as any money changes hands, the gangs see it and want it for themselves."

"Even for something as minor as writing in a ledger?" Fenice asked, knowing already it was foolish to inquire.

"Yes. They will notice that. Anyone who can read and write deserves their consideration," he said with gleeful bitterness. "Have a care, or they will smash your fingers, or blind you if you will not give them what they want."

Fenice nodded. "Thank you for the warning," she said quietly.

"You paid for it," said Libu, licking his fingers. "Go about your work now, so the Greek will not think you laggard."

"Very well." She strode away from Libu, her head up as if nothing she heard had troubled her. Approaching Dorus' stalls, she said, "I am ready, good sir, to begin."

Dorus pointed to a low table where two leatherbound ledgers were stacked. "There they are. Tell me how much sense you can make of them." He stood over her, arms folded, his expression intent.

The writing in the ledger was small and crabbed, making it hard to read; Fenice squinted and pondered, then said, "This column is brasses bought with the price you paid for them. The next column is what you sold them for. I reckon the other ledger is for pottery." She managed a gesture of approval. "You have turned a handsome profit, it appears."

He shrugged, but could not conceal a satisfied glint in his eyes. "The pottery I sell here does not do as well for me, but it is prudent to offer it."

Fenice could think of no reason why this should be so; she kept her expression encouraging and said only, "Prudence is the merchants' virtue."

Dorus laughed aloud. "And tact is the clerks'," he countered. "The potters of Salonika need to sell their wares as much as the brassmakers of Varna do; I profit in serving both of them."

"Truly," said Fenice, adjusting her legs tailor-fashion under her so that she could get to work. "Where are your ink cake and quills?"

"In the drawer under the table," said Dorus, his voice becoming brisk.

"Then I am ready," said Fenice, preparing to write.

Febo glowered at Il Talpa, ignoring Aurelio sitting next to him on the unstable bench; across the rough plank table, Il Talpa regarded the two with cunning eyes. "You have made many claims," Febo said, resisting the urge to shout and blame the man. "You have nothing to support any of them."

"In cases like these," said Il Talpa, smiling egregiously, "support is hard come by. Those who know the truth keep their knowledge to themselves; only gold can loosen their tongues, and only gold is welcome as a key."

Although it was not yet midday, the tavern was full; men sat over their drinks or rattled dice. The smoke from the fire where a pig turned on a spit made everything slightly hazy and left a fine film of grease behind.

"And we pay you and learn nothing useful," Febo said in a flat tone, his handsome face forbidding in its severity. "You may know much, but I think it could be sham, used to deceive us in many ways, so that you can line your pockets with Zucchar gold." He frowned portentously. "You have done nothing to persuade me."

Il Talpa shook his head repeatedly. "You do not understand. I do not deal with bankers and merchants. I deal with men whom the law does not recognize."

"Or who are outside the law," Aurelio added for him; he turned to Febo. "I did warn you about hoping for too much. There are dozens of men like him who claim to know something if only we have money enough to pay to learn it. I have spoken to this scoundrel many times, and while I occasionally credit him with good information, more often I believe he is moved by greed and the desire to have influence above himself." He turned to Il Talpa. "Am I wrong?"

There was nothing Il Talpa could say; he shrugged and pulled at the lobe of his one remaining ear. "You will have to pay to find out," he said brazenly.

"We are retracing steps that have already been walked," Aurelio said to Febo. "Nothing worthwhile can be discovered here." He put a silver coin on the table and prepared to rise. "For your time, Talpa." He leaned forward. "And I warn you not to bring me misinformation again, or it will be the worse for you."

Il Talpa seized the silver coin and slipped it into the pocket hidden in his sleeve. "I would not."

"See that you don't, or you will lose your other ear," said Aurelio with false geniality. "Come, Febo. We have other places we must visit." He plucked at Febo's shoulder and propelled him toward the tavern door. "I had hoped Il Talpa might have heard something useful, but clearly he has not," he remarked as they stepped out into the foggy morning.

"How much of this have you done?" Febo asked, astonished at Aurelio's purposefulness.

"Not enough," said Aurelio, striding to where his gondola was waiting. "We have still not found Fenice."

Fenice's supper was a slab of lamb cooked with onions and served in a thin bread. She washed this down with more of the hot, sweet mint tea as she strolled about the marketplace at sunset. She had five coppers in her pocket and wanted to keep them for a short while, so she decided she would not seek out an inn for the night—not yet; when she had more money, she would find lodgings.

By the time night had taken hold of Varna, Fenice was becoming uneasy; she had not yet come upon a place that seemed comfortable and safe. She did not want to go back to where she had spent the previous night—she was afraid she would be found there and made to move on. Finally she stumbled upon a small stable tucked away at the back of an alley near the market-square; five donkeys were tied there in narrow stalls. Fenice chose the largest stall and made herself comfortable in the bedding straw while the donkey munched hay from a V-shaped manger. The smell of the animal was warm and somehow friendly; she fell asleep almost at once.

And almost at once she dreamed. She was with her hawk-faced companion, soaring over a city beside the sea: Varna? Venice? Or someplace known only to dreams? She watched the place disappear behind her, falling into the distance as she spiraled upward on the air, keeping pace with her partner. Over mountains they sped, and into the fastness of craggy wilderness to a castle as formidable as the peaks around it. Had she been here before? Was this the same castle, or had another been conjured from the tales she had heard as a child? Had she dreamed this place or one like it? She followed the man wherever he went, even deep into the castle, to a hall of fine proportions with a gallery around it.

The man stood before her arrayed in dark purple like a prince, imposing and welcoming at once. "This is where you will find equals," he promised her in sonorous tones.

She went to bow to him, but he lifted her up and put her at his side. She noticed there was an empty chair to his left, but she was too happy with how he had honored her to mention this; she was also afraid of offending him, though she did not like admitting so much.

Suddenly the man caught her up in his cloak. "No one knows your soul but I," he said. "I will give you—"

Fenice did not hear the rest—she was awakened by the pressure of a donkey's nose on her cheek and the first calls to the Moslem faithful to morning prayers.

Over the next several days, Fenice began to make her way in the teaming world of the Varna market. She finished her work for Dorus and was taken over by a gruff-voiced trader in cloth from Cyprus who paid her half what Dorus had done and cuffed her head when she was finished, claiming she had cheated him.

"Don't let it worry you," Libu recommended when Fenice approached him at dusk. "The demon will get him. Besides, everyone knows he never pays what he owes his help." He handed her part of an orange. "Here. You look hungry."

"I am," Fenice admitted as she looked around the market square. "Where have they all gone?'

"Indoors, if they can," said Libu. "They're afraid." He finished his share of the orange. "Of the demon."

"What demon?" Fenice asked with a sarcastic laugh to show what she thought of demons.

"The one they say is in the market," said Libu, and chuckled. "Two merchants—both foreigners—have been found dead, with blood on their necks." He grinned. "So they are saying it is a demon come to ravage the market, and everyone flees."

"You don't," Fenice pointed out.

Libu shrugged. "What demon would want the likes of me?" He held out his shrunken arm. "Not enough meat or blood in me to make me good prey."

"I suppose not," said Fenice. "But aren't they being a bit, well, foolish?" She indicated the empty stalls. "They could sell more if they—" She stopped.

"They would not profit if they were dead," said Libu with ruthless pragmatism. "Only Greeks love profit better than life."

"So the dead merchants were Greeks?" Fenice asked.

Libu shook his head. "No. Turks." He grinned. "It must be a Christian demon."

Fenice laughed aloud. "It must," she agreed, and pointed to where half a dozen young men—the most aggressive of the market-gangs—were slouching in the shadow of an innyard gate. "They are not frightened of the demon, are they?"

"Not they," said Libu with a trace of bitterness. He glanced around. "You know the stable behind the old smithy?" he asked in an undervoice.

"Yes; what of it?" Fenice replied.

"They say that is where the men were found. The smith has offered a reward for the murderer's head." He rubbed his hands in anticipation. "I would like to have ten gold castles."

"So much?" Fenice said, surprised at the generous sum. "The smith must be richer than we thought."

"The other vendors are contributing," said Libu, mocking the vendors with his tone.

"How much, do you suppose?" She saw that the gang was moving in their general direction; she plucked at Libu's sleeve. "Come on; we should be moving."

"I agree," he said, limping after her, only to be cut off by the hard-faced youths.

"You've been paid, Monk," said the leader of the pack, his hand resting on the hilt of his crude dagger.

Fenice hated the way he swaggered as much as she hated the cold fear he engendered in her. "I was given half what I was promised," she said.

"Still, you know you must tithe. All monks know that." He held out his hand. "Pay what you owe, or we will make you sorry."

She knew she could not escape; she looked over her shoulder at Libu and saw he was shaking. "I will give you a third of what I was paid."

"Since it is so small an amount, you will give us half," the leader corrected her, menace in every line of his stance. "Now, Monk. Or we will send you back to the cloister to sing soprano."

Fenice did not want to give them any excuse to fight her, for they would surely discover she was no runaway monk as they supposed, but a female; they would not use her kindly then. She pulled the few coins she had earned from her wallet and handed them to the leader.

"Good little Monk," said the leader, his glowering smile instilling more dread in her. "You will have more for me in three days or you will have cause to regret it." He whistled, signaling his gang to depart, and sauntered away in their wake, tossing one of the coins in the air and catching it with negligent ease.

"They are horrid," Fenice said as soon as the gang was out of earshot. "I wish I had courage enough to say that to their faces."

"You have sense, which is better than courage when dealing with the likes of them," said Libu, resentment simmering in his eyes. "They are disgusting vermin."

"Don't let them hear you say that," Fenice recommended. "They would make an example of you, and then who would share oranges with me?"

He did his best to laugh. "We'd better go."

"Do you think they will come back? Really? Aren't they afraid of the demon?" Fenice smiled to show she was not entirely convinced of this, but there was a question lingering in her eyes that was not completely skeptical.

"I think it isn't safe to remain where we are," said Libu. "You will do what you want to do, most certainly, but I am going to find a place to hide for the night."

"Hide?" Fenice spoke in scorn. "How can you be so paltry?"

"I like to live," said Libu, with such utter seriousness that Fenice was struck by his reply. "This may not seem much of a life, but it is the only one God has given me, and I will not waste His gift. I am not too proud to hide, or steal, or lie, to continue breathing."

It took Fenice a moment to answer. "I didn't mean to disparage . . ." She let her apology trail off. "Yes, I suppose I did. And you are the one who has taught me so much. I should learn from you again." She looked around the market, and satisfied that the young men were gone, she gave Libu her best smile and said, "How do I find a place to hide?"

"I have been sleeping in the shed at the back of the monastery," said Libu. "There's only room for one, so . . ." He shrugged.

"Why the back of the monastery?" Fenice asked as she began to walk beside the slow-moving Libu.

"It is holy ground. The demon will not come there. He will look for those foolish enough to sleep in the open, or in unguarded places." He tried to look amused. "You will want more than a donkey or a barrel to protect you."

"Perhaps," said Fenice, a frisson creeping up her arms in spite of her determination to resist. "I will keep this in mind when I choose a place for the night. I need a new place, in any case. But," she added gamely, "I do not think there is a demon at all. I think it is nothing more than superstition and gossip."

"You may think what you like, but you would be foolish not to take refuge on holy ground," Libu pointed out to her, his tone sharp enough to make her nod in agreement.

"So I would," she admitted. As they walked on along the street leading to the monastery, she glanced down one long alley to where a large house was still alight, figures moving about in the tall windows, open to the treacherous night air. "Someone lives there?" she marveled; she had not seen any sign of life in the house since she arrived in Varna.

"The Russians," said Libu, spitting to show his disgust. "They are in that house."

"Russians," said Fenice, glad to have something other than demons to occupy her thoughts. "What are the Russians doing in Varna?"

Libu's face went crafty, and he lowered his voice. "Well, they *say* that they are here to meet with a Carpathian noble, who wants troops to push the Ottomites off his land. I think he might be better off with the Turks than the Russians, but no doubt the Church would prefer Russians." He snickered. "The Russians want access to the Carpathians, and this noble may let them have it."

"A treacherous bargain," Fenice said as they reached the track beside the monastery. "Well, you have given me much to think about, Libu." She did not like the anxious sense that increased as Libu began to walk haltingly away from her. "I will see you at daybreak."

"In the market," Libu agreed, raising his hand to wave as if to make their usual meeting a special occasion. "May God watch over you in your sleep," he said.

"And you, my friend," Fenice said, unaware that she had spoken this benediction not in Greek but Italian: *e tu, amico mio.*

Libu gave a single, amused laugh, and was lost in the shadows.

Fenice did not linger; she went toward the small Christian quarter, taking care to avoid the Hagia Charis convent; she had no desire to encounter Mother Sophronia again. This made for a more circuitous approach, and caused her to stumble across a small cemetery behind the church dedicated to Saint George of Armenia; there were a number of tombs there, some large enough to provide shelter from the weather and the other dangers of the night. For a short time, Fenice made her way around the cemetery, looking for the most substantial of the tombs. At last she came to one that proclaimed it guarded the mortal remains of Johannes von Eisenbach, knight of Ingleheim, who died while defending the true faith in the 1384th year of man's Salvation. The low-relief sculpture showed a grand figure on horseback with a lance in one hand and a cross in the other. Fenice though about Johannes von Eisenbach, who must have been a mercenary to be fighting the Turks so long after the Crusades were over. She could not keep from laughing at the thought of this German keeping her safe; soldiers or merchants, Germans were the greediest of the lot, she told herself, remembering everything her family had said about them.

She realized too late that it had been imprudent to remember her family, for now missing them came over her like a fever; she huddled down in the shelter of the tomb's deep entrance, her sack shoved under her, and strove uselessly to get the echos of her brothers' and sisters' voices from her mind. "I'm sorry, I'm sorry," she whispered to the memories of Rosamonda. "I never intended to hurt you, Madre Mia. Never. I just had to get away for a while, before I was married and I could not . . . Forgive me for making you worry. And don't believe everything Ercole tells you." The intrusions of her brother's contempt haunted her dreams more dismayingly than any demon could.

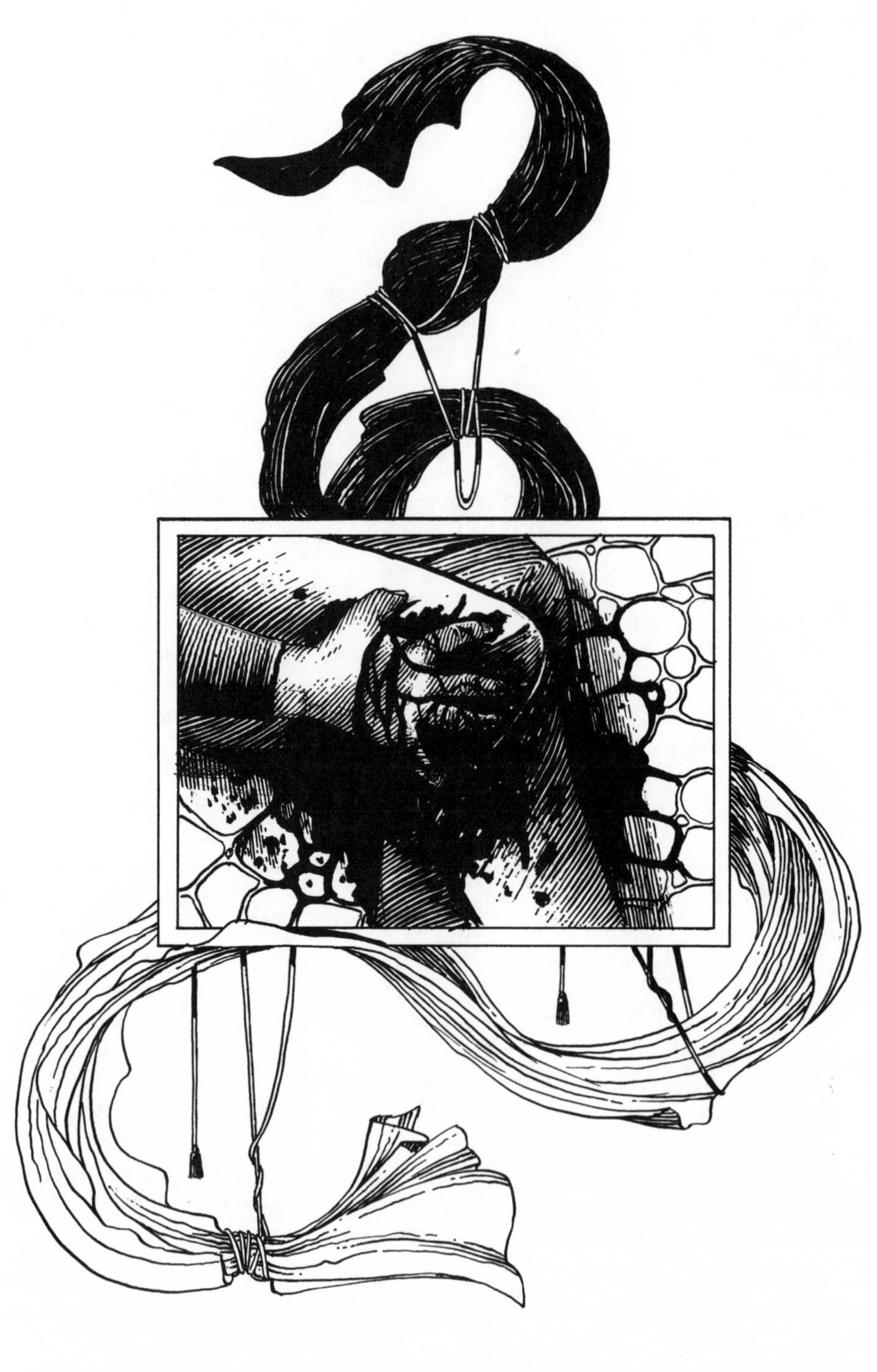

When the sun's bright chariot has fled
Pursued by night's black wake spread
From crag to valley . . .
—Francesco Petrarca

— XVII —

It was raining when she woke, the grayness of dawn overlaid by the low clouds, so that morning seemed only a paler version of night, without colors or the sharp line of shadows to mark sunrise. Fenice shivered in her damp clothes and stretched to ease the stiffness she felt from sleeping on stone; she longed for a *shuba,* one of the heavy cloaks the Polish merchants wore—great long things made of sheepskin with the wool turned in for warmth. As she struggled to come fully awake, she wondered if she should change her adventure enough to confess her disguise to someone who would be willing to protect her while allowing her to go on as she had been; the notion was tempting, for she could imagine an adventuresome lover, like the hawk-faced fellow in her dreams, who would not condemn her for seeking excitement. How much enjoyment they would have, sharing their delicious secret while taking on the world and reveling in all they achieved; they would lie in each other's arms and laugh at the success of their escapades, and their love would be the greatest adventure of all. . . . She sighed. "Yes, I can *imagine* him," she muttered as she left the cemetery. "That's just the trouble—imagination." With this unwelcome realization she made her way back to the market, hoping she would find better employment for the day.

Her relief at seeing Libu at his usual place by the fountain made her uncomfortably aware of the fear which remained with her, as persistent as a cough. The other thing she noticed was that about half the market-stalls were empty. She approached Libu, saying, "The rain is worse than any demon. Look at this place. We might as well be in—"

"It isn't the rain that keeps them away; it is the demon. One of the Genoese was found dead last night, white as an Englishman and empty of blood as a dressed calf. No one is willing to stay here. No one but the few you see, and they will flee if anything more happens." He shivered and looked up at the weeping sky. "This is only an excuse."

"Then . . . then how are we to eat?" Fenice asked, frightened afresh by what Libu told her.

"We may not." He rubbed his face. "You might be able to steal some bread, or a lemon. I don't think the vendors would begrudge us that."

She glanced toward the stall where the sweet pastries were made and was disappointed to find it empty. "Perhaps if the rain stops?"

"Oh, yes. There are those who will brave this place when it is bright enough to drive away anything . . . unwholesome." His chuckle was unpleasant now, suggesting something conspiratorial. He hitched up his good shoulder. "I've starved before. I will do it again."

"How can you be so . . . so indifferent to your . . . our plight?" Fenice demanded, her increasing dread finding release in ire.

"Would my distress change it?" Libu asked bluntly. "It would not," he answered for her. "Then why should I waste my wits and my strength? I will have need of them." He pointed toward the alley where the market gang that had accosted them the night before loitered. "You will have to be careful of them. They don't like starving any more than you do."

She nodded. "I can see them."

"See you don't get near them," Libu recommended, and was about to move away when he thought of something more. "You might want to talk to the Russians. They may need a translator."

Fenice stared at him. "I've only learned a few of the Bulgar phrases. What good will that do?"

"You don't know until you ask, do you?" Libu said, and went to the far side of the fountain where he began his usual cry: "I will hold your horse and water him; I will hold your donkey. I will hold your horse and water him; I will hold your donkey."

By midafternoon, Fenice had earned only one copper martyr for helping a Hydriot captain calculate the worth of his oil lamps in the rates of Varna; no one else had any use for her abilities, not even to letting her earn a single copper galley—half the size of a martyr—for holding a horse or donkey. She had gone through her sack two times in the hope she might find something she had overlooked—a coin or a wedge of cheese—that would sustain her, and once again she begrudged the nuns her four lost ducats. She did not like the sensation of gnawing she felt in her gut, nor did the headache that accompanied it soften her mood. She frowned at the lowering sky and tried to remind herself that this was as much a part of her adventure as escaping over the convent wall had been.

"How has it gone today?" Libu asked in a disheartened voice at the close of the day. "I have three galleys and two martyrs." He laughed harshly. "What success."

"You've done better than I have," she said, wondering if she dared to sell any of her few belongings in order to buy something to eat.

"Go to the monastery gate. They will give you old bread and dry cheese.

It isn't much, but it is better than nothing." Libu held up his hand in warning. "You do not know who might be there. You must watch, so that you will not be set upon by the beggars."

"The blind ones?" She remembered the care Ercole had taken with them.

"And the gangs. They will want charity tonight, make no mistake about that." He rubbed his arms through the thin sleeves of his short, square-sleeved stamboline. "It should not be so cold at this time."

"Perhaps it should not, but it is," said Fenice bluntly. "Damn that Genoese for letting the demon get him."

"If it had not been him, it would have been another," said Libu. "Oh, Aeneo, I hope it does not like crippled beggars."

Fenice stared at him. "Of *course*," she exclaimed. "Of course. I should have thought of this before now. The blind beggars must know something."

"But they're blind," Libu reminded her as if she had suddenly lost her good sense.

"Yes, of course they are. But they hear everything. They might tell us something." She stared around the market, disliking the emptiness of it.

"Not for a handful of coppers," said Libu. "They will want more."

"If I am willing to make them the loan of my eyes, they may be willing," said Fenice, her certainty less than she wanted it to be.

Libu shook his head. "You are well-named, Aeneo; you will venture anything, no matter how reckless." He made an attempt at a grin. "You are a skilled fellow, and I am foolish enough to follow you." Pointing down the street where the blind beggars sat, he said, "I will come with you. Two pairs of eyes may be more welcome than one."

Fenice did her best not to giggle. "Let us find the beggars."

They went a short way down the street only to find the market-gang confronting them once again; the leader had his hands thrust into his belt and he ambled with a nonchalance that was intended to intimidate. "Slow day."

"The demon and the rain," said Fenice. "Tomorrow will be better."

"You had better pray it is," said the leader. "I do not want to be disappointed two days in a row. My men get hungry, and that makes them surly." He smiled to show his approval of their surliness. "They have not eaten much today."

"No one has," said Fenice, knowing defiance would stand her in better stead than weakness. She touched the small of her back for the knife she had hidden there and wondered if she could bring herself to use it.

"But we are hungry," said the leader, coming toward her. "And you have money."

"A few coppers isn't money," said Fenice, scoffing at the notion.

"True enough," the leader said angrily. "But if it is all you have, then it must suffice." He signaled one of his men to move in on Libu. "You have something for us, haven't you?"

"Don't give it to him," Fenice said warily. "Libu. Don't."

She was too late; Libu had already thrown down his paltry earnings and moved to the edge of the gang. "I can't fight them, Aeneo. I'm not strong enough, and . . ." He did not finish before he slipped away into the shadows.

"You might as well give us the money now," said the leader. "We'll take it anyway, and the more we have to fight to get it, the more we'll make you sorry we had to."

Fenice put her hand on the hilt of the short dagger and pulled it out of her belt, brandishing the weapon rather wildly. She gripped the knife tightly and held her ground, trying to be ready for anything that might happen.

The leader laughed, showing his contempt for her knife. He suddenly poked her in the shoulder, thrusting her back from him so that she was off-balance. "The Monk can't fight. Look at him."

Trying to regain her balance, Fenice swung her arms; she had no intention of attacking while she could hardly stand erect, but the point of her dagger slid in at the back of the leader's knee just as he turned away from her to let his gang see how little danger he was in from her. An instant later, he howled and fell clumsily to the pavement, one hand landing in a heap of camel dung.

"You *dead man!*" the leader shrieked as he saw the widening stain of blood spreading around his leg; his face had gone blotchy. He pointed at Fenice. "Kill him. Kill him. *Kill him.*"

Fenice swiped at the air with her dagger, and to her astonishment, the youths in the gang faltered; then one broke and ran, his flight making the others run after him. She continued to hold the knife out, as if she could not believe she had routed the gang so readily.

The leader struck out, trying to hit her, but she danced back out of the way, almost giddy in the aftermath of fear. She stared at the leader as if she could not quite comprehend the kind of creature he was.

"You're dead. You're dead," he repeated sullenly, but shrank back as she came nearer to him.

"It's your fault," she told him.

"You—" His knotted fist missed her by a handsbreadth, but she moved away from him in any case.

"You came after me. I didn't try to hurt you. It's your bad luck you couldn't make me do what you wanted." She saw that there was blood on the blade, and she wiped it off on the sleeve of her giaquetta before returning it to the small of her back, under her belt. "I'm sorry you're hurt, but you brought it on yourself," she said, wondering what she ought to do next.

The leader stared in dismay at the blood around him; he cursed her so vilely that she could only comprehend one word in five, and it was so disgusting that she had no wish to know the rest of what he vowed would be her fate.

"I will try to find someone to help you," she said, and rushed away from him, her bones feeling cold and insubstantial within her. As she passed the nearest of the blind beggars, he called out; she stopped and turned back.

"Have a care, young woman. You have an enemy in that one," said the blind man in German-accented Italian.

This abrupt address brought her up short. She mustered her scattered thoughts and looked around at the beggar who squatted in a doorway, an old cloak drawn around him; there was a faded embroidered representation of an unfamiliar heraldic design. "You are wrong, good fellow; I am Aeneo," she said, making her voice as low as she could.

"You may deceive the rest: it is nothing to me. But I know the difference between the sounds of men's and women's voices, and you are no Aeneo." He laughed harshly. "It would please me to have them learn they have been bested by a female. But"—he held up his hand as Fenice drew in her breath—"I will say nothing. You are in too much danger as it is. I will not add to it." He sketched the sign of the cross in her direction. "May God and His demons protect you."

Nonplused by his strange benediction, she said, "And keep you safe from harm," with the automatic good manners she had been taught as a child.

"I will listen for you," he added as Fenice moved away from him; she headed directly for the Christian cemetery and the protection of the German tomb. All appetite had fled and she was now feeling too chilled and too queasy to do anything more than huddle in her place and pray that the demon she did her best not to believe in would not suddenly become aware of her.

The images in her dreams were fierce, disturbing, and violent. She kept seeing the leader of the market-gang in the alley with blood from his injury smeared on the stones around him from his many attempts to get to his feet. Something in the alley approached the leader, savaged him, and left a husk behind. These dreams, fragmentary though they were, seemed far more real than anything Fenice had experienced before.

By the time she allowed herself to rise, she was filled with abhorrence for what her dreams had conjured, and she decided she would have to be at pains to avoid another such night. She could feel bruises on her arms, shoulder, and jaw, and for once she was glad she had no mirror in which to see herself; she must surely look discreditable. She put her sack over her shoulder instead of leaving it thrust in beside the stone sarcophagus just beyond the door of the tomb. She was careful going away from the cemetery, for she was troubled by what she had imagined in the night and was vaguely uneasy, suspecting that the monks would not allow someone with so disreputable a face, or with dreams such as hers, to shelter in their cemetery.

Once again the marketplace was half-deserted, though the day was sunny enough; the newly arrived merchants from Greece and Italy and the Ottoman lands found the usually bustling stalls mostly empty, and fewer than half the usual number of customs agents waiting for them. They milled about, talking among themselves and waiting for vendors to arrive.

"What has happened here?" demanded a rough-featured newcomer with an Athenian accent and several gold rings on his fingers. "Demons, indeed! Rumors, more like." He turned away from the gathered men with a gesture of disgust. "Madmen, all of them."

Fenice approached him respectfully. "I beg your pardon, good merchant, but they are not as mad as you might think; in the last several days, the market-square has seen a number of . . . murders. The vendors fear for their lives. With good reason, no matter what the cause may be." She ducked her head and wondered if she would be dismissed with a curse and a blow.

The Athenian stared at her. "You don't seem afraid, young man," he pronounced after his short scrutiny. "Do you disbelieve these fables about demons?"

"I am a beggar and I am hungry," she answered. "I can't afford to be scared, no matter what I believe."

"No, I suppose not." He studied her thoughtfully. "But you are out in the morning and many others are huddled indoors. Your Greek is very good," he added.

"I studied it for several years with a strict master," she told him, shivering in spite of the sun's warmth. She glanced toward the alley where she had fought the market-gang and saw a number of Varna officials standing about the place where she had left the leader the previous night. Almost against her will, she asked, "What is the matter today? Has there been another—?" She could not make herself say *murder*.

"Oh, they say the demon struck again," the Athenian informed her in overly dramatic tones. "They say the demon killed a market-tough this time, not a merchant. Hamstrung him first, they were saying. There was a lot of blood, which is not what they said of the demon before. But you know how unpredictable demons are." He shook his head. "These people are superstitious and proud to be so. A demon!" He spat to show what he thought of such nonsense.

"You doubt that is what it was?" Fenice asked, trembling.

"Do not be afraid," the Athenian said. "Of course I doubt it was a demon. Probably all the deaths they say the demon was responsible for were done by the tough, and he finally came up against someone who could fight back. The man deserved what happened to him. I doubt we will hear anything more of this demon preying on market-folk again."

Fenice did her best to smile. "You're right; the demon is gone," she said, fearing what the rest of the market-gang would do to her if they decided she had killed their leader. She began to wonder if she had. She had left him bleeding; perhaps the cut went deeper than she thought.

"What is the matter, boy?" The Athenian studied Fenice. "You're still white."

"The . . . the gangs rob the beggars," she said quietly.

"Ahhh," the Athenian said with a trace of satisfaction. "You are afraid of who might steal from you next." He clapped a hand on her shoulder. "You will have to earn enough to have a room for the night."

"That would be one solution," she agreed, her tone dry at the possibility of that happening. "But look around you. How am I to do it?"

The Athenian chuckled. "Well, you know, the Russians need someone to copy for them. Can you read and write Greek, as well as speak it?"

"Yes. I can," said Fenice, trying not to sound too eager as she felt hope for the first time that day.

"Good. Their copyist fell ill—from the demon, they say—four days ago, and none of them can write in Greek: I suspect most of them cannot read or write Russian, either. The copies are for the Carpathian noble, who demands their records be kept in Greek—he is one of those whose pride is very great, or so the Russians say." The Athenian smiled. "If you were to come with me, I could introduce you to them."

"You do not want the work yourself?" Fenice asked with a sudden rush of suspicion.

"I'm a merchant, not a clerk. And they would not trust me with the task." He considered this and nodded. "Wise of them. They know I would sell anything I learn." His chuckle was louder now, like hail on a stone roof.

"And if you find someone for them, they will pay you for your service," Fenice guessed shrewdly.

"Precisely," said the Athenian. "I am glad you understand these things." He rocked back on his heels. "So, if you want the work, tell me now and I'll take you to them. If you do not, then be off with you." He looked wonderfully unconcerned as he turned away, but Fenice knew he was bargaining with her.

"You will give me a third of what they pay you," she said at once.

"A third?" he blustered. "I think you've got an unreasonably high opinion of your talents, my lad."

"Then you can write for them," said Fenice, shrugging; she was beginning to enjoy herself, for she sensed that this Athenian needed her abilities more than he was willing to admit.

He glared down at her feet. "You'd change your tune if you had to go another day without food."

"So I might," she agreed at once. "But are you so sure I would have to do that? Mightn't I go to the Russians myself and tell them I can do the work they need?"

He shook his head. "Not if I warned them you were a spy." He waited. "Twenty percent."

"Thirty," she said promptly.

"Twenty-five, and I'll go no higher." He spoke in a tone of voice she recognized as final.

"Twenty-five will do," she said as if disappointed. "And it will be for the amount you are paid, not what you say you are paid. If it comes to it, I will know the price. The Russians will tell me. And they will not like it if you cheat me in their name." She recalled how her brothers had occasionally complained of middlemen who inflated their earnings by claiming they were given less than they were.

"Clever boy," said the Athenian. "All right. I will deal fairly with you." He put his hand on Fenice's shoulder again. "You're thin as a rail."

"But capable," she said. "I do not need to be robust to copy accurately."

"No, you do not," he said, and pointed the way toward the forbidding house where the Russians stayed. "They are rough, these men. Not like the toughs in the market, but if you were expecting polished manners, like the Italians or the Egyptians, you had best think again. These men are soldiers more than courtiers." He laughed. "They think themselves formidable."

"And are they?" Fenice asked jauntily to keep her courage up; the dark alley was much like the one in which she had fought the gang leader, which troubled her.

"They would like to think so. And in battle they would be hard to fight; I've heard that the Turks regard them with respect, which is high tribute." He strolled into the dark alley. "That house at the end, with the high walls? That is where the Russians are staying."

"What of the other noble? The one from the Carpathians? From Transylvania?" she asked, needing the sound of his voice more than the information he might offer her.

"He has a house in another part of Varna. He does not trust the Russians enough to sleep under the same roof with them, and who can blame him?" The Athenian reached the thick wooden gate in the protective wall and pounded on it with the flat of his hand. "Ho there!" He added something in what Fenice supposed was Russian, then stepped back, waiting, as the sound of the bolt being pulled back grated the morning.

When the gate opened, the man standing behind it looked as thick and tall as a tree. His costume was exotic, even for the port of Varna: he wore a wolf's pelt over the shoulder of his leather rubashek; his leggings were cut full and gathered into tooled boots. What was most distinctive about him was his long, black hair clubbed at the back of his partially shaven head; he carried a curved sword, like a scimitar but longer. "What is it?" he asked in barbaric Greek.

"You had a man at the market looking for someone to copy Greek documents. This boy says he can do it." The Athenian smiled to show his goodwill. "Tell me that you still need someone and pay this lad well for his service. And give me a fee for bringing him to you."

The Russian frowned as he looked at Fenice. "Come in," he ordered, moving out of the way so that Fenice and the Athenian could walk into the courtyard. He lowered his weapon as he closed the gate and barred it once more. "You can read and write? In Greek?" the soldier asked, taking painful care with his pronunciation. He had to lean down to look Fenice in the face.

"I can," she said, feeling dwarfed by the soldier with the wolf pelt. "I can read and write Latin, as well." This boast made the soldier blink once, which pleased her.

"I will tell my captain," he declared, and motioned to Fenice and the Athenian to follow him.

The house was cavernous and smelled of old mortar; in spite of the sun outside, the interior was dark. There were few windows and most of them were shuttered; there were few amenities beyond an occasional wooden bench until they came to the reception hall, which was vaster than the rest of the place. There, glossy carpets were spread on the stone floor, lavish as anything the Sultan might have. Half a dozen men like the soldier who was leading Fenice and the Athenian sat about the reception hall, busy with cleaning and honing their weapons. On the long table were the remains of at least two meals.

A man in a grander version of the uniforms the rest wore came out of his place in a Turkish hassock and glowered at the strangers. He made a rough inquiry of the soldier and was answered with such a display of ingratiation that Fenice was shocked. The two men spoke briefly, then the superior officer came and looked down at Fenice. "So you read and write Greek and Latin?" he said in fairly good Greek.

"Yes. I do," said Fenice, beginning to wonder if she had made a mistake in coming here.

"And you are willing to copy the agreement we have struck here?" His voice was harsh from long hours of shouting, but he was obviously doing his best to seem more courtly than he was. "The Transylvanian wants it copied out in Greek and our man . . . is very ill."

"So I understand," said Fenice, trying to decide if she needed money enough to remain here. Only the fear of what might happen to her if she attempted to leave kept her from trying it. "I will have to be paid half before I begin," she said, hoping to appear more experienced than she was.

"Certainly," said the officer. "And when you are finished we will give you the rest." His smile had more teeth than sincerity in it, but she did not want to quibble. "You will have a table and lamps for light. We have ink cakes and quills you can cut to your preference." He clapped his hands and issued several sharp commands in Russian, then regarded Fenice. "Are you hungry?"

"I am," she said, hoping that admitting as much would not put her in any danger.

"Then you shall have dumplings before you set to work. Dumplings and eggs." He barked another series of instructions, then stared at the Athenian. "You will wait here until I am satisfied the lad can do the work. Then you will be paid and you will leave."

"Of course," said the Athenian with a determined effort at geniality. "And see you treat the lad well," he added as an afterthought.

"If he does his task well, he will be rewarded," said the officer.

Fenice straightened up and did her best to show purpose in her stance. "I will copy whatever you give me. And you may rely on me not to speak of it to anyone."

The officer laughed nastily. "If you speak of it, I will have your tongue cut out. I am confident you will keep what you learn to yourself." With that he pointed to half a dozen slaves who had come into the reception hall. "There. Your breakfast. I trust you have a good appetite?" He grinned as Fenice, suddenly pale, swallowed hard and did her best to look gratified.

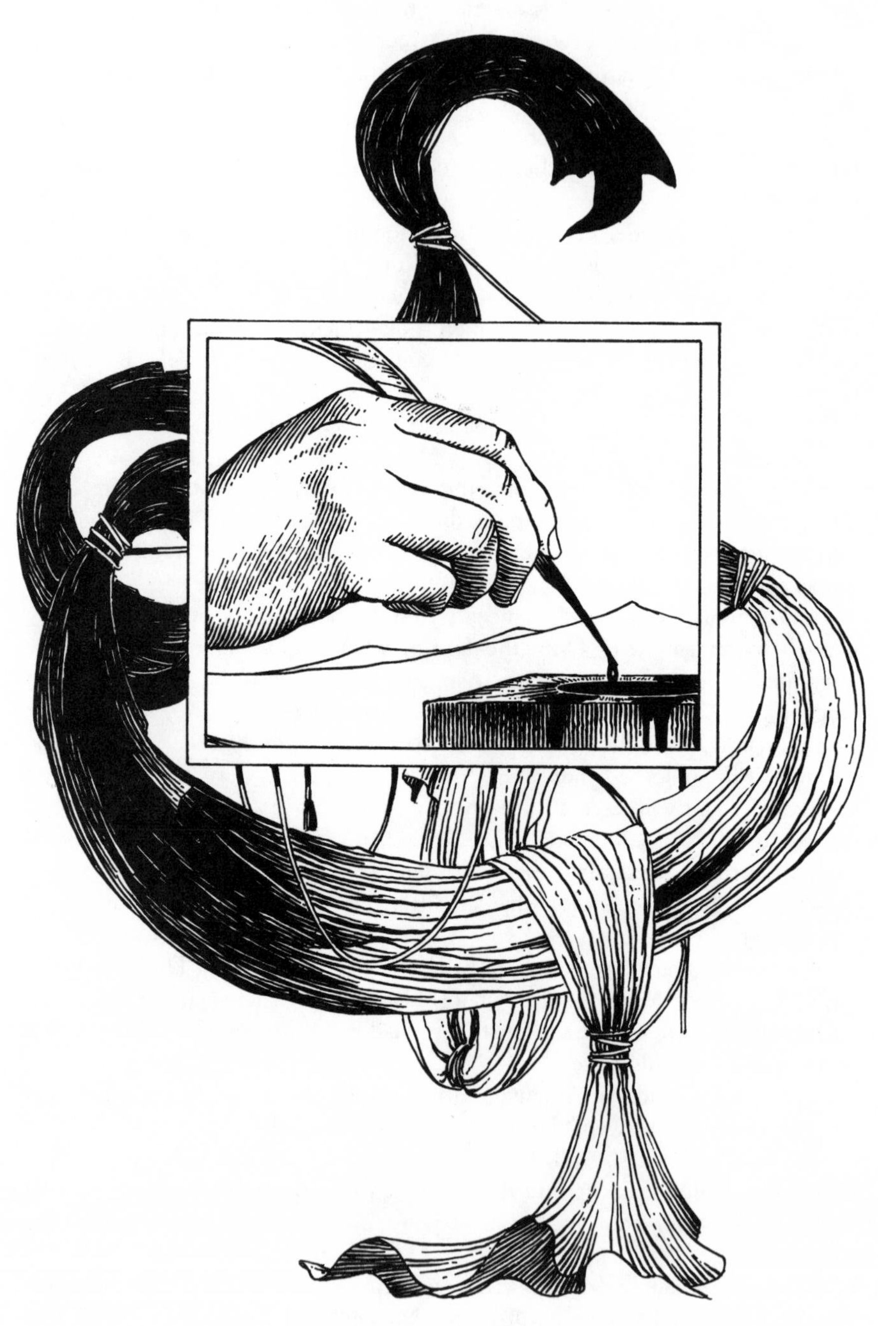

. . . nor no youth so brave
As the stirred heart of woman . . .
—Giovanni Pico della Mirandola

— XVIII —

"I had the oddest feeling I was being watched," Fenice said when she finished telling Libu about her day at the Russians' house. "I thought someone was in the shadows, watching me."

"Well, of course you were watched," said Libu as he gnawed eagerly on the chicken leg Fenice had brought him for his supper. The market-square was growing dark and those few vendors who had braved the demon to sell their wares were now bustling to get away from the place, their courage deserting them with the vanishing sun.

"I was paid . . ." She lowered her voice, then told him almost the full amount. "Two gold castles." The actual figure was three. "And they will give me the same tomorrow." With a chuckle she shoved his arm gently. "So tonight we sleep in bed, Libu, in rooms with doors, and in the morning, we will have yoghurt to eat with our pastries."

He stared at her. "You tell me you will do this for me?" He very nearly dropped the chicken leg in astonishment. "Why?"

"Because you have helped me, and I want to repay your kindness," she said openly. "Without your help, I would have had a much more difficult time of it. This place"—her gesture took in the whole of the darkening market-square—"might have exhausted me in the first two days if you had not been willing to . . . to show me how I could manage."

"At least you have something valuable to sell," he said with sudden bitterness; when he saw her aghast expression, he went on, "You can read and write and you speak Italian as well. And Latin. That makes you more than most of us."

"I do not know the language of the Turks, or the Bulgars," she reminded him. "Greek is useful, but Turkish would be better."

"You will learn," he said, not willing to face her. "You know phrases already, and you will learn more." He held up the bones of the chicken leg. "I should thank you for this instead of carping."

"I didn't buy it for you for that: you may carp all you like. I got you food because I am grateful. I would like to think we are friends," she said, her voice dropping. "If you would prefer to starve, then you have only to tell me."

"Oh, no," Libu replied, and his crack of laughter made her feel less offended. "I will take good fortune when it comes my way. No beggar can afford to do otherwise." He shook his head as he tossed the gnawed bones aside. "I'll let the dogs and rats fight over the rest."

"They are not afraid of the demon," said Fenice, smiling to restore the good humor between them.

"Nor should anyone else be," said Libu, his edgy jauntiness restored. "But the officers of the Sultan have surrendered this place to whatever is killing the merchants. They have gone to the mosque to pray for Allah to make the demon go away. The Christians are no better—huddling in churches and reciting prayers."

"While you and I watch the afterglow of sunset," said Fenice, hoping she did not sound as uneasy as she felt; with the light fading, she could not wholly reassure herself that this place was without danger, for although she had rid the market of the leader of one gang, there were others and they would be vying for mastery among themselves as well as exerting their might on all those foolish enough to fall into their hands.

"It is probably time to find rooms, since you have offered them," Libu said, cocking his head in the direction of the stable that had a small inn attached to it. "Do you want to try there?"

"No," Fenice answered decisively. "It is too near the marketplace. The gangs are still about, and we know that they will be looking for . . ." She did not want to say what they would be looking for. "We will do better nearer the docks. One of the sailors' inns would serve us better; the gangs do not range as far as the docks, do they?"

As Libu fell in beside Fenice, he said, "You're becoming very wise for one so newly arrived here. What on earth did they teach you in that monastery?"

"I learned a few things from my brothers," said Fenice with total honesty. "And I know that sailors are as determined as street gangs; we will be safe where they stay."

"And we'll have fewer questions asked once the rooms are paid for," said Libu shrewdly. "I take it your brothers are sailors."

"Yes," said Fenice, and did not elaborate.

In the morning, the taproom of the Old Lighthouse was filled with sailors wondering about the demon in the market-square. One or two proclaimed their doubts aloud, but the rest were unable to hide their apprehension.

"Another man was found this morning, no blood left in him," a French sailor declared in Greek. "The customs men say they will not go into the market-square while the demon is abroad."

"Then we will not have to pay them," called one of the sailors from a Cypriot ship.

"No one will be there to buy," another predicted gloomily.

From their place at the end of the benches, Fenice glanced at Libu and said, "So it wasn't just the market-gangs."

Libu, his mouth full of figs and yoghurt, mumbled, "Still could be. Lots of them left."

"I suppose so," said Fenice as she downed the dark, sweet tea that was standard fare for the inn; only in the evening did the landlord serve alcohol, knowing the Turkish rulers expected a few concessions to their religion, if only during daylight hours.

"Look," said Libu, and swallowed hard. "Something or someone is killing men at the market-square. That much we know. It may be a demon, it may not, but the deaths are real." He put his scrawny elbows on the splintery tabletop. "You and I will not flourish as long as the dying continues. We must have merchants willing to pay for our services if we are not to starve. Consider yourself, Aeneo. The Russians will give you more money today, and that will be the end of it."

"Until the killing stops," said Fenice reflectively.

"True enough," said Libu. "And it is not wise to spend money you may need later on this kind of housing and food. But," he went on with a shrug, "it is not safe in the marketplace, so why not indulge in these pleasures? Who knows when we may have them again?"

Fenice studied his face thoughtfully. "Do you never resent having to beg?"

His answer was readily given. "Occasionally, as who would not. But I would rather be an honest beggar than live with the monks who feed you and work you like a slave in return for their prayers and cheese." His features darkened. "The monks must accept those who cannot fend for themselves, as it is one of the Seven Acts of Worldly Virtue: clothe the naked, feed the hungry and give drink to the thirsty, visit those in prison, tend the sick, ransom captives, shelter the homeless, and bury the dead. The Seven Acts of Spiritual Virtue are: teach the ignorant, counsel those in doubt, console the grieving, forgive those who trespass against you, bear with oppression, acquiesce in God's Will, and reprove the sinner." He smiled. "You are not the only one who knows something of monastery life. I left it, too, but I was not a novice."

Fenice shook her head. "Why does everyone think I was a novice monk?" she asked the air.

Libu laughed aloud. "Well, it's obvious. You are too naive to be anything other than a monk, and too educated. You're as beardless as a eunuch. You conduct yourself as if you were in church." He wagged a finger at her. "You're as protected as a girl, and you have no more sense than a toddler, but you have the courage of lions. What else can you be but a runaway novice? I've supposed you were one of those unfortunates whom the Turks castrated, and who was consigned to monastery life. What else could you become but a monk, and why else would you flee so guarded a life?" He winked. "One of the older monks tried to bugger you, is that it?"

Fenice had learned enough aboard ship to know what Libu meant; her face went scarlet and she coughed on her hot tea. "It wasn't . . . that bad. . . ."

"You needn't fear me, Aeneo, or whatever your name is. I know what monks are, and I know what they do." His jesting turned to sarcasm. "Saying prayers while their habits hang on tentpoles, denouncing the Devil for taking their holiness away. As if a tonsure led to holiness. I saw it—every day one of the monks would—" He stopped, apparently aware he was causing her distress. "You are not the only one monks have used shamefully. They have trouble with Seven Virtues, particularly chastity." He ticked them off on his fingers. "Humility, chastity, honor, honesty, courage, charity, fidelity."

Fenice was baffled. "Why do you work so to show me how much you know about—"

"Monastery life?" he interrupted. "So you will know that when I say I know what you have endured, you will not doubt my sincerity, or think I am misrepresenting myself to earn your sympathy." He waved his hand at the sailors in the taproom. "Any one of them would probably be willing to tell you any tale they thought you wanted to hear to gain your goodwill. At least for as long as you had money."

"You're quite the cynic," said Fenice, amazed at how much compassion she felt for Libu; his revelations would have shocked her even four months ago, but no longer. She drank the rest of her tea, and then said, "About the demon—what do you think is happening?"

"I think the customs agents are too afraid to find out, and I think the merchants aren't frightened enough to pay to have the demon hunted down," said Libu. "And the market-gangs will use their hesitation to make themselves the law in the square."

"Do you believe it is the market-gangs who are doing the killing?" Fenice asked, remembering what the Athenian had said.

"I think it doesn't matter who is doing the killing; the gangs will use it to their advantage. We will have to watch ourselves, for they will be watching us." He was almost finished with his breakfast and grinned with contentment. "You have every reason to be careful, Aeneo; do not imagine otherwise. They probably think you killed that bully the other night. They will want to make sure you don't do anything like that again."

"They?" Fenice echoed, though she knew the answer.

"The other gangs. They may hate one another, but they will stand together against a common foe. You may well be that foe." He wiped his lips with his fingers and prepared to rise. "The Russians are waiting for you."

Preoccupied with all she had heard, Fenice rose, oversetting the bench behind her. "So they are," she said as she righted the furniture. With doubts for companions she went out of the Old Lighthouse and made her way toward the walled house of the Russians.

In dismay Febo stared at his father in shock. "What do you mean, you want me to leave in ten days?" he demanded, his handsome features growing pale. His tone roughened. "Who is going to fetch Fenice when we have discovered where she has been taken? I assumed that would be my task. Don't tell me there are others who will do it—she must be brought back to Venice by her own family. Anything else is unthinkable, for everyone would think the worst of her. She will be frightened and in want of comfort." He paced the length of the study, so restless that his sleeve swept a loosely rolled map onto the floor. As he paused to pick it up, he went on less urgently, "I want to be the one to . . . find her and bring her home. Not Ercole, not Lionello, me."

"She will not have much of a home to return to if we do no business and waste our money in futile searches for her," said Gaetano sadly. "She would not want any of us to do that."

"But she is still gone," Febo accused.

"And we have had no demand for ransom. Even Aurelio says that we must leave it to him; we have work to do." Gaetano expected an outburst from Febo and was not disappointed.

"Aurelio! And what does he know about it?" Febo was about to pound his fist on his father's desk when he stopped. "Not that Aurelio isn't changed by what has happened. Who would have thought he would take his task so much to heart and work so tirelessly on it?"

"His father has said that our tragedy has been the making of his son." Gaetano sighed and made a gesture to show his resignation in the face of the whims of fate.

"It may be so," said Febo, somewhat mollified by this observation. "Who would have thought Aurelio of all of them would be so able to put himself to the search?" He did his best to smile, but did not completely succeed. "Fenice must have known, for she saw something in him that the rest of us did not."

"And that will bring her back to us if anything can," said Gaetano heavily, adding, "I have heard rumors that the Sultan's agents have paid men outside the law to harry honest Christian merchants with misfortunes so that their fortunes will decrease, leaving more for the Ottomites to claim. I cannot say if this is one such, but I would not be astonished if it should turn out to be so." He sighed. "So it is time we returned to our work and let Aurelio keep at his. If anyone can discover where she has gone, it will be Aurelio. And no one will be more committed in his search for her." He motioned to one of the chairs in the room. "Sit down, Febo, sit down. You're making me nervous, pacing about like a lion in a cage." He waited until Febo sat. "I will not send you far: Sicily, Corsica, Sardinia, and back along the coast. The Doge will approve the Galley, so that you will not be far from Venice; I can do that much for you."

Febo nodded, new shock in his eyes. "What of Ercole? Does he even know about Fenice yet?" He crossed himself. "To have gone so far, and with such acclaim, and to come home to this." His impatience increased. "You have reports waiting for him at Corfu, I know, and you think this may serve to tell him what has happened, but I doubt it, Padre Mio. No one could receive such news and not be moved by it. No triumph of the *Impresa* could be great enough to offset the news that Fenice is gone."

"It may be the *Impresa* that brought about our loss," said Gaetano with a slow nod of his big head; the new gray in his hair shone in the bar of morning sunlight from the window.

"How?" Febo demanded. "Who would think that?"

"The Doge, for one," said Gaetano. "He has told Aurelio that ships like the *Impresa* inspire envy, and it is possible that taking Fenice on the very night before the *Impresa* sailed was intended to show disapproval for the ship. Aurelio is certain now that Fenice's kidnaping was a threat, warning us to launch no more ships like the *Impresa*. The Doge is afraid the culprits behind the crime might well be Venetians, but Aurelio does not agree." He put his hands in his lap. "I fear we will never see her again."

Febo, who had entertained much wilder theories than the ones his father mentioned, kept the most extreme to himself; he told Gaetano, "The informants Aurelio has dealt with have not been very reliable."

"No, they have not." Gaetano coughed once, determined to shed no more tears. "And we have Artemesia's wedding to prepare for, so it is fitting that we do not mar the occasion with unavailing reflections on the loss of Fenice. Bianca has promised her Sisters will pray for Fenice's return morning and night every day, and you will look for her when you are able. I will say this to you again, Febo: we have ships that must sail or we will soon face ruin. No ransom, no matter how minor, could be paid if we did not have profits from trade. If you want to be helpful to your sister, then do your duty to our business."

Febo rubbed his face with his hands. "I cannot tell you if . . . But it is galling to think that I cannot look for her myself." He scowled suddenly. "There must be some way that I can help, even if I have to go to sea again."

"If you can think what it is, I will applaud your efforts and I am certain Aurelio will do so, as well." Gaetano regarded his son levelly. "You are a good son and a good brother. You know how hard this loss is for all of us. Do not make our burdens worse by refusing to sail; our competitors would take this as a sign of weakness and I fear none of us would be safe again."

"Why should we not be safe?" Febo asked bluntly.

"Because if any of our competitors have done this, either by their order or through their instigation, then our inability to persevere will show that all that must happen to ruin the House of Zucchar is to prey on their women. Your mothers and your sisters would never be safe again, nor your wife when you take one. This must not happen."

"Do you think our rivals did this? Who hates us so bitterly that they would steal Fenice? Have you learned something you haven't told me?"

"No, but I do not put it above some of them to use such methods now that it is apparent they work. Not all merchants are upright and fair, not even all Venetians. Think of Ca'Duro if you doubt me: he killed his uncle in order to get his business, though no one could prove it. Everyone knows, and he has boasted of it more than once, though not in Venetian waters." He did his best to be philosophical. "If not the Venetians, then the Calabrians, or the Sicilians, or even the Greeks; they have easy access to this city, and they have no obligation to honor our laws if they can get away from la Serenissima. They have warehouses here, and they learn things. The Germans have been closely checked and if they were part of it, Aurelio cannot discover it. And he tried most diligently."

"But you are not certain?" Febo's expression was searching, as if he needed to know more of what his father was thinking.

"I am satisfied that Aurelio will do all that can be done; I also realize he may make inquiries that would not be possible for us. He will continue his search for her while there is breath in his body." He held up his Jupiter finger to forestall any interruption. "Anyone known to be her relatives must attract notice to the search for her that would make all of us the objects of exploitation. And while many know that Aurelio was her affianced husband, more do not, and do not associate him with our family." He would not let Febo speak. "Think about this carefully, figlio mio, and we will talk again tonight. And prepare to sail in ten days."

Febo knew it was useless to argue; he rose and left his father alone, thinking, as he had done since he came home, that all the joy had gone out of the house.

Three oil lamps gave the parchment a dim, uneven light that left Fenice with a headache as she put the finishing touches on the copying she had begun the day before; she marveled at the complexities of the treaty, which provided the Russians would join with the Transylvanians in opposing the Ottomans, if the Serbians did not protest, or if they did not have need for Russian assistance. It also assured Tsar Ivan a haven in Transylvania should he need one, and the Transylvanian a place in the Russian court, if he were exiled. The Transylvanians—in the person of the Dragon Prince—promised to help the Russians if the Ottomans turned their armies on the Russian borders, if there were no standing conflicts in the Carpathians, either with the Ottomans or the Austrians. The Transylvanian nobles, although technically part of the vast Hungarian Empire, were an independent lot, balancing Hungarians and Ottomans with apparent ease while they struggled to keep their autonomy: this treaty with the Russians was a major concession for any Transylvanian to make.

"The mountains make them wild, for they think they have a fortress made by God that no one can conquer. These Transylvanians are the worst of the lot," muttered the elderly Russian nobleman as he read over Fenice's copying; his Greek was very good, but the cadences of Russian put odd stresses on some of the words so that Fenice was hard-put not to correct him. "The Moldavians are more reasonable, more flexible."

"But the Dragon Prince agreed," Fenice pointed out.

"Dragon Prince," the nobleman scoffed. "Fine title for a man living in the remotest part of those mountains. What is he prince of, I ask you? The cadet branch of his House are veiovodes, which is reasonable—but Prince?" He sanded the parchment, nodding. "Very well done. You have an elegant hand, my boy. Your tutor taught you well." Patting Fenice on the shoulder, he went on, lowering his voice as if he expected to be overheard. "We must have a care, for the Tsar will not be pleased if we fail to secure the terms he commands to set forth." He looked at once satisfied and apprehensive.

"Are the Carpathians so important?" Fenice wondered, looking at the nobleman and seeing his anxiety.

"They are," he said. "Tsar Ivan says so. At least, he said so when he dispatched us here." He shook his head repeatedly. "He wants allies to whom he can turn if the boyars rise against him. They have tried it before." There was a slight hesitation in his speech, as if he was unsure of Fenice. Then he shrugged. "Well, this is what we were sent to get. Tsar Ivan cannot dispute it."

"Why would he?" Fenice asked.

The nobleman frowned. "The Tsar is our Little Father, our master in all things. The people think him a link to God, and the Metropolitans allow it. Tsar Ivan is . . . very clever. He reads and writes in many tongues. His temperament is . . . mercurial. I must say that it is. When he secures a thing, you cannot always know how he will . . ." He turned away abruptly. "I should not say these things to you, boy."

"Why should you not?" Fenice asked with genuine curiosity. "I know no one to whom I may speak of these things, and even if I did, no one would believe me. I am nothing more than a . . . a beggar from the marketplace who knows how to read and write in Greek." She blew the sand from the page and said, "There. All it lacks now is the seal. When will it be done?" Fenice hoped she would be able to see the signing and sealing of the treaty, but she knew the chances were slim; she was too foreign and too unimportant to be allowed to witness so monumental a moment.

"Later today," said the nobleman, discouraging any more questions.

"How much longer will you need me here?" Fenice asked. "Will the Transylvanian come while I am here?" If she could see this Dragon Prince, she would feel she had gained something more than coins from the work.

"He has been here for some time. He has been observing you at your work," said the nobleman, gesturing to the shadowed doorway beyond this room in which she had been working. "You have earned his approval."

Fenice felt a rush of anger and vulnerability. She stood up. "Well, that is gratifying," she said through her teeth. "How good of him to trust me to do the work I was paid to do."

"Don't be so mettlesome, boy," the nobleman advised. "He is the one who would not allow us to hire a Russian to copy the work."

"Can he read?" Fenice asked with heavy sarcasm.

"Yes. Latin and Greek and Russian as well as Hungarian and his own Transylvanian tongue. But he is wary of those who seek to please two masters. You are only working for the gold. The Tsar does not impress you, nor does the Transylvanian. Or if they do, you are clever enough to say nothing about it." His smile was more to console her than to show his approval. "You're young, boy; you don't know what the world can make men do."

"I'm not that young," said Fenice brusquely.

"But surely you understand that there are men, powerful men, who must be very careful as they go about the world. They have enemies, my lad, who would stop at nothing to harm them. Be grateful that God has not put such a heavy burden upon you, and all you must endure is the scrutiny of the Dragon Prince." He took the copy of the treaty and held it up. "And you can rest content in the knowledge that you helped the powerful in times of trouble."

"Dear me," said Fenice, her pride still smarting. "How fortunate that chance should turn out so to my favor."

The nobleman laughed. "What chance? The Athenian was paid by the Dragon Prince to bring the new youth from the market-square, fair as a eunuch or a girl, who spoke Greek and Italian to write for us. No one else would do; the Athenian proposed two others, who were acceptable to me, but the Dragon Prince insisted on Aeneo."

Now Fenice felt the slither of a grue up her spine and in spite of herself, she shivered. It was all she could do to keep from turning toward the doorway in the hope of catching sight of this Dragon Prince. She turned to the Russian nobleman and said, "Do you know why he did this? Why would he want me above any other? What did he tell you?" The most disturbing question she kept to herself: how had he known about her in the first place?

The Russian made a gesture of ignorance. "Only that you were the copyist he would accept. It was a small enough thing to concede." His chuckle was low and private. "He was grateful to have you brought here. He is a man who is not often grateful."

This was not enough information to satisfy Fenice, but she knew it would be unwise to press the matter; she took the money she was paid, and was pleased when an extra gold piece was added to the others. When she left the room, she turned back once and saw in the far door a shape that might have been a man in a cloak, but might as easily have been the shadow of a curtain.

Libu shook his head, not disapproving but shocked. "You're asking for—I don't know what. Trouble is the least of it." He shaded his eyes against the afternoon sun; in the half-empty market-square the heat of the day imparted a languor beyond anything the demon had brought about.

"I know," said Fenice, her demeanor lively with anticipation. "It's so exciting."

"Do you think so?" asked Libu, his doubt increasing as he saw her enthusiasm.

"I am certain of it," said Fenice; she lowered her voice. "I will follow him tonight, and see where he goes. They told me he is in a house in another quarter of the city. I only want to get a *look* at him. I don't intend to *talk* to him."

"Men of his sort don't like being watched," Libu said, frowning. "You do not know what he might decide to do if he suspects you are . . . are trying to learn more about him."

"Well, he seems to have spied on me," said Fenice. "And if I can find that Athenian again, he will owe me an explanation. And a few coins as well, not that I shall ever see him."

"He's probably long gone. Or the demon got him." He saw the alarm in her eyes; he glanced over his shoulder, then said, "Another one died last night: the same thing, drained of blood. All I know is the man was a foreigner. Nothing else has been revealed. The customs officers are furious and terrified, and who is to blame them?"

"They have never had such misfortune, have they?" she asked, then went on, "They are being foolish, but it is hardly surprising."

"Why is it not surprising?" Libu studied her, cynical amusement making his face look older than his years.

"Because they cannot control the market-gangs. Why should anyone think they would know how to deal with murders?" She folded her arms. "We have lodging for tonight again. I will come to the Old Lighthouse after I have followed the Transylvanian." She saw he was about to protest and took up a more bantering tone. "Oh, don't put on such a face, Libu. I am only proposing to watch him, not to rob him or anything of the sort. Turnabout is fair play."

"It may be among your people; here it is often the road to disaster." He refused to join her laughter as they started toward the docks in order to secure their quarters for another night.

When Fenice had explained her plan to Libu, it had seemed an easy one, something that would have more thrill than fear in it; now that she was making her way along the deserted streets, she could not summon up the same lighthearted enjoyment she had had when she had decided to undertake to follow the Transylvanian. After finding her way back to the Russian house, she had waited for the Transylvanian to leave, and was shocked to see how quickly he moved; she almost had to run to keep up with him. The streets he chose were old ones, twisted and unpaved; in winter most of them would have been impassable. Fenice stumbled on the uncertain footing more than once, and had to bite her lip to keep from crying out when she twisted her ankle on an ancient rut.

Twice she had nearly been waylaid by men with weapons; both times she was able to elude them, but the necessity left her rattled, a sensation that increased when she realized how far she had gone beyond the streets around the market-square: much as she hated to admit it, Fenice knew she was now lost. Wherever the Transylvanian Dragon Prince was staying, Fenice would never be able to find it again—assuming she was able to make her way back to the Old Lighthouse; that was becoming a more remote possibility with every halting step she took through the close-leaning houses that fronted the passage.

Then ahead there was a wide avenue leading to a gate; Fenice saw the

Dragon Prince striding away from the gate, as if going back the way he had come. Slipping out of the protective darkness into the baleful glare of the waning moon, Fenice felt as if she must be instantly visible; the Transylvanian made no sign that he was aware of her, for he continued on his way, relentless as a hunter in the field. Fenice stared after him, and began to follow him, this time at a greater distance. There were fewer places to conceal herself along this thoroughfare and she did not want to be caught.

The avenue ended at a plaza of good size and irregular shape, more trapezoidal than rectangular, with a mosque at one end and a church at the other; Fenice had never seen it before. All the houses around the plaza had shops on the ground floor, and, though boarded up for the night, Fenice could see they sold much finer goods than were offered in the market-square. She hoped she would be able to find her way back in the morning so that she could explore the plaza; her Greek might be more valuable here, and the surroundings were more to her liking than where she had been making her way.

A lamp marked the house of a silk merchant. The Transylvanian stopped there and knocked on the closed door; in a moment it swung open and a man in the costume of Tana stepped out, bowed deeply, and indicated one of the alleys near the house. Fenice could just hear a few words, but they were in a language she did not know, so she had only the courteous tone to guide her. When she was almost certain she would not be seen, she scurried across the plaza and ducked into the alley.

She had to wait a moment for her eyes to adjust to the darkness, and when they did, she had to clap her hand over her mouth to keep from screaming: in the flickering illumination of a lantern, Fenice saw that the Transylvanian, like a monstrous shadow, had the silk merchant in a deadly hold as he bent over him, his mouth to the gory ruin of the merchant's throat. Blood gouted from the wound, hot in the hot night, and the Transylvanian drank it greedily.

Numbed by horror, Fenice backed out of the alley; she was unable to take her eyes from the grisly sight. Only when she was in the plaza once again did she have volition enough to turn and run. And as she did, she heard a voice behind her, rich and mocking: *"Buona notte, ragazza mia."*

Remote in the crowd, I see
Your face, a lamp at midnight.
—Cassandra Fedele

— XIX —

Libu was aware something had happened, but neither questioning nor teasing could make Fenice tell him what she had seen when she followed the Transylvanian. "You cannot know," she said when he tried to pry some information from her. "You would not be safe."

"But what could be so terrible?" he wheedled as they stood by the fountain in the market-square four days after that unthinkable night.

"He spoke to me," she said, trembling in spite of her resolve not to. "In Italian."

"And what is so bad about that?" Libu had heard this much before and still could not grasp why Fenice had been so badly frightened. "Why should Italian be worse than another tongue? What if he had spoken Greek?"

"He *knew*, don't you see? He *knew*." She could not tell Libu what troubled her the most—that the Transylvanian had not only spoken to her in Italian but he had called her *girl*; she knotted her hands together and stared blankly across the market-square to the tables where the customs officials sat: if only she could get up the courage to approach them. She had to earn some money soon; the two gold pieces she held in reserve would not keep her forever, and the Old Lighthouse was paid only through the end of next week. Yes, she insisted to herself, she would have to make some money, and soon, if she was not to be out on the streets at night, or sleeping in the cold porch of the German soldier's tomb once more, anywhere she could be sure was safe. It was now very important to Fenice that she be protected at night, for she knew the danger that waited in the dark: she had seen it.

"Aeneo—what *is* it?" Libu persisted. "You're jumpy as a mouse in a cat's bed." His face showed more than concern; there was fright in his eyes as well.

"It's nothing," she snapped.

"How can it be nothing when you are so changed?" He was ready for rebellion or denial; he was appalled when she started to cry. "Saints and Devils! Aeneo!" he exclaimed, not knowing what to say or do to help her.

Ashamed of this outburst, Fenice turned away and forcefully composed herself; when she turned back to Libu, she was once more in control of her fear. "It is all the murders. Try as I will, I cannot keep from wondering if you or I might be next."

"I will believe that if you like," said Libu, clearly skeptical of this explanation. "But I think the market-gangs have more to do with your fright than the dead men."

She could not resist asking, "Why do you think that?"

"Because you are a sensible fellow and sensible fellows are afraid of the market-gangs; there is one murderer and there are many market-gangs, and those of us who sell our skills—such as they are—in the market-square are more likely to be harmed by the gangs than by any hungry demon." He gave her a smug smile to show he was not angry with her. "I think you know they will want to teach you a lesson."

This had not occurred to Fenice until now, not as a genuine threat, and she made herself stare at him without showing any more fright. "They won't bother with me," she said at last.

"I hope you may be right," said Libu, doubt in every aspect of his body. "Just the same, I should be careful. The market-gangs have little reason to wish you well and many reasons to harm you." He studied her face. "If you like, I will stay close to you for the next several days, until the worst is past."

The generosity of his offer made tears come to her eyes; she wiped them away with the back of her hand. "Oh, Libu. You don't have to do that."

"And you didn't have to pay for my room at the Old Lighthouse, but you did," he said. "I am not a very reliable creature, Aeneo. I am a beggar, and that means I will sell even my soul if the price is high enough; all of us would. But I know real kindness when it is before me, and I will respect it for all those times when there was no kindness at all."

Fenice had to bite the insides of her cheeks to keep from weeping. She could not make her voice as gruff as she wanted, so she only gave him a terse nod before she went to offer her translating skills to a young customs official who could not read Latin.

That night Fenice kept to her room at the Old Lighthouse, the door closed and firmly latched. She lay huddled on the bed, the sour-smelling blankets drawn up to her face, trying to keep awake in case someone—she would not let herself think who—should try to break in. As the night deepened her resolve grew weaker, and without knowing it, she drifted asleep.

Once asleep she dreamed: *A city lay at her feet, which she saw from a great height, as if she hovered in the air. Its dark shapes were unknown to her, but she did not find this troubling; she noticed spires and domes, minarets and cupolas, some with a moonlit glow of gold or silver.*

Then a voice spoke behind her. "What do you say? Shall we plunder them?"

She spun around to see the hawk-faced companion of her other night-fancies. She faltered as she saw the ferocity lambent in his eyes.

He touched her shoulder. "Come, come," he chided her. "Has your spirit forsaken you? Have you let fear sap your courage?"

Fenice shook her head repeatedly, though she knew she worried it might be true. "I have not lost my—"

"Bravado?" he challenged. "Is that all you have? Or can you seize the world by the throat and wrest all good things from it?"

In her dream she was briefly transported to the place where she had seen the silk merchant die at the hands of the Transylvanian; she banished this memory with a valiant cry. "I will have the good things," she declared.

"Then you must take them," said the man, his arms going around her, stronger than arms could be. "As I will."

She had not thought she wanted his kisses, but her dream showed her she was wrong; she could not deny the rising need that gathered within her. As his kiss deepened, she began to struggle as if against drowning, but he would not release her; slowly, as if against her will, she returned his passion, and when he loosened his hold, she swayed on her feet as if the embrace were real and not the work of a dream. Her pulse fluttered in her throat as she contemplated her companion. "Why did you do that?" she asked him at last.

"If you are to have all the good things of this world, you must begin with the flesh, for it is all of life." He stroked her short-cropped hair. "Be reborn, like your name, from your fires."

Fenice heard his voice as if it came from the sky and her veins at the same time. She made herself face him, trying to contain her strength for his testing of her; at the same time she felt her will suborned to his, and she chided herself in her dream for this weakness. She spoke no words, but she summoned up defiance and flung it back at him in silent accusation.

"You have borne much," he agreed. "Now claim what you have earned for yourself." This time when he touched her it was to direct her toward the city beneath them. "They have imposed upon you; why should you not have recompense?"

"How can I?" she asked, and dreaded the answer as much as she longed to hear it.

"I will help you," said her companion. "Look there, where that powerful man has bartered away his daughter for greater fortune. Should he not answer for what he has done to his child? Has she not become as much merchandise as the dyes he trades in?"

"It is the way of the world," said Fenice, hating herself for admitting it.

"The world will not change without . . . incentive. If this man suffers for what he is doing, he might not do it again. If no one gives him cause to question his decision, he will do the same for all his daughters." He laughed angrily. "Is your rebellion nothing more than pique?"

Fenice shook her head vehemently. "I would not have done so much from pique."

"Then demand what you have earned," said her companion, insinuation turning his meaning ambiguous.

Somehow they were now in a grand house, filled with treasures. A man in robes of silk and velvet lounged on a Turkish divan, although he appeared to be Greek. His ample body boasted of his wealth as much as the jeweled rings on his fingers. He held a sheet of parchment in his thick fingers that Fenice realized was a marriage contract; the man pursed his lips as he read over the terms of the agreement, nodding critically.

"There he is," said her companion. "Make him pay for all he has done to his daughter, only to increase his wealth."

"But how?" Fenice asked, aware her dream would provide what she sought if her desire was great enough.

"You can kill him," said her companion as readily as if he had recommended she wring the neck of a chicken.

"I have no weapon," Fenice protested, her voice sounding strange to her ears, neither apprehensive nor affronted.

Her companion shook his head as if dealing with a recalcitrant child; though the room was bright with lamps and candles, Fenice could not see his features clearly—he continued cloaked in his own shadow. "Then I will teach you. Watch me, and learn."

Not knowing what would happen, Fenice stood aside as her companion advanced like a mass of night on the unsuspecting man. Reaching out he dragged the man to his feet, seized him, and bared his neck.

As the blood pulsed out, Fenice awoke with her fist in her mouth to keep from screaming.

For the next two days, Fenice did not venture beyond the market-square and the Old Lighthouse; her dream haunted her with an intensity that she found it difficult to shake off. To her chagrin, she discovered she could only feel truly safe in the most familiar places. She told herself that the reason for it was that the dream so exactly repeated what she had seen the Transylvanian do to the silk merchant that her revulsion sprang from her horror at the memory and not from the dream itself; the rumors that there had been more killings kept her emotions in turmoil, for she could not rid herself of the anxiety that she might in some way be responsible because of what she witnessed, both on the street and in her dreams. These reservations increased at night, when she worried that her dream might be repeated.

After an intolerable morning, Fenice decided she had to rid herself of her misgivings or succumb to dread. Over a silent breakfast with Libu, she upbraided herself for cowardice and then suddenly declared aloud, "I'm going to follow the Transylvanian again," as if speaking her intentions aloud would make them more real.

Libu stared at her. "So that's what you've been thinking about," he said.

"Yes." She brought her chin up in order to seem more determined. "I didn't find out what I wanted to find out." It was a lie; she feared Libu would sense it, so she went on. "I think he may have done something . . . something very wrong."

"You mean you think he might be the mysterious murderer?" Libu's question was so uncannily accurate that Fenice gasped. "Why would he do anything so reckless, Transylvanian or not? Everyone says they are wild men, but that does not mean he must be the killer."

"Still," said Fenice indirectly. She drank her tea and did not say anything more until just before they left the place, when she could not keep from reiterating her request. "Keep watch for me, will you, Libu? On what the Russians do?"

"They are going to be leaving soon," Libu said, glad to have a bit of information Fenice apparently did not know.

She stopped him with a frown. "Who says so?"

"The butcher who sells them meat," Libu told her. "If the Russians leave, so will the Transylvanian."

"Perhaps," said Fenice, making herself smile to reassure him. "All the more reason for me to follow him while I have the chance."

Libu shook his head, amused by her emphatic manner. "You will live up to your name, won't you?"

Similar words from her dream shocked her as they echoed in her mind. "I . . . I suppose," she replied, and tried to regain her composure. "If I do not, how can I keep my name?"

Libu laughed and gave her ribs a friendly poke. "If the Russians had any sense they would take you with them. But they won't. They're Russians," he said, and chuckled as they walked out into the hazy morning: he made a grand, ironic gesture to take in the weather. "It is going to be hot by noon but the mist may still linger," he said. "When we have this kind of mist at dawn, the day is sweltering."

Fenice recalled the low-lying fogs of Venice and for an instant she suffered a pang of homesickness that was as painful as it was unexpected; she longed for the sight of the domes of San Marco and the sound of the monks singing across the canal. "Are there mists in winter, as well?" She did her best to sound lighthearted.

"When the wind permits," said Libu. "But we have more still days in summer, and the fog comes then."

She nodded, wondering distantly if she had been wrong about leaving everything behind. It would be hard never to see her family again—and she knew in her bones she had gone beyond anything they could forgive—yet she had to resign herself to it, or all of her enterprise was wasted. She stood a little straighter. "Then we had best get to making money before the day is too hot for anyone to move."

Libu set off beside her; if he had any questions, he kept them to himself. As they approached the central market-square the mists grew brighter, making the whole area seem a place of brilliant phantasms. Libu shook his head. "They could give me a dragon to hold today and I would not realize it."

The unreality of the market-square reminded Fenice of her dream the other night, and she winced at what she recalled. She stared into the glowing mist and made herself move along with a jaunty stride; this was not the way to defeat her fear. "I'll see if any of the customs men know about the Transylvanian," she told him as they prepared to separate for the morning. "I'll make my plans when I find out."

"Remember, Transylvanians are a strange, mad race. No one knows what they may do, and no one wishes to offend them, for they are not forgiving.

You may decide it isn't wise to follow him." Libu held up a warning finger which he cocked at Fenice. "And be careful of the Russians, Aeneo. They're mad, too."

"Is there anyone who isn't mad—other than you, of course?" Fenice asked, and hoped he would answer her.

"Oh, I don't think so. And I may be the maddest of all." He waved as he went to the fountain in the center of the market-square, becoming indistinct and shining in the hazy light.

Fenice felt the hair rise on her neck, as if Libu had turned into a ghost before her very eyes. Without thinking, she crossed herself before starting toward the customs tables, where she hoped she would earn a few pieces of silver.

The first employment she got was with a trader from Otranto who could not read in any language: he was patently relieved to hear Italian spoken, even in the Venetian dialect. He shoved half a dozen sheets of vellum at Fenice and demanded to be told what they meant.

Fenice managed five of the six, but could not help with the one bill-of-lading in Turkish. She admitted that her command of the local tongue was slight—she had learned many words and phrases since her arrival, but anything more than basic conversation was beyond her—but that she could conduct his inquiries in Greek, if that was acceptable; the customs officials would be able to understand Greek and they would not cheat him too badly. She came away from those tasks with one golden florin and two silver ships: the Greek had been generous. He had also confessed a fondness for young eunuchs and might have paid much more for more personal services.

While she shared noonday fruit and cheese with Libu, she recounted her morning, saying, "I think he would pay several gold coins for having me . . . meet him."

"You'd do better with the trader than the Transylvanian," said Libu. "But monks don't sell themselves easily, do they?"

This observation made Fenice very uncomfortable. "I . . . I could not."

"Not to a trader from Otranto, in any case. You might give yourself to a bishop, or a high-born lord." He winked. "They probably pay better."

Fenice found her cheese hard to swallow. "Probably," she said, and coughed.

"But if the trader is very grateful, you could make a tidy sum," Libu went on mercilessly. "You might find yourself kept in style. Until he grew bored with you, and sold you to a brothelkeeper on Cyprus or in Spain." He relented, knowing Fenice was very uncomfortable with such raillery. "Follow the Transylvanian. It's what you want to do."

"I suppose it is," she said quietly. "I have to know what I saw was . . . what I saw."

"The ever-mysterious," said Libu, rolling his eyes. "If the Transylvanian did it, it could be almost anything."

Fenice nodded twice. "I know. Strange people, the Transylvanians." She made herself laugh, not wanting to put Libu too much on his guard. She would find a way to deal with him later, when she was certain that the Dragon Prince of Transylvania was the ruthless slaughterer of merchants she thought he was. She could not forget the mockery in his voice as he had called after her in Italian, and she had done all she could to persuade herself that she had imagined it—that she had heard Italian words when he had said something else that she could not understand. If she followed him again and nothing happened, she would know that she had not seen what she thought she saw. All the while she knew beyond all doubt that she had not been mistaken, that he had drunk the blood of the silk merchant just as her companion had done to the wealthy man in her dreams.

If she were ever to have her dreams back, she had to prove she had erred.

"You look tired," said Libu. "Do you have to work any more today?"

"It's the heat," said Fenice. "I'll come back in the afternoon, when it's cooler."

"Go to Ipani's stable. He'll let you sleep in the loft for a copper. The market-gangs won't bother you there; Ipani is too important for them to try to steal from him. Tell him I sent you to him," Libu said, shoving her gently in the direction of the stable. "If you're determined to go out tonight, you'll need your rest now."

She managed to show amusement. "One trouble at a time. I know."

He took a bite of fruit, and while the juice ran down his chin, he said, "Go on. I'll see you when you get up."

Gaetano rose from his knees and crossed himself; beside him his family did the same. The echoing interior of the Basilica of San Marco still rang with the last notes of praise to God and blessings on His people. There was white in his beard and his hair that had not been there six months ago, and the line between his brows had deepened. He smiled wanly at his wife as he helped her to her feet, saying, "Aurelio will call at noon."

"Again?" Rosamonda asked. "Has he learned something new?"

"I don't know," said Gaetano, sighing as he knelt in the aisle to cross himself. "I cannot let myself hope any longer. It's too painful."

Rosamonda also knelt and crossed herself. "Should we do as Padre Danare suggests, and have the *Requiem* sung for her, in case she . . . in case she needs it?" She could come no nearer to admitting her daughter might be dead.

"I don't know," Gaetano said, becoming testy as they left the basilica and stepped out into the morning heat of the Piazza San Marco.

Much of Rosamonda's vivacity was gone. She followed her husband as submissively as a nun would, and her expression was somber. They walked through the crowded piazza and along the Rio Sant' Angelo, saying nothing. Eloisa brought up the rear, her Testament clutched in her hands so tightly that she might have been intending to tear the little book in half.

A meal was laid out at their house, but none of them had much appetite; they sat down together and picked at the food, their silence making the occasion more glum than any conversation would have done. Finally, as they sipped Lachrymi Christi, Aurelio was announced.

"Do not disturb yourselves," he said as he bent to touch cheeks with Gaetano and Rosamonda. "I will not be here long."

"You have learned something?" Rosamonda asked in spite of her intention not to.

"Nothing that you do not already know, and nothing that Febo or Lionello could not have discovered for themselves while they were here," he replied regretfully. "But I have come upon a new source of information, and I am off to ask questions. I am hopeful that these men may have learned something that will assist me." He saw the skeptical light in Gaetano's eyes, and said, "These men are pilgrims and have traveled far; they hear many things. I cannot say if they will tell us anything of use, but they are known to be reliable."

"Pilgrims?" said Rosamonda. "What sort of pilgrims are they?"

"They have been told to visit every healing shrine between Paris and Jerusalem." He coughed. "They have the French Disease and nothing has helped them thus far. They will bear true witness as long as they are unhealed; their bishop vouches for them." He glanced at Eloisa. "I am sorry to speak of such things before her."

Eloisa shrugged. "I know about the French Disease—who does not?"

"But mightn't they be mad, and tell you madmen's fancies as the truth?" Gaetano asked, not wanting to let himself hope again.

"They are not, according to the bishop who authorized their pilgrimage. Don't worry," he said with as much encouragement as he could summon up, "I will not be led astray by crazed maundering. I have every desire to winnow out lies, deliberate or accidental." He bowed to Fenice's parents. "I still believe she will be restored to us."

"May God reward your faith," said Rosamonda, ashamed of her own doubts. "If you discover anything that may lead to . . . to recovering her, come back as soon as you may to let us know."

"Of course," Aurelio promised. "I could not keep anything significant from you." He lowered his eyes. "I have a few questions to ask them on the Doge's behalf, as well. We will garner something of value, no matter what; it may only be which harbors the Turks chain closed at night, or how many galleys are being built at Famagusta, which will aid the Doge. I pray most devoutly that they will tell us where to find Fenice."

"And the Doge?" Gaetano could not hide his worry that Aurelio would put Venetian concerns above those of Zucchar.

"He knows my purpose; I have made it plain that I am more eager to find your daughter than to advance his struggle against the Ottomites. I am sure he understands this. He has only asked that I do what I can to assist him in concert with my inquiries about Fenice." Aurelio looked from Gaetano to Rosamonda to Eloisa and back to Gaetano once more. "You have endured much, and I am honored that you allow me to share your grief. If I had the power to summon up the spirits of the air, so that they would show me where Fenice has gone, I would do it. As it is, I must confine my inquiries to men who have been about the world and have gone places where secrets are whispered. I will continue in this manner until I have learned her whereabouts, or that she has perished. You may rely on me."

Rosamonda's eyes filled with tears. "I pray we may find her, so she may know how fine a man she chose. Most suitors would not want to claim any woman as his bride who has been gone as long as Fenice has."

"May God shine His Face on you," added Gaetano.

"If God will show me how to find her, I will be grateful for His Mercy all of my days," said Aurelio as he bowed once more and prepared to leave.

Eloisa's question stopped him. "Do you really think she's still alive? After all this time?"

Aurelio turned to her. "If God is merciful, she is," he answered, then left them.

The room was still; then Eloisa asked, "Do you believe him?"

"I want to," Rosamonda admitted, her voice dropping to just above a whisper.

"I believe he believes," said Gaetano at the same time.

"Well," said Eloisa with a toss of her head, "I believe he is enjoying himself. I believe Aurelio is becoming more a servant of the Doge than he was ever suitor to Fenice. That's what I believe." So saying, she rose and left her dumbstruck parents alone with the remains of their meal.

By nightfall the mist had thickened, filling the air with counterfeit brightness. The lamps at the market-square were fuzzy balls of luminescence casting no shadows; Fenice stood with Libu at the fountain, feeling as if she were a vast distance from the lamps, perhaps adrift on the sea. The fog changed everything, making everything indistinct. "I'll come back to the Old Lighthouse when I'm done," she said, handing him a silver coin. "Make sure they hold my room for me."

"You're determined to do this, aren't you?" he asked with resignation.

"Yes. I have to, Libu." She closed his fingers around the coin.

"You could always sleep with me, you know, and save the money," said Libu, fingering the silver as if unwilling to give up so easily. "You'd be safe. I'm not like that merchant this morning. I won't do anything to you, Aeneo."

Fenice was glad the fog hid her face; her cheeks were scarlet. "Have them save the room," she repeated. "Tell them I will be very late. The watchman will have to let me in."

"All right," said Libu. "Are you sure you can find your way in this?" He was reluctant to part from her. "Another night might be clearer."

"Another night he may well be gone," she said, adding to herself that she would never free her dreams from that terrible murder if she had no answers from the Transylvanian.

Libu surrendered. "Well, it should not be so thick away from the water."

"I hope so," Fenice said, stepping away from him into the fog. The echoes of her feet striking the paving stones seemed to be louder because of the mist. She stopped to listen, and heard other footfalls; she chided herself for the flare of fear within her—it was obviously Libu leaving the market-square. She reminded herself that she would have to be levelheaded if she was going to succeed tonight. "The fog is good," she murmured. "It gives me somewhere to hide." This reminder did not reassure her as she intended it should, but it was enough to keep her from losing heart completely and abandoning her search for the night.

She left the market-square behind for the darkness of the streets; she made her way to the house where the Russians were, and from there set out in what she hoped was the right direction. As she got further from the waterfront the fog did become less enveloping, as she had hoped it would; the streets were unfamiliar, but the greater visibility made her go on. Once she thought she heard other footsteps, but she could not be sure where they came from; she also had to stop and peer into the filmy night several times in response to the unpleasant sensation that she was being watched. Eventually more by accident than design she stumbled upon the house with the emblem of the Dragon Prince hung above the gate. The shield was lit by torches and the massive gate was shut.

Fenice stopped, perplexed. Was the Dragon Prince inside the gates, or was he out roaming the streets searching out stray merchants to drain of blood? The question now seemed absurd, and Fenice did her best to laugh; the hollow sound shuddered along the stone fronts of the houses, fading into the mists.

Then she heard a scuffle of feet nearby, and she swung around, her back to the gate, to face what was emerging from the haze; her pulse was loud in her ears. "Who is there?" She was glad her voice was steady; her hands were trembling.

There was no answer at first, and she was beginning to think she had been scared by nothing more than the city watchman when she saw two young men coming toward her, like wraiths taking on bodies. She pressed against the gate again as she recognized them as companions of the market-gang leader who had been killed. The knife she carried now seemed woefully inadequate.

Two more young men appeared, one of them holding a sling with a stone in it, the other caressing a heavy length of wood. Both of them were smiling in lupine anticipation. Fenice recognized them as being part of a larger gang—there were nine or ten of them; these were the most dangerous.

"You killed Jed, eunuch. You killed him." The tallest of the young men was more than a head taller than Fenice, and used to threatening people with his height. He deliberately loomed toward her, casually making knots of his hands.

"I didn't kill him," said Fenice, keeping her back to the gate. "He was alive when I left."

"You let him die," said the one with the length of wood. "It makes no difference. He is dead because of you."

Fenice did not dare to take her eyes from the four young men; in the time it would take her to find a place to bolt, they would be on her. She swallowed hard against the growing tightness in her throat.

"Eunuchs are useless," said the young man with the sling, hefting his weapon experimentally. "No one would miss you."

"Tell us what we should do," said the tallest in a low tone intended to frighten her. "Should we kill you or sell you to the Greeks? They *like* eunuchs."

"If we sell him, we get something for Jed," the youngest pointed out, jeering. "But will they pay enough for such a scrawny boy as he is? We would have to divide the money among all eleven of us, and that would not leave much for each. Why don't we just kill him?"

It was hard for Fenice to think; she was panting in fear, and her body felt heavy and unwieldy, as if she were moving in water. She tugged her knife out of her belt and held it in front of her. This simple act ended the sensation of impotence, but it also made her so jumpy that she could not concentrate.

"Oh. A knife," said the one with the sling. "I'm so frightened." He sniggered as the others joined him in taunting her. "What're you going to do with that b-i-i-i-i-g knife?"

"Make you a eunuch, too?" the tallest suggested, his hands covering his groin.

"Look!" cried the one with the sling, and swung his arm so that the sling became a blur.

"Don't get too close," the one with the length of wood warned in exaggerated dread. "He might hurt you."

Fenice gripped her knife more tightly and prepared to run at the first opportunity. She did not waste breath on words; she would not give them the satisfaction of answering their challenges.

"Let's try him out first, so we can tell the Greeks if he's worth it," the tallest suggested.

The terror that flooded through Fenice's veins made her bones hurt. She hated them for their laughter, for being amused by her plight. Goaded by panic to action, she flung herself toward the small gap between the first two young men and the second two, hoping to confuse them enough to have a few precious heartbeats to run.

The sling snapped, and something struck her a glancing blow above the temple; light painful as splintered glass burst inside her skull. With a wail of despair, she fell forward, rolling, unconscious.

Love and the noble heart are the same thing
As the sage has said . . .
—Dante Alighieri

— XX —

Hands were groping for her belt as Fenice came to; before she knew what she was doing, she kicked out and slammed her heel into a bent knee. The joint made a scraping pop, and the man dropped his weapon. Howling, he went down, curling up with his hands over the joint, which bent at an unnatural angle. His face was pasty in the golden torchlight, and his forehead shone with sweat. Slowly he began to drag himself away from the fight he had thought was won.

"Look out!" shouted the tallest as Fenice continued to kick and strike out with her fists.

"Not a bad fighter for a eunuch," said the youngest one, trying to confine her hands so that they could get the clothes off her.

Fenice realized with sudden, cold certainty that she would be raped and killed if they discovered she was not a eunuch. This gave her strength as no fear could. She struck upward with the heel of her hand and slammed the youngest one's nose back against his face; there was a crunch of breaking cartilage and the youth fell back screaming, his hand pressed to his face to stop the stream of blood. There were two more to fight, and Fenice knew they would be the most difficult to defeat.

"Want me to smash his head again?" asked the one with the sling.

"Not yet. He's still good for some fun," said the tallest, stepping back far enough to get out of range of Fenice's hands and feet. "Feisty."

"Some Greeks like them that way," said the slingbearer.

"Then let's find out if we do, too," said the tallest, bending down and reaching for her hair. "I'll bang his head on the stones and he'll be more reasonable."

Fenice kicked out at his leg, but the man moved back, muttering a curse as he did. "Don't touch me!" she shouted at them as she rolled away from his sudden kick. She wondered if she should have tried to grab his foot and trip him, but knew that he was big enough and heavy enough that she was not likely to succeed.

"Don't let him get away," the one with the sling ordered sharply.

The youth with the broken nose hunkered down against the wall, whimpering as he held his hands out, staring aghast at the blood that filled his palms and ran through his fingers.

"Be quiet, Mocti," said the tallest one. "You did a stupid thing."

Mocti's face was red with gore. "I . . ." He stopped as the tallest one shot him a threatening look.

Fenice took advantage of this brief distraction to feel for her knife: it had been knocked out of her hand when she was struck with the stone, and she hoped she could find it in time to use it. She thought she saw the gleam of steel at the edge of the light cast by the torches, and she rolled toward it, afraid to try to get to her feet while the men were still close enough to knock her down again. She felt the blade as it cut her finger, and she stifled a cry of relief as she grabbed the hilt; she did not care about the cut, for it meant she was armed once again.

"Look out. He's trying to get away," the tallest one said with scorn. "Grab him."

The man with the sling readied another stone. "That bruise is pretty bad. He won't get back on his feet. He can't run back to the market-square: the rest of us will stop him there and make him regret running at all." He approached Fenice almost casually, swinging his sling suggestively. "If you don't fight, we won't have to hurt you. If you surrender to us, you will not have to face the rest of our gang."

Fenice cursed him in the roughest terms she had heard the sailors on the *Impresa* use.

"The boy can swear—that's something," said the tallest one.

"Not that it matters," said the man with the sling; he reached out suddenly and caught the front of Fenice's clothes, ripping the giaquetta down the front.

Because of the heat she had worn nothing beneath it. Fenice tried to pull the cloth across her chest, but it was too late.

"Oho," said the man with the sling. "This makes a difference."

The tallest one leered in anticipation. "We must teach her a lesson." He came nearer. "Are you going to cut me?" His chuckle said he thought this was impossible.

"If I can," said Fenice, pulling herself into a low crouch; her head throbbed where the stone had struck her and she had to swallow against nausea as she prepared to fight them.

The man with the sling was moving to her right, while the tallest one was going to her left; she would not be able to face them both at once. They would come from the sides, or from behind, and they would win. She could not endure that. She ran at the tallest man, striking out with the knife, not upward, but down into his thigh; she tugged the knife toward her as it sank into his flesh, slicing a long gash from the edge of his hip, across the side of his leg and almost to the tendons at the back of his knee.

As he roared with pain he flung his arms up, preparing to bring them down on her.

Fenice pulled the knife out of his flesh and scampered away from him, horrified and pleased as she saw him stagger and then collapse; he tried to staunch his wound, but could not.

Surely, she thought, someone must hear this. Someone must know that a dreadful fight was taking place. Surely the Dragon Prince would not allow her to be raped and murdered in front of his gate.

The man with the sling had kept his distance, trying to gauge how to bring her down; he was no longer taunting her. Anger showed in his deep-set eyes and he maintained his distance, a rock loaded into his sling. "You will pay, bint."

She had no doubt he meant it, and she knew he was by far the most dangerous of the men she had faced; she was sure he intended to kill her. She kept her knife at the ready, frustrated by the distance between them and at the same time glad to have a little time to prepare for the most demanding contest of her life. Three things, too ephemeral to be thoughts, flickered through her mind as she faced her tormentor: she might have been pregnant by now had she stayed in Venice and married Aurelio; no one in her family would ever know what happened to her, or how she had ended her life; it wasn't fair to have so few months for her adventure after all she had risked—all she had given up—to achieve it.

The man with the sling was weaving a bit, dodging so that Fenice had to concentrate on his movements and could not plan what she could do to escape him; she realized he was trying to get her confused enough that he could attack her with limited danger to himself. She forced herself not to be too caught up in his movements—to watch him without being distracted from her own task: she had to escape him, somehow.

"Your crippled friend told us where to find you," said her attacker, his words aimed with the same deadly intention as his rock would be.

"Libu?" she could not stop herself from asking: she would not give him the satisfaction, or the advantage, of seeing how this distressed her. Had Libu really told them? What had they done to him? Why had he told them? Why would he— She made herself ignore these questions, fixing her mind on her knife and the man with the sling.

"We only had to smash one of his hands before he gave you up," he said. "The rest of our company has him as a prisoner, and he will suffer if you cause any more trouble."

Nausea hit Fenice like a fist. She gagged and felt tears smart in her eyes. "It's a lie," she muttered, not wanting him to hear her.

The man with the sling laughed. "See if it is. If ever you meet him again." He increased the swing of his weapon. "You must know what is going to happen to you, bint. Why not make it easy on yourself and give yourself to me? I won't have to hurt you if you do."

From some unknown reservoir of strength, Fenice found the power to laugh in return. "You will kill me. That is what you will do. I will not make that easy for you."

He shifted his stance slightly: she had surprised him. "If you insist," he said. "Remember when you are bleeding and your bones are broken that you chose it."

"You haven't got me there yet," she answered back, too desperate to keep from this act of audacity; she needed to hear her contempt for him more than she needed to husband her breath.

"Very well," said the man, moving a little closer, his sling spinning.

Fenice moved back until she was up against the gate of the Dragon Prince's house; she could not convince herself that it provided her any real protection. Her head ached wretchedly and she could feel her courage beginning to ebb. She held her knife as tightly as she could, not caring that her hand cramped.

The man let the rock fly; it struck Fenice low in the chest, driving the air out of her: the knife flew from her hand. As she bent double, he rushed her, and slammed her against the gate, raising his knee to separate her legs. Panting with excitement, he shoved her upright as he wrestled her torn giaquetta off her.

"Get. *Off!*" she hissed in his ear through bruised lips, struggling to break free of his weight.

He cuffed her where his first rock had struck her head, and chuckled when she cried out. "Do what I say, bint. I'll hurt you if you don't."

Through a haze of pain, she felt him grope for the cord of her hose and knew he would soon overpower her; she could not bear it. Then something Febo had told her long ago came back to her: she had been not quite fourteen, and he had taken her aside to tell her how to protect her honor if ever she were attacked. Repugnant as it was to touch this predator, she did not doubt it was the only thing that would save her. Summoning up the last of her fortitude, she reached between his legs and grabbed his penis and testicles and twisted them as far around as she was able to as hard as she could.

The man pounded his fists into her shoulders, then went still. Very slowly he dropped to his knees, his face quite white, his mouth open, his eyes wide and set. As his knees touched the ground, he vomited.

Repelled and exhausted, Fenice stumbled a few steps away from him; she had to get away, but where could she go? She was almost naked. If she went back to the Old Lighthouse she would be turned away or welcomed as a harlot, and she could not endure either. She huddled under the torch and tried to make herself think over the keening in her skull: she did not know if it was the pain of her injury or the sounds her attacker was making. She became vaguely aware that the other young men were still now, and she could not understand how that should be.

She tried to take two steps without the support of the gate and discovered that her knees would not support her. But she had to get away. The realization that her peril was not over struck her with renewed force; she looked about the dark streets for an escape. She felt her eyes become as penetrating as lanterns as she pierced the darkness; her vision was intense as she swept the entrances to the three streets converging on the house of the Dragon Prince: it tangled on the gaze of demanding, charcoal-colored eyes.

"You did well," said the man in the long, dark Hungarian robes as he strode into the circle of light from the torches; his Italian was very good, and she recognized the voice.

Fenice was appalled. "You saw?" she gasped as she held her arms crossed over her small breasts. "You?"

"All of it," he told her, looking back toward the young men who were so very still.

Anger fed her next question. "And you did nothing?"

"You did not need my help," he said, nudging the last of her attackers with his foot. "What do you want done with this offal?"

She could not grasp all of what he told her. "I . . . what do you mean?" She began to shiver as the command she had had over herself slipped away.

"I mean: what do you want to happen to him?" He reached down and dragged the man to his feet; the youth made a futile attempt to break free of the newcomer's hold. "He was ready to rape you and murder you afterward. What should I do to him?"

In the light from the torches, Fenice glimpsed the hawk-face she had seen only in dreams. Surely that was impossible: she had conjured up a face she knew to reassure herself. She could not make herself speak.

"As you like," said the stranger; he lifted the whimpering young man in the air and with a sudden action, broke his neck and bent over his exposed throat.

Fenice crossed herself, remembering the fate of the silk merchant and the things she had seen in her dreams. "But—how can you?" she said quietly, so wholly aghast at what she witnessed that she had nothing more to remark upon.

"You wanted this," said the stranger, blood running from his mouth as he spoke. "Do not deny it; you wanted him as dead as he wanted you."

Fenice was unable to speak, unable to move; all the horror of the night pressed in upon her, and she closed her eyes so that she would not have to watch the stranger feed. Bad enough that she had been attacked, bad enough that they had found out she was female, but worst of all was that they should die like . . . sheep. Her body felt cold, far colder than the night air. She put her shaking hands to her face, aware that the man who had attacked her had paid a dreadful price. Much as she wanted him dead, she could not feel anything but humiliation at what had become of him. She wanted to offer some excuse for what she had let happen, but words failed her.

The stranger released the young man, letting his body fall like so much refuse. "It was what you wanted," he told her.

"I . . . I don't know," she admitted, unwilling to look at the heap at the stranger's feet. "You killed him." She spoke without emotion, as if the accusation were too encompassing for her to express; she wanted to see his face clearly, convinced she would be less afraid if she could see him plainly just once.

"He would have raped and murdered you. He does not deserve your consideration," said the stranger. "If you have pity for him, you waste it."

"But you—" She had wanted him dead, she knew, but not this way, and not at the hands of this stranger. Shadow still obscured his countenance; she wanted to see him, and at the same time she wanted to escape. The night had been too full of terrors for Fenice to grasp them all. She was appalled to realize that her face was wet with tears. Lord of Angels, for whom did she weep? She despised the market-gang that had waylaid her, and she would have not hesitated to kill them if she could, but it was nearly impossible for her to look on the bodies now that they were dead—she had no doubt they were dead, for the stranger was all too confident for any of them to be left alive. "My head—" she said, to account for her consternation. She was able to stop shaking, but the effort was tremendous.

"Yes," said the stranger with the face from her dreams. "You have been injured."

"He hit my head," she pointed out, unwilling to touch the injury. "He used his sling."

"I saw," said the stranger.

She had no answer to give him: she could not account for her reaction, and did not want to. More than anything she wanted to be gone from this place, from Varna itself. She did not care where she went if only she could get away from . . . She shook herself inwardly. This would not do, she reminded herself sternly. "My giaquetta is ruined," she said, hoping this would account for her silence.

"So it is. And you haven't another with you," said the stranger, and stepped into the light.

Fenice gasped. She could no longer pretend it was not the hawk-face from her dreams. "It can't be," she cried out, beginning to tremble again. Feeling very stupid, she said, "You're not real."

"You should be grateful that I am," he corrected her, his demeanor severe. "You would not enjoy what they would have done to you."

"You're a dream," she protested.

His laughter was low and insinuating. "And what are dreams, but our desires?"

"But you were . . ." Her confidence evaporated at once. "I am grateful, of course," she said, striving to fight down the panic that returned.

"How prudent you are," he said quietly.

"You disdain my efforts?" Fenice demanded.

"No. I admire them." His face was too near hers.

"You . . . you delivered me from . . ."

"Ruin," he said bluntly.

She felt very naked now, and holding her arms over her breasts did not seem enough for modesty, let alone for protection. Her head hurt more fiercely than before and she had to fight the impulse to burst into tears. "Ruin," she repeated, agreeing.

"But you were not ruined," he said, indicating the bodies. "They paid the price for assailing you; be proud of what you have done."

She lowered her head. "I am not sure I could have managed . . . to get away if you had not come."

His sly chuckle made his answer more sinister. "Oh, you would have dealt with them all: you did. But you might not have killed them, and that would have been a mistake." He saw the flash of anger in her averted eyes. "If they had lived, everyone would know you are not a eunuch by first light, and you would have been put into a brothel or a prison. No nunnery would open its doors to you now, not after what you have done." He came a step closer to her. "With them dead, your secret is still secret."

"But for you," she said with a trace of hostility; she dared express nothing more.

"But I, ragazza mia, have never been deceived." He held out a hand, not to touch her, but so that she might touch him.

Without warning she began to cry, not soft, gentle tears, but deep, hard sobs that made the pain in her head much worse. She took his hands to steady herself, and was terrified and relieved when he pulled her against him, supporting her, his arm enclosing her. The comfort he gave her was mixed with a command that troubled her, for she could not put her dread aside; she was in his power and that was as frightening in its way as the four from the market-gang had been: she doubted she would escape from him as she had from those men. Her crying became a keening and she struggled to break free of him. "I can't. I can't. I can't," she repeated as she twisted in his grasp.

"I have you now," he whispered to her.

"I can't," she insisted, failing once again to break his hold on her.

"Contain yourself, Fenice," he said; at the sound of her name she went rigid in his grasp. "Fenice Zucchar, you are safe with me, as you are safe nowhere else in the world." He lifted his hand to stroke her head.

She winced as he touched the blood-matted hair where the rock had struck her; she tried to speak through her weeping, striving to overcome the welter of confused emotions that went through her like a malign tide, pulling her from strength to weakness, from relief to despair, from giddiness to melancholy with such abrupt shifts that she could not keep any sense of balance in her. If she could ignore the bodies in the street, she might be able to work out her feelings, understand their complications. She could not keep from resenting her companion's masterful calm that made her uncontrolled fluctuations the more despicable to her. "I . . ."

This time his chuckle was indulgent, as if she were a recalcitrant child. "You will leave these things to me, Fenice."

"To you? And what will you do?" Another, sharper fear sank its fang in her heart: she was now wholly within his power, and he could do anything—*anything*—with her and no one would ever know. More than anything she had done, he would make her vanish from the face of the earth.

"I will take you into my house," he said.

"And then?" Apprehension put an edge in her words that made her voice breathless and shrill.

"My housekeeper will look after you." He laid his hand on her head again; she shrank as the hurt welled. "You would not prefer to remain in the streets, would you?"

The prospect appalled her. "No," she said, chastened.

"Then let me look after you until you are . . . better." There was a kind of purr in his tone, a low, satisfied rumble that was at once consoling and threatening, like the presence of a great yet untamed cat.

Defeated, she could think of no response that was not spiteful or hazardous. She looked over her shoulder once more at the dead men, and shuddered with abhorrence and wrath. "What about them?"

"They will be gone before morning," he said soothingly, turning her in his grasp so that she could walk beside him. "They need never concern you again."

"You couldn't have let them live? Dear God, four men are dead. Did you have to—?" She knew as she asked that she was glad they were dead, and that she would have never been able to feel safe if they were alive.

"They know you are female. If they had told anyone—and you may be sure they would—you would be in terrible danger. As it is, you will not be entirely safe from them when these bodies are discovered." He turned her face toward him, his fingers hard on her jaw. "What do you think?"

She hated herself for wanting to cling to him, for taking such comfort in his presence which might be the greatest deception she had ever encountered; she hated the unsteadiness of her steps and the way she cringed as he kissed her forehead. She had never thought she could be such a paltry creature, soft and without fortitude. When she faltered, he held her up; she hissed her thanks and felt revulsion at her response.

He was not offended. "Your anger is good. It will purge less worthy feelings from your soul."

"I should not be angry with you," she said, shocked to realize she was.

"Your anger cannot hurt me," he told her, amused that she would think it might. "It will lend you strength and you will flourish as you embrace it."

Fenice could think of nothing to say; she had to resist the urge to strike out at the corpses in the street, and disgusted that she could feel such rancor for the dead. "Do we have far to go?"

"Not tonight," he said, turning toward the house of the Dragon Lord. As they walked toward the gate he made a gesture; the doors swung ponderously open in response. "You are welcome to my house," he said.

"Then you are the Dragon Prince?" Fenice asked, amazed that she was not surprised.

"Yes," he said as they entered the courtyard and the gates closed behind them. "I am Dracula."

[How can] . . . a light, vital and pure
Come from inky shadows, or from cinders
Burst forth such shining flames?
—Giambastisa Marino

— XXI —

It was closer to midday than dawn when Fenice woke, her head aching and tender, her body bruised and scraped, her pride in tatters. She was in a curtained bed, on linen sheets, with a feather pillow and a night rail of fine cotton: she could not remember how she came to be here. This was so much like her bed in Venice, and yet so much unlike it that she felt disoriented, anxious; she began to fret, sensing an ill-defined danger that hung about her like a bad odor. Her first attempt at sitting up did not succeed; she lay back groaning while the world rotated around her. The second effort went rather better. By pushing herself up against the headboard, she was able to lever herself upright without making her vision buckle and sway. Turning the pillow up behind her, she pulled back the curtain and looked about the austere chamber. There was a fireplace on the far wall, flanked by shuttered windows. A chest stood next to a clothespress on the right wall. The left wall had a candle sconce on either side of the door. A single chair stood near the fireplace. There was a nightstand next to the bed with a guttered candle in the simple brass stick. Fenice touched the cold puddle of wax at the base of it, hoping it would bring back some recollection of what had happened to her, but without success.

Pushing the sheet back, she lifted the night rail and flinched at what she saw on her skin: bruises and scrapes were everywhere. There was a welt on her hip and another at the base of her ribs *where the man had jabbed her when he had forced her up against the gate, trying to—* She gave a little cry, striving to recall the rest of it, but the images slipped away, turning into dream-wraiths of her hawk-faced companion.

Outside the window there was the distinctive, ominous croak of a raven, and a moment later a handful of pebbles spattered on the outside wall to scare the ill-omened bird away.

Fenice began to slide her legs out of bed, down the side of it; she could not look at the injuries she saw. Averting her eyes, she slipped down to the floor and nearly collapsed from pain and weakness. Dear God, what had happened to her? *Four of them had surrounded her, one with a crude club, one with a sling, and . . .* Again the images evaporated, and she was left clinging to the bedpost as if to a floating spar after a shipwreck.

A respectful tapping at the door brought her attention back to the unfamiliar chamber and the nagging question of how she came to be here. "Open," she called in Italian, then in Greek, and finally in the admixture of Bulgarian and Turkish that was the language of Varna.

"Good day, young woman," said a middle-aged woman in the nondescript, dust-colored clothes of a domestic servant. The woman carried a tray with a bowl of figs and a large, soft bun filled with soft cheese. "The master said you would be hungry."

The sight of food made Fenice salivate but also stirred a twinge of nausea. "I suppose I am," she said warily. Her body ached from her head to her feet, and that penetrating hurt made her chary of eating. "I don't know where you are to put the tray." She spoke in Greek, hoping the woman would understand.

She answered in the local dialect. "I understand Greek well enough, but I do not speak it well. If you can comprehend what I say, you may speak to me in Greek and I will speak my own language."

"That is fine with me," said Fenice in Greek, feeling relieved. "About the tray?"

"If you sit in the chair, the tray is wide enough to rest on its arms," said the woman. "If you need help, I will help you, young woman."

"No. That isn't necessary," said Fenice, finding the notion of help galling.

"Very well, young woman," said the servant, waiting while Fenice did her best to get from the side of the bed to the chair.

Tottering across the space that seemed vast, Fenice thought how strange it was to be called a young woman again; she had just become used to being Aeneo, and now she was being returned to the female sex. What about that sickened her? she asked as she grabbed the back of the chair. *Her giaquetta was torn, and the young men from the market—two? three? four?—had gloated at what they saw—* She felt sweat on her face; she was panting.

"You poor thing. The master said you had been waylaid by outlaws." There was a hint of a question in what she said, although her seamed face was impassive enough.

"I . . . I don't . . . really remember," Fenice confessed, and felt color mount in her face, as if her lack of memory were a greater fault than the cause of her injuries. She got into the chair and waited while the servant put the tray in place. "Thank you."

The woman remained beside her. "I am Olena; I am the housekeeper here." She ducked her head. "My master bought me when I was younger than you are."

Fenice did not know what she was supposed to make of that admission, so she coughed experimentally. "Is there any of the mint tea? I'm very thirsty."

Olena bobbed her head again. "When you have finished your food, I will bring some. The master said that you were to eat before you drink."

This struck Fenice as a bit high-handed, but she held her tongue. "This is his house," she said, making allowances for the man who had saved her from—*from what?* "When I've done, may I have a mirror? I want to see how badly I am—"

"Pardon, young woman, but the master will have no mirrors in his house." Olena shook her head to add emphasis to what she had just said. "He will not allow them."

"No mirrors?" Fenice repeated this, somewhat bewildered. She remembered that Libu had told her that the Transylvanians were wild and strange; perhaps he had been right. *There was something about Libu, something about his hand. The men had told her something about his hand.* The rest was gone as quickly as the recollection had risen.

"Eat, eat, young woman," said Olena anxiously, as if she were responsible for Fenice's appetite. "You must eat."

"All right," said Fenice, breaking off a section of the bun and biting into it slowly; her face was sore and chewing proved more uncomfortable than she thought it would be. Her mysterious host might have been right to insist she eat before she drank.

"The figs are very good," said Olena, as if this were in doubt. "They were preserved in honey from last year's harvest." She leaned forward. "I can bring you more of them if you like them."

"I will have to eat these first," said Fenice. "Allow me a moment to . . . to enjoy them." What did this woman want of her? She took one of the figs and began dutifully to eat it.

"You will have to eat well if you are to recover. This is the time of year of the bad air, what the Italians call the *mal aria,* and you cannot afford to remain weak or the air will poison you. It is essential that you—"

"All right," said Fenice, taking a second fig. "I will eat." Chewing was becoming a little easier in spite of the soreness of her face. What must she look like? She would not know without a mirror. But it could be that ignorance was kindness.

Satisfied that Fenice was not going to refuse her meal, Olena ducked her head again. "I will go fetch tea for you."

"Thank you," said Fenice as the raven croaked again, this time from somewhere overhead.

Olena scowled upward. "The guards should kill it."

"Why won't they?" Fenice asked, disquieted by the reminder of the bird's presence.

"It is bad luck to kill one. It will haunt you if you do," said Olena, as if explaining the obvious.

Fenice had never heard this, but knew each place had its own beliefs. "I doubt they can frighten it away."

"So the master says," Olena told Fenice as she left the room.

Despite her intentions, Fenice did not finish the breakfast Olena had brought: she consumed half the bun and all but two of the figs, but could not endure more. She hoped that the housekeeper would not refuse to serve her tea, for she was very thirsty.

Olena eyed the uneaten food with ill-concealed dismay, but served the tall cup of hot, sweet tea. "The master gave orders you were to be bathed. The bath will be ready in a short while. You will want to prepare."

"I'll be glad of a bath," said Fenice, and wondered who had cleaned her off the night before; she knew she had been dirty and bloody. How had she come to be in a night rail in a bed?

"I will come for you when it is ready," said Olena. "Until then, you might as well rest."

The suggestion that eating a few bites of food might have enervated her to the point of needing sleep made Fenice indignant; for that reason alone it was the more shocking to realize that she actually was tired. Her head felt as if a rat were gnawing on her skull from the inside and her ears rang quietly but persistently. She decided to make her way back to the bed, resolved to nap until she was summoned.

This proved to be more difficult than she had anticipated. After she had pummeled the pillow into a variety of diverse shapes, none of which seemed to give her any repose, she gave up; fixing her gaze on the canopy of the bed, she did her best to reconstruct the previous night. She remembered following the Dragon Prince—Dracula, he called himself, she could recollect that much—through the foggy night to a tall gate. She had been followed. That was also clear to her. Four men from the market-gang had come after her, to take vengeance for the death of their leader. She felt her pulse beat more rapidly. They had goaded her into a fight. She could summon up an image of their jeering faces. She had injured two of them, and then the remaining two had become more . . . dangerous. She had to struggle to keep the thread of her memory intact, for the vision she had of what had happened became more chaotic, and her thoughts shied away from the full event.

The Transylvanian had come when one of the men was . . . was beating her, and something else: something worse than anything.

"Young woman," called Olena from outside the door. "The bath is ready. If you will come to the door, I will take you there."

Walking was less painful than it had been at her first attempt, but Fenice had to go slowly, as if balancing herself on a narrow plank. Her right ankle was swollen and the foot felt swathed in rags. She was proud of herself for reaching the door without stumbling. Now all she had to do was get to the bath and back without incident, and she might have reason to think she would recover.

The bath was in the rear of the house behind the kitchen. No servant was present in the house, no cook worked in the kitchen, as if the house were deserted but for the guards and the housekeeper. There were two large sunken pools, more Turkish than Roman; one was steamy, the other not. The room was dark and smelled of mold and sandalwood.

"There," said Olena, pointing at the two pools. "The hot first and then the cool. Ring that bell"—she indicated a small brass bell near the door—"when you're through and I will bring you fresh clothes."

Fenice stood very still. Clothes. She had no clothes left; even the night rail she wore was not her own. "I . . . I have nothing to wear," she stammered.

"The master has provided clothing for you," Olena informed her as if Fenice should have known this. "Go. Bathe."

As she sank into the warm water, Fenice could feel her muscles try to ease; they ached ferociously for a short while, then began to let go. There were sponges for washing, and salts to apply to her skin. She began tentatively, as if worried she might hurt herself. But gradually she began to scrub with purpose, as if to expunge some terrible blemish from her flesh. Her skin grew rosy, then red and mottled as she wielded the salty sponge with a desperation that baffled her. What was she trying to wash out? She began crying and she told herself it was the sting of the salt that made her weep. If she could remember what had happened, she would be able to be rid of it; as it was, she felt as if it had retreated into her vitals, where it would fester.

"What is it? What is it?" she demanded of the warm, cloudy air.

"Are you all right, young woman?" called Olena from the other side of the bath door.

"Yes! Yes!" Fenice shouted rather wildly. "My cuts hurt me."

"Do you need help?" Olena asked.

"No. I will manage. You are very kind. I am all right." The words came too quickly, but Fenice was unable to stop them.

By the time she emerged from the bathhouse, Fenice was nearly overcome with langor; she had examined the hurts she could see and knew she had been in a serious fight, but she was no closer to bringing it into sharp relief in her mind than she had been when she first woke up.

In the small dressing room, Olena met her with a fine sottana of dull gold damask silk, somewhat old-fashioned in cut, but of superior quality. There was also a simarra of brocaded satin in a deep bronze shade which made Fenice think of the sea just after sunset. She touched the fabrics as if she expected them to vanish.

"The master wants you to wear these," said Olena, as if stating the obvious might cause Fenice to reveal something more about herself.

"Then I will," said Fenice, unsure of herself now that she was being restored to her femaleness.

"You will have to go barefoot for a day or so, the master told me," Olena went on. "He did not know how large your feet are."

"Your master has been generosity itself," said Fenice, and could not help but wonder what the price of that generosity might be.

* * *

Under the hot sun the Black Sea shone like molten brass; the *Impresa* moved steadily across the flat water; in his cabin, Ercole waited for his midday meal, his thoughts caught up in all the events of Varna. He had not been able to put his decision behind him, and it troubled him that he could not.

A scratch on the door told him his food had arrived; at his command, Niccola came into the cabin carrying a tray with a trencher filled with salt cod in a sauce of green peas. He put this on the table but did not turn to go. "I've been thinking about Aeneo," he said, his boldness belied by a tremor in his voice.

Ercole swung around to stare at him. "You dare to talk of my sister?"

"I said Aeneo," Niccola told him, determined to finish now that he had begun. "Aeneo is the boy I knew. I never knew your sister."

"So." Ercole snorted. "You expect me to listen to you?"

"I hope you will, for all the days we have sailed together," he said, and waited for Ercole's answer.

Ercole came and sat down to eat his meal. "Very well. If you must, you must."

This was a daunting beginning, but Niccola folded his arms and began to recite what he had so carefully rehearsed. "I have been thinking that it is a shame that Aeneo cannot continue to be Aeneo." As Ercole shot a disgruntled look at Niccola, he took a deep breath and continued. "I have been thinking that Aeneo is an intrepid lad who has courage and pluck, and that I have not seen many like him in all my years at sea. He is not unmanned by hardships, he does not complain when the voyage is hard, he is not made testy by long hours of solitude and tedium."

"What is the purpose of this catalogue?" Ercole demanded, a wedge of cod on the end of his knife. "Or are you trying to change my mind about the convent?"

"I am," Niccola said without apology, and before Ercole could find words to express his indignation, Niccola hurried on. "Think about it, Captain. This boy could serve on the *Impresa* for years and no one would be the wiser. Who would suspect such a deception? No one. Say that this is a eunuch rescued from the Ottomites, and who is to contest your claim? She loves the sea, Captain, and she is happy when she is sailing. You know what that love is—all your family has it. Why should you be surprised that your sister is like you in this respect? She is not made for life on land, as someone's wife. If you were to keep Aeneo on the ship, who would it hurt? Certainly not you, or her. You would be able to watch over her while the ship plied all the Galleys from Romania to Flanders, and you would be able to keep her from harm."

"Are you insane?" Ercole asked incredulously as he stared at Niccola.

"No. I am being sensible, Captain, if only you would realize it." He glanced at the sea through the open window at the back of the cabin. "Aeneo was so eager to see it all, and I know that no one would be more loyal than he."

"Aeneo is my *sister,*" Ercole reminded Niccola. "What female can serve aboard a ship?"

"Not a female," Niccola said persuasively. "Your brothers all sail. Think of Aeneo as another brother and bring him back to the ship when we return to Varna. You can do it. You need say nothing about your sister unless your father demands it. And Aeneo can continue with the crew."

"That's impossible," Ercole said, laughing to show how absurd he thought it was.

"Only if you will not do it," Niccola said. "The boy has a talent for the sea. You must have seen it had you not been so angry. We will be in Tana soon; on our way back to Varna, think about what I have said, that's all I ask. Go to that convent and bring back not your sister but Aeneo, and make everyone happy."

"I can't do that. I am offended at the very notion." He began to chew on his food with tremendous determination; he said nothing more.

Niccola made a gesture of resignation. "Then, Captain, flog me if you must for saying this, but I hope you will never find her again."

Night had fallen and Varna was once again shuttered and barred against the evils of the dark. Rumors about the deaths of more market-gang men had spread from one end of the city to the other and had spurred even the most complacent inhabitants to take refuge behind stout doors and imposing locks.

In the main hall of Dracula's house a fire illuminated the room where Fenice waited for her host to appear. She was dressed in the fine clothes he had provided; she had done what she could with her cropped hair, but without a mirror, she feared the results were far from satisfactory. She was certain her face was bruised, and she knew there was a lump on her skull where the stone had hit her.

A chill wind came from high above, rushing past her like a silent scream; Fenice felt as if the heat had suddenly been sucked from the main hall, leaving her as cold as a merchant coming from Vienna to Venice in the middle of January. She told herself this was foolishness: it was high summer and the day had been stiflingly hot; now that the sun was down the city was only just beginning to give up the warmth of the afternoon.

"You are feeling better?" Dracula said in Italian as he came out of the shadows, a grand figure in Hungarian court dress of a deep, dusky purple.

"Thank you, yes," said Fenice trying her best to maintain her composure; she could not stop herself from shaking. She had never thought she would have lost her nerve so completely as she appeared to have done.

"I am pleased you are here; I thought you might want to recuperate for a day or so." He came up to her, gallant and remote. She was still amazed by his face; he was aware of it. "You need not be surprised, Fenice. I have longed to know you better for well over a year."

"A year ago, I was in Venice," said Fenice, her eyes fixed on him.

"And you were dreaming of being gone from Venice," he agreed. "You were a wild girl then and you will always be a wild girl." His smile had no mirth in it; she was fascinated.

She let him take her hand; when he kissed it instead of kissing his thumb as custom demanded, she blinked. "You—"

"Surely I know you well enough not to need to stand on ceremony with you? If your brothers can kiss your hand, why not I, who have served you better than any of your brothers have." He did something with his mouth that was not quite a smile. "You have been coming to me for a long time, ragazza mia."

"Why do you call me your girl?" She had not intended to confront him, but his presence left her so perturbed that she spoke before she had planned to.

"Because you are," said Dracula, unflustered by her question. "You have been mine since you began to yearn for adventure. You could not keep away from me once you set your heart on rebellion." He sounded neither approving nor condemning.

"But how?" Her voice rose.

"There are many things that cannot be explained in a few words." He went away from her toward the hearth. "You may not believe it, Fenice, but your journey has only begun."

"My journey where?" she asked, feeling that everything was moving much too fast for her; she could not keep up with what he told her.

"Your journey to me," he answered. "You have come this far and I will take you the rest of the way."

Fighting a rising dizziness, Fenice said, "I was not aware I was coming here. It was by chance that my brother discovered me aboard his ship and put me ashore here." She did not like the way he shook his head, or his indulgent expression.

"If it pleases you to think this was chance, then do so," he offered with a courtier's bow. "You will learn otherwise in time."

She shook her head, unwilling to hear him out. "You are wrong. You are taking advantage of my . . . my enterprise."

His expression was not affable, but his manner was polite. "You may think so."

She rose from the chair, although it made her come far too close to him for her comfort. "I know I am willful and that I have long resisted the wishes of my family. I know that when I determined to leave Venice, I did so in secret, for no one would have helped me, not even Febo, if he had not been at sea. I know that it was Ercole's decision to put me ashore here. If he had not known I was aboard, I would have gone on to Tana and seen the wild people of Russia and the blue tiles from Samarkand." Her eyes shone as she recalled all she had heard as a child. "But ill-luck and a storm brought me here, and I, on my own, left the convent of Hagia Charis. How can you think that you had anything to do with any of it?"

Dracula shook his head. "In time you will understand." He waited a moment. "You think you will be able to travel in four or five days?"

"Travel?" A frisson went through her, half excitement, half horror. "Where should I travel, my lord?"

If the title pleased him, he did not show it. Instead, he put his long, large hand over the center of his chest and bowed to her again. "I am going to take you with me when I return to my homeland. I trust you can ride; you will have to."

Fenice had only twice ridden a horse in her life—in Venice, travel was done in boats, not on horses or in carriages—and had no idea if she would be able to, but she gathered her courage and said, "I will learn, my lord," as she walked past him to stand directly before the fire, which now seemed inadequate to heat the warm evening.

"That you will," he approved. "I have arranged for remounts between here and my castle. We will not be delayed by lack of mounts." He came up behind her and put his hands on her shoulders, apparently unaware when she stiffened. "It will be a long ride, and we must ride as if devils were after us." He laughed a little. "Come, Fenice. You had purpose enough to hide in the hold of your brother's ship and remain there for days. This, surely, is no worse."

"How did you—" she began, determined not to face him, for that dream-familiar face was not one she would trust. She tried to shake free of his hands and could not. "You guessed what I had to do. How else might I remain aboard the ship, but by hiding in the hold?"

"You had to hide, I grant you that," said Dracula, indulging her. "But to say that you chose the hold when you might have gone to the food locker or some other place." He studied the line of her neck. "You are delectable."

She wrenched free of his hands. "As those merchants were, no doubt," she accused him from halfway across the hall. "As the man you killed last night was?"

"I killed him because you wished it," Dracula reminded her as if she had forgotten a ring or some other paltry gift. "He would have told the world you are a woman, and you would be—"

"—branded for a harlot or sold to a Turk. Yes, I know," she said, weariness coming over her. "No woman can be in the market for long and not know these things."

Dracula considered her. "You hesitate to put yourself in my hands, yet you know what will become of you if you do not. Why is this?" He came up to her again, touching her dark hair, teasing out stray tendrils to frame her face.

Fenice sighed. "I suppose if I remembered everything that happened last night, I might be more grateful. But as it is, I cannot have come through so much to want to put myself in your hands—yours, or anyone's." She frowned down at her clasped hands. "When I was very young, I learned my brothers would travel. They would know the liberty of leaving Venice behind and striking out into the unknown world, dangers and all. I understood I would not have such an opportunity. I would remain in Venice, marry, and have sons who would enjoy the same freedom my brothers did. And I could not bear it." She began to weep. "I told them when I was young that I would follow my brothers, and no one believed me. Now that I have done it, the doors of my past are closed to me. My brother Ercole holds me in contempt, and no doubt my family would wish me at the bottom of the sea—or they will when Ercole returns to Venice. The adventures that bring honor to my brothers bring shame and vilification to me." She took a long, deep breath and wondered why she was telling Dracula so much, unless she believed him, at least in part.

"That which the world finds odious, I admire," Dracula said to her. "And you will find that being my bride is not the imposition you fear it may be."

"I have no wish to marry," she said at once, adding in a less strident voice, "Not even Aurelio." She stared directly at Dracula. "He is my affianced husband."

"Your promise to him means nothing, not now. He would not touch you if you went back to Venice, and he would curse you for bringing humiliation upon him." Dracula touched her hair again. "The man who almost raped you last night would bring you into such disrepute that no one would consider you unstained."

She raised her chin, her lower lip not quite steady. "When you say nearly raped, what do you mean?" The things that had niggled at her mind all day long now began to take form, to show the appalling events in sharp detail.

"He tore your clothing off and had you pinned against the wall, his knee between your legs as he unfastened your underhose." He made no attempt to soften his report, and no apology for what he told her. "You twisted his genitals so he released you. But had I not killed him, you could not have escaped him, and he would have killed you most cruelly."

"And I am to follow you to your castle for killing him?" Fenice asked sharply as she swayed on her feet. It came back to her now in a rush, so clear that she put her hands to her eyes as if to shut out what her mind showed her. "I disabled three of them—four, if you will allow me the last one."

"Disabled but not silenced," said Dracula. "They would have taken keen delight in telling the world that you were female; you cannot doubt that they would say you had been used by them all, and that would make you a harlot, and a . . . Chri—Catholic harlot at that, one the followers of Islam already think lustful and immodest for showing your face. To dress as a boy and succeed in your deception is a most serious offense. You would not be received well in the courts."

"So you killed them to spare me?" Her sarcasm made her voice harsh. "You took no pleasure in . . . drinking their blood?"

"Oh, come, come, Fenice; I took blood only from the last. What sense was there in draining more than one?" His eyes shone like splinters of black glass. "They are chaff. Only a fool would glut himself on them."

"And you are not a fool," she said. "You are my protector. You make my welfare your utmost concern. Why am I not overcome with obligation for what you have done?" The sensation of the dead assailant's hands on her body made her want to retch. She clamped her teeth shut and attempted to break away from him.

He would not permit it. "I am your protector, whether it suits you to have me or not. I did not summon you all this way to turn you over to a fat Ottomite with a dozen women to service his needs, to grow old and die in the course of a decade or two. No, Fenice. I have guarded what is mine, and I will keep what is mine." The veneer of courtesy was gone. His raptorlike countenance was so close to hers that she felt his cold breath on her cheek.

If he kissed her, she would gag; she could taste bile at the back of her mouth. Dracula's nearness and her memory of the man with the sling fused in her emotions and she struck out with the heels of her hands, intending to bloody his nose or blacken his eye. His hands went around her wrists as inexorably as manacles.

"Listen to me," he said softly, his words thin and cutting as wire. "You have come to me. I claim you. I am your only sanctuary in this world, and the next. If you leave me, you will be degraded in life and in death." He lifted one of her clenched hands and kissed it and then the other. "You are not a foolish girl."

"Let go of me," she muttered, pulling against his strength.

"You were taken advantage of in the marketplace. You may have brought death to a few of the gang that tormented you, but there are more of them, and they will not let you triumph." He released her so suddenly that she staggered backward. "You are vulnerable as long as any of them remain alive; they will want vengeance."

"You cannot be certain," she said, hating the fear that filled her heart with a coldness that was more dreadful than any winter storm.

"You think you will be permitted to win any battle against the men in that gang? What of the crippled boy in the market-square, the one you have been looking after? They will exact a price from him for what you have done."

She brought her fear under control, doing her best to meet his gaze without recoiling from what she saw in his eyes. "You said you were going to take me to your—"

"So I am, but not like a cur-bitch, slinking away with your tail between your legs, but as the victor you can be." He smiled more broadly. "Think of it: you may claim vengeance for all you have endured on their account. Those nights spent in shivering dread inside the German's tomb, the days you had to pay half of the money you earned to those cowards so that they would not beat you or your friend. They have much to answer for, and they will. None of them will ever forget Aeneo, if you have the fortitude to do what must be done." The expression on Dracula's face was a mixture of enthusiasm and fatalism. "What are you made of, Fenice? Are you weak as milk or strong as fire? Have you water or lava in your veins?"

She stared at him. "You know what I have in my veins—you, better than anyone."

He laughed. "Yes; I do. I know it runs sweet and hot, and that you have passion you have not plumbed. But you have not discovered it for yourself."

Then he caught hold of her again and pulled her into his embrace. "As I know you are mine."

It was foolish to fight him; she knew it was, but she could not stop herself. Her struggles were nothing to him, even when he pressed his mouth to hers, burning as ice burns. She had never known strength like his, and in that comprehension, she conceded her weakness. As he lessened his hold on her, she put her arms around him and kissed him, telling herself that it was on her terms, that she was accepting the alliance he offered and not sacrificing her autonomy to his will.

"A good beginning," Dracula approved as he looked down into her eyes. "A very welcome promise."

"I promise nothing," Fenice said, her haughtiness sounding petulant even to her ears.

Dracula answered her with a cold smile and a deep, insulting bow.

PART III

VARNA AND TRANSYLVANIA

1573–1575

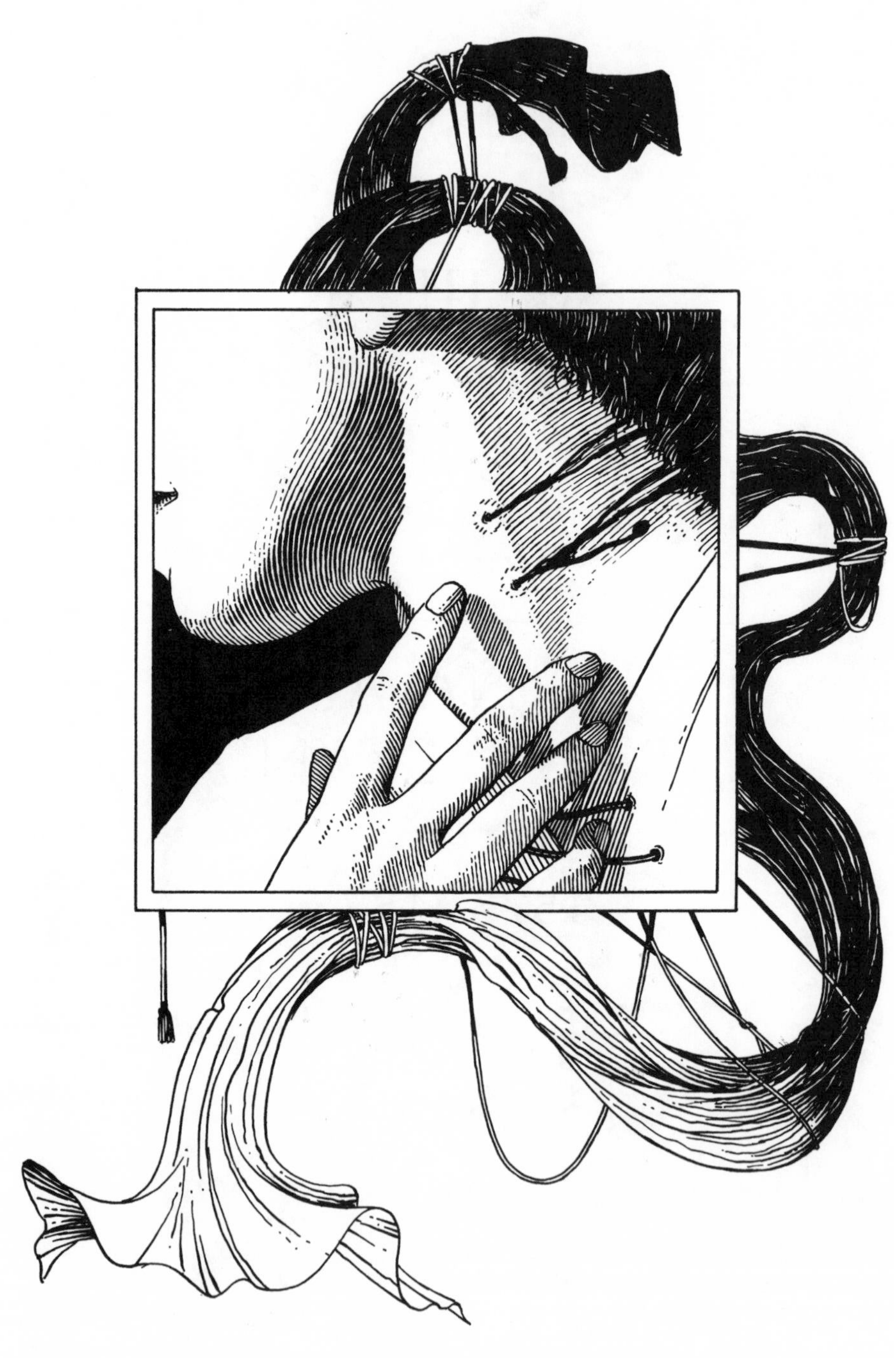

If I were fire, I would ignite the world;
If I were winds, I would flatten all with storms;
—Cecco Angioliere

— XXII —

By the evening of the third day at Dracula's house, Fenice was less frightened of her host; she no longer winced when he touched her, nor did she cringe when he spoke of killing the rest of the market-gang that had attacked her. She passed the time in dreamlike hours when she was not reading one of the books in the small book-room in the house, books which allowed her to escape the lingering hold of her nightmares and the occasional sharp recollections of what had happened to her outside the gates to this house. Her bruises—the ones she could see—had faded to shades like rotten fruit, and she was certain her face had the same shades of yellow and green that her body did; her head no longer ached constantly and the scrapes on her knuckles had begun to heal. Her spirits were not recovering quite so well: she had hours when she felt her old exhilaration, but increasingly she was thrown into sudden onslaughts of wrath, or into the darkest melancholy. She could not anticipate these lapses, and that added to her mercurial state of mind. She felt a degree of sympathy for what Dracula had said now, as if her anger at what had been done to her—and to Libu—had been locked in a stupor and was only now beginning to well within her. Dressed in the newest garments she had been provided, the court regalia of a Hungarian noblewoman in deepest red embroidered brocade over a dark olive color, Fenice paced the main hall, fussing with the expansive skirts and longing for her boy's clothing again. How on earth had she managed all those years in skirts? She tugged on her padded sleeves, trying to make herself more comfortable, when she heard Dracula's voice deep in the shadows.

"Fury becomes you," he said, dangerous amusement making his tone light. "You are a woman to be reckoned with."

Fenice did not give him the satisfaction of seeing her startled by his arrival. "I assumed you would be here, my lord; the sun has set." She glanced around the main hall, as if she were being received there for the first time. "We are still in Varna. I thought we should have gone by now."

"You have not been quite ready," he said, not quite teasing her. "When you are, we will leave."

"Why do you wait? What more do you require of me before you arrange for our traveling?" She conducted herself with the kind of behavior her father would have approved of, which seemed to amuse Dracula.

"You know what you have left unfinished," he said, coming a little closer so that his shadow loomed out of the darkness.

"What might that be?" She dropped him a slight curtsy. "You tell me I have unfinished matters to deal with, and leave me to exhaust myself trying to discern your meaning? How am I to know what you intend, if you will explain nothing?"

He threw back his head and laughed as if she had said something very amusing. "What a general you would have made, had you been a male."

"You mistake, my lord," she told him coolly. "In Venice we have admirals; we leave generals to those who fight on land." She approached him as he came into the light; she wanted him to see that she was not frightened of him.

"I am corrected," he said, taking her hand to kiss it.

The chill of his lips still disquieted her, but she did not reveal her emotion. She realized he would not be entirely fooled, but she wanted to keep some portion of her autonomy. "I don't know that I would like to be an admiral," she said. "I would rather be one of the navigators going to the New World, or to China." Her smile was automatic, to make sure he did not get too close to her; the memory of his embraces made her apprehensive, and she had no wish to encourage more of them.

"Not battle but adventure," Dracula acknowledged. "Yes, that is more your character." He clapped his hands. "You must be hungry."

"Your housekeeper has fed me very well," said Fenice. "I can tell that I have added flesh to my bones."

"It would not take much to do so; you were like sticks tied at the joints. I have seen toys with more flesh to them than you have, even now." His nearness made her uneasy; he came a step closer. "You have not forsaken your courage, Fenice; like your name, you rise from the flames."

"If to be your prisoner is to rise from the flames, then I suppose you are right." She was surprised at how bitter she sounded, and how tight her body felt, as if confined within chains instead of fine garments.

"Prisoner?" He did his best to look shocked. "Nothing of the sort. If you want, I will find you rags so you might return to the market-square. You are not constrained by me. I would not stop you leaving, though you may doubt it. You see, I know you would return to me. The market-gangs will make your life miserable, and with Libu dead, you will have to—" He broke off. "Oh," he said with exaggerated concern. "You had not heard. Of course."

"How did Libu die?" Fenice asked, uncertain that he was telling her the truth. "You said he was hurt, not dead."

"Yes: you knew about his hand, and that he was a captive of the gang of market-rogues," said Dracula, dismissing the matter with an impatient gesture.

"I know you did. His hand festered, as you might expect in such weather. And when the four young men did not return, his companions went and clubbed Libu's back and his malformed leg, to find out if he knew anything of the matter. They spared him nothing, but he could not tell them what they required of him, for he knew so little. What could he tell them, but that you had followed me and they had followed you? The boy was already feverish, and because he could tell them nothing, they rubbed his wounds with dung and let the fever take him."

"Libu—" She could not—she refused—to think of him dead. "I—"

"So you have not only yourself to avenge, but Libu as well, if you are to be satisfied. Your honor and his memory require you have vengeance on—" said Dracula, breaking off as Olena came silently into the main hall bearing a tray with Fenice's supper on it, along with a tall bottle of wine in Venetian glass. This luxury caught Fenice's attention as she knew Dracula had intended it should. "Eat, my lovely guest. We will talk more later." He turned as if to leave the room, but took up a place in the alcove beside the fireplace.

Fenice did not want to be watched as she ate; she tried to angle her chair to provide her some protection as she sat down. She signaled to Olena to come nearer. "It smells wonderful," she said, recalling all the times Rosamonda had reminded her to thank the servants for doing their work well; in this place she suddenly felt a need to preserve the amenities she had been taught.

Olena put the tray down on the table; she leaned toward Fenice and said very softly, "Do not let him persuade you. You will be a living ghost if you do. He will make you like me."

Fenice jumped at these dire words. "I . . . I am on my guard." She took the service-cloth and put it high in her lap. "He is a very powerful man."

"That is not all," said Olena, then raised her voice. "I am told the last of the Russians will leave in a day or two. Most of them have departed already. The master will not stay here for much time after the Russians have gone."

"Are you sure of that?" Fenice asked, no longer willing to pretend she did not care about these things.

"I am," Olena answered, and lowered her voice again. "He will command you."

"He cannot do that," said Fenice, speaking a bit too loudly. "I am grateful to him for all he has done," she added, hoping to make her intention less obvious to Dracula.

"He will do what you are not grateful for," said Olena. "He will make you like him if you remain here."

From the darkness Dracula's voice echoed. "You are already half mine."

Fenice rose to her feet, nearly oversetting her chair. "I—"

Olena hunched over and fled from the room without speaking again.

"You have taken me into you," said Dracula, ambling out of his alcove. "Do eat the food while it is hot. Olena will be upset if you wait."

Very slowly Fenice sat down again; she bent to retrieve her serving-cloth from the floor, and this time tucked it into the front of her bodice. "Why do you torment Olena this way? She is frightened of you."

"Ah, yes," said Dracula. "So she is. But she came to me willingly, offered herself to me. Then she lost her nerve, and would not accept what she had sought. She lacks your strength. She thought she wanted to serve me, and so she does, but not as you will. You are more than she will ever dream of being. You know that you have courage. You will become my ally, my comrade, my second self. You will take the gifts I give and you will not shrink from their price. You will know what it is to live beyond death." His words wound sinuously around her. "You are not shaken by the force of what you were taught; you question your place and your nature. You know that the world is not the way your tutors said it is. You know that your brothers are favored over you, and you know that this is an injustice." He came to the far side of the table and faced her. "You do not tremble at your desires, but for their might. You do not hide from the truth in your soul. Your wildness rules you."

Fenice stared up at him. "How can you—" She made herself begin again. "I will not surrender to you: I did not surrender to my family's wishes."

"Very staunch," he approved. "You are beyond price, beyond praise. A man would better have you than an army." He lifted the lid from a crockery pot. "I am told this is very good. You will have to give me your opinion."

The aroma of the dish was enticing. Fenice did not like to be put off-guard in this way, but she was too hungry to ignore the wonderful smells. Before she tasted the food, she warned him, "I am not going to capitulate."

"Of course not," Dracula said. "But you have not yet considered what difficulties you face. If you will permit me an hour or so, we may discuss what lies before you. Have your meal first, and then, if you are willing, we will talk. If not, then tomorrow or the next day." He poured some of the wine into the goblet Olena had provided and held it out to her, his courtesy more oppressive than gracious. "This will restore you."

She took the goblet and sniffed at the contents. Reassured that it was truly wine she was to drink, she put the goblet to her lips and tasted it. "This is very good. You keep an excellent cellar," she said as if she were at a fine banquet in Venice and not a lone guest in Varna.

"Did you think I would give you anything that was not excellent?" he demanded, stung by her confident manner.

"I do not know what you will do, my lord." She put the goblet down as a feeling of pride gave more color to her cheeks than the wine did.

"Then do not fear me until you know. I have done nothing to deserve your fear." He leaned forward, his shadow falling across her.

"I know what you did to the silk merchant, and to the man who attacked me, and to others." She lifted her fork, determined to behave as if she were truly a guest and not a captive.

"What is that to you? Did you want me to spare the market-ruffian? Did you think the silk merchant was a man of virtue? Why should you question what I have done?" He turned away from her. "You will not goad me, Fenice.

I know what you want; I learned it in your dreams. I know how great your soul is, and how much you long for the freedom I give—"

"Freedom?" she challenged, her food still untasted. "As your sworn handmaiden? As your slave?"

"Yes, as both those things. I can give you more freedom than anyone you could know in a hundred lifetimes. I can break the bonds of death that all men fear. I can promise you all the nights in eternity for your enjoyment." He swung back toward her. "You are like me."

Fenice made herself take a bite of her food; she chewed, not watching him while she thought with determination. Finally, after she swallowed the morsel of meat, she said, "How can I be like you, my lord?"

"You do not allow the world to define you: you define yourself. This is rare in men and much more rare in women. You will not accept the limits of cowards, or the rules of celibate men." He motioned for her to drink again. "Not tonight, but perhaps tomorrow night you will be ready to put your resolution to the test."

"How do you mean?" Fenice asked as she caught another bit of meat on her fork.

"You will want to make sure the youths who killed Libu answer for their crime. Will you not?" He bowed with a flourish. "In such a contest, I am yours to command."

The meat seemed suddenly to have the savor and texture of straw. "Tomorrow night?"

"Why, yes. You will be over the worst of your hurts. You will have to do the work quickly, for we will be leaving soon after." His wolfish smile made her want to disown her anger, to deny its gnawing reality, but she could not. "There—you see? You know you must do this. Your hurt and Libu's death will haunt you until you do. Free yourself and come to me without those burdens, that we may be happy. It is what you want, Fenice."

"I suppose so," she answered, and concentrated on her eating.

It was long after midnight when Fenice finally fell into restless sleep. She began to dream in sporadic images: *The hold of the* Impresa *and the odor of the oarsmen on the deck above her; the rush of the sea in storm; the domes of San Marco glistening in the pale winter sunlight; Aurelio's uncertain smile. This gave way to another smile, more immediate and more rapacious. She had a vision of four venal faces; she struggled against them only to have them vanish and be replaced by the raptorial grin she had sought to elude. She lay on the bed in her dream that was the same as the one she slept in, and the smell of the logs burning in the fireplace permeated her dream, making it seem so real that she wondered if she had wakened without knowing it, and found Dracula parting the curtains of her bed.*

Her body was still tender and his demands were not gentle. He did not woo her; he roused her, drawing on her pain and her despair to bring her to an intense surrender to his passion that left her breathless. The pain of her injuries fused with the frenzy of his appetite, becoming anguish and anodyne at once. Never had her dreams awakened her desires as this one had, and never had she felt the presence of the dream so keenly with her senses.

"You will revel in our hunger," he said. His voice was low and persuasive, supple as a melody in a reed pipe. "My need will be your need."

Blearily she watched him as he rose from her supine body; she could feel something both hot and cold on her neck, slightly sore and slightly pleasant; she could not decide what he had done to her neck, though she had no doubt what he had done to her flesh. Her lassitude was too great for her to summon up outrage enough to accuse him, but she felt it within her, like a banked fire. *How odd,* she thought, *to have a lover who thrives on my hatred and embraces my misery.* When she woke in the morning, she knew she would be furious, but now she was strangely content, almost euphoric. "Why have you—"

"You are mine, Fenice. I am claiming what is mine. You will be mine until Judgment Day, and beyond." He put his hand on her head as if bestowing a blessing on a child. Then he stepped back and pulled the curtains closed, laughing exultantly as he did. "You are not made for mortal men; you are made for me."

Fenice shivered and pulled the covers more closely around her, wanting only to escape into dreams where he could not reach her, and where her fury and despair had no power.

Olena's visage was set as if hewn from stone as she pulled back the shutters and let in the afternoon light. "You did not send him away," she said to Fenice, disapproval in every aspect of her presence. "After I warned you."

Fenice huddled away from the light which was so bright it hurt her eyes. "Please. Close the shutters." She brought up the corner of her coverlet to shield her eyes. "It is hot today."

"Hum," said Olena. "I have brought you cheese and bread to eat, like a good Christian." Her tone was condemning, making it certain that she doubted Fenice was deserving of any such consideration. "The master is . . . asleep."

"He sleeps during the day," said Fenice, wondering how she knew this. As she levered herself upright, she saw a red stain on her pillow; her hand went to the place on her neck where she had felt pain at the end of her dream. She touched a pair of small cuts, very small, each with a thin trail of dried blood falling away from it.

"You let him do that," Olena said condemningly. "You did not refuse him."

"He . . . he came in the night . . . when I was . . . dreaming," said Fenice, struggling to recall when her dream had begun and when she had found Dracula with her.

"He came in the night when you were ready for him," Olena accused her. "You knew he would take you, and you would be his. You *knew*." She closed the shutters. "Since you will have your darkness, there it is."

Fenice nodded her head as a sign of her appreciation. "You are kind, Olena. I hope you will not continue to be vexed with me."

"I am not vexed," Olena responded sharply. "I fear for your soul, child."

"My soul?" Fenice laughed. "How could my soul worry you?" She got out of the bed. "I have put myself in danger without Dracula's help, if my Confessor told me the truth." Her hand went to the little cuts again. "How can this hurt me now?"

Olena sighed and put her head down as if to shield herself from blows. "You have let yourself become one of his creatures. Shortly you will feel him in your veins. Oh, not today, or tomorrow, but shortly you will know what it is to be his creature."

"And you are not?" Fenice challenged, her emotions roiling without warning.

"I am," said Olena quietly. "As much as he permits me to be. He will let me die in time, when he has had enough of me. But for now, I give him what he wants, and he spares me." She pointed to the cheese and bread. "If you have not given in to him, then eat what I have brought you and tell me you are nourished by it." Her thin, wrinkled lips parted in a smile that revealed missing teeth. "If you do, then I will go to the church of Saint George of Armenia—let the master say what he will—and pray that Saint George will banish this dragon as well as he did the Devil's serpent." She looked squarely at Fenice. "Do not tell me you are not hungry."

"Of course I am," said Fenice sullenly. "But why should I eat to please you?" She found it hard to admit that the prospect of cheese and bread left her feeling slightly ill. She got out of bed, and making a point of staying out of the occasional bands of sunlight that brightened her room, she went to the chest where the food had been set out. Carefully she broke off a section of the bread and ate it, thinking as she did that it was too hard and dry; then she pulled a bit of cheese from the wedge Olena had brought and stuffed it between her lips, resisting the urge to gag on it.

"You are not lost—not entirely," said Olena in a measuring way. "You have so much strength. No wonder he wants to bend you to his will." She came up to Fenice. "I will do as I said I would—I will pray to Saint George for you, and hope he will protect me from the master, as well as protecting you."

"Why should I need Saint George to help me?" Fenice asked.

Olena leaned near to her. "Saint George defeated the dragon," she said as if speaking to a child. "Dracula is the dragon's heir. Dracu, draco, they are the same, and so is he." Her voice dropped lower still. "You do not think you can stand against him on your own, do you?"

"I should not have to stand against him at all," said Fenice, staring at the food and wondering why her hunger was so acute. "He has saved me. I am grateful to him."

"And he will use your gratitude to drag you into damnation." She crossed herself with an effort. "I can still do this, though he drinks my blood when no other is available. But you are more than sustenance to him, you are one he wants to make like him. You do not know what danger he has placed you in; you are going to lose your soul."

"You've said so before," Fenice told her with a burst of spite she could not completely explain. "I am not damned."

"Not yet, perhaps, but in a week or two, as he seduces you with words that were promises in Eden, what then? God will not mind, he tells you. God cannot hurt you, he says, God will never condemn you for what is my sin. Well?" She crossed the room to the door. "Finish as much as you can, for the good of your body, and I will do as much as is possible to feed your soul, so that the master will not have you to delight in."

"If you must," said Fenice, disinterested in Olena's concerns already, and preparing to make herself eat more of the inadequate food.

"If he tells you that you are about to leave this place, be sure you are in the greatest danger of all. No prayers can save you once you become his ally." She had her hand on the latch. "You are a fine, brave girl. I would not want him to conquer you."

"Yes, yes," said Fenice impatiently as she sat down to eat. "Do what you must."

Olena lowered her head. "I pray it will be enough," she declared as she let herself out of the room.

Rosamonda knelt before the lovely little altar in the Madonna chapel in Sant' Angelo. She had taken to coming here every morning to pray for the return of her daughter; she knew she was the only one of her family who still wanted her back: her husband and her children all had resigned themselves to her loss, and did not want to face the potential embarrassment of her return. She prayed with automatic piety, which she feared might offend God. "I don't care where she has been or what has been done to her, I only want her back. You are a mother; You can understand that, can't you? If she is dead, then it is God's Will, but I would like to learn of it so she can be mourned and remembered. If we have the *Requiem* sung while she is still living, we will offend God by our lack of faith: if she is dead, we should have Masses for the repose of her soul." She looked up at the image of the young woman above the altar, thinking that God's Mother was much too young to know what their family was enduring, with all but one of the children grown, and their fortunes established in the world. "You lost a Son, and You suffered for Him. My daughter is not like Your Son to anyone but me, and I know that Your Sacrifice was greater than what I have endured, but You know that my daughter is precious to me. Tell me what has become of her."

There was no answer. A short while later Rosamonda got to her feet and went out of the chapel, noticing that Eloisa was engaged in conversation with a well-dressed young man whose face was faintly familiar. Just the sight of Eloisa with a stranger was a keen reminder to Rosamonda that strangers had abducted her Fenice, and she moved more quickly, trying to deny the fear within her. This was a church, and should be safe. But so should Fenice's bedroom have been. As she approached, Eloisa blushed and nudged her companion; the young man bowed and stepped back.

"Who was that?" Rosamonda asked as she approached her youngest daughter.

"Gualtiere Pontesasso," she said, a trifle too readily. "He is—"

"Enrico Pontesasso's nephew," said Rosamonda, recalling the young man's identity. "Why was he talking to you?"

"He was being polite," said Eloisa, doing her best to keep her temper in check. "Is there anything wrong with that?"

"Wrong?" Rosamonda asked. "You were by yourself. He should have kept his distance."

"As if I had the pox?" Eloisa challenged. "Isn't it bad enough that everyone is saying that Fenice is in a Turkish harem, and that she disgraces us all?"

Rosamonda slapped her before she realized what she was doing. "You will *never* say such things! *Never!* Do you hear me?"

Humiliated, Eloisa put her hand to her face and mumbled something that might have been an apology. "But that's what they're saying. Everyone but you and Aurelio."

"And what if we are right?" Rosamonda demanded as she looked about the church, suddenly aware of her surroundings. "Come, Eloisa. We can discuss this at home."

"There is nothing to discuss," said Eloisa. "Fenice is gone. There is nothing more to say." Her pretty face took on a sullen cast as she stepped out into the sunlight.

The morning heat was not as overwhelming as it would be later in the day, but it still struck like a soft, invisible wall that absorbed them into its furnacelike interior. The whole of the city shone, the colors brilliant, the water as dazzling as shards of a vast broken mirror. Most of the people gathered in the Campo Sant' Angelo were showing signs of the heat, from wilting ruffs and collars to tracks of sweat through face powder, to a reluctance to move too quickly. By noon most of the city would be in a stupor, within doors until afternoon offered a breeze for relief.

"You don't mean that," Rosamonda said as she headed toward their house. "Fenice is your sister."

"And so is Bianca, and Artemesia. You never seem to give them any thought," Eloisa said as she followed her mother. "Artemesia is pregnant, but do you show her any distinction for it? No. You only pray for Fenice, who probably shames our name."

"Eloisa," her mother warned, "mind your tongue."

"Why? Everyone says the same thing. Everyone." She folded her arms in her stiff, slashed sleeves. "I don't want to do this anymore." She nodded toward the church. "I don't want to have to spend all my mornings praying for Fenice to come back. I don't want her to come back, not after so much time."

"So much time?" Rosamonda echoed. "If you were the one who was missing, would you think this has been too much time? Well?" She had reached the entrance to their house; as she waited for the door to be opened, she stared at Eloisa as if she did not know the girl.

"She's probably dead," Eloisa muttered, as close to an apology as she was willing to give.

"Living or dead, I want to know."

Oh, more than other harmonies of instruments and song
This sweet silence . . .
—Lorenzo de' Medici

— XXIII —

"Have you decided what you want to do to those young men?" Dracula asked Fenice the following evening. "Your injuries are better now and you are gaining strength. If you are going to be revenged on them, you must do it soon, or lose my protection and this house as a haven. I have delayed my departure on your account, waiting for you to act." He paced in front of the fireplace, his tall figure moving in front of the leaping flames like smoke but more solid and more dangerous; his dark purple, long-hemmed dolman seeming darker for its color than blackness would have been.

Fenice looked up from the Greek text she had been reading. "I suppose I must do as you have told me." She did not want to talk about the young men who had attacked her and had killed Libu; she wanted them out of her thoughts and her dreams forever. She set the book aside, a frown gathering between her brows.

"For your sake," said Dracula emphatically. "You must not do it for mine, but for yours. You were the one they wanted to rape and kill. Remember that, Fenice." He came up to her and leaned above her, ominous as the thunder-clouds that had gathered in the afternoon sky. "It is your life they wanted to take."

"Not only my life," said Fenice dully; she could not remember the four young men without a coldness coming over her that numbed the humiliation and rage that lay beneath it. "And they killed Libu."

"They have much to answer for," Dracula declared. "But only you can hold them to account. If you do not, then we must assume you are willing to let them have the victory over you."

She bristled. "Nothing of the sort," she declared. "I have not yet decided on how they are to die." It was partially the truth: her dreams had been filled with bloody visions of murder.

"You will have to decide shortly," Dracula told her. "I will not wait here forever while you find the courage you need to do what you have sworn to do." He was pacing the hall without apparent purpose but to release the energy coiled within him.

Fenice did her best not to wince at this accusation of cowardice. "I do not want them to escape me," she declared.

"You will let them die of old age, I fear," he responded, enough mockery in his voice to make her ire come to the surface.

"I will not!" She swung around to face him; she did not like his moving behind her as he did.

"How can I believe that?" Dracula asked her as if she had failed him already. "You sit here reading while they strut about the market-square, boasting of their deeds."

"Four of them are silent," Fenice said as bluntly as she could.

"Four. There are many more of them who have not been held to account, who would not hesitate to use you as the four wanted to." He reached down and brushed her untidy hair back from her neck. "Your work is not finished."

She felt her face redden. "I have said I will kill them. I will." She wanted to hear more purpose in her own voice, for she was afraid she would not be able to summon up the ferocity she would need to face the men.

"They will try to hurt you," Dracula reminded her unnecessarily.

"I know," she snapped, and looked down at the half-healed cuts and bruises on her arms and hands. "I know."

"And it is up to you to keep them from their satisfaction." He bent and kissed her on her exposed nape. "You must be as bloody as they are."

Had she not been so troubled, she might have lashed out at Dracula. As it was, she only said, "I will be."

"I want to believe you," said Dracula, his fingers caressing her face from behind her. "If you cannot do this, tell me now."

She shoved herself out of the chair and away from him. *"I will,"* she muttered, her hands locked in combat with each other.

"You tell me; you do not show me." He came up to her, and without touching her in any other way, bent to kiss her mouth.

Fenice stood as if nailed to the floor, too distressed by her feelings to do anything more than look aghast; there were tears on her face, tears she knew came from wrath, but which seemed an admission of weakness nonetheless. She put her hands to her head and fixed her fingers in her hair. "Do not touch me," she said when Dracula stepped back from her.

"I only wish to remind you that you have had my regard until now. I understand your wish to regain your strength, but I do not understand why you hesitate now that you are healing. If you do not want to continue in my esteem, you may leave this house." He spoke softly, but with such underlying purpose that Fenice shivered again.

"When I leave, it will be to kill those . . . those wretches." She did her best to regain her composure, but there was a brightness in her eyes that revealed the precarious state of her temper. She smoothed the front of her clothes as if this ordinary gesture could make her moods less volatile, for in the days since she entered this house, she had been unable to find the stability she had always known before, even in danger; her excitement had been bound by her judgment—now it no longer answered to her will.

"You will be much relieved when you do this," said Dracula. "They will not be able to haunt you as they do now, once you have rid the world of them."

At the suggestion of haunting, Fenice started. "They will have ghosts," she exclaimed.

Dracula's laughter was insinuating. "Not they. They will vanish, leaving no trace." He moved away from her, circling her as if to drive her into a trap. He kept his voice low, dark as the shadow he cast along the floor like a massive finger pointing at her.

"But—" Fenice had been taught that those who died violently haunted those who caused their deaths.

He answered her without hearing her question. "They are nothing more than rats. Kill one and others will come, but those that are dead are gone."

Fenice felt herself impaled on the power of his eyes: she was transfixed by the potency of his gaze. "Then why—" She broke off, unwilling to admit she might not want to kill them. "Rats should be exterminated."

"And you must vindicate your honor," he reminded her. "If you do not, then you are as they are, worth nothing." His relentless tone struck her like a blow. "It is not their lives that are at stake here, but yours." He came up to her once more. "You do not know what fires burn in your soul, Fenice."

She nodded several times, trying to make herself consent. "They will die," she said at last. "I will see to it."

Dracula was directly in front of her, blotting out the brilliance of the fire and haloing himself in flame. "When?"

As if from a great distance she heard herself say, "Tomorrow night."

Lying awake that night, Fenice did not trust herself to succumb to sleep; she did not want to dream, for she knew that her anger would spur more hideous visions. A dull ache settled behind her eyes and sank into her neck and she drew back the curtains that enclosed her bed in order to have some distraction from her wandering imagination: the room in darkness provided an ordinariness to her musing that she trusted would hold her furies at bay.

She did not know when she became aware of a luminous presence in her room; the air seemed spangled with ephemeral light. Something that was like a glowing fog slid through the room toward her bed, moving like an incoming tide. She reminded herself that often in Venice when the mists were thick they would invade the houses, bringing their gelid wraiths to dim the lanterns and chill the fires in the hearth. Varna was a port, and surely it occasionally had thick fogs. Her own arguments did not reassure her: Fenice watched, trying to convince herself that she had fallen asleep and this was her dream, but she could not persuade herself that this was nothing more than a vision conjured by her disordered senses. To prove she was not awake, she tried to sit up and found that she was unable to move. She tried to speak, but the words would not come; they stuck in her throat, making her hiss like a cat.

The glistening fog drifted nearer, shining darkly as it neared her bed. Fenice thought she detected an odor, not quite pleasant, emanating from the fog, and she tried to resist the strange sensation that began to make itself felt in her spine; it was as if minuscule sparks were striking her flesh, making her tingle. She reached behind her for one of the pillows, then clutched it to her chest when she had got hold of it.

Slowly the fog reached her bed, now glowing blackly; it began to coalesce, rising up in a gleaming column that began to take the form of a cloaked figure. From within the shape of the head, two chatoyant eyes gleamed, fixed on her; Fenice tried again to speak, but only a sigh escaped her. A frisson, as intense as agony, went through her, making her body ache with something that was not quite pain but could not be called pleasure. There was a familiarity to the emotions she felt, as if she remembered the sensations she now experienced from some earlier event; the whole of her response was dreamlike, and she gave herself to it as if to the pleasure of a dream.

Ephemeral arms reached out to envelop her; the touch of those insubstantial limbs sent a thrill surging along her body more impressively than the sparks had done. Deep within her, she wanted to struggle, to resist the lassitude that was coming over her, but her determination deserted her, and she was unable to overcome her growing lethargy. As the embrace deepened, her one salvation against it was the anger burning deep within her. Even when her body moved pliantly against the insubstantial figure that held her, she comforted herself with wrath, recalling her battle against the young men; she would not succumb to the pleasure that soothed her flesh.

No gentle blandishments were offered; the tweaking of her cheeks might have been kisses, but they were too sharp to encourage complete surrender; they demanded something more, something harrowing and strengthening at once, something she would not let herself recognize. The heat she had thought was rage spread through her, making her quiver with anticipation, but of what, she refused to contemplate. Then there was a coldness on her neck, and the distant alarms in her soul grew immediate. She could not let herself capitulate to his demands, no matter how coercing his presence might be, or how much she longed for his desire; such things were unthinkable. And all the while she knew he could require this of her at any time, and she would not be able to resist him.

"Sleep, my phoenix," the very air murmured to her. "Sleep; dream."

More readily than she would have thought possible, Fenice began to drift, carried by the incorporeal arms now wrapped around her. Beneath her unwanted compliance, her temper gathered. No one had ever dissuaded her, and she would not allow this . . . this imaginary presence to do what her family and hardship could not. Steeling herself to retain her dedicated wrath, she slipped into her dreams of revenge with a satisfaction that might have been less certain had she seen the vulpine smile on the immaterial lips that were bright with her blood.

She could have passed for a nobleman's page, someone in the company of Hungarians or Austrians or Croats; her giaquetta was brocade, a deep, dusky shade of blue that made her seem like a shadow in the fading light of the hot afternoon. She wore slashed upper hose, the slashes lined in dull purple, which made the blue less distinct; her underhose were the same dull purple, and her boots, reaching to mid-calf, were of soft black leather. Her hair was newly trimmed, framing her face in a dark halo. She had her hand on her dagger, and her eyes moved restlessly as she neared the market-square. Her posture was haughty; she looked at the people milling around the stalls and the customs desks as if she were watching ants at work.

When she reached the fountain where Libu was accustomed to stand, she felt the smarting of tears in her eyes. She lowered her eyes so that no one would notice she was crying.

Only those who had intended her harm would know her wrath. She fingered the quillons of her dagger and promised herself she would use it well. As she lingered by the fountain, she heard another whisper of a merchant found drained of blood.

"The demon has not left," said one of the men in Greek. "The priests have not exorcised him at all."

"But it has been a few days since he struck. Perhaps he is becoming weaker," said a man in Croatian dress, his accent rough but understandable. "With such a powerful demon, it may take time to banish him entirely."

"Well you may think so, and pray God he does not dine on you," said the first sharply. "You are a fool to think he is gone."

"Not yet," said the Croat with a shrug. "But he will be. In the meantime, keep a crucifix about you and rub your face and hands with holy water. And hang garlic at your bedposts at night." He crossed himself for good measure.

"I have Confessed today," said the Greek. "If any ill fate should come to me, I am readied for Heaven."

"You may be canny, readying yourself for Heaven; me, I'd rather stay alive." He chuckled and cocked his head in the direction of the customs desks. "Them. What do you think they do? Wrap themselves up in their prayer blankets and hope that Allah will send the dancing girls of their Heaven to claim their souls?"

The Greek shrugged. "Their Allah is supposed to keep them safe from demons. So they say." He spat to show his opinion of Allah.

"Including those who haunt the market-square and have a taste for merchants?" The Croat made a rough gesture, taking care that no Islamite could see it. "They are a thousand times worse than any demon."

"Because there are a thousand times more of them," agreed the Greek, then noticed that Fenice was listening. "Be off with you, boy," he ordered.

"I meant no offense," said Fenice, bowing enough to be polite. "I wanted to . . . to warn my master of the danger in the marketplace."

The Croat did not quite smile. "Looking after his interests, are you?"

She nodded. "He is a foreigner, as I am, and I would not want him to fall into danger because of it." She stood very still as the two men took stock of her, one of them nodding slowly. "My master sometimes is abroad at night; I thought it best to warn him of what is being said about this demon."

"And earn yourself an angel or two for your trouble, no doubt," said the Greek with an indulgent shake of his head. "Well, you would get the money in a good cause, no doubt." He pointed toward the mosque towers. "If he deals with the Islamites, your master would do well to be careful. They are beginning to say the demon is Christian and that it is the Will of Allah that a good Islamite drive the demon away. It gives them the right to accost strangers. Your master will want to know that, if he is a foreigner and a Christian."

"My master comes from Transylvania," said Fenice, wanting to see the response this would bring.

"Ah," the Croat exclaimed, "one of those Hungarians. No doubt a fierce fighter; he could give the demon a bit of his own medicine, I think, if what I hear of Hungarians is true." He slapped his thigh and looked Fenice over again. "He must have some . . . substance, to keep as fine a servant as you. A page in brocade. We might as well be in Italy, or France." He laughed at his own humor and shoved Fenice in the arm. "You've heard enough, lad. Be off with you. We have to discuss the delivery of goods."

"You do not want to hear what we say," the Greek added in more sinister tones.

At that, Fenice realized the men were smugglers as well as traders and knew it would be wise to get away from them. She ducked her head respectfully. "I thank you on behalf of my master and I hope you have good profit here."

For the rest of the afternoon she wandered the market-square, searching out the young men she was becoming more determined to find with every passing heartbeat. By sundown, she began to hunger for the hunt, for the joy of confronting them, for the moment she would kill them, to imagine how their blood would taste—

Taste?

The idea caught her up short. How could she want so repellent a thing as to taste their blood? That was for Dracula, not for her. She considered her emotions with apprehension; so much of what she felt was new to her, and she could not discover why she should have such powerful, and such conflicting sensitivities warring within her: why should she long for what repelled her? Had she been tainted by Dracula's lusts as well as gaining some of his courage? She lingered in the shadow of the warehouse used by Russian merchants and pondered what had become of her.

She would have to kill at least one of the men in the gang before she returned to Dracula's house that night. If she failed to do it, she might end up like Olena, a creature enslaved by Dracula's will as well as his needs. That was unendurable. No: if she were to prove herself to Dracula, she would continue in his esteem, which she realized now was very important to her. Setting out carefully, she made her way toward the most noisome taverns where the cutpurses and bullies drank when the day was done. Most of the market-gangs spent their evenings in such places, readying themselves for their nights of mayhem. She maintained her grip on her dagger.

The first tavern she reached was so ill-lit that she could not recognize any of the faces; she took up a rickety stool near the door, ordered wine, and hunched over the cup they brought her, wrinkling her nose at the sour smell of it. She kept careful watch while pretending to drink the wine, and in a short while was rewarded: one of the men from the market-gang came reeling from the back, exclaiming loudly that he had to piss.

With an attempt to look drunk, Fenice teetered off her stool and wove in the direction the man she was following had taken. She flung out one arm as if to steady herself, swung out of the door, and then, out of sight of the patrons of the tavern, took up her pursuit in earnest. There was a certain thrill, illicit as fornication, in hunting this man. The alley where he went was dark. No lights shone from the windows above; no sounds came from them. Toward the latrine, the alley doglegged, ending in a small courtyard with old stone basins on the far side, and a long trough for vomit and turds: this place struck Fenice as an appropriate place for her quarry to die.

The man swung around, noticing footsteps behind him for the first time. Seeing Fenice, he laughed. "Got to . . . do this," he said as he prepared to urinate. "Then I'm . . . at your service." His gesture left no doubt as to which service he meant.

Fenice felt herself blush, but continued toward the ruffian. "Finish your business," she said as her hand closed on the hilt of her dagger. She glowered at him, waiting for the satisfaction of killing him.

"Don't be . . . bashful," the man said, indicating one of the basins near him. "I won't . . . tell how long yours . . . is." He was having trouble speaking clearly, and he had to concentrate on his aim, his brow furrowed with effort.

Certain he was distracted, Fenice struck him in the small of the back, leaning into the blow so that the dagger sank deeply in the space between his ribs and the top of his hip. She had recalled Febo saying it was useless to try to stab a man through his ribs; much better to get him where no bones could interfere. She was mildly surprised at what strength she needed to drive the dagger into the man's flesh.

Bellowing with pain, the man swung around, his fists balled, his face contorted with rage. His breeks were around his ankles now, so that when he tried to lunge at Fenice, he fell heavily, hobbled by his own clothes. Cursing in a mix of Bulgarian and Greek, he reached out to grab her ankles and was rewarded by a kick in his shoulder; he howled more loudly.

Fenice was shaking with excitement as she danced back from him; his arms were flailing now, but from pain not from purpose: she watched him writhe at her feet, and she was nearly overcome with giddiness that was part triumph, part disgust. She was astonished at the amount of blood that came from the wound. Surely, she told herself, he would have to die soon.

The blood had a fascination that held her attention as his agony could not. It shone in the faint moonlight, and steamed. She was certain she had never seen so much blood, that the man must have more than his share of it. She moved in closer to him as his movements became torpid and hands went slack; she was disappointed that he had fallen prone, for she wanted to see his face. She wished she could bring herself to move him, to roll him onto his side so she would be able to watch the life fade from his eyes.

Her ferocity appalled her as she let herself think about it. She had never believed she would take joy in seeing anyone murdered—let alone that she would be the murderer. *No,* she told herself as the man slowly gave in, his voice nothing more than a ragged breath, which was already faltering. No, she was not one to revel in such crime. But here she was, with her own dagger sticking up from the man's back, and she could only exult in his dying, and take pride that she was the cause of it. *It was for Libu that I did this,* she reminded herself. *For Libu. And for me.* The second realization was more troubling than she wanted to admit.

At last he was still—no movement in his limbs, and none in his lungs. She approached him tentatively, feeling queasy now that it was all over. The night around her was colder and her shaking was not from excitement now, but from the chill that cut through the last of the heat of the day, leaving her feeling exposed and vulnerable with her victim at her feet.

She had to brace her foot against his back to pull her dagger out of him, and when she had done, there was blood on her fine, dark clothes. She was glad now that she had worn such dark colors, for at night the blood would not show. Her smile was more a grimace as she slipped out of the alley and made her way through the streets of Varna to the house where Dracula, the Dragon Prince, waited.

Olena had brought a barrel to Fenice's room and filled it with hot water. She worked in silent disapproval as Fenice skinned out of her clothes and tossed them aside, saying they would need cleaning at once.

"The stench of death is on them," said Olena, grudging even these few words of condemnation.

"The man who died was more guilty than I," Fenice said, thinking she was defending herself needlessly; she had no reason to account for her actions to a slave. "See you get the blood out of them. If you can."

"Perhaps," said Olena, adding the last bucket of hot water. "You had better wash. It will get cold shortly." She pointed to a large sheet. "For drying."

Somewhat puzzled by this unusual service, particularly when it was apparent that it was service she was reluctant to give, Fenice asked Olena, "Why did you not heat the bathhouse?"

Olena's face was averted as she said, "The water is running there."

"Yes?" Fenice said, hoping to receive more of an explanation than she had been offered.

"You would not like it, not any longer," Olena said as she went to the door.

This declaration surprised Fenice; she said, "I don't know why that should be."

"He doesn't like it," said Olena, and there was no doubt whom she meant.

"Does it follow that I would not?" Fenice asked, irritated by Olena's disfavor, yet unwilling to be left alone.

"Yes. Now it does," said Olena, her voice as flat as her eyes. "I will tend to the barrel in the morning. When you will be asleep." With this last remark, she left the room and closed the door behind her.

Fenice drew up a chair so that she could climb into the barrel; the water rose almost to the rim as she lowered herself into it, welcoming the embrace of its warmth as much as the security of the wood around her. She closed her eyes, wanting the tension to fade from her body, and was immediately distressed to see the man at her feet once more, his body jerking—had he really done that, or had her memory added it to her recollection of the event?—and his damning oaths fading to slow, shallow breaths. She blinked, and was reassured to see the fire in her bedroom hearth shining before her. Resigned to being unable to stop the images of death from clouding her thoughts, Fenice set about rubbing herself with the cloth Olena had supplied; she went over every part of her body, scrubbing until her skin was ruddy from her ministrations. Even her short, dark hair was wet and her scalp tingled from the work of her fingers.

She had to struggle to get out of the barrel, although the water provided some buoyancy; she had to haul herself up on her arms, and scrabble one leg over the edge before she could get on the chair, and wrap herself in the sheet Olena had left. By that time, she was chilled and she went, swathed in the sheet, to huddle in front of the fire, hoping for warmth to return. Without being aware of it, she dozed and then slept.

And in her dream, Dracula came into her room through the window, and found her bunkered at the side of the hearth, her damp sheet clinging to her like cerements; he bent and lifted her in his arms and bore her to her bed, his dark cloak wrapped around her.

In the bed he lay beside her, stroking her and speaking encouraging words of praise to her while she drew the covers up. He would not leave her side even when she begged him to let her sleep. "You have no reason to sleep and much to celebrate, Fenice. You have done well tonight. The stain on your honor is already fading. When all of them are dead, you will have no cause for shame."

"But I do not feel shame," Fenice protested, knowing it was less than the truth. "I do not know what I feel, there is so much of it, and so much . . . conflict."

He kissed her brow. "You are permitting the lies you were taught to rule you. Think, Fenice, what was done to you. And to your friend. You were used disgracefully. Why should you not take vengeance for those things done to you, and to the boy? If you were a man, everyone would expect it of you. Why should your being a woman make the insult any more tolerable?" His kisses wandered lower, to her mouth, her throat.

She had no answer as his lips lingered just below her ear.

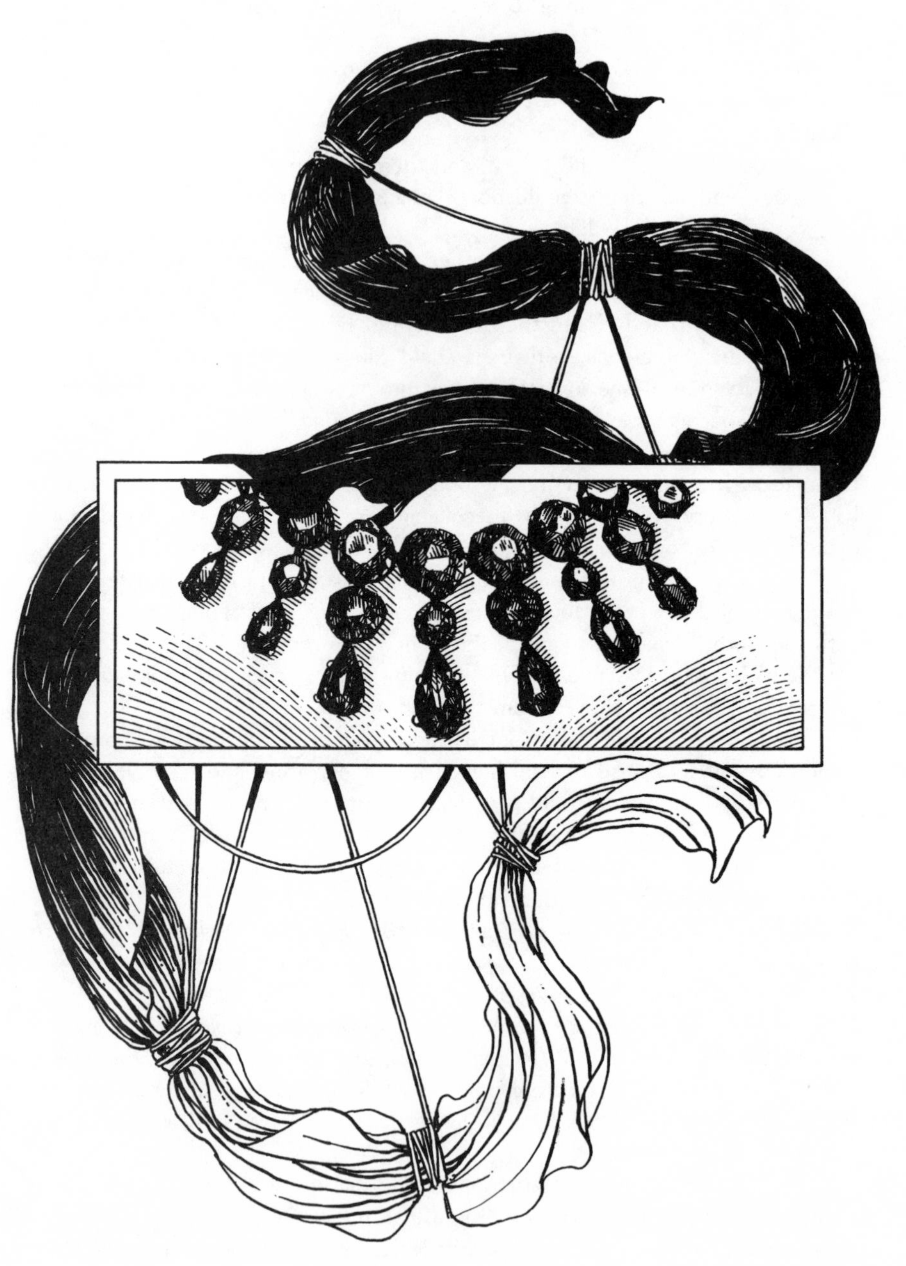

The Seraphim are nothing
To one who is in love.
—Jacapone da Todi

— XXIV —

Fenice found her afternoon meal oddly tasteless. She dutifully ate the braised lamb rolled in allspice and pepper, but could not bring herself to do more than taste the bread and the figs Olena had provided. The wine seemed to have lost its potency as well, for Fenice drank it like water and had no effect from it.

"Dracula expects you to join him in the main hall at sundown," said Olena in a tone that was not quite respectful. "He requests that you wear women's clothes." She pointed to the fine ropilla laid out on the bed. "He will give you jewels to wear with it."

"I will be pleased to do as he asks," said Fenice, toying with the slice of cheese that accompanied the bread. "I am sorry," she went on with a show of contrition that was greater than what she felt. "I have insufficient appetite to do justice to your meal."

"May you not regret it," said Olena, becoming nervous as she spoke. "If you decide you would like to have . . . anything later, you will summon me and tell me."

"Of course," said Fenice quietly. "And I thank you, Olena, for looking after me so well." She would have said the same thing to a servant at home, she knew. This woman made such common courtesy difficult, and Fenice had not yet made up her mind why that should be so.

"Will you need help dressing?" Olena asked.

"I don't think so. If I do, I will call you," Fenice answered, glancing at the ropilla.

"It is very grand," Olena said, making it plain that she did not intend this as flattery. "You will have to thank him for it." This was more a warning than a reminder.

"I have never seen anything finer," Fenice said, knowing it was true: not in all her life had she seen anything like that ropilla of black-and-gold Antioch silk with its pattern of hawks and wolves worked in the weave. The sottana that she would wear beneath it was a glorious dark bronze that set off both the black and the gold in the ropilla. She would not be reluctant to wear these clothes at the court of the Holy Roman Emperor himself. "Dracula is very good to show me such . . . such kindness." As she said this, she wondered if kindness had anything to do with it.

"As you say," Olena's voice was completely neutral in tone.

"I will dress shortly," Fenice said. "You need not linger."

Olena hesitated. "You . . . you will have to be on guard."

Fenice swung around to look at Olena. "On guard? What do you mean? Against whom should I be guarded?" Had someone witnessed her killing the night before? Had questions been asked by the authorities? Was she in danger from the men in the market-square?

"Nothing," said Olena as she backed out of the room, leaving Fenice to imagine and worry while she donned the gorgeous sottana and ropilla, preparing to meet with Dracula in the main hall at sunset.

Aurelio sat at his desk, an intent frown on his regular features making him look older and more dutiful than his brother Andrea thought possible.

"Still searching for Fenice Zucchar?" he asked as he came into the room.

Looking up, Aurelio shook his head. "Not entirely, no. I have been looking over some information the Doge has given to me. It is nothing to do with Fenice Zucchar, but he thought, with all I have done to find her, I might be in a position to advise him."

Andrea looked puzzled. "Arrigo said you were . . ." He floundered, looking for words that were less condemning than those his oldest brother had spoken. "He said you have been more devoted than any woman deserves."

"Did he?" Aurelio asked dryly. "He has said something of the sort to me, only much more crudely." He motioned to the chair on the other side of his desk. "Sit, sit. I am not so busy that I cannot spare a moment for you."

Reluctantly Andrea did as he was told. "You have been looking for her, haven't you? You want to find her, don't you?"

"Yes," said Aurelio a bit too quickly. "Certainly. I will hunt for her until I find her. But I have discovered a few things that are useful to the Doge. Can you fault me for lending him my knowledge when it is so beneficial to Venice?"

Andrea shrugged. "What could you know that the Doge does not?" It had been Arrigo's question the evening before, and both brothers knew it. "And why should he come to you?"

Aurelio decided to answer the question. "In searching for Fenice Zucchar, I have sometimes spoken with men who are at the edges of the law and who deal with those who are beyond it entirely. I have maintained my contact with them in the hope they may hear something of Fenice." He looked at his younger brother with such concentration that Andrea was startled. "They often learn of other things, and they know those whose activities lead them to discover much that is important to Venice that could not be learned more directly." He put his hand on the sheet of vellum he had been studying. "Here there is news of the Sultan's work in Crete; I had hoped to discover Fenice had been carried there, but in asking, I was told of matters that the Doge will want to know." He gave a tight smile. "I know which men we may rely on and those we may not."

"So you are a . . . servant of the Doge?" Andrea asked, uncertain whether to be impressed or skeptical.

"I aid the Doge when I can. And contrary to what Arrigo has said, I am not his tool." He did not smile this time and the humor in his eyes was hard. "Nor am I holding out false hopes to the Zucchar family to keep my actions from being questioned. You see, I have heard Arrigo, too."

"Arrigo says many things," Andrea said in oblique defense of him.

"And you listen to them." He put his elbows on the desk and leaned into his linked hands. "You think I am a fool to want to find Fenice Zucchar, because she has been missing for so long. I understand why you have such reservations; I occasionally share them. But she was the first to see worth in me beyond my skill for building bridges and boats, and for that I am grateful. I owe her more than I can repay. So I will do all that I can to return her to her family, and to marry her if the Doge and the Patriarch will allow it, after so much time."

"You're serious about this, aren't you?" Andrea considered Aurelio with an interest he had never shown his older brother. "Arrigo thinks it is only a flight of fancy. He says the Zucchars don't want her found anymore; they would rather mourn her as dead." He said this gingerly, not wanting to anger Aurelio. "I like the Zucchars. They are a . . . a fine family."

"I like them, too. If that is their wish, that I continue to look for their daughter, so be it; if it is not, I will search on my own behalf," said Aurelio, as if wholly uninterested in what Fenice's family thought. "They have said nothing of the sort to me."

"But they wouldn't, would they?" Andrea suggested. "If you will do their work for them, and save them embarrassment, why should they stop you?"

Aurelio sighed and leaned back in his chair. "True enough," he told his brother. "You cannot fault them for such a decision." He watched his brother from the tail of his eye. "Do you think I am being a fool?"

"I think," said Andrea after a moment's cogitation, "that Fenice Zucchar, wherever she is, has given you a purpose that you did not have, and I can see why you would want to show your appreciation to her. But I can't comprehend why you would want to marry a woman who is so compromised as she must be. That is where I think Arrigo is right." He ducked his head in apology. "I do not want to offend you, Aurelio, but I don't think you would be wise to marry a woman who has been—"

"I have to find her before I can marry her," said Aurelio. "Your worry may yet prove moot." He made an impatient gesture. "I told the Doge I would have my report ready by tomorrow and I am not yet half done with it."

Andrea stood at once, glad of the excuse to leave. "I hope the Doge knows how dedicated a . . . an advisor he has in you."

"If I continue to show my use to him, he will acknowledge it," said Aurelio, putting his attention on the words on the vellum.

"And the Zucchars: do they know what they owe to you?" It was a risky question and he framed it with much consideration. "Are they grateful?"

"That is unimportant to me," Aurelio said curtly.

Andrea realized he had overstepped himself. "Well, I hope they will thank you when you find Fenice," he said.

Aurelio glanced up from the page. "So do I," he admitted as he waved his brother out of his room.

Dracula bowed over Fenice's hand, and kissed it; his mouth was cool on her flesh, and she resisted the impulse to pull it away. "You have done well," he approved as he led her to the high-backed chair before the hearth. "I am proud of your courage, Fenice."

"You have shown me much . . . distinction," she said, meaning the clothing she wore. "I must tell you that I am grateful."

"It is nothing more than you deserve." He indicated she should sit down. "You have shown yourself worthy of much more than this trumpery." He held out a necklace of rubies. "You will want to put these on yourself."

Fenice stared at the jewels, astonished at their beauty. "They are . . . too fine," she protested, unable to bring herself to touch them.

"I am the one to decide that," he said, leaning over her. "I wish you to put them on; if you would please me, you will."

It was harder to resist him than to comply; Fenice took the necklace in her hands and worked the clasp open. "I will wear them to please you," she said as she put them around her neck and did her best to secure the fastening.

"In time you will know you have earned them," he said, smiling at her.

For an instant, Fenice could see the dead man in the malodorous alley-court; she gave a tiny shake of her head, banishing the image and the apprehension that the jewels were a kind of recompense for the killing of the man from the market-gang. "I cannot think how I should do this," she said warily.

"In time you will," Dracula promised her, and touched the roll at the top of her sleeve. "You would shine in the courts of the great: in this house, you make me humble." He touched her under the chin and when she lifted her head, he kissed her full on the mouth.

Filled with equivocal responses, Fenice could not bring herself to act. She remained in his arms, unmoving, her passivity more troubling to her than to him. At last she pushed on his shoulder and managed to break free of him; she muttered something about feeling faint and steadied herself against the high back of the chair. "You . . . you surprise me, Prince."

"Ah, no; you need give me no title," said Dracula. "My name will do." He caressed her breast through the rich fabric of her ropilla. "Dracula. Say it."

"Dracula," she said, as if the name had an unsavory taste to it. She could not help but feel she had made a dangerous concession to him, letting him command her to name him as he had. At first she had thought he was providing protection, but that was no longer the case: his name itself seemed to have power over her for reasons she could not quite explain to herself. She frowned at her hands, unable to look him in the eye for fear of what she would find reflected there. The heat from the fire was suddenly too hot for her, and she raised her arm to shield her face.

If Dracula was perturbed by any of this, he did not reveal it; he stayed uncomfortably close to Fenice and said to her, "There. You do me honor to call me by my name."

"And I am honored to be allowed to use it," she said, more for form's sake than from honesty. She forced herself to look at him.

"You have eyes like storm clouds, Fenice," he said, his voice silky with meaning. "Now they are almost black; I have seen them green as the sea."

"Perhaps it is because I am troubled that they darken," she suggested, unwilling to expose herself to any other criticism. She had to fight her urge to touch him, as if she would be contemptible for so minor a gesture.

"You have no reason to be troubled," said Dracula, once again leaning toward her. "Rather, you have reason to rejoice. You have taken the first step to expunging the stain on your name."

She laughed, the sound wild and without amusement. "Which name? Fenice? Aeneo?"

Dracula lifted her hand and kissed it. "The name of the bride of my blood," he said, unwilling to let go of her hand.

Fenice stared at him. "Bride?"

"You and I will be united," said Dracula. "When you have completed your mission, you will be mine." He did not wait for her to speak. "You will come with me far away into the mountains where I reign, and you will be with me, my comrade and my lover. You will be respected through all of Transylvania, and you will live very long in my protection." This time he kissed both her hands.

"Why do you say such things?" Fenice asked, her words breathless. "I will not be mocked, my lord."

"Dracula," he corrected. "You do not know what delights we will discover together, what adventures we will have."

She could not deny that something in his words stirred her, making her want to listen. It took an effort of will for her to say, "I do not know that it would suit me to go away into Transylvania with you, Dracula."

He shook his head, faintly condemning as he said, "You will be content to beg in the market-square until someone kills you trying to take your money, or finds out your sex and sells you to a brothel? Is this the life you want for yourself?" He shook his head. "No. You are made of better stuff than that. You are one who had dared all, and must have the rewards of her dare. You could have had a comfortable, even pampered, life in Venice. But you chose the life many boys haven't courage enough to live. You have mettle, and you have tested yourself against all adversity. Now it is time you assumed the place where you need not worry about being found out, the place where you will have the regard of all who know you, and my esteem." He held her hands and pulled her up out of the chair without effort. "You have every reason to come with me, and none to remain behind."

"I will vanish, then?" She realized as she spoke that she had been assuming that one day she would confront Ercole and show him how wrong he had been to condemn her. That was not likely to happen, she knew now.

"From Varna, yes," said Dracula.

"And I would be with you in your Transylvanian stronghold?" What sort of place was on the other side of the forest? She tried to imagine what kind of country it might be.

"There are mountains, great mountains, in a vast, sweeping curve. In the center there is a high plateau, rich in grains and other bounty of the land. My keep is in the mountains, on a crag above a river where no enemy can reach it. Eagles fly beneath it." He smiled at her, this time winningly. "Gypsies come every year to do me homage, and the common people speak of me with awe. It will be the same with you."

"Because of you?" She could not hide her disappointment.

"At first," said Dracula at his most persuasive. "In time they will know you for what you are and they will value you as you deserve to be valued." He enclosed her in his arms, her head beneath his chin, and he went on, "You will be revered by all who hear of you, Fenice. No one will dare to voice anything against you, and no one will slight you in any way, for they will understand that to complain of you is to complain of me."

"How can you say this?" Fenice asked, finding it difficult to breathe; his arms held her tightly and she could not move.

"I am lord of that land. I have ruled there many, many years. The cadet branch of my family has caused the Ottomites some trouble, but no longer. I, on the other hand, have withstood conquerors for centuries." He gripped her more securely. "Think what that can mean to you, Fenice: to live for decades beyond anyone you have ever known, to be all but immortal. You will see nations rise and fall from my castle, and you will sustain all. You will have the mountains to measure time by, and the generations of gypsies." He relaxed his grasp enough to look down into her face. "You will venture abroad without hindrance, and together we will share the excitement of the hunt, and of exploration."

Fenice was tempted by what he said, but she could not bring herself to express the doubts that lurked in her mind, just beneath the longing she had for the opportunity he offered her. "I cannot tell you anything, not yet," she said. "I had no thought to . . . to leaving Varna, or to . . . to taking a husband."

"Then it is appropriate for you to consider your answer," said Dracula; it was clear he had already decided what her answer would be. "Shall we say in three days, at sundown? I will leave Varna then, with or without you."

"Why three days?" she asked, in order to say something so that she would not feel so truly lost; the ruby necklace was heavier and tighter than it had been a breath ago.

"That will give you an opportunity to kill the rest of them," Dracula said, and favored her with a smile that made Fenice go cold in her bones. He stroked her hair. "Tonight you need not venture out, unless you are eager to kill the others."

Fenice shook her head repeatedly, her head beginning to ache. "No. Not tonight. Not tonight."

"Wise," Dracula approved. "They may be on their guard tonight. But tomorrow night it will be easier to waylay one or two of them and do what must be done. You will be more ready and they will be less." He made a gesture of encouragement. "They will not have long to boast of their triumph over you."

"Triumph?" She thought the word sounded hollow, and she wanted to challenge Dracula's insistence on using it; instead she said, "I would not have thought that I would mean so much to any of them, given that they maim and steal every day. Why should they take any pride in accosting me, when they are always searching to do the same, or worse, to others?"

Dracula regarded her with approval. "I knew from the first, when you were nothing more than an adventuresome child, that you were unlike most females. You do not suppose that you must be the cause of all that men do."

She shook her head again. "Indeed, how could I?" she asked. "I had my brothers to show me otherwise from the first."

"And you knew what you saw—you understood it." He stepped away from her and strode down the room. "You need no illusions to cling to. You do not require vows and promises for every occasion. You do not have to be coddled and cajoled." There was a kind of petulance in his remarks that held her; she was convinced he was speaking of his own experience. He swung around to face her. "You have earned my admiration."

Fenice did not know whether to curtsy or giggle: it was so absurd, she told herself, to be so much at the command of Dracula. "I am no child, my lord," she said, taking care to maintain a serious demeanor, for she suspected that he would mistake laughter for mockery.

"No, you are not," said Dracula with an expression that was difficult to interpret.

"And if I agree to go with you, I will not become one," she added.

Dracula came back to her side. "I rely on you not to," he said.

Well after midnight Fenice went to her room, too restless to sleep, but so tired she could not stay awake. She found Olena yawning by the fire, waiting to help her undress. "You need not have waited," Fenice said as she saw the slave totter to her feet. "I am not so encumbered by clothes that you must help me out of them."

"I have been told to tend you, and I will do it," said Olena with a stern passivity that Fenice could not counter.

"Then I thank you for your service," she responded, and began to unfasten the rubies hanging around her neck. "These will have to be locked away, I suppose," she said as she held out the jewels. "I do not know where Dracula would want me to put them."

"I know," said Olena, taking the necklace and dropping it into the capacious pocket in the front of her apron. "He has a place where he keeps all his fine things."

"And you have seen much of them, over the years?" Fenice suggested as she began to unfasten the brooch that held the ropilla closed. "He has had other women he has given gems to?"

"One, while I have been here. Before, who can say?" Olena admitted. "Her name was Muna, and she came here shortly after the Dragon Prince bought me and took me into his service."

"Muna," Fenice repeated, as if speaking the name would reveal some of the woman's character.

Olena nodded as she prepared to take the rolled and padded sleeves off the ropilla. "She was from Smyrna, a dancer of great repute, or so I was told."

"And what are you telling me happened to her?" Fenice stared at Olena, daring her with her eyes to reveal all she knew. Bending at the waist, she let Olena tug the ropilla off her, then straightened up. She continued to undress, loosening the ties at the wrists and neck of her sottana.

Olena shrugged. "Dracula took her away with him, pledging everything to her that he has promised to you. In ten years Dracula returned, without Muna." She busied herself folding the ropilla, putting the sleeves atop it, and then waited for the sottana to be handed to her.

"She did not wish to travel here again," said Fenice, making light of the disquiet she felt dawning within her; she pulled the sottana over her head.

"She might have children, too, but he has never spoken of any." Olena tossed her head. "No, girl. He took her with him and now she is dead. I would stake my soul on it."

"Have you still one to stake?" Fenice asked with acrid sweetness. "You say he has mastered you, and you tell me that you have given up your soul to him. Yet now you give your oath to me on what you claim you do not have. What am I to think?" The dismay she assumed was comic, something that the commedia del' arte might approve. She abandoned her mockery and looked directly at Olena. "You have spoken against Dracula, yet you claim devotion. May I never depend on the loyalty of servants like you." She was almost naked now, and she made no effort to hide her body from Olena, as much to show her how little importance she gave the slave-woman as to express her defiance.

"So-ho!" Olena exclaimed. "You are defending him now. That is the beginning, and you know where it will end. You will be like him, taking the blood of the living to keep you in your damned existence. You will prey on mankind as wolves prey on sheep and goats. You will make yourself one of that dark legion that has followed him down the years, to everlasting perdition."

"Perhaps I will," said Fenice as she tugged on her thin night rail and skinned out of her underhose and hose-belt beneath the voluminous garment. "And if I do, I will have my own caprice to blame; you need not fear I will put my fall at your door." She tossed her underhose to Olena and folded her arms. "There. You have made yourself plain to me and I have heard you out. You have betrayed the trust of your master in doing it, and I suppose I am expected to put more weight on your warning for your treason. I regret to tell you I cannot endorse what you have done. Nor can I believe you."

Olena seemed terrified and furious at once. "You must believe me," she insisted. "You must. And you must leave here tonight and never come back. Go to the good Sisters at Hagia Charis. Let them shelter you."

"Thank you, no," said Fenice bluntly. "I have some experience of the Sisters, and I would rather put my whole dependence on Dracula than spend one more hour in their care."

"You will be lost," said Olena, with a trace of satisfaction in her voice.

"Perhaps I will," Fenice agreed. "But it will be the loss I sought, not one foisted on me." She shook her head. "You have done what you came to do. Now leave me."

Olena ducked her head in a servile manner and left Fenice alone.

But when Fenice climbed into bed, she could not conceal the apprehension that took hold of her in the still darkness. She had to admit that Olena had given voice to fears that had troubled her since she had first followed Dracula and seen him attack the merchant. Surely he must have stalked others over the years, and some of them must have liked what he evoked in them; some must have wanted to share his life, to be like him. She could not be the first woman who had responded to his strength and his freedom from limitations. She began to wonder who these other women might be. This Muna—if she were real and not some tale invented by Olena to frighten her—must have wanted some part of what Dracula offered. And if she did, what had become of her?

Another, less welcome, notion struck her at almost the same instant: what if Olena had told her those things on Dracula's instructions? What if he had wanted to test her, and that instead of opposing his will in talking to Fenice, Olena had been fulfilling her service to him? What might have happened if she had succeeded in persuading Fenice to turn away from this house and all Dracula offered? The memory of bodies drained of blood filled her mind.

So much of what she felt about Dracula was contradictory: Fenice realized this was part of her inability to resolve her questions about him. She was pleased and relieved that he was not repelled by her adventures, that he seemed to endorse them; but she knew he would not allow any rival for her devotion, not even her love of adventure, which he would have to share if she were to continue to enjoy it. This recognition of the ambivalent state of her mind provided enough surcease to let her drift into an uneasy slumber, in which she pursued unknown figures along unfamiliar trails, taunting them as she ran them to ground.

She woke with a start. "I am not like that," she said to the leaden predawn light. "I am no hunting dog, to run my quarry to earth. I have . . . I have . . ." Character? Principles? Scruples? She could not decide which would apply. The increasing light troubled her and she drew the curtains more closely around her bed. She had much on her mind, and yet she could not force herself to remain awake.

This time her sleep was deep and still, like the slow, deep rest of bears in winter; if any dreams perturbed her, she could not recall them to mind when she wakened at sunset, her thoughts clear and her attention sharp.

She found Olena waiting for her, food on a tray, and new clothes laid out. "He will join you shortly. Here."

"Then I had better dress before I eat," said Fenice, no longer willing to be swayed by the stories Olena might tell her.

"I thought as much." She frowned at the clothes, for they were made for men, not women, and Olena was still capable of disapproving of such irresponsible behavior. She pointed to the loose, smocklike top. "At least he does not put you in a giaquetta like the one you had on when you came here. This is more . . . seemly."

"Because it is Greek and not Italian?" Fenice challenged, but decided it was not worth arguing about. "I am sorry this offends you, Olena. It is in accord with Dracula's wishes that I wear it, not to distress you."

"You flout the way of the world," Olena complained.

"It must seem that I do," Fenice allowed mildly. "I will ask you to make allowances for me." With this careful and courteous remark, Fenice began to dress, glad to be putting on men's clothing again; she began to experience a resurgence of excitement as she adjusted the underhose tied to her belt, and then pulled on the short-hose, not complaining at their longer, looser fashion than the Venetian ones she had had before. She realized she would be less conspicuous in these garments than in what she had worn before; Greeks were everywhere, but Venetians were not as common a sight. She liked the deep, dusky gray of the clothes; they were like smoke and, she thought, would provide a kind of invisibility by their very color.

"He said he likes you dressed that way. He says it causes less comment." The scorn in her voice was eloquent. "He likes to have you deceive good, honest men."

"That may be," said Fenice. "But I doubt he is concerned for the gullibility of others."

Olena made a snort of disbelief. "If you think that, you are not as wise as you assume you are."

"Tell me," said Fenice with cordiality as she put on the outer belt, buckling it so that it hung on her hips instead of her waist; she had seen more sailors with this manner of wearing them than those who tightened them at their waists. "Since you are determined to tutor me."

Having permission granted so readily made Olena suspicious. She frowned at Fenice, her brow drawn down in disapproval. "You do not want to listen to me."

"No, I don't," Fenice agreed. "But you are determined that I should hear you. So while I eat, you may speak your mind." She sat down and pulled the tray toward her. "Meat. Good."

This did not reassure Olena as she came up to Fenice's side. "You don't know what he is. Oh, you think you do. You think he is your champion, your defender, and he can be, but at a price. The price is much too high—you must believe me."

Fenice broke off a piece of bread and dipped it in the heavy juices around the slab of rich, dark meat that filled most of the bowl in the middle of the tray. She let the bread soak up the savory sauce, and popped it into her mouth, signaling Olena to go on while she chewed.

"You have been smitten by him. You think you love him, and that he loves you. Ah!" She made an impatient gesture with her knobby hands. "Girls always think they are loved when they do what they know is wrong."

"I don't think I love him, necessarily," Fenice said around the last of the morsel. "Nor do I think he must love me. I do know he excites me, and that I seem to interest him." She saw how scandalized Olena was and tried to make things better. "You think I do not know that he is a hunter, without any regard for those he hunts? I know this. I know he is teaching me to be like him by helping me find the men who wanted to harm me, and who killed my friend." She cut off a wedge of meat and fixed it on the end of her knife, then nibbled at it, the way the sailors on the *Impresa* had eaten. She did her best to soothe Olena's distress. "There is no reason to think I am seduced by Dracula. If I surrender, I do so willingly."

Olena's features became more seamed and lined as her anxiety increased. "Then I will hope that you will find mercy in the afterlife, for there will be none for you in this world, no matter what side of the grave you are on."

Fenice would have said *amen,* but there was meat in her throat and the word would not come.

Perhaps your soul, with greater faith than mine
Observes more truly the fire within me.
—Michelangelo Buonarroti

— XXV —

"There. Ahead on your right," Dracula said softly to Fenice as they made their way through the market-square. "Do you see them? In the doorway?" It was night and the last of the torches set around the place were burning low; only their footfalls disrupted the silence of the marketplace, made eerie by the echoes from the stone-fronted buildings around them.

Fenice squinted into the darkness, then smiled; the feathery touch of the breeze made her skin feel more hot than cool as she readied herself for what was to come. "I see them. Four men, perhaps five. One is supposed to be on guard, but he has fallen asleep. I think I recognize one of them," she added, a grimmer purpose putting an edge to her whisper and making her eyes dark as charcoal.

"The one with the scar on his jaw. Yes," said Dracula, his approval making his voice warm. "You will be able to demand much from him. You have that right."

"I do not care about right; I care about vengeance." She said it to please him, and was somewhat surprised to realize she spoke the truth. Now that she had the chance to exact recompense for her ordeal, and for Libu's death, she was hard-pressed not to give some sign of it. She put her hands together as if to contain her excitement; she thought she must be shining in the night like a torch, so great was the thrill rising within her.

"Be careful," Dracula cautioned her. "There are more of them than you. They are ruthless; you know this already."

"So I do," Fenice agreed. "But they are not expecting me, and I know who I am to fight." She looked at him with the vestige of a smile. "You have no reason to doubt me, my lord."

He laid his hand on her shoulder. "No; I know I do not. I am concerned for the doubts you have about yourself." If he had intended to alarm her, he could not have chosen more effective means to do it. "Your purpose must be fixed, or you will fail for lack of it." He bent down and kissed her mouth once, roughly; as he released her, he said, "You have triumph and defeat within you. Which it will be is yours to decide. Not them. They are chaff. You are—"

She stopped him. "When it is done, you will tell me which I chose." With that, she pulled the dagger from its sheath and began to run toward the broad doorway where the men slept.

The dozing sentry was her first target: she rushed up behind him, put her hand over his mouth and used her hold on his jaw to spin him around, lifting her dagger as she did. She set her teeth in a hard grimace as she made herself plunge the dagger into his throat, silencing him as she killed him. Stepping back to keep from being drenched in his blood, she let him stagger and fall without concern; her attention was now on the next man, a Turk with a cast in his eye who barely opened it when Fenice's dagger went down into his neck and chest.

One of the men was wakening, surly and combative. He rubbed his eyes as he pulled out an Oriental knife, bent and deadly; he scythed it before him, cursing as he prepared to fight.

"Keep them busy. I will kill them." It was the man with the scar speaking; he had not given himself away until then; Fenice guessed he had been awake since she began her attack. She crouched low and struck out, aiming for legs in order to disable a second Turk. She realized he had slipped back from her, and she was now between two dangerous ruffians who were ready to fight. There was no sign of Dracula.

For an instant, Fenice imagined herself back before Dracula's gate, with the men she had fought there once again opposing her; the memory was so repugnant that she was determined to banish it with this battle or carry it to her grave.

"Hold him. It's that Aeneo!" the one behind her cried in a hushed tone.

"He's good with the knife. Get his arms," the other ordered, his voice a bit louder.

Fenice kept moving, weaving, ducking, lunging, making sweeps with her dagger, trying to hurt them without putting herself within range.

"The lad's cautious," one of them marveled.

"Two against one," said the second, taking up the tone.

"Might as well fight a woman as him," the first said, trying to goad Fenice into a reckless attack.

This almost worked. Fenice kept herself from striking out with an effort of will: she would not permit herself to behave as if she were a green boy, fighting his first time. She had seen enough, and done enough, that she could not be distracted by the slights and insults they flung at her. She kept her mind on her work, her hand on the dagger steady.

"What is he doing here?" one wondered aloud, trying to take Fenice's mind from their battle.

"Come back for Libu, no doubt. He's angry that we took his boy from him." The second man laughed. "What man wants to give up his pleasure to death?"

"You would think Aeneo would want to join Libu. The afterlife would be a reward for their fidelity." He was moving nearer, keeping in the shadows to conceal what he did. "He's got to die. He might as well go to Libu when he enters Paradise."

"Boys and houri everywhere," the other said with smacking lips. "What a good place. Better than this one, surely."

"Do they have boys in the Christian Paradise?" The voice was behind her—either one had moved more quickly than Fenice realized or she had been right in her estimate that there were five, not four, of the gang sleeping in the broad doorway. She lowered her stance again, pulling the muscles in her back and legs until they quivered from strain.

"Why make this so long?" The third voice sounded both angry and bored. "You two grab his arms and I'll dump his guts on the paving." They ceased their jeering and began to fight in earnest. "Try for the knife-arm first, or you could get hurt. Break the elbow."

Fear went through Fenice like a horde of stinging insects, almost holding her in place. She scowled, making up a front of belligerence that was wholly fiction. This was too soon; she had too many bruises from the last time.

Then she heard the low, ferocious laughter, and knew Dracula was testing her. She leaped suddenly at the nearest of the men, slashing at his abdomen with fast, intense swipes of her dagger.

He screamed and staggered away, then fell on his knees, his hands pressed to his body as if trying to hold back the welter of blood with his fingers. He began to wail, a high, thin sound that was eloquent of agony and despair.

Fenice could not let this success make her lax in her defense; she heard one of the men curse, and felt more than saw him strike out in her direction. She dodged his arm only to find herself backed against the corner of the building; she could not make herself move away from it, comforted by the false safety it offered.

The nearer man kicked out, trying to knock her legs from under her; Fenice protested with a sound that was more a growl than anything else. She slipped away from the wall and skulked into the deepest night-shadows she could find. There, instead of crouching, she climbed a short way up the irregular stones of the wall, above where the men hunted her. Holding her breath, she waited until one of the men was beneath her—she dropped on his shoulders, using her dagger on his throat as she landed.

He jerked like a gaffed fish, dislodging her from her place and almost falling on her as he collapsed, spasming as he strove to breathe one more time.

Fenice was disoriented by this abrupt end of life; she had caused it, but she had not thought it would happen so quickly, so irrevocably. This death was different from the rest, although she could not say why, and could not afford the time to consider it. She scrambled to her feet, alert to every sound, every motion in the darkness. An instant before a hand jerked her ankle, she became aware of the last man creeping toward her on his belly; had she not seen him, she would have fallen. As it was, she kicked out, hopping to remain upright, and stamped down on his arm. There was a nauseating snap and the man howled.

Stepping away from him, Fenice warned herself that, even with a broken arm, the man was dangerous. She waited a moment while the last man began to moan, curling around his broken arm like a fading leaf; swiftly Fenice stepped over him and, with a quick motion, sliced the Achilles tendons at the back of his ankles. As the man wrenched from the pain, Fenice moved away from him. "This was for what you did to Libu. And what you were going to do to me." She had to contain the rush of pride that came over her. "You thought it would be easy to kill me." Finally she was aware of the smell of death that filled the air, and the dead and injured men strewn about like refuse. She could not keep her fear from raging now, and she ran from the place.

"You see?" Dracula said as she careened into his arms; terror made her eyes huge and her pulse loud. "You have it in you to exact revenge."

Fenice could only pant, her body suddenly watery and rickety; she leaned against him. "Where were you?" she demanded.

"Nearby," he answered, undismayed.

"They might have hurt me. They wanted to kill me," she declared, her hands fixed in his dusky purple cloak like talons.

"You did not allow them to hurt you; you knew already they wanted to kill you." He regarded her calmly. "If I had helped you, you would have doubted your own strength. You doubted it before." His arms went around her and he crushed her against him. "You should know how much I value your strength. It is what captivated me; that, and your wild soul."

This praise was disquieting, and for a moment Fenice was filled with uncertainty about this sinister savior. Then she felt his mouth on hers and her questions vanished as her senses flamed.

"Yes; this is as it should be," Dracula said when the kiss ended. "You show yourself as you are, fierce and brave."

"I was frightened," she admitted.

"In time you will not be," Dracula assured her. "You will remember how you bested these men and you will lose the fear." He stroked her hair. "Are you angry with me now, for making you take revenge?"

She glanced at the men. "They deserve what happened to them," she declared. "They have reaped the harvest they sowed."

Dracula kissed her again, his arms like vises around her. "I am proud of your courage," he said. "You deserve to be mine."

Fenice felt this praise with rapture and misgiving. She took pride in his admiration, but how could he provide her what she sought if she were in his thrall? She struggled in his embrace. Where was the adventure if her spirit were tethered to his? She let his mouth cover hers again. She felt transfixed by him, and all the vitality that had sustained her in the fight now turned to an immobility, numbing and passive.

"We should not linger," Dracula said as he released her.

"We are not in danger," Fenice responded as she looked at the corpses again. "Dead or dying, they are no—"

"Others will come, and we cannot risk discovery." He went to the man whose Achilles tendons Fenice had cut; he bent over and ripped out the man's throat, taking the blood with such eagerness that Fenice found it difficult to watch. When he was finished, he straightened up. "There. He will say nothing now, and there will be no hunt for us."

"But why should we be hunted at all?" Fenice asked, and knew the answer as she spoke. "You do not want to be flayed in the market-square and left there to rot. They would do that, wouldn't they, to prove you are no demon."

"They would not find me easy to kill," said Dracula. "They would have to do more than flay me. You would die well before I did."

Fenice blanched at this harsh remark. "You would not let them catch me, would you?"

"Not if I could stop it, no; but the Guard might come upon us." He started into the shadows again. "Come with me and live, Fenice. Remain and die."

She was not certain his threats had any substance, but she was reluctant to put them to the test. She broke from her stillness, running after him with more determination than she thought she could summon. The effort of moving was more enormous than the fury that had carried her through her fight; she felt as if she were carrying the bodies of all those men on her shoulder as she followed Dracula along the narrow streets.

Sitting at the table in the main hall of Dracula's house the next evening, Fenice could not get warm. In spite of the fire on the hearth, and the magnificent ropilla of soot-colored velvet over a sottana of heavy dark russet silk, she felt as if she stood on the quay at Venice as a gale roared in from the north, all stinging sleet and cutting wind. She had tried to eat the steaming soup Olena had put out for her, but she had no appetite for it; she put her hands to the sides of the bowl as if hoping that heat would warm her.

"You are as cold as the dead," Olena remarked as she touched Fenice's brow.

The mention of death made Fenice shiver. She could not convince herself that she had been justified in the killing she had done so readily the previous night; those men had not harmed her, had not done anything to her, but she had killed them. She managed a wan smile. "Small wonder," she said, as if this should be explanation enough.

"You should have wine. It will warm you." Olena went to get the jar of dark Hungarian red wine. "It is said to keep the heart lively."

"I'll have some. Later." She stared into the flames and thought she saw the men she had killed in their leaping brightness. "It's just the logs," she muttered.

"Logs, you say?" Olena asked sharply. She put down the jar and scowled at Fenice. "You did his bidding, didn't you? Whatever it was, you did it."

"Nothing of the sort," Fenice snapped. "I accepted his guidance. He was right, I know that now that I have acted. I would never have known it if I had not heeded him."

Olena made a distressed sound. "You speak so readily about something you do not comprehend," she said, more sad than vexed. "You say that you acted on your own, but guided by him? You must think what that means. You have made yourself his creature. He is making you one with him, and you have been deceived."

"I think not," said Fenice quietly. "I think he had seen that within me that makes me want what he wants." She frowned, and went on more to herself than to Olena. "I have always been reckoned wild, and I have done things that no young woman ought to do, and I have been proud of doing them. So why should I be puzzled when I realize that I am more willing to take up disputes as a man would? My brothers would have done the same, and been praised for it. You look askance that I would want to listen to Dracula, but I am coming to think that it was more my desire than his that I should exact vengeance for what I suffered. I am ashamed that the images of those men haunt me. I am out of patience with myself that I let old fears possess me." She slapped her hand down on the tabletop. "I am grateful to Dracula. I am annoyed with myself."

"You should pray," said Olena. "You should stop your fall before you are in the Pit. The harm is of his making, and you are not willing to hold him accountable." She shoved Fenice, more brazen now that she had heard Fenice's ruminations. "You have fallen into the hands of a great evil and you will not do what you must to save yourself."

"I have done that already," said Fenice, and picked up her spoon, willing herself to eat and trying to convince herself that she enjoyed the savor of the meat, peas, and onions.

Olena shook her head. "You are embracing your damnation. You will be lost if you do not shun him and all he commands you to do."

"And why should this trouble you?" Fenice challenged. "Pour me wine."

As she filled a chalice for Fenice, Olena said, "You do not know how great your sins are. You think he serves you for your sake. He does nothing that is not to his good. Nothing else matters to him. He helps you only to make you rely on him." She held out the chalice. "Drink it. See if it will warm you."

Defiantly Fenice drank about half the contents, the strong taste making her smile. Setting the chalice down, she said, "It is good wine. I like it." She regarded Olena with narrowed eyes. "You are once again trying to confuse me."

"I am trying to show you how dangerous your circumstances are," Olena said piously.

"And you say you are not jealous that he aids me and leaves you his slave?" She drank more wine. "You have done nothing to earn my trust and he has done much. You say he is trying to make me like him. If that would give me fortitude and honor, why should I refuse to be like him? You have nothing you can say to me." She made a sign of dismissal, then held up her chalice. "Refill this before you go."

"You are seduced," said Olena as she filled the chalice and put the jar on the table beside the chalice. "Be careful that you—"

"Leave me," Fenice interrupted. "And take the soup with you. It is tasteless."

Olena took the bowl and, with a look of reproach, went out of the main hall, leaving Fenice alone with her thoughts and the wine.

Somehow Fenice found her way to bed and managed to get out of her clothes. She had no clear notion how she had managed it; her recollections were disordered and her emotions were in turmoil.

She did not notice the shutter opening, and the tall, lean figure that slipped through the window into her room; when she did become aware that she was not alone, she thought she was imagining Dracula standing beside her. "My lord," she said muzzily.

"Fenice," he answered, and bent down to her.

This startled her into near-wakefulness. "You are here," she said, reaching out to touch him as if she expected him to vanish like smoke.

"I am," he said, moving swiftly to lie next to her. "You should have expected me."

"I hoped you would come," she said, as if to account for her lapse.

"I will always come where I am wanted," he said, and moved to embrace her.

This was what she had longed for, and she strove to make him show her some comfort and care, or at least, some kindness. "I will do anything you wish," she said to encourage him.

He kissed her slowly, his mouth hard on hers as if using his passion to rouse her from the lassitude of the wine. His hands took her body captive, enforcing his need of her. The passion he revealed was like the burning cold of ice, not the heat of fire; it roused her as her fears had done, and she let him use her, hoping she would be rewarded with some sign of affection when he had achieved his craving. His mouth went to her throat, and she steeled herself for what was to come, telling herself that it was his way, that he deserved this of her, that he had earned the right to claim her. "You will make me proud of you," he said when he was done.

To her surprise, he did not leave her bed when he had finished; he lay back and opened his cloak and camisa. "What?" She could not guess the reason for this.

He drew his fingernail across his chest, opening a narrow furrow of blood. "Drink it," he said, his hand on the back of her neck to guide her to his wound; his strength was formidable as he moved her inexorably toward the cut.

For an instant she had a pang of revulsion. She had seen too much blood—drinking it was too dreadful to contemplate. If she was capable of drinking blood, then she was no longer the woman she thought she was; a half-formed protest formed on her lips, but she could not voice it. Then she saw the adjuration in his eyes, and she did not resist. If this would ensure his devotion, she would comply gladly; it was a small enough thing to please him. And she realized then that she wanted desperately to please him.

The taste was metallic and strong, more intense than any meat she had eaten. She found it difficult to swallow, as if it were too rich after all the wine she had drunk.

For some length of time they lay together, her mouth against his chest where his blood welled. Neither of them spoke, although Dracula sighed deeply once, and his hand on Fenice's neck relaxed. Something thrummed in the air around them and there was a wail in the distance that might have been wolves while Fenice sank into a stupor that was not quite sleep.

It was afternoon by the time Fenice awoke; she sat up in the bed suddenly as if disturbed by a sudden intrusion. Frowning a bit in uncertainty, she flung back the curtains and saw the red stains on the pillows and the sheets. With a cry of dismay she clapped her hand to her neck as if she feared she was still bleeding. She was about to call for help when the events of the night came back to her in a rush. She clung to the bedpost as the enormity of what she had done came over her. Absently she wiped her mouth and found something crusted on her lips. She spat involuntarily, and chided herself inwardly for such a useless reaction: whatever had been done could not be abjured now.

Sounds from the courtyard below claimed her attention; she went to the window and opened the shutters, wincing in the brilliant sunshine that flooded in. Gingerly leaning out, she saw to her amazement that horses were being put to wagons, wagons that were being loaded with trunks and cases. Fenice recalled Dracula's intention to leave Varna, but seeing these preparations, she was struck with a deep sense of fear—what if he should abandon her?

"You silly child," she admonished herself aloud. "Why should being on your own trouble you? You have acted on your own for months now. You can do it again." But the words were hollow in her ears, as if she had lost her courage. "He will take you with him," she said, trying to convince herself that his promises had been sincere.

"Yes," said Dracula from the doorway. "I will." He came into her room, a bundle of clothes in his hands. "We leave at sunset. Be ready."

She caught the clothing he tossed to her. "But . . . it will be night."

"And we will travel at night." He cocked his head toward the courtyard. "The men will follow; the wagons are too slow for my purposes. There will be remounts for us along the way, never fear."

"But I thought—" Fenice began, trying to recall what day he had finally decided upon as their departure.

"At sunset. In the courtyard." With those terse orders, he turned on his heel and left her to dress for the night.

Fenice stood, ambivalence holding her to the spot. How could he speak to her so . . . so unfeelingly after all that had passed between them the night before? What offense had she committed that he regarded her without a trace of affection? Had it meant nothing that she had tasted his blood? She put the clothes on the bed and was mildly pleased to discover they were boy's garments: a camisa of good linen, which she pulled over her head as soon as she had got out of her night rail; over it a Hungarian dolman of tooled leather; leather breeches and leggings; last of all, high rawhide boots. When she had finished dressing she longed for a mirror to see how she looked. She raked her fingers through her hair, hoping to put it in some order.

She was rolling up her night rail and puzzling how to pack it when Olena came into the room, her face stony with disapproval. "So you are leaving," she grumbled. "You, and the faithless fools who have gone before you. Well, you have chosen destruction, and may you not despair when you know what you have done." She held out a basin of water and a comb. "I will tend you for this horror you have embraced."

"Strange sentiments from someone who could not be worthy of him," Fenice heard herself say in a tone as daunting as any Dracula had used.

"You are not with him yet, not entirely," said Olena as she motioned Fenice to the chair where the slave could wait on her.

"Better to be with him than alone in Varna without any to support me." Where were these haughty words coming from? Fenice started to apologize but was interrupted by Olena.

"Remember there have been others and they have never returned." Olena dragged the comb through Fenice's short dark hair with more energy than necessary; Fenice winced as a knot was ruthlessly dragged out of the strands. "You have something matted in your hair."

Fenice kept her head still in spite of this mauling. "Then get it out," she said bluntly.

Olena dragged the comb through the strands again and finally pulled a small wad of them out on the comb's teeth. "It looks like blood," she declared at her most condemning.

"Then it may be blood," said Fenice, and fell silent while Olena finished her work.

"You will have no one to pray for you if you leave here," Olena warned when she was done.

"Perhaps not," said Fenice and was at once struck with a vivid impression of the face of her sister Bianca, who would be a nun by now, and devoted to praying for all those who could not, or would not. She found little consolation in this recognition, and wondered why.

"When you are gone from this house, I will forget you," Olena warned as she prepared to leave Fenice alone.

"You did not forget the other—what was her name?" Fenice said with pronounced unconcern.

"Muna," said Olena grudgingly. "No, I have not forgot her, nor should you."

"Of course," said Fenice, adding with spite that shocked her inwardly, "She must have failed where I shall succeed."

Olena glowered at Fenice. "You may deserve him, after all," she said as she opened the door. "I wish you well of him."

Fenice bowed to Olena as she slammed the door shut.

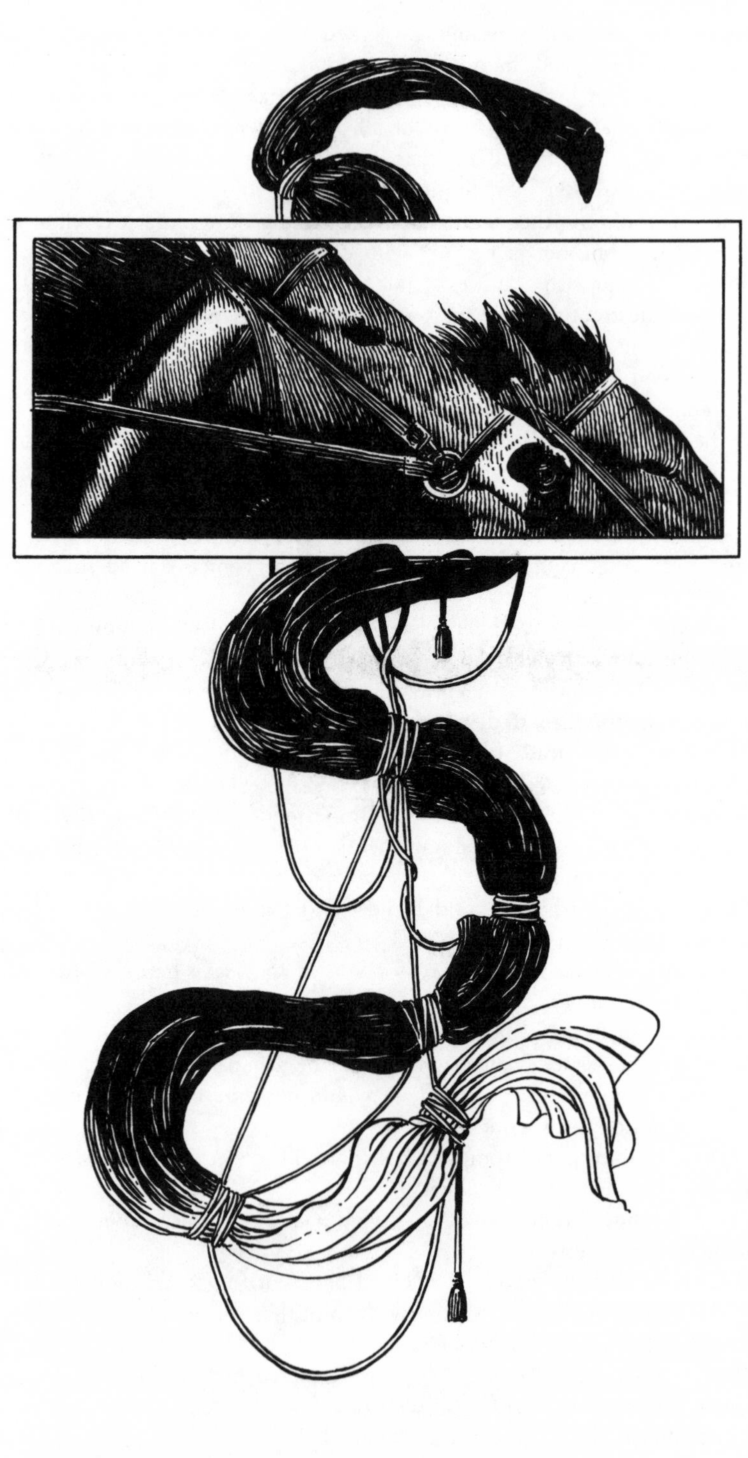

Go, song, pierce her breast like an arrow:
Thus vengeance and art are both served.
—Dante Alighieri

— XXVI —

Two big-shouldered black horses were standing in the courtyard, their bridles held by grooms who needed all their strength to keep the animals from sidling and stamping in anticipation of their coming journey. Dracula strode up to the larger of the two and put his hand on the high pommel, testing the security of the girths with a sharp tug; the saddle remained in place and he nodded his approval to the groom.

"They were fed and watered?" Dracula asked.

"An hour since," said the first groom. "They will be ready to run when you leave here."

"Good," Dracula said, and turned as Fenice strode out into the courtyard. "You are ready?"

"I am," said Fenice with more confidence than she felt. She stared at the horses and once again tried to quell her doubts. She went up to Dracula, her stride long and boylike, to show how glad she was to be back in male garments. "What do you want me to do?"

"Mount that gelding," said Dracula, pointing to the second horse.

"How?" She hated to admit her ignorance.

"You put your left foot in the left stirrup and swing up," Dracula said, a cold amusement in his eyes. "Then you take the rein in your hands, tightly enough to feel the horse's mouth, but not so tightly that you pull in his head."

It was another test; Fenice knew it as soon as she heard Dracula's tone. "Very good," she said, and went to the animal Dracula had indicated; she lifted her leg to put her foot in the stirrup, reached for the pommel and hauled herself upward. She had to struggle to get her right leg over the cantel, but finally she settled gracelessly onto the gelding's back. Then she reached for the rein, a thick leather strap leading from one side of the bit to the other. She took the strap in her hands like grasping a rope; the groom shook his head and mimed the proper grip, which she did her utmost to duplicate.

The gelding was released by the groom and immediately began to back up, his nose tucked into his chest.

"Use your knees," Dracula told her. "And your heels."

Fenice found the movements of the horse much larger than she had expected, and she realized she would have to sit in the saddle as if she sat in a boat, accommodating the roll and pitch of the movement or she would exhaust herself in a matter of hours. More instructions were shouted at her; she gathered in the reins, kicking the horse tentatively.

"Use force!" Dracula ordered, and she kicked again, clapping her heels with authority against the black flank.

The gelding halted and stood; Fenice could feel his eagerness in the gathering of the big muscles under his shoulders. "I'm ready," she said, and hoped it was so.

Dracula vaulted into the saddle of his mount, brought up the reins, and turned the horse in a single, practiced movement. Then he shouted, "Open the gate!"

His order was obeyed at once. As soon as the gate was open, Dracula and his horse lunged through it; Fenice's mount plunged after them, Fenice clinging to the reins with one hand and the pommel with the other.

The streets were nearly empty; those few people abroad scattered like autumn leaves as the two black horses raced for the city gates, where the guards shouted in vain for them to stop; they rode through the gates and onto the road that led north from Varna.

Jolted and rocked in the saddle, Fenice put all her attention to staying on the horse's back. She clung to the reins with hands like claws as the gelding cantered onward. She paid little attention to the cluster of buildings just outside the gate, and less to the farms that lined the road with their barns and sheepfolds; night was falling and the shapes were becoming indistinct: a hut was no different than a large shrub. She could not call out, for that would reveal her inability to ride.

The road continued into the countryside, a deeply rutted track wide enough for two laden wagons; Dracula kept to the verge where the footing was better. As the last of the light faded from the sky, the horses fell into a trot; Fenice panted more than her gelding as the steady pace slowed.

Watching Dracula ahead of her, Fenice was struck by how much his cloak looked like wings as the wind lifted it. She could just make out the shape of it in the night. She had the odd sensation that she was following a huge bird of prey, and that vision brought home to her how much she was in his power. She could not make herself believe that she was free now. She toyed with the possibility of taking the horse and setting off on her own, finding another road and following it instead of Dracula. But even as the thought crossed her mind, she knew it would do no good to make such a foolish attempt: Dracula had set his seal upon her and he would find her no matter where she fled; she had chosen this path.

The road turned, leading to steeper inclines. Their pace slowed to a walk as the horses climbed. The open lands began to give way to forests and the trees blocked what little light the stars provided. A cold wind cut through them, making the leaves whisper urgently among themselves as Dracula set their path along the narrow track. The trees encroached on the roadway until it seemed they were going through a dark, steep tunnel, with nothing ahead of them but blackness.

Yet Dracula was unhampered by the night; he held his horse on the path as if he carried a lanthorn. Fenice felt almost blind, for she could see nothing but the neck of her horse, and that was more because of the movement of his mane than anything more visible. As Dracula kept on, she began to imagine they had left more than Varna behind, that they were going to places so remote that no names existed for them. Her hands no longer belonged to her; they clung to the rein like talons, so rigid that they might have been carved in wood; she swayed with the movement of her gelding as she would sway with the rocking of a boat, but she could sense already that her muscles would not recover quickly from the unfamiliar exercise. The wind grew colder and keener, slicing through the trees, its touch making her bones ache. Once an owl swept over them, its huge, silent wings fanning them as it passed, and once there was the distant cry of wolves.

On they went, deeper into the forest, along the narrow mountain trails, until the space above the trees began to pale, and the rustling in the undergrowth changed to the calls of birds high in the branches. Only then did Dracula rein in his horse and stop Fenice behind him. "There is a place ahead. We will change mounts and sleep for a while."

Fenice was so tired she could barely nod in acquiescence. She was so exhausted her skeleton felt limp. She had to make herself pull on the rein as if she dragged a laden barge against the tide.

The place Dracula led them to was not much more than a lean-to put up between two large, burned-out stumps of ancient trees. The structure was as unruly as a bird's nest; Fenice was surprised that it had a real door instead of an unprotected opening. There was a paddock with a small barn at one end; these buildings were far more regular than the hovel, and Fenice was not surprised when she heard a sudden whinny from the barn. Her own mount answered the greeting, only to have Dracula swing around in his saddle and bring his crop down across her mount's nose; the horse shied and tossed his head.

"My horses are taught to be silent. We need no announcement of our presence, and it could betray us to my enemies," he said in answer to the shocked expression Fenice could not hide.

"But here . . ." Her words softened.

"If they forget the lesson here, they will forget it elsewhere." He swung out of the saddle and took the rein in his hand. "Dismount," he told Fenice.

"I don't know that I can," she said as tears smarted in her eyes.

"You can," said Dracula, and waited for her to comply.

Just taking her foot from the stirrup was difficult; swinging down from the saddle was an arduous project, a complex negotiation among worn muscles, painful hands, stiff back, and fatigued legs. When she finally lowered herself to the ground, she tottered and her thighs shook. When she tried to walk she almost collapsed; she leaned against the black gelding and hung onto the stirrup until she was able to stand erect. Dracula motioned to her to come with him, and so she pulled on the rein and led the gelding toward the barn.

The building was large enough to accommodate half a dozen horses in its stalls; in the hayloft above there was fodder enough for many days. Dracula clapped his hands and a small, wizened man of indeterminate years rushed out, bowing double to Dracula before scurrying forward to take the rein from him, and to lead the horse away.

Dracula said something in a sibilant tongue, and indicated Fenice's gelding. Then he said to her, "The groom will tend your horse and ready our mounts for the evening." He indicated the stabled horses; all were as black and strengthy as the two they had ridden all night. "He will decide which are most ready for us." He came and laid his hand on her shoulder. "How have you fared?"

"I'm tired," she admitted. "I'm not accustomed to riding."

"You will become more used to it as we go," he said without a trace of sympathy. "You will have to make yourself get back in the saddle tonight, but tomorrow you will not mind as much." He did not laugh, but there was a lightness in this prediction that might have been amusement. "You are game, Fenice, I will give you that."

"Did you think I was not?" Fenice asked, making it more a challenge than she had intended.

"No, I thought you were or you would not be here." The starkness of this admission banished all good humor from his demeanor. He shrugged. "More women are of Olena's cut than yours. I have rarely found a woman like you."

Being too worn out to guard her speech, she said, "Was Muna like me?"

If she had thought to shock Dracula, she was disappointed. "Yes," he said as the groom came to take her horse in hand. "She was not as courageous or as . . . resourceful as you are, but she was more like you than Olena."

Fenice was too drained to respond with more than "Was?"

"She died," said Dracula. He started out of the barn, leaving Fenice to stumble after him.

The shelter they were offered was kept by a stern-faced old woman. She showed Dracula such obsequious deference that Fenice wondered what she feared in him. The woman bowed Dracula to a small room against the inner curve of the larger tree stump where a rough bed was made. A cover of wolf-pelts served as its blanket. "I will summon you before sunset," she promised Dracula, and looked at Fenice with great curiosity as she went into the room with Dracula.

When the door was closed, they were in near-darkness. Dracula indicated the bed, saying, "Choose where you will sleep."

This was unexpected: Fenice hesitated. "Do you not—"

"You are more tired than I am. You will have to select the place you want to sleep. I will retire shortly, but not yet." He made no suggestion that she undress, so she only pulled off her boots and looked over at him. "Go to sleep," he told her.

Fenice was distantly aware of doubts within her, but the pull of enervation was too great. She would talk with him later, when she was rested, when her body did not ache so much, when she could order her thoughts. She nodded as if in gratitude, then sank back on the furs, closing her eyes almost at once; she was vaguely disturbed when the door to their room opened, but she was asleep before it closed again.

The second night was a repeat of the first: a long ride through the engulfing forest to a place that seemed to be as much part of the wilderness as any of the surroundings did. Fenice ached more fiercely than the previous morning, and she fell asleep more utterly, waking to a new, black horse, and Dracula's grim approval.

"You learned well from the sea, Fenice," he approved as he watched her haul herself aboard her remount. "Your stamina bodes well."

At another time she might have been curious about this remark, but with her shoulders protesting and her back sore enough to make sitting an ordeal and her thighs hurting from strain, she paid little attention to Dracula's equivocal compliment.

"We will be into the mountains tonight," Dracula said as he set his horse trotting.

Astonishment overcame Fenice so that she could not help but ask, "Mountains? What have we been riding through?"

"We have not reached the crags yet," he said to her. "You will see before the night is done." His expression became more feral. "And tomorrow night we will hunt."

"Hunt?" Fenice could not imagine riding after hunting dogs as the aristocracy of France were said to do. She felt the trot in every bone and began to hope for the rocking ease of a canter or the slower demands of a walk; to ride after prey seemed horrid and intolerable.

"You and I," said Dracula, swinging around in his saddle to look at her; even in the dark, she could see his eyes like hot coals shining ahead of her. "Surely you are hungry."

She could think of nothing to say—she was hungry, very hungry, but she had supposed she was being tested again and that he would reward her with food when he was satisfied that she could go without. But his implication brought back memories of the market-gang and she winced. "What will we be hunting?" she asked. She decided she would not be able to hunt: she was too tired and too sore.

"There is prey for us, never fear. And we will not have to go far to enjoy it," he promised her. "You will have what you need, and so will I." With that, he kicked his horse into a canter as they crossed a long, stream-fed meadow;

deer sprang out of their way as they approached, crashing away through the underbrush as if fleeing from wolves.

Fenice was glad of the pace; she found it possible to move with the rhythm of the horse so that her discomfort was minimal. She let the steady, three-quarter beat soothe her, and did not think about what might be ahead of her. She could sense an excitement growing in her that sprang from a need that had been growing since she tasted Dracula's blood.

Once they entered the trees again they slowed to a walk, and this night Dracula was content to let his horse set the pace—a long, reachy walk that ate up the leagues as the night went on.

Sometime near the end of the night, when the waning moon hung above their right shoulders, they left the trees behind. As Dracula had promised, the road led along high peaks on a road cut into stone.

The horizon in the east was stained red, making the moon look ruddy, when they arrived at an ancient inn, its old stones weathered and mossy, its stone roof uneven from long years of weather. Dracula entered the innyard and was at once met by the ostler, who took their horses in charge while he called for a groom; a moment later the innkeeper bustled out of his hostelry and abased himself before Dracula. "Your rooms are ready, my lord," he exclaimed in a language that was enough like Latin that Fenice could understand him.

"Good. Go in and fire the bathhouse; we have been on the road three long nights and we must wash the dust from us." He signaled to Fenice to dismount. "Our clothes will need beating to clean them, and the camisas will have to be washed. See it is done."

"Of course, my lord," the innkeeper assured him, and went off to issue orders to all his staff.

"They know you here," said Fenice, looking about with narrowed eyes; she felt exposed now that she was off her horse, for in this strange place anything might happen.

"And they respect me," Dracula said. "Go in. They will serve you well, for my sake."

"You're not coming?" She could not conceal her apprehension.

"Not yet. You want food, which they will provide. I have other hungers that must be satisfied. When you have finished bathing, I will wash, and then I will sleep." He turned on his heel and strode away.

Fenice stood, wondering if she should enter the inn. The door was open and she was very tired; the opportunity to bathe was as seductive as a kiss, and her need for sleep was enormous. Reluctantly, on stiff legs, she made her way into the taproom where she saw a spent fire in the hearth; its warmth attracted her and she made her way toward it as if drawn by its power.

A young woman came toward her and spoke in the same, Latinlike language. "You will want your bath." She pointed in the direction of a long, dark corridor, so much like the passage through the trees that Fenice stared at it.

"I'd like to get warm first," Fenice said in Latin, hoping she would be understood.

The young woman giggled. "You talk funny," she said. "I'll come back for you shortly, when the bathhouse is hot."

"Thank you," Fenice said, and lowered herself carefully onto a bench in front of the fireplace. Her muscles trembled and her eyes burned in her head while hunger gnawed at her entrails like a rat making an escape. She folded her arms and huddled as near the heat as she dared.

In the family chapel, Rosamonda rose from her prayers, her sense of duty fulfilled more than her faith. God had not answered her plea to bring back her daughter, and she was growing tired of asking what was clearly an unanswerable question. She smoothed the front of her brocade stomacher and curtsied to the altar before leaving the chapel.

Gaetano was waiting in the dining room, his morning cheese-and-bread on a plate before him; Eloisa was seated to his right and the servants hastened to bring her breakfast to her as she sat down opposite her husband. "You were up early," he remarked as she drank the watered wine poured for her.

"I was in the chapel," she said, her voice calmer than her thoughts.

"Why don't you admit Fenice is gone?" Eloisa asked, sounding bored with the whole issue. "If she isn't dead, she ought to be."

For once Rosamonda did not upbraid her daughter for her lack of concern; she knew Eloisa was only saying what the rest of the family was thinking. "I still have . . . faith," she said, wishing it were true.

"And God is pleased that we persevere in faith," said Gaetano. "But we have had no word and it has been so long . . . I no longer hope to see Fenice again in this world."

It was all Rosamonda could do not to say the same thing. "If there is any chance of it, I pray it will come to pass. If only we knew where she was, that would be a beginning."

"Or an end," said Gaetano heavily as he smeared honey on his bread-and-cheese; crumbs clung to his beard and mustache and he wiped them away as he chewed.

"I fear that may be all we will have," Rosamonda admitted as she accepted her food. She murmured a short prayer and began to eat.

"I wish we didn't have to talk about her every day," Eloisa complained. "If she had married Aurelio, we wouldn't. It would be like Artemesia and Bianca—we would talk about them sometimes and sometimes we wouldn't. It's as if you try to keep her here by talking about her." She was not quite pouting, but she was not acquiescent either.

"Eloisa," said Rosamonda, trying to be patient, "you miss Fenice, don't you?"

"Yes," she admitted. "But not every hour, every day. I did for a while, but not now." She looked at her mother. "Do you?"

"When you have children of your own, you will understand," said Rosamonda, and glanced at Gaetano to see his reaction.

"It is true, you always feel you must look after your children," said Gaetano, doing his best to look concerned.

Eloisa sighed. "I won't have any children if we remain in mourning until we hear something about Fenice. It may be years and years and years before we discover anything, and by then I will be too old to find a husband." She reached for one of the apples set on a tray in the middle of the table. "I am getting old enough to marry."

"Not quite yet," said Rosamonda, grateful to have something else to talk about.

At this, Gaetano coughed diplomatically. "Aurelio has mentioned that his younger brother might be a suitable match."

"And whose idea is that?" Rosamonda asked. "Did Andrea suggest it, or did Aurelio?"

"Aurelio says it was his brother's notion. And it may be," said Gaetano. "You must know he is not one to impose on his family."

"That was certainly true once," said Rosamonda cannily. "I do not know that it is so now."

Eloisa slapped her hand on the edge of the table. "Do either of you care what I think?" she demanded, color mounting in her face.

Rosamonda considered her daughter. "What do you think?" she asked after a silent moment.

Now that she had her parents' attention, Eloisa swallowed hard before speaking. "I think I am able to secure a suitor for myself. And if he is Aurelio's brother, what of it? We have had times to talk when you were busy with Aurelio. I like Andrea. I think he likes me."

It was Gaetano's turn to look surprised. "Andrea Pirenetto. Well, you could have found a much less suitable fellow, I will give you that." He rubbed at his beard. "If Andrea is truly interested in having you to wife, I will not refuse out of hand. But let him wait a while. We would not like the world to think that we had substituted one match for another."

"Who cares what the world thinks?" Eloisa scoffed.

Gaetano shook his head. "You will not want anyone whispering that you are a bride only to salvage the contract arranged for Fenice, will you? No, you would prefer the world to see that you were the choice of your husband. You do not want it said that you were married for pity."

Eloisa looked abashed at this suggestion. "No one would think that, would they? Not if we did not look like everything was arranged."

"Which it would have to be," Rosamonda reminded her.

"Very well," said Gaetano. "If Andrea is sincere in his attachment, have him speak to me. Not just at once. You will need some time to discover if you know your minds. But if he is determined to have you, I will make your betrothal known at the Nativity. To do so sooner," he went on, his hand raised to silence her protest, "would appear unseemly, not only for your suit, but for Fenice."

"Fenice again," Eloisa muttered.

"If she had died from fever, you could not have become engaged before then," Rosamonda pointed out reasonably. "It is foolish to think you must wed at once. That could lead to disappointment in the future."

"Yes, Madre Mia," Eloisa said, sighing to show how much of a burden this was.

Gaetano rose from his place at the table. "Rest content, Eloisa. I will not refuse an honorable proposal. And you will please me to show some respect to Fenice, for without her calamity, you might not have Andrea Pirenetto courting you." He prepared to leave the room.

"Sposo," Rosamonda called after him. "I will want to speak more of this with you."

"Of course, of course," said Gaetano, and left his wife and daughter to finish their breakfast without him.

With the night came storm clouds, big as mountains, towering above the crags, rumbling as if with celestial avalanches; lightning spiked the darkness, vanishing as blackness bludgeoned it. Wind sang battle songs and thredonies to the rising tempest.

Fenice woke to the tumult, sitting up in her rustic bed so swiftly that she was briefly dizzy with the effort. She looked about her, trying to recall where she was; the whole returned to her at once and she stumbled out of bed, calling for Dracula.

"I am here," said a voice in the shadows.

She spun around to confront him. "How long—"

"I came when I awoke, not long ago." He stepped out of the shadows into the light from the fire in the small hearth. He was dressed for something more than riding: his short cloak covered a leather tunic and leggings and low boots not intended for stirrups. He indicated her clothing hanging over the back of a chair. "You will want to dress."

"I will," Fenice agreed. She strode up to the chair and picked up the camisa. "It's not quite dry." She hurried on. "Never mind. It is not too damp to wear." Why did she suddenly want to show him she was not finicky about such things?

"Very good," he said.

"Those are not the clothes you wore before," she remarked as she tugged her borrowed night rail over her head and reached for the camisa.

"No. I keep clothes here and in other places." He studied her body. "Your bruises are nearly gone."

"Possibly," she said. "But I ache nonetheless." She tied the camisa at her neck. "The ride has not been easy."

"But you have done it," Dracula said. "This pleases me."

His praise made her flush. She reached for the rest of her clothes. "It is becoming easier. I will be ready in a short while."

Dracula made a gesture to remind her they would not leave yet. "Tonight we hunt, and in the morning we come here to rest again. Then we will go on." His demeanor became more feral. "Tonight we will hunt prey as our kind must."

Whether you flee or pursue
Sweetly you lure me to my destruction . . .
—Torquato Tasso

— XXVII —

Stones and pebbles were cold underneath her as Fenice lay in wait behind a spur of rock that loomed at a bend in the road. Dracula had climbed atop the huge boulder and he lay on it like a slice of the night, hovering like some vast, malignant bird of prey. The storm had not broken and the battle of the lances of lightning and the cannon of thunder continued above them.

What traveler, Fenice asked herself for the twentieth or thirtieth time, could be out in this? And she answered herself with two replies: a desperate one, or a lost one. She did not want to think how Dracula would behave if they failed to find prey tonight; his restlessness had increased to the point that he could remain still only when in ambush. She realized that he had denied himself since they left Varna and now he was at least as hungry as she; his hunger was more specific than hers, and she hoped she would not have to provide what he sought when she herself was as exhausted as this journey made her.

After what seemed double the length of night, there was a light in the distance. At first Fenice had mistaken it for lightning, and then she thought that perhaps the forest below them had been set ablaze; but the light came bobbing, growing no larger than a pail—someone was trying to find his way with a lanthorn, and judging from the way it moved, he was mounted on a slow-moving animal, perhaps a donkey or one of the squat, tough ponies used in this region: few horses would tolerate such weather as they encountered now.

Finally a man huddled on an undersized mule came into sight some distance down the road. The mule kept on at a steady walk, paying no attention to the rambunctious sky. The traveler was wrapped in a sheepskin cloak, his head down, one hand on the rein, one on the handle of the lanthorn that lit the road with a single, feeble oval of light. There was such a quality of misery to that lone figure that Fenice would have let him pass but for her fear of Dracula's displeasure.

The mule faltered as he approached the tall rock; his long ears lay back and he almost crouched on his haunches, preparing to spin and run.

Then Dracula dropped on them from above. The mule reared and the traveler swore as he tumbled from the saddle.

Fenice rushed from her hiding place, prepared to try to halt the mule, but the animal had already swung around; as she approached, the mule bolted, clattering away with unexpected speed as Dracula dragged the traveler to his feet.

The lanthorn went out.

Fenice blinked, trying to fix her eyes on the struggle going on two steps away from her; she gained focus just in time to see the traveler lifted off his feet, shaken severely, then dropped. Dracula fell upon him at once, worrying at the man's throat.

There was a single, gurgling scream and then the man went limp beneath Dracula's body. Fenice hesitated to move closer, for she sensed the ravenous need in Dracula's feeding. She had seen dogs and cats fight over kills and wanted nothing of that for herself.

"Come," he said at last as he rose from his kill. "There is some left for you."

A wave of nausea swept over Fenice; just as quickly she banished it. She could smell the metallic tang of the blood, and she knew to her chagrin that she thirsted for it. She longed for enough disgust to refuse the blood, but could not discover it in herself. More eagerly than she liked, she got down on her knees beside the man and lowered her head to the gory ruin of his throat.

The first taste made her retch, but the second had quite the opposite effect; she suddenly could not get enough of the blood.

Dracula stood over her, stern as a Confessor, watching her. When she wiped her mouth, he gave a single nod of approval. "You will need time to get used to this life. You have begun well."

Emboldened by his praise, she said, "Have I done as well as Muna?"

"Oh, better than she, or Eudike, or Asenath. Not as well as Kelene, however." He bent down and picked up the corpse, taking it to the edge of the narrow road and letting it drop, to roll and slither away down the rocky slope. "The wolves will finish him off. No one will know what became of him, if, indeed, anyone bothers to look for him."

These names took Fenice by surprise. "Muna is not the only one?" She finished wiping her mouth. "There have been others?"

"You knew there were," said Dracula. "As this is not the only traveler I have ever hunted."

This indifference struck Fenice with a renewed dread, which she sought to conceal with indignation. "He made it possible for you to go on. Have you no gratitude?"

"I am grateful, I suppose, as lions are grateful for gazelles, or as you are for chickens and fish. Come. It will be raining soon and you will not want to be out in it. You will find rain is hard to endure as you change. It can unnerve you; it is disquieting." He brought his cloak up around her shoulder and pulled her in close to him. "You have done well by me, Fenice."

"Then I am glad," she said as if reciting by rote. The whole incident, brief though it had been, troubled her. She had not thought she would be able to join in the hunt, but she had; she thought she would be unable to share the kill, but she had managed to do that, too. And now she felt so little remorse that she was dismayed.

Dracula began to walk, taking Fenice with him. "There are a few more hours until dawn. Let us hope that the storm is over by the time we wake at day's end." These calm observations chilled her more than the night had done. She huddled closer to him in the fold of his cloak, seeking vainly for warmth.

There were puddles in the innyard and ragged clouds in the sky when Dracula took Fenice out to mount up for another night's ride. The horses were the same as the ones they had ridden in on, but now they were rested, reshod, and eager for activity. Fenice mounted with more ease than before and pulled in the rein without fuss; she began to think she would be an accomplished rider by the time she reached Dracula's castle.

"The road will be narrow tonight, and the mountains steep. The moon is waning, so we will not have its light at first," Dracula warned her as he signaled to the groom to open the innyard gate. "You will have to be alert."

"I will be," Fenice promised, her words emphatic and her expression determined.

"Good," Dracula said as he spurred his horse out of the courtyard and into the night; he did not bother to look to see if Fenice was behind him.

She managed to keep up with Dracula, but she became aware of their precarious route as they rushed on. Moonrise came late and only served to show how great their hazards were. The track they were on would not accommodate two horses abreast; they were winding their way up the side of the mountain, going deeper into the range. Although it was summer, the night wind had a chill bite in it, as if it came off distant snow. The howls of wolves provided the only counterpoint to the beat of their horses' hooves.

Once, when they stopped at a high spring to let their horses drink, Dracula rose in the stirrups and made a wide gesture with his free arm. "All this was once my domain. No man could set foot upon it without my grant. I commanded soldiers and the obedience of lords from the Dniester to the Danube; everyone trembled at my name. Even the cadet figures of my House were men to reckon with." He shook his head twice as if to rid himself of his memories. "But no matter how much of my land they claim, no matter how many of my subjects bow to them, they still fear me."

Fenice listened with mixed emotions: she could almost feel sympathy for Dracula in his great isolation. She remembered how they had waylaid the traveler, and her sympathy changed to something less forgiving. "You—or your House—has ruled long here?"

"I. I am my House. I have held my lands against foes you cannot imagine.

Not even the Huns could conquer me. The Ottomites say they are lords here, but the people know better." He made a sound that was not quite laughter. "You will see how they will turn away from my lands. They may think they have conquered, but they are wrong." He looked directly at Fenice. "Do you fear me?"

She thought about it. "Sometimes," she answered.

"And you have earned my regard," Dracula said with a nod of understanding. "Think how you must feel if I were your sworn enemy."

She did not want to consider the possibility. "You were the enemy of the men in the market-gang," she observed.

"Hah!" His jeering was as powerful as a slap across her face. "They were not my enemies. They were not worthy of being my foes. To oppose me, they would need courage, not bullying, and they would have to be willing to battle gladly." He spat. "They were vermin, to be killed and disposed of. They were not your enemies, either, Fenice," he added less vehemently. "They were foolish men who knew nothing of what power truly is; they knew only brutality and supposed it was power. You have a taste for power; I can feel it in you."

Fenice could not tell whether she was being complimented or insulted. She studied Dracula and frowned at him as he moved his horse closer to hers. "I do not like killing."

"Because you don't understand it, not yet. When you do, you will not think of it as you do now." He reached out to her, taking her jaw in his hand and kissing her.

She did not want to respond, aware that resistance would make her less his servant than he assumed she was; but the cold-burning passion of his mouth roused the wildness within her, and she could not deny it. When he pulled back, she made a small sound of protest, and despised her own weakness.

"We must go on," Dracula announced, satisfaction making his words smooth and caressing. "Night will fade and we must be sheltered when it does." He nudged his horse back toward the trail.

"You must," Fenice said, though she realized it was folly to remind him of her greater endurance of the sun. "I have no reason to—"

"You have more reason than you know," Dracula interrupted her harshly, turning in his saddle to look at her. "You have been changing since you drank my blood. There is only one thing left to complete your transformation to my kind."

Fenice shuddered but could not keep from asking, "What thing is that?"

"Your death," Dracula said as he kicked his horse into a trot.

As Fenice awakened in the abandoned fortress, she knew this would be her last night on the road. Once the sun rose again, she would be at Castle Dracula and her life would change forever.

"What will I become?" she asked the darkening sky. This was not what she sought when she had set out on her adventure. Or was it? Surely when she put her name and family behind her forever she made herself more than a Venetian outcast. This notion, once admitted, grew in significance as she sat on the musty straw which had served her as a bed: what had she thought would happen when she put her past away? She had wanted freedom from the strictures of the world—how had she thought that would come about?

"You are awake," Dracula said as he came from his bed.

"I am," she said, stretching to prove it was so.

"You will have to saddle your horse tonight," he told her. "There are no grooms to tend to the task." He was about to turn away when she stopped him.

"When are you going to kill me?" The question hung between them, all but visible on the air.

He answered her in an even voice. "After we reach my castle. Once we are there, I will decide." His eyes were lambent. "Are you so eager to die?"

"It's not that," she said, trying to match his calm with her own. "But I would like to be ready when it comes." She stood up and brushed the straw from her clothing. "I don't want to die like the traveler we killed."

"I would not waste your death that way," said Dracula. "You will not have to suffer as he did." He smiled at her, reminding her of the maw of wolves. "You will not be—" He stopped.

"I will not be what?" Fenice prompted when he did not go on.

"Unwilling," Dracula said in a flat voice.

Fenice could not rid herself of the impression that he had intended to say something else.

By the end of the night they were riding along the rocky crest of one of the high peaks; the road was a bit wider here, wide enough for a carriage to pass. Dracula had said something about the gypsies using it; Fenice thought she could feel the earth roll beneath her, bringing her nearer to sunrise. The remoteness of the place staggered her as much as its splendid beauty: nothing but rocks shouldering the sky; no sign of any habitation anywhere.

And then she realized that what she had mistaken for a formidable outcropping of rock was the wall of a castle; the road bent around it and led to a massive oaken door braced with huge metal staples. It was impossible to guess the castle's size from the wall, for it was part of the mountain itself; impregnable as the highest crags. Dracula rode up to the gate shouting in a language Fenice did not know. A harsh-voiced clarion sounded and the gates were slowly opened.

The courtyard inside the gates was spartan: it was a marshaling yard, with no other purpose than to ready the castle for defense. There was a stable on one side, an armory on the other, and a smithy in between. Dracula dismounted and handed the reins of his horse to the groom who seemed to materialize at his feet. "Tend them."

"My lord," said the groom, bending double in homage and speaking the language with Latinlike words that Fenice had heard before.

"Is everything prepared?" Dracula asked, imbuing the question with ramifications Fenice could not fathom.

"All is ready, my lord," said the groom.

"Then alert the castle," Dracula said, giving the order without any clarification.

The clarion sounded again as Dracula strode toward the inner door.

Fenice watched this with mild interest, as if it had nothing to do with her. She had assumed that Dracula would have servants and that they would be devoted to him—why else would they consent to remain in so solitary a place as this castle? That she would excite some curiosity did not surprise her. As she dismounted, the groom took her horse in hand as well. She noticed that there were half a dozen men-at-arms standing in the courtyard, still as statues; they watched her without any sign of emotion. She let herself walk with a slight swagger to show she was not intimidated as Dracula motioned to her to follow him.

The corridor they entered was narrow, curving, descending; it appeared to be cut from the living rock as it led deeper and deeper into the castle. The corridor moaned and sighed with the wind, giving the impression of many voices echoing along the stones. Torches gave sporadic illumination to the hallway, but revealed little else about the place; how many rooms they passed, or other corridors, Fenice could not tell as she strove to keep up with Dracula down the uneven steps. There were no servants anywhere.

Finally they emerged into a great hall with a gallery above and a great hearth blazing; two tremendous brass candelabra stood near the hearth, their dozens of candles adding to the luster of the room and showing the wealth of its master. Even the weapons hung on the wall were jeweled in the hilt and quillons, and the single tapestry glowed with gold and silver threads. Two chairs were high-backed and elaborately carved, with silken cushions in their seats. The setting was as grand as the outer castle was austere. In front of the immense fireplace a long table was laid for a banquet, lacking only the food to begin the feast.

Not even the extravagant ambitions of Rocco degli Urbanesei could match this magnificent display. Fenice stared in unabashed awe at what she saw around her. Suddenly she felt shabby in her leather riding gear; she stepped back into the shadow of the gallery as if trying to hide her dusty garments. For an instant she missed her home in Venice so keenly that she had to blink the tears from her eyes.

Dracula tossed his cloak aside negligently. He strode to the table and looked at the gold plates set out in the single place setting. He picked up a golden chalice and scrutinized it as if searching for a flaw.

"It is very fine," Fenice said at last, feeling she had to say something. "I have never seen anything to equal it."

"From a Venetian, that is praise indeed," said Dracula with supreme indifference. "Do not mourn too much, Fenice. You have gained far more than you have lost."

Whether it was from fatigue or homesickness, Fenice began to cry, her sobs wrenching through her as she strove to conceal her shame.

"It is late. You will want to sleep. When you waken, my servants will bathe you, and then you will come here and they will feed you." He paid no attention to her sobs. "You will learn more in the evening. Now you should sleep."

"But—" Fenice was able to say. "But where? How?"

Dracula clapped his hands sharply; a dark-haired woman of uncertain age came rushing into the great hall, her face flushing and then going pale as she saw Fenice with Dracula. She abased herself. "My lord."

"You know where my guest is to be taken. Give her what aid she requires and ready the bath for her use at sunset, when she wakens." He frowned at the servant. "Well?"

The woman faltered. "You . . . you gave orders about . . . accommodations?"

"Yes, I did," said Dracula, his voice purring with menace. "You have not failed to make the necessary arrangements, have you? Everything is in readiness, is it not?"

"Oh, certainly, certainly," said the woman. "But you will have to . . . to . . ." She dropped to her knees. "We did everything we could," she said in a wail.

"No doubt you did," said Dracula, sounding unexpectedly weary. "But you were unable to complete them all—that is what you are telling me, I surmise. And I suppose I must attend to the matter myself." He folded his arms. "For the sake of my guest I will not punish you now as I would at another time. Think of this as Fenice's mercy, not mine." With that he made an abrupt gesture, dismissing her. For all the notice he paid to her now, she might have vanished in a puff of smoke.

The woman hurried away, muttering thanks and praise as she went. Fenice watched her go, wondering why any servant would remain with Dracula if he was so feared.

"I will have to leave you shortly. There is something I have to do, and quickly. I leave you in the hands of my servants; you may trust them as you trust me." He made a swift gesture of his hand as if to push away an annoyance. "This need not concern you; I will deal with— You will be taken to your room. I will send for another to escort you—it seems I have business to attend to." The purpose was back in his tone and his stance was rigid with determination. He clapped again; this time a club-footed man of gypsy lineage answered the summons. "My guest. Show her where her room is."

"I will," said the servant, and bowed awkwardly to Fenice. "If you will follow me?"

Fenice shrugged and prepared to go with him. "Will I have a basin, at least, to wipe the grime off my face and hands?"

"See she has it," Dracula said, adding, "Our soil does not yet nurture her."

Fenice was too tired to question his meaning, but she could not shake the remark from her mind. The servant led her with crablike steps to a room off the gallery, one of three, with an elegant bed, two covered chairs, a chest, and a washstand; all that was missing was a mirror. But bringing fine glass to a place as remote and arduous to reach as this one, she told herself, would make having mirrors prohibitive, so expensive and fragile were they. When the servant left her, she got out of her boots; she was debating whether or not she should undress when the club-footed servant returned with a ewer of warm water which he put on the washstand. "Thank you," she said.

"There is no reason," said the man in the same Latinate tongue the other servants spoke.

"I have been taught to acknowledge service," Fenice said in Latin, and saw the surprise in the man's face.

"Where are you from?" he demanded sharply, looking once over his shoulder as if he feared intrusion.

"Venice," said Fenice, pride in her origins making her raise her head.

"Venice," the man marveled. "So far away."

"Yes," Fenice agreed, suddenly forlorn as she realized she would not be likely to see her home again. Until they reached Castle Dracula, a part of her had always assumed the time would come when she would return to her family, to tell them farewell and to explain why she had done what she had done; she wanted them to understand. But now that she was inside the castle, it was borne in upon her that this would not happen; no matter how far she might stray from Castle Dracula, she would never see Venice again.

"What was the master doing in Venice?" the servant wondered aloud.

"He found me in Varna," she answered, trying to conceal her fatigue.

The man's curiosity was piqued. "How did you come to be there?"

"I . . . It is a long story, and one your master can tell better than I," she said, afraid that she might begin to weep again if she said too much.

"I will leave you," said the servant as if he had offended her and wanted to apologize. He began to back out of her presence. "If there is anything, there is a pull for the bell. It will bring me or one of the others at once."

"Very good," said Fenice, looking at the logs burning in the fireplace. "They should last a while, shouldn't they?"

"And a new fire will be laid before you waken," said the servant, pausing in the doorway to tell her this. "We will look after you."

With the closing of the door, Fenice felt exhaustion take possession of her; she managed to clean her face and hands, though it seemed a Herculean effort. Then she undressed, so very slowly, and set her garments aside; they each felt as heavy as a pillow filled with sand and she shook with the effort of handling them. When she pulled back the curtains of the bed, she was only slightly surprised to find a night rail laid out for her, this one of Egyptian cotton. She put it on, thinking it was a shame to wear something so fresh and fine when she had not yet bathed herself free of the road. Then she forgot about these matters and sank down onto the bed, managing to pull the coverlet to her chin before she succumbed to sleep.

In her dream, she was once again aboard ship, not hiding in the hold, but standing boldly on deck, her face into the wind, the sailors bustling around her at her order: she was not with her brother—she was Captain in her own right, and the port to which they sailed was fabulous beyond the conception of any traveler. Not China and the islands lost in the vast ocean between the New World and Orient could hold the splendor as the port of her dream, where she would walk the spice-scented markets without fear, where she would be received with the honor due an experienced traveler. So sweet was her dream that she resented the coming of dawn that summoned her back from the exploits of her fancies.

. . . And no more lovely seduction
Than the promises I would make myself.
—Guido Guinizelli

XXVIII

By the time the bathhouse was heated, Fenice was awake enough to hear nervousness in the voice of the servant—this time a young woman whose prettiness was marred by a harelip—as she showed Fenice the way from her room to the bathhouse. She had supposed at first that the nervousness had to do with having a stranger in their midst; now she was not so sure.

"And this will take you out into the courtyard," the servant-woman was saying, pointing to an alcove with a door at the back. "I will lead you this time."

"You are very good," said Fenice automatically, trying to summon the nerve to ask the woman what was upsetting her so. As they went out into the courtyard, Fenice made her first attempt. "I suppose you do not have many visitors to this place." In the torchlight the woman's features were hard to read, for the flickering created its own expressions on her flesh.

"No," the woman answered obliquely. "Few come here."

"And when they do, it must be a trial for you." This was almost a question, and she waited for her answer; she could see it was not easy for the woman to answer.

"A trial. Yes, visitors can be a trial. For themselves as well as for us." She shoved the bathhouse door open and pointed to the dark interior. "You will find everything you need here; the drying sheet is set out for you. There are clean clothes in that press. When you are done, you may use the bellpull to summon aid if you need it. The master says when you have bathed you are to dress and join him in the great hall."

Fenice shook her head. "I am not certain I can find the great hall," she confessed. "This castle is . . . confusing."

"That it is," said the woman, peering uneasily toward the bath where steam was rising from the surface of the dark water. "It is ready."

"I can see that," said Fenice, and prepared to take off her night rail.

The woman stopped her. "Not yet. When you have put your foot into the water, then take off the sleepwear. Not before."

Fenice regarded her with interest. "Is this your custom?"

"It is how we do it here," the woman replied. She made a clumsy curtsy and headed for the door to the bathhouse. "If you do not come in a while, I will return for you; I will listen for the bell, but I will come when the time for your meal grows near. You can leave without summoning help, if you prefer: come to the door on the other side of the courtyard. It is there I will find you when you come in from this place." Without waiting for Fenice to speak, she was gone.

The bathhouse echoed every sound so that it was awash in noise. As Fenice stepped into the bath, she flung her night rail onto a low seat carved into the stones of the bath. Lowering herself into the hot water, she found herself huddling, as if afraid of being watched. "You're being foolish. You have let yourself be scared by a servant." This rallying helped her gather her courage as she let the heat begin to ease the last of the fatigue from her body. It was lovely to stretch out in the bath, to be supported by the water while she cleaned the smirches of travel from her body. She gave special attention to her hair, washing it twice and running her fingers through it to rid it of the worst of the tangles.

A sudden noise brought her out of her enjoyment: a sound like the slamming of a metal door echoed and eddied through the bath, and suddenly the warm water seemed cold. Fenice rose quickly and reached for the drying sheet that had been left for her; as her fingers closed on the thick material, she thought she heard a low snicker. "Who's there?" she called out, doing her best to sound curious instead of frightened. "Muna?"

The snicker became a chuckle, equivocal and sinister.

Fenice came out of the bath with haste, wrapping herself in the sheet as if to shield herself from danger. She contrived to tie the enveloping cloth so that she could move without having to hold the material shut with every step. The water now seemed clammy, making the drying sheet cling to her and chilling her at the same time. The whole room had lost its warmth and the drying sheet could not hold out the cold. Try as she would, she could not stimulate warmth in her skin. She dried hastily and dressed in lustrous silks and dark, rich brocades without attention in her need to get warm; the sumptuous fabrics seemed too light, too insubstantial to restore the heat she sought. She hugged her arms across her chest and only then noticed the jewels—sapphires, moonstones, and amethysts—worked in the sleeves of the ropilla, and the dark gray seed pearls sewn on the cuffs of her sottana.

She hurried out of the bathhouse into a twilight that disoriented her; no wonder the bathhouse had gone suddenly cold: the wind cutting through the courtyard was keen as steel. Fenice looked about her in consternation, unsure of which way to go. She heard a door slam somewhere behind her and was about to try in that direction when the servant-woman who had taken her to the bath appeared in a lit doorway. Gratefully Fenice stumbled toward her, waving to show her relief and her attention. As she came into the room behind the pantry, she said, "Thank you. I was confused. I thought I heard—"

"There's been mischief," said the servant-woman with a hard look.

"Mischief?" Fenice repeated.

"The master gave orders. They were ignored." She shook her head. "Why he should think it would be otherwise, I do not know." With a click of her tongue, she indicated the corridor they were to take. "Come. He is waiting for you."

Fenice went obediently, trying to learn the way. She counted the number of doors on her right, and had reached eleven when the servant-woman stopped her.

"The next door on the left—take it and turn right at the double arch. You will be in the great hall." She made a gesture of subservience and turned away.

"Thank you," Fenice said quietly; she felt she owed the servant-woman more than an appreciative word, but she had nothing more to offer.

"See you watch yourself," the woman warned, something about her stern mouth softening. "You are not safe yet."

These cryptic words alarmed Fenice; as she followed the instructions to find the great hall, she tried to think what these odd warnings could mean. Stepping through the arch into the shadow of the gallery, Fenice was struck again with the luxury of this one place. The great table had been turned at an angle, and now the chairs were set between her and the gaping fireplace where two enormous logs blazed. The candelabra were flanking the chairs, all candles lit, and the torches in the sconces by the doors added their brilliance to the vast chamber. Fenice saw the jewels in her garments wink, and for the first time she noticed that the brocade pattern, worked in dark red and slate-blue, was of hawks and falcons, the jewels providing them with eyes. The felt slippers she had been given made no sound as she walked forward; only the hem of her ropilla whispered as it touched the flagstones. She curtsied to Dracula, who sat in the larger of the high-backed chairs as if enthroned. "Good evening, my lord," she said, certain that formality was called for.

"Come here, Fenice," he said. His voice was low.

"I thank you for your courtesy in receiving me," she went on, trying to discover what he expected of her in so grand a setting. "I hope I may deserve the honor you do me."

"And you do, my phoenix," he said, ferociously smiling. "Tonight you will finish your journey to me. We will celebrate the occasion."

"Of course," said Fenice, wondering what he meant. "I am pleased to do as you wish."

"Are you?" he asked her with abrupt intensity. "Are you truly willing?"

"Should I not be?" she countered with the kind of easy banter she had learned in Venice.

"You must be," he said in a tone that ended all levity.

She tried to smile. "I have followed you to this place; I have put myself in your hands. I have . . . I have drunk your blood. What else must I do?"

His smile did not fade. "Die," he answered.

Her attempt at incredulous laughter failed utterly. "Die?"

"And become like me, one of those for whom death has no dominion." He leaned forward, reaching for her hand. "You will die and, like your name, you will rise from your death. I offer this gift to you, Fenice. You will enter the life of the un-Dead at last."

She blinked as if closing her eyes and opening them again would change what she had just seen and heard. "Must I . . . die?" She began to cross herself, but her hand would not complete the protective gesture. The cold she had finally banished from her flesh returned tenfold, as if her bones had become ice.

"Don't tell me you are afraid?" he challenged; he made a vast gesture with one arm, but he did not move away from her. "You have fought off assassins, yet you falter now, when an eternity of power is waiting for you?" He came out of his chair and stood directly in front of her. "You have lost your faith in me."

"No," she said quickly, making herself stand her ground though she wanted to step back from him, from the enormity of his shadow which cast her into darkness.

"You do not fear me?" He made the question an imperative.

"I fear what I know you can do," she said carefully, still determined not to be put to flight.

"As well you should," said Dracula, making no apology for his manner. "All who are mortal are wise to fear me. But you, Fenice, you have nothing to fear." He stroked her shining dark hair; she managed not to flinch at his touch. "You will have the power to instill fear yourself, as soon as you are fully one with me."

She raised her head, daring to look at him. "Am I not that now?" she asked, pleased that her voice did not shake as her hands did.

"You are very nearly, but you have not completed your transition: you will do that only when you cast off your mortality." He laid his hand on her shoulder. "Take that step now, so that you will share all with me. Why did you come here with me, if not for that?"

She swallowed hard: yes, why had she come, if not to make herself like him? Or had she thought that she would be able to take only a part of him for her own, and would be free to do as she wished while under his protection? She had hunted with him, and she had killed with his approval, but that was not sufficient. Had she assumed that her blood would be recompense enough for Dracula? She realized he was waiting for her reply. She sighed and said with conviction, "I came to be one with you."

"Very well." He bent and kissed her mouth; he did not put his arms around her or touch her in any other way, yet she felt as bound as if he had wrapped her in hemp ropes. When he drew back, he held out his arm for her to lay hers on, and with a show of pomp led her back to the two chairs, seating her in the smaller of the two before taking his place in the larger. "This is your place, Fenice: at my side."

Fenice could think of no response; she was still trying to comprehend what he had told her about her death—she would die tonight. Die tonight.

Die tonight. No matter how often she told herself, it made no sense to her. Surely he could not mean she would be dead? Dead? The word had no meaning. How could she be dead?

But he had said un-Dead. Suddenly she understood what he had told her, and what he was. Had she not known him, she would have been terrified, but he had shown her that he was not a ravening monster from the Pit. When he said she would die, he was telling her she would become un-Dead like him. She finally comprehended the significance of all he had revealed. He had not offered her an adventuresome fiction to strengthen her when her fears were greatest; he had not urged her to revenge to soothe her injuries. He had wanted her to become like him; once she died, that transformation would be certain.

Her first rush of anticipation stopped almost before it began: she would become like him. That would mean a salvation that was not that promised by the Church, and she recalled the many times her Confessor had admonished her to cling to . . . to . . . she could not bring the name to mind without anguish. She took a long, deep breath and tried to call upon one of the . . . company of . . . those to whom churches and lives were dedicated. She trembled, trying to think of the name of a Saint, but even the word eluded her. If she could not call upon the source of the Church's redemption, then she must take what she could have. "The Church abandoned me," she said without any preamble. "You saved me. No heavenly messenger, no canonized holy man came to my rescue. You did."

"Yes. I did."

"Then you may have my life; if it is forfeit, I will not refuse it." She said this in a rush so that she would not lose her courage. "You kept me from a terrible death, and the sin it would have left me."

"Yes. I did." He leaned back as much as his chair would allow.

She continued to persuade herself. "You took me in, you helped me exact revenge, you took me away from beggary."

"Yes," he said a third time. "I did."

"To make me like you," she said with conviction.

"And you will be. Only one thing is lacking," Dracula said, his voice thickening with desire. "It will not be long."

She gathered her hands in her lap. "I ask . . ." she said with less conviction, "that you be swift. I would not want to linger once . . . once you begin."

"I will see you have no pain," said Dracula grandly. "Do not dwell on it." He clapped his hands. "For now, you will enjoy the pleasures of the table and the senses; you will want to remember these delights when you acquire my tastes; you will want to relish all you do in my name." As his servants appeared, he indicated the table where the platters they bore should be laid. "Let them move our chairs—mine to the head of the table, yours to the foot, as suits a House of rank." He rose and indicated she should do the same.

Fenice did as he bid as if sleepwalking. She could not imagine that this was the last meal she would ever eat. She sat down in the chair when it was put in place at the foot of the huge table; her arms seemed to be made of wood, and her legs did not feel part of her at all. The covers were removed from the platters and the servants began to offer the dishes to her; one man filled a golden goblet with dark, sweet wine.

"Taste it all, Fenice," Dracula said. "You will be glad of this when you no longer dine on mortal viands." He dismissed all but one of the servants with a wave of his hand. "You will give your orders to Marcu here; he will wait upon you. He will deny you nothing if it is his to provide." Dracula raised one foot, bracing against the table, then leaned back in his chair, one arm dangling over the side of it, the other extended so that his hand rested on his bent knee. He wore an expression of idle amusement mixed with cynicism.

"I don't know where to start," Fenice said, her voice remote.

"The soup is good, they tell me," said Dracula in a tone that meant it had better be.

"Then I will start with soup," said Fenice, reaching for the tureen, only to have Marcu reach past her and fill a bowl for her; he was brown-haired and lean, young enough to be unable to conceal his admiration of Fenice.

As he put it in front of her, he said very quietly, "You need not fear Kelene tonight; she is hunting."

Fenice nodded, unable to make sense of this information. "It smells delicious," she told him, to cover her bafflement. What did he mean, *Kelene is hunting?*

"Then make the most of it, Fenice," said Dracula.

Obediently Fenice picked up her spoon and began to eat the thick, dark soup; it had a savor that was strong and subtle at once, and a texture that was thick without losing fluidity. "Very good," she declared as she had another spoonful; all the while she pondered what Marcu had whispered to her: *You need not fear Kelene tonight*. Why should she fear Kelene? What could her hunting mean? She recalled the name: Dracula had spoken it once or twice. But what was there to fear? She had more soup until the bowl was half-empty. "I must stop, or not do justice to the rest," she announced. While the bowl was removed she had a sip of the strong wine; she knew it could easily go to her head, and she told herself that she would have to be as circumspect with it as with the dishes she was offered if she was not to sate herself to insensibility. Then she wondered if that might not be the best way to greet death—replete and swooning with the pleasures of life? It would be easily done, and she would not have to confront the end. She shook her head.

"Does something displease you?" Dracula asked, his sharp words cutting through her reverie.

"No," she said at once. "It is hard to make up my mind with so much bounty offered." The lie came readily and that gave her a sense of accomplishment. At the same time, the wildness that drew her to Dracula rebelled: if she had to die, she would not be insensate. No, that would be capitulation beyond anything her pride would tolerate. She pointed to the sausages wrapped in cabbage. "Marcu, those look wonderful. Will you put two or three on my plate?"

"Only two or three?" he asked with a covert glance at Dracula.

"Only two or three," said Fenice. "And then, those collops of lamb in basil and cream." She was sorry there was no fish, but so far into the mountains, and with the river leagues below them in a canyon, she was not surprised. "I would have liked scallops in saffron," she said wistfully. "But no matter."

Dracula scowled. "This is not to your liking?"

"It is excellent," she replied promptly as she cut one of the wrapped sausages in half. "And I am wrong to complain of what cannot be had. It was churlish of me to speak of it." She began to chew, and finally the taste flooded her mouth and she discovered how great her hunger was. Before she realized it, she had drunk half the wine in the goblet and Marcu was refilling it. "Not so much," she protested.

"Fill her goblet," Dracula ordered, and rose from his negligent repose to come toward her. "You may go, Marcu. I will be her servant now."

Fenice did not know how she ought to react to this announcement. She had been trying to maintain the deportment she had been taught was appropriate to splendid banquets, but she was not prepared for the intimacy Dracula clearly intended they share. Recklessly she had more of the wine and reminded herself she had been able to deal with the rigors of shipboard life and the hazards of the Varna marketplace: this could be no more dangerous. She had been protected by Dracula and now there was only one thing left unfinished between them: she was not frightened.

With a deep bow, Marcu withdrew, casting a last, admiring glance on Fenice before the dark of the corridor swallowed him up.

Standing behind her chair, Dracula leaned forward and slid his hand down inside the front of her ropilla; his hand rested over her breast with only the silk of her sottana between his fingers and her flesh; the caress brought an immediate response: her nipple swelled, the soft fabric making its excitement more pronounced. "There are more pleasures to come," he promised her as he gave her the goblet with his other hand. "Drink," he ordered.

Disconcerted by the unanticipated stimulus of his touch, Fenice took a deep draught of the wine, hoping to steady herself. She put the chalice down and reached for her fork once more.

He tweaked her nipple with his thumb and forefinger.

"What—?" she exclaimed; it should have been painful, but instead she discovered her body was becoming awakened and sensitized. She tried to concentrate on her meal as Dracula withdrew his hand but only to undo the brooches holding the ropilla closed at her neck and breast. He tossed the jeweled ornaments aside as if they were nothing more than nutshells; Fenice could not let him do this without a murmur of protest. "They are beautiful."

"They are shiny stones, nothing more," he said as he pulled the front of her ropilla open and worked loose the knot at the neck of her sottana. "Have another bite, Fenice."

This offer confused her; Fenice cut into the lamb as Dracula opened the front of her sottana exposing her flesh. He began to stroke her as if she were a tame panther. With the back of the chair between them, it seemed as if disembodied hands ignited her; the wine blurred her senses so that the taste of the food and the touch of Dracula's hands ran together, making it impossible to know which was the greater enjoyment, or the greater confusion. All the candles seemed to be stars, burning as places on her skin burned from his touch. She stopped trying to separate them and let the gratification and terror carry her. Only one question continued to niggle in a distant part of her mind: why should she be afraid of Kelene? When Dracula gave her the goblet again, even that last reservation vanished.

When her body had been raised to a pitch of fervor, Dracula came from behind the chair and in a single motion swept all the platters, plates, bowls, cutlery, cups, and the goblet from the table. Then he turned and lifted Fenice onto the place he had made for her, and with a passion compounded of hunger and fury, fell upon her and glutted his need with her life.

Fenice woke in darkness, enclosed in a narrow bed that would not allow her to turn or roll in any direction. She tried to raise her hand to her face only to encounter a covering that stopped such movement as well. Fright brought her wholly awake, into the most profound darkness she had ever known; it was relieved by nothing: no flicker of distant stars, no spark of light of any kind. She jolted in place as if trying to run. Where was she? How had she come to be in this . . . this trap? This was far worse than the hiding place she had made for herself in the hold of the *Impresa*, and she had to grapple with her fears to keep from giving way to panic. Gradually she began to take stock of her situation. She thought back to the night before, to the spectacular feast that had ended in a rapture of . . . pain? She recalled the magnificent food and the wine—she had had too much of it, she was certain of that—and there had been something more. Dracula had been grandly attentive, he had dismissed the servant so that he could serve her, he had come to her, and then he had . . . The next slipped away from her like fish in the canals of Venice. She fingered the clothes she was wearing: the ropilla and sottana from the night before, to judge by the quality and hand of the cloth. The two brooches were back in place, making her wonder how much of her fuzzy recollection was memory and how much was dream. She frowned and tried to raise her hand again. This time she felt the texture of the surface immediately above her. It was plush, like the finest velvet, but behind it was unyielding wood or stone. She strove to recall what had happened to her.

She could not keep from screaming, though the sound reached no ears but hers.

Dead. She was *dead*.

The confinement was her coffin.

She brought her hands up as far as she could and tried to press the lid upward, but it would not budge. She summoned up all the strength she could

and struggled again to push the lid away, and again she was unable. Her confines now seemed to grow tighter than when she had wakened, and her efforts became desperate. What if all her un-Dead life were to be spent in this black box? How soon would it be until she was mad?

Squirming in the strict limitations of the coffin, she was finally able to shift enough to be able to have slightly more leverage on the lid. Summoning all her strength, she pushed, expecting resistance; she nearly tumbled out of the coffin as the lid swung up and open.

The place that she found herself in was only slightly less daunting than her coffin had been: she was in a vault, with a low ceiling of ancient stones. There were impressive stone slabs on which coffins were set—her own and two others, both closed. Thick pillars rough-hewn from the stones seemed to labor to hold the vault open, serving to convince Fenice she was in the very depths of the castle. On each pillar was a single bracket with a torch burning fitfully, supplying just enough light to make the place alive with shadows. The smell of ruins was thick in this oppressive chamber. The sound of wind moved through it with a steady moan as if the stones themselves groaned under their burdens.

Fenice staggered to the nearest pillar and leaned against it, as if it might provide her some strength; the stones were cold and slightly damp and provided no succor at all. The place was so cold that her breath became fog before her face.

Breath! She nearly laughed. If she breathed she was not dead. She must be alive! Dracula had changed his mind, and for some caprice had spared her. Then her relief fled as she recalled that Dracula breathed, and if she had become like him . . .

There was a sudden fluttering and from the hidden recesses of the ceiling hundreds of bats came flying, darting and skittering through the gloom with the eerie certainty of their kind; Fenice huddled against the pillar and watched while the tiny flying horde left the vault. She had a fleeting impulse to follow them, then reminded herself they could depart through a chink in the roof; she would require a larger, more accessible egress.

With the hope that she would not have to remain in this dreadful place forever, Fenice made herself begin to explore. She had become somewhat accustomed to the low light, and her searches took her into the deepest recesses of the vault. She found a stack of large chests, each stoutly bound and sealed with the arms of the Dragon Prince; she recalled the device from the gate of the house in Varna. Beyond the chests were a number of broken, empty coffins; Fenice noticed that a few were so old the wood they were made of was rotting and falling to pieces, but the rest were somewhat newer. She picked up one of the boards and held it in her hands as if it might reveal to her something about whomever it had held. Nothing. She put the board down and continued to wander, wanting to discover the limits of this place.

The torches became fewer and fewer and then she was once again in enveloping darkness. She resisted the urge to strike out blindly—for in this place, she was very nearly blind—making herself stand, turning slowly until she could find a distant spot of light to guide her back to where she had been. The stones underfoot were uneven, with no regular path cut into them, and so she had to go slowly, her hands out in front of her. As she became aware of the flicker of torchlight ahead of her and slightly to the right, she made her way toward it.

The susurrus of the wind changed subtly, beginning to rise and fall, like the sound of the sea in a shell. Fenice slowed her pace, guessing that this could portend trouble or something so unexpected that she would need a moment to recruit her wits. She stood by the torch and listened. Did she hear voices? Was someone talking, or was it only the soughing of the wind? Gradually she thought she heard Dracula's voice, deep and imperious, but only the tone of it. There might have been another, but if so, it was almost as light as a child's and was easily lost in the wind. With great care, Fenice began to move closer to the sounds, retracing the steps she had made in her exploration. She came to the empty coffins and the chests and there she paused again, all her attention given over to listening. At last a few words reached her; she recognized the language after a moment: they were speaking in Greek.

". . . you will not," Dracula pronounced. "If you are . . . mischief. I will know and . . . punishment."

". . . so bold?" challenged the childlike voice.

Fenice recalled the second coffin, and Marcu's warning: *You need not fear Kelene. Kelene is hunting.* Was this treble-voiced taunter the Kelene she had been warned about? She might as well be warned about Eloisa. She came close to laughing, but could not quite achieve real mirth. She moved away from the concealing bulk of the chests and began to move closer to the voice.

". . . none of the others have," jeered the high voice.

"I will not allow you to harm Fenice," Dracula ordered. "If I have to lock you in your coffin for a century."

The shriek of indignant laughter that greeted this had more bravado than courage in it. "You would not dare. You would be bored in a year. You would miss me."

"I will have Fenice," Dracula said, his words becoming silky. "She is not an erratic and sullen child."

"If that is all I am to you," the higher voice said, suddenly as seductive as a courtesan, "you have forgotten—"

"I do not forget." Dracula's tone made it clear that he wanted to hear nothing more from the voice Fenice did not recognize. He started to turn away from the speaker, but she caught the edge of his sleeve. He swung back and glowered down at her.

"You took me from my home, from my family, from everything, so that you could be all that for me." She was more insistent than pleading. "But you do not realize what you are doing to me."

"I owe you no accounting for my actions. I am Prince here." He pulled his sleeve away.

She stretched out her hand to him. "The angel that lured me here promised me an eternity of devotion in return for my adoration. That was not so very long ago," she went on, ignoring the finality in his last words. "Did that angel lie?"

"You followed no angel," Dracula said brusquely.

"Another lie," said the unknown voice. "Unless the angel is an infernal one." There was a tense silence for the space of three heartbeats. "I have kept faith with you. Why will you not keep faith with me?"

"You have deceived us all," said Dracula.

Her laughter was filled with mockery. "Why should you protest when I learn from you?"

Whatever Dracula might have replied was lost when Fenice stepped into the light.

What messenger could bring so reprehensible
A message, but one from infernal angels . . .
—Giovanni Boccaccio

— XXIX —

Beside Dracula stood a fair-haired, blue-eyed woman barely out of childhood, her body showing the first promise of maturity. She was dressed in the finery of earlier days—a blue-green gonella that brought out the color of her eyes and made her golden hair shine more brightly in contrast. Small pearl earrings and a pearl-and-sapphire necklace were her only ornaments, appropriate to her apparent adolescence. Everything about her bespoke youth until one looked more closely and saw the practiced airs of seduction she could assume, and the decadent line of her lips. This juxtaposition of concupiscence and innocence was perversely attractive. She stared at Fenice, outrage coming over her. "You insult me for *this?*" She gave Fenice a look of scathing disdain.

"You have said you are lonely." Dracula spoke with the weariness of old disputes. "I told you of my plans."

"And you think another mistress for you will placate me? How am I to be less alone because you have another bride?" She glared at him. "Or did you think she would take my place here? Did you have other plans? Are you intending to supplant me with her? Is she your new bride? Have you decided to—"

"Kelene," Dracula said, very quietly. "Stop."

She went silent at once, and though her chin came up in defiance, her blue eyes were glazed with fear; she was too angry to pout and too frightened to protest. She remained rigidly alert as Dracula strode to Fenice's side.

"This is Fenice. She comes from Venice, much farther away than your Salonika." He took Fenice by the arm and half led, half pulled her toward the blond young woman. "This is Kelene. She is Greek."

Not knowing what was expected, Fenice gave a short curtsy, as she would to any guest of her host in Venice. "I hope my coming is not an inconvenience," she said in Greek, thinking how incongruous her manners were in this place.

"Answer her, Kelene," Dracula ordered.

Kelene did not comply at once, but as Dracula took a step toward her, she obeyed. "If Dracula brought you here, you must be welcome. This is his castle: all we within are his devoted vassals," she said with a smile that was as wide as it was false.

Fenice tried to think of a response, and finally said, "I am pleased to be here." As she said it, she thought it was as fraudulent as Kelene's smile.

"No doubt," said Kelene, looking straight at Dracula. "Is that all? May I now go in search of sustenance?" She folded her arms, for all the world like a girl having a fit of pique; only the depths of her cerulean eyes betrayed her.

"Yes," said Dracula, his very curtness a kind of surrender.

She straightened the front of her gonella as if adjusting her armor. "I will not go near the two villages. I will avoid the gypsies. I will stay out of direct sunlight." She recited this by rote, as if it were a lesson long since learned.

"You know where the travelers are to be found," Dracula said as if unwilling to indulge her. "I want no complaints of you coming to me."

"You will not have them," she said, and turned without acknowledging Fenice. "I will be back before sunrise. That is a promise."

"I expect nothing else," said Dracula as Kelene stormed out of the vault, going toward an indentation in the wall which proved to conceal a door. There was a burst of wind as she went out; the stones screamed as the air rushed through. Then the door shut again and Kelene was gone.

Fenice did not say anything for a short while. Then she remarked, "I knew I was not the first. But I thought it would be Muna."

For the first time Dracula seemed unable to answer directly. "Muna was here after Kelene came. Before Muna was Eudike, and before her Asenath. They are gone now. Only Kelene remains."

This evasiveness puzzled Fenice. "They disagreed?" she ventured.

Dracula shrugged. "They made themselves rivals." He released his hold on Fenice's arm. She studied the place where his fingers had been. "What happened to them?" She held her breath as she waited for his response.

"They met with accidents," he answered, clearly unwilling to say more.

"Accidents," Fenice echoed.

"Muna did not return until after sunrise one morning; she died outside the door, burned to nothing. She was still much too sensitive to sunlight. Eudike fell from the battlements and was impaled." He made a gesture to show that nothing could have been done to save them.

"How did she come to be impaled?" Fenice asked incredulously. "Surely that could be no accident?"

Dracula gave her a condemning stare. "The gypsies were here and they had set up their camp near the wall. It was a cloudy night and Eudike did not realize her danger. She fell on the tether stake holding the leads of the gypsies' goats." He shook his head. "The gypsies were terrified. They were afraid they would have to answer for her death. Kelene persuaded me not to make an example of them." He said nothing for a short while, then added, "Asenath was foolish enough to hunt a priest; he overpowered her with the cross and his other protections, and then he beheaded her."

Fenice frowned. "Why would she hunt a priest? She must have known it could be dangerous." She thought of how difficult it was for her to try to turn her thoughts to holy things; would it not have been the same for Asenath?

"I do not know. Kelene told me she warned Asenath of the risks, but Asenath wanted to test her powers." Dracula strode away from her toward the coffin with the elaborately carved lid displaying the arms of the Dragon Prince.

"But on a priest?" Fenice knew it was foolish to speak so directly, but the words were out before she could stop them. Hastily she amended her outburst. "Of course I did not know her; she might well have wanted to undertake the greatest challenge before she was capable of confronting it. I have no way of knowing. But I should have thought she would know it was folly to . . . to put herself at such risk."

"Perhaps she did," said Dracula quietly. "But she had set herself a task that Kelene said she would hesitate to undertake." It was the only concession he would make to giving credence to her dawning apprehension. "Kelene is more of a child than you may think; I claimed her when she was fourteen."

"And fourteen she has remained," Fenice said. "As I must assume I will remain seventeen?" Saying this aloud made her feel cold again: to be decades or centuries old and remain fourteen, or seventeen! She could not grasp the enormity of it, but she realized she had seen the shape of her future. If, indeed, she had a future to see.

"Yes. You will always be as you are now." He came to her and bent to kiss her, more to demonstrate his mastery than to show affection.

Fenice did not resist him, though he did not rouse her senses as he had done the night before; was that because she was now un-Dead, or had there been a greater change than that? She was not sorry when he stepped away from her, nor did she object when he told her that Marcu would provide her with what she needed tonight.

"Wait until he is deeply asleep. You will not have to drain him—not yet, in any case. Use him well and he will last you for many nights. Just be sure that when he dies, he dies utterly. I will not have him rise within these walls." He held up his hand in a warning. "Do not look to the living for allies. They are weak and their time is short. You will find no haven without me."

"Certainly not in my coffin," Fenice said, nodding toward hers. "It could be a prison cell as easily as a resting place."

Dracula nodded. "I see you understand."

She had no idea how to go about the duty Dracula had set forth for her: Fenice remembered the traveler they had waylaid and she could not convince herself that Dracula intended her to attack Marcu in that brutal fashion. But what was she to do? She could fight him, as she had done the market-gang, but that would be clumsy at best. She thought of how Dracula had come to her in Varna, and how he had wooed her. Perhaps she could do the same with Marcu. She had little faith in herself as a seductress, but she supposed she would manage that better than fighting the handsome servant every night she became hungry. "Besides," she said aloud as she made her way up into the main floors of the castle, "he might object to nightly battles, and if he complained, the results might be unwelcome." Attacking unknown travelers was one thing; preying on servants was another. She had never considered that she might have to follow Dracula's example in obtaining nourishment; now she realized she had little choice in the matter. She was un-Dead now and would have to survive as the un-Dead survived.

The servants of the castle had their quarters in the rooms above the kitchen. Each had a bed, a chest, a table, and a washstand provided them, along with two oil lamps that were refilled twice a month. This was stark housing by Venetian standards, but Fenice supposed that for Transylvania the conditions were acceptable. She entered Marcu's room after she had waited by the door, listening to his breathing to be certain he was asleep. She saw him lying on his side, his straw-filled pillow shoved between his head and shoulder in the bend of his elbow; he looked younger than he had when he served her the night before. She came to his side and studied him. How to take blood without rousing him? She considered trying to be inconspicuous, but could not think of any way to do that. He must surely be aware of a bite on his neck, which would waken him, and there would be an outcry . . . She folded her arms, perplexed. What would silence him? She could smother him, or clout him on the head and take what she sought while he was unconscious, but that again would lead to an outcry, though it would be less immediate. She would need his cooperation and his silence. She pursed her lips and glowered. How was she to achieve her ends? She raised her head and bent over him: masters seduced servant-girls all the time, if the rumors she had heard in Venice were right. Then why not seduce a manservant?

Carefully Fenice lifted the rough coverlet and slid into the bed next to Marcu, facing him. His elbow brushed her forehead and she teetered on the edge of the mattress, afraid of waking him if she moved much nearer. She could not make up her mind what to do next, for she did not want to startle him, or give him reason to summon help. She knew what went on between men and women, but had never experienced it for herself—her brush with rape and Dracula's peculiar methods of making love did not strike her as applicable to her present task—and did not know how to begin.

He sighed and pulled the pillow more tightly against his neck.

Fenice lay utterly still until he was once again breathing regularly; she considered briefly leaving him to rest undisturbed. But she was hungry, and tomorrow she would be ravenous if she did not do something tonight to mitigate her hunger. Then she might not be so circumspect. So she brushed her fingers lightly along his naked thigh, hoping that he would be tantalized instead of startled. She made her touch as soft as she could, ephemeral. If he was excited he would not be in a hurry to chase her from his bed when he realized what was happening.

He grunted, turned and shoved the pillow under him, then lay atop it, trembling.

Fenice was perturbed. This was not what she had expected, but she decided to make the most of it. While Marcu's sleeping body rocked on the pillow, she pushed herself onto her elbow and, after a few awkward attempts, managed to nip the side of his throat enough to raise a little blood. Wincing at her need, she put her mouth to the two little cuts.

It tasted *wonderful*. Her senses flooded with its palingenesy; vitality surged through every part of her as if propelled by some arcane spell, giving her a vivacity of spirit she had not experienced before. So this was the wildness of her soul. No wonder she had longed to live by its desire, and no wonder so many had feared it in her: Fenice knew now that this was the vindication of all she had done. Nothing she had ever consumed had been so profoundly gratifying as Marcu's blood. She drank greedily, growing annoyed when the wounds did not flow readily. She was tempted to try again, but she remembered Dracula's admonition to make him last. With a reluctance she could not have imagined before this, she drew away from Marcu and slipped out of the bed as the servant slipped into a deeper sleep, his pillow still mashed beneath him.

Two nights later when she woke, Fenice could not open the lid of her coffin; the latch that Dracula had showed her how to operate did not release the lid. She did not panic as she had three nights earlier, but she was annoyed enough to make a petulant kick at the foot of her coffin. To her astonishment, the coffin moved, jerking a handswidth along the stone slab on which it stood. Pleased at this result, Fenice kicked again, and once more the coffin slid a short distance. Fenice tried to imagine where the coffin was now on the high, flat stone, but could not. With a quick shaking of her head, she recommenced kicking until she felt the coffin teeter. She kicked again and it fell; inside she was banged about, but the lid sprang open, which was what she had hoped for.

As she got to her feet, she saw Kelene disappearing up the long corridor into the main part of the castle. For a moment Fenice wondered if Kelene had done anything to the lid of her coffin. It was obvious the Greek girl was jealous, but Fenice supposed it was no different than the occasional fits of dudgeon Eloisa indulged in; she might try to show her pique by locking Fenice's coffin lid as a childish prank. "How tiresome," Fenice said to the empty vault, for she saw that Dracula's magnificent coffin was empty, the lid raised and waiting for his return.

Doing what she could to put herself in order without a mirror to help her, Fenice was soon ready to begin her nightly adventure. Since she knew it would be some time into the night before she could visit Marcu again without waking him, she decided to explore the castle, for she had had no opportunity to do it when she arrived. As she reached the great hall, she looked up to the gallery and decided she would take it one side at a time, going along the various corridors and into the vast, silent rooms that appeared to comprise most of the castle.

After discovering a number of unused bedrooms and sitting rooms on the south side of the gallery, she came upon a muniment room, with records of the castle and the House kept in enormous leatherbound volumes chained to bookcases and high, canted desks. Shields of various ages hung on the walls, each with the dragon device of the House blazoned on them. Fenice opened the nearest and what seemed to be the newest of the record-books, only to discover it was written in a language she did not recognize, though from the groupings of numbers, she supposed it must be accounts. She shook her head once in disappointment, then put the book back in its place. She had not realized until then how much she would miss reading if she was to be deprived of it for any length of time. Perhaps Dracula would be willing to purchase some books for her when next he traveled to Varna. The hope was a forlorn one, but she clung to it as the only consolation she had. Leaving the muniment room, she slapped the dust from her hands and clothes before she started in the direction of Marcu's room and the sweet, restorative elixir she would find.

The next night Fenice woke to Kelene bending over her with a torch in her hand. "It would be a pity," the blond girl whispered softly, "if your lovely clothes should catch fire. You must take care not to—"

"I am not reckless with lamps and candles," said Fenice with asperity as she got out of the coffin and brushed at her clothes. "But I thank you for your warning."

"You must take care," Kelene repeated, displeased at being interrupted. "Accidents can happen so easily in a place like this." The sympathy in her voice was at odds with the hot glitter of her blue eyes.

"So I have been told," she said, the image of Eloisa strong in her mind. "You have been a most fortunate guest to have suffered no injury."

"I was *first,*" Kelene said with pride. "Before you came, or any of the others, he summoned me." She held the torch out, almost touching the sleeve of Fenice's ropilla.

"Be careful," Fenice said brusquely.

"I just wanted to show you how easily accidents can happen. Muna and Leonaline and Asenath were careless. Eudike was stupid. Ruera was stupid. Thalis was too reluctant." She turned and thrust the torch back into its bracket.

"I'll keep that in mind," said Fenice. She tried to think of some way to relieve the girl's anxiety, but nothing suggested itself to her. When Eloisa was in a taking, she recalled, the best way to end it was to pay no attention to it; for an instant she missed her youngest sister fiercely. Then she glanced at Kelene and put her mind to getting along with this more senior but much younger inamorata of Dracula's. "I thank you for pointing this out to me. In a new place, one can overlook matters of true importance because they are not recognizable amid the novelty of the place." She thought she sounded remarkably stiff, but she saw Kelene nod.

"Just so you know," said Kelene, and hurried toward the door to the outside without another word.

* * *

Four nights later, Fenice discovered the library. It was on the north side of the castle, a huge room with shelves reaching to the ceiling; ladders gave access to the volumes on the highest shelves. To Fenice's dismay, she saw the room was thick with dust and the smell of old parchment was strong in the stale air. Determined not to be discouraged by the library's obvious neglect, she searched greedily for books in Greek, Latin, and Italian, and found well over a hundred of each. She grinned with anticipation of the many hours of pleasure that lay ahead of her. Between this room and Marcu's blood, she knew she would be happy in this place if no other adventure was offered her. *At least,* she added to herself, *for a while.*

She was halfway through a centuries-old *Arcanum* three nights later when Dracula found her. She looked up, startled, as if interrupted in some guilty act. Then she said, "You have treasures here."

"Collections of words," he said. "But it pleases me to know you value them."

"Have you read them?" she asked, incredulous that he should be so indifferent to such treasures.

"Many times," he said, making no excuse for his boredom. "They pall, after time."

"How could that be?" Fenice asked, gesturing to the room. "There is so much here. When I finish what you have, I will start over and read them again." Her enthusiasm was so great that it evoked a wintery smile from Dracula.

"When you have read them again for the hundredth time, tell me again what treasures they are," he said, and changed the subject. "Marcu is to your taste?" He showed his teeth to indicate he wanted to amuse her.

"He is . . . I cannot tell you how wonderful he is." She felt as if she might be blushing. "It is nothing like what . . . what you and I did. This is . . ." She shook her head, running out of words.

"When we hunted together, you were still living. Now you are un-Dead and you know what makes our existence worthwhile." He sat down in one of the large, dusty chairs. "But you do not wake him. You wait until he is asleep."

Fenice was startled; she had not thought she had been observed. "No. I . . . would not know how to . . ."

"Persuade him?" Dracula suggested. "Influence him? Seduce him?"

Fenice shook her head. "Any of those things." She looked away from him. "I never learned such arts; I wanted my adventure instead. Was I wrong?" Her eyes came back to his.

Now Dracula laughed; the sound was low and sly. "Not then, since your adventure brought you here. But now you will have to learn to lure your prey to you. It is not for us to wait upon the pleasure of the hunted, but to bring them to us."

"As you brought me?" she asked sharply.

His nod was almost a bow, very grand and stately. "You were seeking me. Now that you are with me, you would do well to turn your attention to learning how to make your prey welcome you." He made an idle gesture. "You cannot spend all your time waiting for your prey to fall asleep so that you may slake your thirst."

Fenice brought her head up; she coughed to cover her sudden gasp. "How can Marcu be prey?" She could not hide the indignation she felt on Marcu's behalf.

"What else is he? Oh, yes, a servant, but there are many more who can take his place. Even here, in these mountains, I can find servants, for I pay very, very well." He stretched out his legs as if he intended to nap in the chair. "But Marcu is your prey, and you behave like a wolf-cub, waiting until what you hunt is asleep before you dare to attack. You do not command his obedience."

"As you have commanded mine?" she asked, stung by the implication.

"You were never prey, Fenice; you were always destined to become one of my own." He reached out and touched her negligently, as if reassuring himself that she agreed with him. "But as one of mine, you cannot falter when you are in need. You will have to learn to be more assertive of your place—your place and right—if you are to remain under my wing. You will have to put aside those gentle notions of courtship unless they will bring you greater rewards than plunder will. How can you wait upon the whims of sleeping servants if you are lord here?"

"I did not realized I was lord here," said Fenice with heat. "How could I?"

"You have my favor. Everyone in these mountains knows what that means. You are clinging to your dreams of escapades, of grand exploits, of masquerades, and ambuscados." He shook his head. "This is no tale to make children marvel: this is the realm of the un-Dead and all living must go in fear of us."

Offended by what she recognized was an insult, Fenice rose from her stool. "I do not deserve such censure."

Dracula was unimpressed. "I say you do, and in this there can be no dispute. You came here to be with me, to be of me. Very well. I have made you one of my own. You must learn what that entails; all of what it entails, or you will be lost. Not today, or this year, or next, but you will be lost."

This dire prediction struck a chord. "Kelene warned me about accidents." Then something occurred to her, something so monstrous that she hesitated to speak of it for fear of being proved right. "Did Muna and Eudike and Asenath refuse to learn to hunt? Did you leave them to the . . . accidents that—" She stopped, aware of what she was saying. Had Kelene made the other women her prey? Kelene was a child, a petulant, sensual child: how could she set out to murder her rivals in that callous way? But then, a capricious child could easily destroy something that provoked her; Fenice had broken her favorite doll when she was six for no reason other than Artemesia had a newer one: were Kelene's acts so different from her own childhood dissatisfaction? Fenice stared at Dracula. "You let her do it, didn't you? You knew and you did nothing."

"I did not give her permission. Nor do I know for certain that she did anything." He was as aloof as a cat, and as unctuous. "They would have died somehow. They could not live as the un-Dead must. They wanted to be grand ladies, bestowing favors. You, at least, want high adventure instead of languishing suitors." He shook his head and the feral light returned to his eyes; his face was raptorlike. "We seek no favors. We take what we need. If we fulfill desires as well, it is our right."

"And you permit Kelene to . . . to test your conquests?" Fenice demanded.

"If that is what she is doing, why should I not? She is living according to our ways; how can I not accept what she does—if she does anything?" He stared at her face without any emotion she could discern.

Had she been able to, Fenice would have crossed herself. As it was, she withdrew into thought, saying only, "I understand what you have told me, my lord. I will consider what I must do."

Dracula rose from the chair. "Kelene is clever in her way." It was all the caution he would give her and Fenice knew it.

"As I am, in mine," said Fenice, and opened her book again so she would not have to watch Dracula leave the library.

The *Impresa* left Trebizond in fine weather and made good speed back to Varna; Ercole was more than satisfied with the speed of his voyage and was already looking forward to boasting of his ship's remarkable swiftness when he returned to Venice. What he was dreading was retrieving his sister from Hagia Charis and the necessity of confining her like a prisoner all the way home. He hoped Mother Sophronia had been able to instill Fenice with some humility and penitence for her mad escapade. He did not want to have to spend the last of his voyage—until now a triumph—in continual arguments with his sister; that would spoil all he had achieved, and he begrudged her every instant he was deprived of his accomplishment.

"We can keep her out of sight at least; that will spare us more embarrassment. If the crew does not get to see her, we can bring her into Venice and get her to a convent without exposing her to the kind of attention we must deplore." He drank his wine and looked out over the twilight sea. He did not want to punish Fenice: the nuns would have done that already. But he was determined to make her comprehend the magnitude of her errors.

"Of course," Niccola said tonelessly. Niccola had offered to keep Aeneo with him in the kitchen as before, but Ercole had refused: he had convinced himself that Fenice would have acquired enough shame to refuse such an offer even if it were made to her. He did agree to let Niccola bring her meals and generally tend her to keep from exposing her to the lascivious speculation of the crew, and with that concession he told himself he was doing more for his wayward sister than she deserved.

"We will be in port in a day or two," Ercole said. "We must be ready to have her aboard."

"I am ready," Niccola promised, thinking that Fenice would suffer for her escapade more than she deserved to suffer.

"I wish I were," Ercole said heavily as he had a third cup of wine.

Arriving at Varna, Ercole had success with the amber he brought from Tana; his prices were lower than those of the Russian merchants and he traded for dyes, spices, and perfume, making a handsome bargain with a loquacious Turk for half the leather he had brought from Tana in exchange for a small chest of lapis lazuli. Then he took the time to meet with other merchant-captains to boast, complain, and exchange information. It was all a delay to keep from going to Hagia Charis; when he had run out of excuses for avoiding his obligation, he reluctantly took a second cloak and made his way to the convent, remembering to pay the beggars who lined the streets.

Mother Sophronia looked distressed when she was summoned to the gate to speak with Ercole. She crossed herself repeatedly and called on the saints to witness her blamelessness in this terrible event.

Ercole listened, appalled at this shocking display. "What is the matter?" he insisted several times. "What has happened?" He crossed himself Roman style. "She isn't . . . dead?" He hated himself for the leap of relief that swelled in him.

"No, no, not dead. Better dead," Mother Sophronia said with great emotion. *"Gone."*

"Gone?" Ercole repeated blankly; of all the calamities he had imagined, this was not one of them. "Gone—how?"

Mother Sophronia sighed. "Who knows? She was here, and then, one morning shortly after you left, she was gone." Now that she actually admitted this hideous truth, she began to weep.

"She has been gone . . . some time?" Ercole asked, trying to grasp the significance of what Mother Sophronia was saying.

"Yes. You had been gone a few days, only a few, when she vanished." She clasped her hands and held them up to Heaven. "I swear on my eternal soul, we were diligent in her care. We guarded her as we swore we would. She simply . . . went."

"Where?" Ercole was unable to believe she could be completely gone. It could not happen. Fenice disappear? That was impossible. And as he thought about this latest trick he grew angry. "I will go—"

"We do not know how she went, or where she has gone," Mother Sophronia admitted, and lowered her head in disgrace. "We have not seen her. No one has seen her."

"But she's in Varna," Ercole said, encouraging the nuns to tell him she was.

Mother Sophronia shook her head. "If she is we have not found her, and the beggars do not know of it." She knelt down at Ercole's feet. "Forgive me, I beg of you, for the sake of your soul and mine. We did not mean for this to happen. When we realized she was gone, we tried to find her, but to no avail."

Staggered by this information, Ercole could not answer her at first; when he did, it was in an absent way. "I don't . . . hold you responsible. I have nothing to forgive. It is her . . . ungovernable nature that has brought this about. You have not." He shook his head as if trying to clear it of confusion. "I will . . . I will leave you now." He would have to search for her in places the nuns would not go: taverns and brothels. Perhaps, he thought, she had disguised herself again and signed aboard another ship. "Thank you. For all you tried to teach her," he said to the nuns as he hurried away down the alley.

Niccola heard the news a short time later and did not respond at first. When he had thought it over, he remarked, "Plucky thing to do."

"Foolish, stupid, wilful thing to do," Ercole corrected him. "She'll regret it. She will regret it, I promise you. I'll beat her black and blue when I find her."

"And do you think you will? Find her?" Niccola asked remotely. "If she wants to be found, perhaps; otherwise—"

"She won't escape me," Ercole vowed.

"If you insist," said Niccola, shrugging his shoulders to express his doubts.

For the next two days Ercole remained in Varna, trying to discover where Fenice had fled to; the more he searched the less he found, for no one had heard even a rumor about her. All the speculation Ercole pursued failed to provide any hint of what had become of Fenice, and gradually Ercole became despondent. His anger turned to worry and then to grief as it was borne in upon him that his sister was lost to him forever.

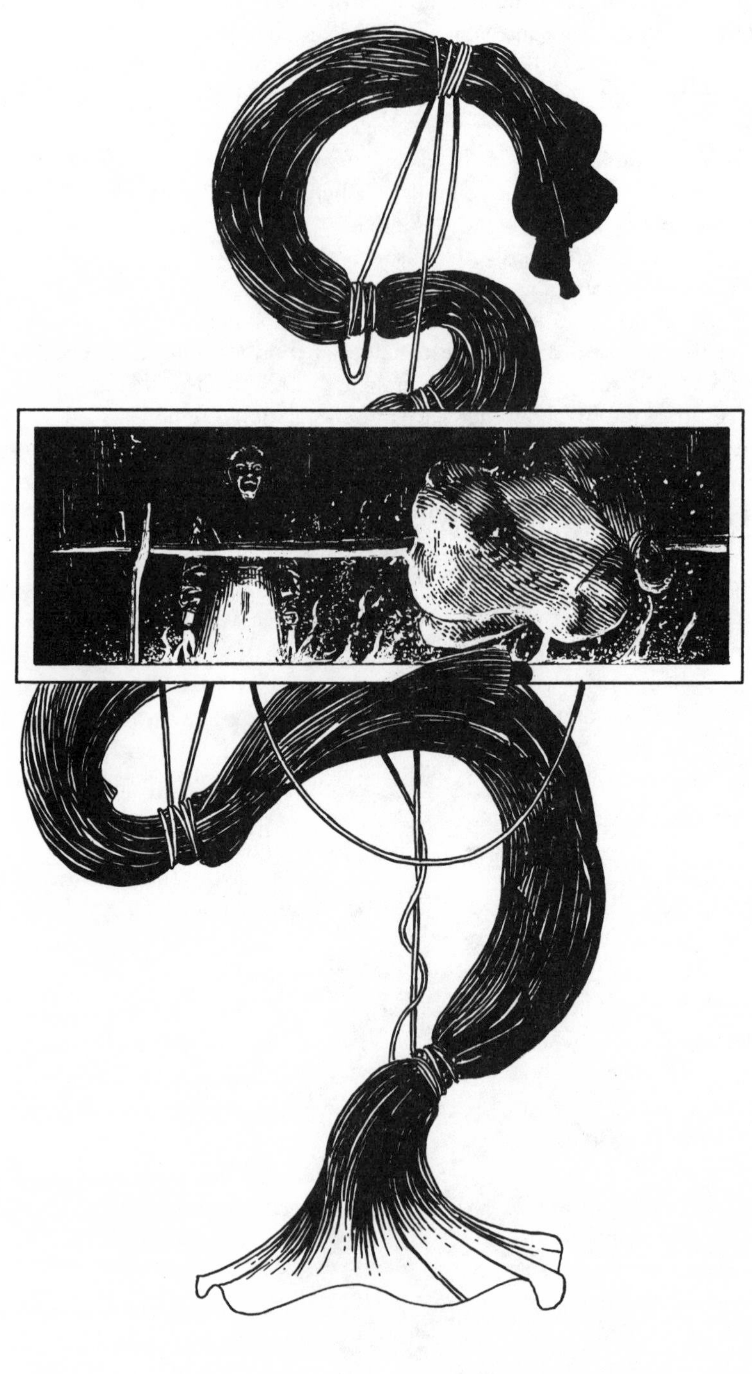

Say that you are happy here,
Wild, roaming wild mountain tracks?
—Franco Sacchetti

— XXX —

She had taken too much of his blood, she could tell by the inert sprawl in which he lay, by the thready way his breath came and went. But it was so *good*. Dracula had been right about that. Fenice straightened up as she wiped her mouth on the cuff of her sleeve. Poor Marcu would not be able to get out of bed in the morning, she was certain of it. And it would be her fault. She almost reached down and touched his brow as a kind of apology, but she recalled Dracula's admonition and did not. She started toward the door, then paused. Had she heard something in the hall beyond? Had someone been waiting for her to leave? Might there be an accident waiting for her just outside?

Fenice paused, her hand on the latch. She gave all her attention to what was on the other side of the door. She heard a whisper, then a silence, then another whisper, and the soft padding of bare feet, followed by the gentle closing of not one but two doors: two of the servants had been taking their pleasure of one another. Satisfied that she was in no danger, and grateful that she had not been discovered, Fenice slipped out of the room and made her way to the library, where she spent the remainder of the night reading in Greek of the wide travels of an Islamite called Ibn Battuta; some of her longing for strange places returned as she followed the remarkable narrative, and she wondered if she would ever be able to persuade Dracula to allow her to go with him on his forays beyond Transylvania: it did not seem likely, and she sighed with regret as she considered her prospects, consoling herself with the reminder that she was in Transylvania, in a place no one else in her family had ever been.

As she made her way down to the vault shortly before dawn, she encountered Kelene coming in from the night. The girl was in high spirits, her cheeks flushed as with a fever, her movements wild and restless as she offered Fenice a hectic greeting.

"Isn't it glorious? I found two travelers. Actually, I think they were probably bandits, but they were looking for new places where they could rob. They were impudent enough to think that Dracula would permit bandits to flourish in his region. I let them think that they could ravish me, and then I took their lives for their audacity." She smiled angelically. "They assumed I was a child."

"Foolish mistake," Fenice said, wishing she could feel more dismay at these revelations—had she done anything better in her time with Marcu? She knew any reservations she felt about Kelene's boasting were only a question of degree, not of action.

"It was, it was." Kelene was almost crowing. "They were ready to subdue a girl to their will, but they could not. They could not." She tossed her hands up, the frivolous implication revealing a little of the sham the two bandits had believed.

"So," Fenice said, not knowing what Kelene expected of her. "You have done your work."

"Happily," said Kelene, smiling in predatory contentment. "And in three nights when I hunt again, I hope to be so fortunate."

"In three nights?" Fenice repeated. They had been ambling down the twisting corridor toward the vault; now Fenice halted.

"Why, yes," Kelene said, turning to look back at Fenice. "I have fed well. I am not a glutton that I must stuff myself night after night. When I have supped deeply, I fast until the hunger returns." Her smile widened. "I am not so fastidious as you seem to be. I am willing to take what I require. There is always more prey."

Fenice pressed her lips together as if to keep herself from a rash retort, or to deny the hunger they shared. Finally she spoke. "I don't know how to forget they are like us."

"But they are *not. Like. Us,*" Kelene said, her vehemence as acidic as it was sudden. "They are nothing. They are sheep. They are fodder. Why should we do anything but prey on them?"

"Have they no shepherds?" Fenice asked sadly as they entered the vault.

"There are those who claim to be. Those who serve at their altars and tell fables about the Saints and Angels who watch over us." Her laughter had more of rage than mirth in it, and she tossed her golden hair defiantly. "There is one salvation, one resurrection, and it is the one Dracula gives. All the rest is coercion and superstition." She reached her coffin and climbed into it; Dracula's was already closed.

Fenice knew she ought to be scandalized by this denouncement, but she could not find it in her to reprimand Kelene, or to come to the defense of her faith as she had been taught to do. She cocked her head and regarded the Greek girl with curiosity. "Why do you say that?"

"Because I know it is true. Because Dracula kept his promise to me, and no one else ever has." With that, she pulled the lid closed.

Fenice went more slowly to her coffin, and for a while sat in it, staring into the wavering torchlight in thoughtful silence. Then she lay back, pulled the lid closed, and gave herself over to dreamless rest.

Six weeks after Fenice arrived at Castle Dracula, the gypsies returned, their wagons drawn up in a circle near the high stone walls, the smoke from the fires blending with the gray skies overhead. Their songs echoed through the high peaks, lonely as the cry of wolves.

"You must be careful if you choose one of them for fodder," Kelene warned Fenice with a show of concern that might have been convincing if Fenice were not on her guard. "They know how to deal with us. Usually they allow us one of their foundlings, but no more. And the foundling is mine." She spoke as if she had claimed a new toy.

"I will not forget," Fenice said; she had ventured outside the castle walls twice, and once had waylaid a tinker going from remote village to remote village; she had lured him to an empty barn and waited until he slept before taking what she required. The second time she had come upon a drunken mercenary half-asleep in his saddle. She still visited Marcu in his room, but he was weak now, and the sustenance he offered was no longer as satisfactory as it had been at first. She would have to seek other nourishment, and soon.

Kelene studied Fenice a moment. "You have not learned to love it yet, have you?" She chuckled with contempt.

"No," Fenice admitted, knowing precisely what Kelene meant.

"You will," said Kelene. "Or you will not survive." She waved lightly and rushed out of the vault and into the night.

Dracula opened the lid of his coffin and rose, stepping out of its confines in one practiced movement. "You are a very prudent woman," he observed. "One might not think so at first, but it becomes apparent with knowing you." His smile was cold. "Will prudence be enough, I wonder."

"Enough for what?" Fenice asked, although she already knew: Dracula was speculating on the outcome of the contest between Fenice and Kelene.

Dracula only smiled. "You will be going out tonight?"

"Yes. I think I must. Marcu is in no condition . . ." Her words faltered; she did not know what to say beyond that.

"You have been very careful with him," Dracula said. "Another sign of prudence. I was certain he would be dead by now." His approving nod made Fenice want to scream. "So tonight you will have another adventure."

"Do you approve?" Fenice inquired with scathing sweetness.

"If you need my approval, you have it," Dracula said, shifting the fit of his cloak on his shoulders so that it fell like folded wings along his back. "But I am not the one you have to consider, am I?"

His smugness caught her off-guard. "You go to the trouble of bringing me from Varna and then you . . . you throw me to the wolves," she cried out in protest. "Why?"

"I have not thrown you to the wolves; I am discovering if you are worthy. Any knight had tests to pass before he gained his spurs. Would you have me demand less of you because you are a woman from Venice? After all you have done?" He shook his head.

"But I have done so much," Fenice protested. "When will it be enough?"

"Kelene will tell you," Dracula said softly.

"No doubt she will." The bitterness in her voice took her aback.

"You did not think you would have me to yourself, did you?" There was something in his voice that made her stare at him.

Mustering her courage, Fenice countered with, "Why not? Kelene has."

Now she caught Dracula's interest. "If you would join that battle, you had better prepare to fight to the death." He leaned toward her. "Do not begin what you are not prepared to finish. For Kelene is in earnest; you had better be as well."

"I know she is hoping to have me dead," Fenice said, refusing to show any trace of fear. "I have taken your warning to heart."

"Wise of you," said Dracula, striding toward the small door leading to the outside of the castle. "But let me advise you not to put all your attention on her; starvation makes us weak, as it does the living. When you become desperate, you become careless." He held up a warning finger, then let himself out of the door.

Left alone a second time, Fenice frowned in concentration. She would have to get food, that was of first importance. Which, she reminded herself, would mean hunting tonight. She had hoped to finish the travels of Ibn Battuta tonight, but she had no hope of it now. Instead she would have to search along the few roads in the region for lone travelers who could be— She would not let herself think *attacked*; she shook her head once. There had to be a better word for it. Attack was what the market-gang had done to her: she had no wish to be like them. What would the traveler be? Detained? That was too tidy a thought. Secreted? That was more acceptable; it had a sinister yet playful tone, much more to her liking: hadn't she secreted herself aboard her brother's ship, and kept up the game in the market-square of Varna? Tonight she would have to find someone and *secret* him for her own purposes. Satisfied that she had found a worthwhile term for what she had to do, Fenice let herself out of the same door Kelene and Dracula had used.

The night was cold, but that no longer caused Fenice much discomfort; her magnificent ropilla was enough to keep her warm. She slipped past the gypsy camp to the steep road leading down to a long defile where shepherds maintained a small hamlet; this she passed by, for it was understood that the lord of Castle Dracula would protect those dependents living in his shadow. Onward she went, her speed faster than a running horse. She covered the ground without effort, silent and tireless in her hunt. She was out of the defile quickly, and soon reached the crossroad to the next village; she hesitated only a moment, then struck out toward the stockaded houses, hoping to find a straggler outside the walls.

Tonight she was in luck: less than a league from the village she found a solitary traveler in foreign clothes huddled by a small, smoking fire, contemplating a roasting duck as it turned on a spit above the flames; he had a small pack on the ground beside him and a large dagger thrust through the strap of his belt. He looked miserable and cold as he sat there, with nothing to look forward to save a night's sleep on the cold ground. His face was large and square with deep-set eyes and an ugly knot of scar tissue under his lip. He was neither old nor young—perhaps about thirty—and he carried himself with the general demeanor of a man who has seen more roughness than ease in life; he would not be unsuspicious of any intruder.

Fenice approached him carefully, taking stock of him. He was far enough from the village, and the few huts immediately outside it, that any alarm from him would not rouse the inhabitants. She noticed that while he was not stout, he was not scrawny either, promising sufficient nourishment for her. A man of this sort would not willingly succumb to her needs, so she would have to use guile to gain access to him, and to put him off his guard; she wished now she had put on her boy's clothes, so that she could approach him directly without giving him any cause for apprehension: a boy on the road was just another wanderer like him—a woman in fine fabric would demand more than curiosity from him, increasing her risk. Had she hope of finding another, more promising traveler, she would have passed this man by. There was nothing for it; she would have to manage as she was, but she decided that in future she would present herself in male guise. Thinking about it a moment, she tore her sleeve and rubbed a little dirt on her face, then she rushed out of the darkness, crying, "Oh, thank goodness!" hoping as she did that he understood Greek.

The man started up with an oath, almost kicking the duck into the fire. "God on the Cross," he said in astonishment, then summoned up a few words in Greek. "What is . . . wrong?"

"My coach. It was overturned. I was thrown out." She saw he was following the gist of her tale and went on. "I think the coachmen and postilion were killed. I know three of the horses were. I have been wandering since sunset." She dropped down onto her knees. "Help me."

The surprise he had shown changed subtly. "Of course. I will." He reached out.

"How good of you," Fenice exclaimed. "I have been so frightened, so alone."

The man stared down at her, his features crafty in the firelight. "No one is with you?" he asked, his accent rough but understandable.

"I am alone," she exclaimed, and buried her face in her hands as if overwhelmed with the enormity of the calamity that had befallen her. "And I am too tired to go any further tonight. If you have a little food and water to spare, I would be grateful, very grateful."

"Alone," he said as if he had not heard the rest, his hand going to the dagger in his belt. "I am alone, too."

She looked up at him, and saw the intent in his eyes. "What—?"

He held out the dagger. "I do not want to use this," he said. "But I will if I must." He caressed the hilt. "I have before."

Fenice stared at him, oddly grateful that he had made her decision so easy. She started to rise. "No. You must not. For pity's sake—"

"Go to the priest for pity," said the man, adding more in a harsh language Fenice did not recognize. "The priests showed me no pity when the women at home complained about me."

Although she did not comprehend the words, the man's intent was clear enough for Fenice to strike out at him, slapping his chest. "You cannot. You are cruel; I come to you for help, for mercy." Her ambivalence about hunting him was entirely gone now.

"You will get what you deserve," said the man in his own tongue, trying to grab her.

Fenice eluded him, putting the fire between them. If he had been compassionate, she would not have enjoyed preying upon him; as it was, she reveled in the contest, so much more direct than her continuing conflict with Kelene.

"Damn you for a whore," the man yelled as he tried to get around the fire to her.

She wanted to taunt him, but she did not want to take the risk of inciting him to throw his dagger, so she pretended to weep and plead with him, begging him to show her a little kindness. "I have lost my servants and my friends will not know where to find me. If you will not help me, I will never return home."

The man laughed. "You may not want to when I've finished with you," he said, half in Greek, half in Czech.

Fenice brought her head up. "You are despicable." She spat at him, and stood very still as if preparing herself to surrender.

He started around the fire to claim her, but she circled the flames again, and he could not reach her. "You sow," he growled, his Greek making the word sound worse.

"Better a sow than a beast," she shot back, and moved around the fire again.

"You will not be able to do this all night," he told her. "You will get tired, and I will be angry. Stop now and I will not beat you."

"Will you not," she challenged. "Then put your knife down and stop making threats." She saw him grin. "But that would not please you, would it? You want to frighten me."

"And I have done it," he said with pride.

"You may think that if you like," she said, doing her best to sound disheartened. She pretended to stumble and right herself.

The man saw his chance; he reached out across the fire and seized her arm.

She was on him in an instant. Before he could resist, she had him by the shoulder and was pulling him toward her through the fire, her desire more inexorable than his lust and her strength so tremendous that he could not believe it even as she dragged him to her; sparks took hold of his breeches and the cloth began to smolder as she bared his throat to her teeth. "You will give me food and drink," she said as she struck.

In the flames, the duck blackened and burned as a cold wind ruffled the fire.

* * *

Rain came, and after it, the snow; the gypsies gathered more closely about their fires while in Castle Dracula the long nights gave more time for hunting—a necessary thing in these days of sparse prey. Fenice set the seamstresses among the servants to making her a long, loose, sleeved tunic in a heavy silk the color of dark plums, with long breeks in a heavy cotton the color of her hair.

"Still adventuring," Dracula told her the first time she wore these clothes when she went in pursuit of nourishment. He was in the great hall in his thronelike chair, Kelene beside him, childlike and disturbingly seductive in her out-of-fashion finery.

"It sufficed aboard ship and in Varna. It will do me now," she replied, refusing to be provoked; she strode to the fire, wishing vaguely that it would alleviate the profound cold within her, although that could never happen.

Kelene laughed aloud at her garments. "They will mistake you for a player, or a eunuch strayed away from the harem."

"So long as they do not assume I am un-Dead, or a whore, I do not care what else they think." As soon as she spoke, she saw she had made a mistake, for Kelene's face became set and her blue eyes grew hot as the heart of a flame.

"So you think I am a whore, do you?" She approached Fenice slowly. "Do you?"

Fenice did her best to recover. "I meant only what I feel about myself, and how I have been . . . responded to."

Dracula held up his hand. "Fenice is not like you, girl," he said to Kelene. "She has ever been as rambunctious as a boy; she has not your skills. Do not fault her for knowing where her strengths lie."

Kelene achieved a dissatisfied smile. "If she wants those who prefer boys, she may have them." Her petulance was so like Eloisa that Fenice chuckled, making Kelene bridle again.

"It isn't you," Fenice said as quickly as she could. "You remind me of—"

"You have said you have sisters. So had I, but you are not like any of them." Kelene had intended this to be insulting, but instead Fenice smiled.

"Do you miss yours? I sometimes miss mine." She glanced at Dracula as she admitted this.

"No," said Kelene disdainfully. "They have all been dead a long time." Her laughter was harsh and faded almost at once.

"Did you ever miss them?" Fenice pursued, sensing a mystery here.

Kelene hitched her shoulder. "I suppose I did, at first. But it didn't last."

Dracula made a gesture to silence them both. "All that is in the past," he said imperiously. "You are here now, and that is the whole of it."

"It is better than where I was," Kelene declared, leaning a little closer to Dracula's chair.

Dracula looked at her with unconcealed annoyance. "Stop baiting her, girl. Fenice is not like you. Your tricks will not work with her."

"And you like her better. She is a novelty." Kelene turned to Fenice. "You think you can claim my place, but you cannot. I am senior, for all you think me still a child."

"Yes, you are senior," Fenice agreed, seizing on this opportunity to smooth over the difficult moments between them. "You have been here far longer than I, and you have had many years to develop your . . . skills. I am still a beginner, and I will always be less experienced than you are." She indicated the clothes she wore. "This should make that plain to you. I do not have your attractions, and so I must use the ones I have made for myself."

Dracula offered her a swordsman's salute. "How apt."

Fenice realized that he was provoking them both; she resolved to keep from responding as he tried to make her do. "Kelene," she said, paying no apparent attention to Dracula, "you have nothing to fear from me. I know I could never take your place, nor do I want to."

"So you say," Kelene said sulkily.

"Because it is true," Fenice insisted. When there was no further comment from Kelene, she said, "I am going to see Marcu one last time tonight; before then, I will be in the library."

"And what do you do there?" Kelene challenged. "Hide?"

"I read," Fenice answered, already turning away so that she did not see the look of raw envy that came into Kelene's lovely, youthful face.

In Corfu Ercole had read the letter from his father describing Fenice's abduction and all that was being done to find her; on the last leg of his Galley, he spent many hours wrestling with his conscience about what he should or should not tell his family upon his return home. Would they be consoled or shamed to learn that Fenice had stowed away on his ship? And if they were willing to excuse that audacious act, how would they respond to learning that she had got away from him at Varna? Would knowing where she was last seen increase the chance of finding her, or would it be more prudent—and kinder—to let them believe she had been kidnaped and was now Heaven-only-knew-where?

His mind was not yet made up when he stepped off the *Impresa* onto the family dock in Venice; he was relieved to have his father and cousins around him to offer their congratulations and marvel over the cargo he brought.

The one awkward moment came when he found himself confronting Aurelio Pirenetto; Fenice's betrothed put his hand on Ercole's shoulder and said, "It is hard to come from such success to such sorrow, isn't it?"

Ercole took a long, deep breath. "I have been . . . troubled since I learned of—" He did not go on.

"I should suppose so," Aurelio said, adding, "I would appreciate an hour of your time this evening, if you are willing to spare it for me."

It was the very thing Ercole dreaded most, but he nodded in acceptance and allowed his mother to summon him, giving him an excellent excuse to break away from Aurelio and the confusion of his arrival.

Rosamonda did not keep him with her for very long; she listened to his accounts of the ports he had called in, and the cargo he brought back. When he had summed it all up, she said, "Your father will be proud of you, as I am."

"But something is bothering you," Ercole added, reading her frown correctly. "It has to do with Fenice, doesn't it?'

"No," said Rosamonda, surprising her son, "not directly." She looked down at her skirt. "I have realized of late that God has been very good to the Zucchars. We have prospered and we have remained well. Only one of our children died in youth; none of you have been killed, or drowned, or filled with fevers or pox. I am grateful to God for His Mercy," she said, crossing herself.

Ercole echoed her action. "What has that to do with—"

"Hear me out," Rosamonda interrupted him. "Losing Fenice as we have—and I am resigned to her loss—has shown me as nothing else could how fragile our prosperity is, and how little it would take to extinguish the Zucchar House in the world." She looked directly at her oldest son. "You have not married. We have not urged you to because we have been pleased that you have been making your way in the world for the House. But riches from distant ports are not the sole worth of any family. I want you to remain ashore long enough to arrange an appropriate match for you. I will ask the same of Febo when he returns home." There was a sternness about her mouth that brooked no argument.

"I . . . I confess I had not thought this was . . . that you wanted to talk to me about . . . that you want me to . . . marry. I supposed you . . . had other things on your mind." Ercole nearly lost himself in the tangle of words his confusion brought on him.

Rosamonda smiled. "You have not had to think about these things and so you assumed I had not." She rose and went to his side. "Figlio mio, you do not know how mothers long to see their families happy and thriving. When I think of you far away on the seas, I cannot keep from fearing that I will never see you again, that your life will be snuffed out in some foreign place and I will not hear of it until long after. So you must marry, so that your children may perpetuate you in the world. If you would make me happy and console my old age, you will do this for me."

Ercole was so relieved that he would not have to lie to his mother about Fenice that he said, "I will do it for myself, Madre Mia, and I will thank God for your kindness."

"You are a good son," Rosamonda said, patting his shoulder. "We will speak more of this in the next few days. Your father will want to begin to make inquiries on your behalf once you and I have settled on the women you would prefer."

"And gladly," said Ercole, relieved that he had escaped this interview unscathed, and certain his conversation with Aurelio would be more arduous.

It took place well into the night, in the smaller withdrawing room in the Pirenetto house. Aurelio had a roll of maps in his hand and he greeted Ercole with more warmth than he had ever shown Fenice's oldest brother. "I have told the servants to bring hot wine and then go to bed. I will see you out myself."

Ercole coughed diplomatically. "If it is no imposition. I could come another time. Given the lateness of the hour—"

"No, no," said Aurelio quickly. "We might as well get this over with now." He took the seat on the right side of the fireplace and indicated the chair on the left. "Please. Be comfortable."

Comfort was the last thing Ercole hoped for, but he did as Aurelio bade him, marveling at the change the last ten months had wrought in him: he could hardly recognize the abstracted dreamer he had been in this purposeful young man; it was disconcerting to have to answer his questions. "I had a letter from my father. At Corfu." His beginning was tentative, for he had to feel his way with Aurelio.

"I know what he told you," Aurelio said with a slow nod. "I am certain you are aware that the possibilities of finding your sister are now very slim. Forgive me for being blunt, but there can be no benefit in avoiding the truth."

Ercole was stunned by Aurelio's direct speech. "I have not been here for some time," he said carefully. "What you know of old is new to me."

Aurelio accepted this. "You are still trying to accustom yourself to her loss; I have had months to deal with it." He looked up as his servant brought the two tankards of hot, honeyed wine. "Thank you, Maurizio. You may retire."

The servant bowed and withdrew.

"You may speak frankly here; no one will listen, and the servants are retired," Aurelio said as the door was closed. He took his tankard of wine and lifted it. "Shall we drink to Fenice, and to the hope that she is worthy of her name?"

"Zucchar?" Ercole asked, trying to sort out his jumbled thoughts.

"No; Fenice," said Aurelio with mild rebuke. "I hope she will rise from her ashes." He lifted his tankard in salute. "Though I may be the only person in Venice who still hopes she will one day return."

"To Fenice," Ercole seconded, glad of the hot, sweet wine; he did not need to remark on Aurelio's addition to his toast. He set the tankard down. "What do you know?"

Aurelio sighed. "Only that she disappeared on the night you sailed. It must have been done then because of the disruption in your household. What better time for such a crime? It was possible for the kidnapers to get in and get away without attracting the attention they must have done at any other time." He was staring into the fire, as if he could read the story in the flames. "I have tried to find out who took her, or where she was taken, but so far I have learned nothing of value." His expression darkened, then he made himself look directly at her brother. "What of you? Has no word come to you during your travels?"

Ercole made up his mind; he shook his head. "I have heard nothing." He dared not ask if anyone had considered the possibility that Fenice had run off, stowing away on his ship; if the notion had been considered and rejected, so much the better. If it had never been thought of, he saw no benefit in mentioning it now and beginning inquiries that would be fruitless and painful.

"I did not think you would," said Aurelio. "If you had, you would have acted at once." He put the tankard aside. "No, what I wanted to ask you about, as you have been into the Black Sea not many days since, has to do with the Sultan's armed ships. It seems there may be a new problem there. We have heard rumors that there is a new navy being built in the Black Sea, to avenge Lepanto. War galleys would mean that we would have to prepare for more sea battles. Did you see anything that would support that fear?" He began to unroll one of the maps he had held. "Reports place the building here. You have seen the place for yourself: what did you observe?"

It took a moment for Ercole to realize that he was not going to have to fabricate any more tales about Fenice; her loss was now accepted, as final as her death would have been. Indeed, she was as dead as if she had been laid in her grave and the *Requiem* sung for her; to have her resurrected now would cause disgrace to those who still loved her. Shame went through him, mixed with relief, and he vowed to keep her escapade locked in his heart forever. It was kinder to say nothing than to create new distress, since he would not be able to restore Fenice to her family to have her sins acknowledged before all the world; his own failure would not have to be admitted to anyone but his Confessor, and not for years to come. No, he decided, the truth about Fenice must remain locked in his soul until he made his last Confession, for to speak now would tarnish her honor and the honor of their family beyond any restoration. Better to think her dead and gone than know she had brought so much shame on them all. He swallowed more of the wine, then leaned forward to look at the map and to answer Aurelio's questions about the Sultan's navy.

And what enemy more deadly
Than one lurking in a smile?
—Agnolo Poliziano

— XXXI —

Fenice regretted killing him, though his blood was hot enough to warm her and its savor was sweet; he had fought her and cursed her, forcing her to end his life. She sat beside the cart in which he had been riding, a juggler and clown going from market to market to earn his bread; the cart would be disposed of, the mule pulling it left in the fields of one of the peasants nearby. She had found him on the road trying to repair a broken wheel-rim and had fallen into easy conversation with him, conversation that had led to a companionable evening; the juggler had assumed Fenice was a eunuch and had guessed he had lost his position, a supposition Fenice did not deny. The juggler had told interesting tales of his wandering, encouraging Fenice to remain with him for company's sake.

"We are both alone on the road. We would be safer together," he had said with a hearty smile. "Bandits would rather attack a man alone, and a manlet as pretty as you would have more than robbery to fear."

"It is kind of you to offer," Fenice had answered, hoping he would fall asleep so that he would never know what she had come for. But the juggler continued to talk, and when it was nearly midnight, Fenice could deny her need no longer. She had tried to explain only to have the juggler damn her and call the curses of Heaven upon her. So he was dead and she was no longer hungry, but she could not rid herself of the nagging sense that she had betrayed him. Dracula would laugh at her for such emotions; she could not look at the supine body in the colorful clothes and think his death was anything but a sad waste.

Melancholy had taken hold of her by the time she returned to Castle Dracula, not long before dawn. She made her way to the door to the vault only to discover it was locked. She pushed on it, then pounded on its stout planks, all with no results. She remembered that one of the women Dracula had brought to the castle had been shut out of this door and had died in the sunlight. She shuddered. This had to be an accident; Kelene would not try to kill her, not the same way she had done away with another: Dracula would know she had done it and that the death was deliberate.

But would he mind? That single question all but immobilized her, calling to mind many unpleasant recollections of her time with Dracula. She knew he tested her; perhaps this was another test, to determine if she was capable of living the life he demanded of her. Kelene would be a glad ally in such an endeavor. She struck the door one more time, expecting nothing. The guards would not open the main gate to her, not without Dracula's express permission. So she would have to find some other means to save herself. She looked up at the stones above her and was disheartened. The nearest window was four stories up. Glancing along the wall, she remembered it was lower where it bowed around the kitchen garden. Making up her mind, she struck out for that area, and when she had reached the place, she decided she would have to climb over; her clothes would suffer, but she could have new clothes made. Taking great care, she felt for the irregularities in the wall that would give her purchase enough to climb; she could not hesitate, for dawn was coming: already the sky was turning gray and the first birds were singing in the wood below.

After one look down over her shoulder she had to wait where she was on the wall while the queasiness of vertigo faded; she would not look down again. This was more difficult than climbing the wall of the convent. It was higher, and the stones were much larger and smoother than the convent stones had been. When she finally made it to the top, she scrambled over and began the descent down the other side. The drop to the ground was too far to jump. The jagged mountain peaks in the east were red-rimmed by the time she stepped down into the kitchen garden, every muscle quivering from the effort of her climb. She knew the door to the castle would be shut and barred, so she made up her mind to take shelter in the bathhouse. It was not as secure as her coffin, but it was enclosed and dark and during the day she doubted any of the servants would come inside. If they did, they would not harm her. The warm dampness did not bother her as she lay down on a bench and prepared to sleep.

She sat up again at sunset, feeling as if she had just closed her eyes. The day had passed as if in a heartbeat. She got up and slapped at her damp, scuffed clothes, then raked her fingers through her hair. It was time to go into the castle, to ask Kelene why she had shut her out and to insist that she never make such an attempt on her life again. If only she could believe she had the fortitude to do this as she imagined herself doing it. Speaking directly to Kelene would make it possible to forestall any more attempts on her life, but it would make them enemies, which Fenice did not want. She frowned as she thought this over as she went to enter the castle through the kitchen.

Two of the servants goggled at the sight of her, which Fenice realized meant they had not expected her to return; Kelene's campaign must have been more successful than Fenice had assumed. She made a sign to the servants that she had come in from outside just now. "I am well," she said in Latin, trusting them to understand her.

She went to the great hall, took a seat in a Turkish chair away from the hearth and the table, and waited; little as she liked the Turks, the chair was very comfortable, and she lounged in it more easily than she would have waited in either of the high-backed chairs. She used the time to think of how best to deal with Kelene in order to prevent outright enmity that would require decades to resolve. She asked herself how she might have dealt with Eloisa if she had done something spiteful and dangerous.

Some while later she heard Dracula and Kelene approaching; they were arguing and trying to keep their voices down for privacy, but the stone walls caught their words, magnified and distorted them so that they sounded like a storm within the castle walls.

"—losing so much of the night over this," Kelene protested.

"Some attention was given to Muna and Eudike: the same should be done for Fenice," Dracula overruled her grandly. "And you are to comport yourself with dignity, girl," he added critically. "You have no cause for celebration, or so you swear to me."

"She did not realize the time; she was caught in the open. How can I be held responsible for that?" The petulance was back in her voice.

In her shadowed chair, Fenice leaned forward, her attention held with perverse delight to their vying; she had an instant of regret that the game would soon end.

"You ought to have no reason," Dracula said. "But you do not show yourself touched by grief or regret."

"I am not: would you have me lie?" Kelene demanded, turning to face him as they reached the two chairs. "And given the time, I must be out hunting, and so must you. The hour is advancing and our prey will go to ground before we can find them." She did not quite stamp her foot, but she took a mulish stance and dared him to deny her.

"How can you behave so callously?" Dracula asked. "When one of our number perishes, all of us have cause to mourn."

Deciding she could have no more appropriate moment than this, Fenice got to her feet. "I am sorry my absence has caused you so much trouble," she began.

The two turned toward her, Dracula beginning to smile in his lupine way, Kelene clenching her fists in disbelief. Dracula recovered soonest and spoke first. "I am the one who must apologize," he said with elaborate gallantry, "for having so little faith in your resourcefulness." His laughter was intended to sting Kelene, and the girl's expression revealed that it did.

Unwisely Kelene lashed out. "You were outside! How could you return?"

"And you know," said Fenice calmly, "because you shut the door against me." She was careful not to make this a condemnation. "You wanted to cause mischief."

Kelene very nearly spoke, the stopped herself. She nodded. "It . . . it was . . . supposed to be a game."

"And you would have opened the door again at dawn," Fenice went on, looking directly at the golden-haired girl.

"I . . . I intended to," said Kelene, faltering as she strove to discover what Fenice was doing. "But I fell asleep."

This sounded so like something that Eloisa might say that Fenice chuckled a bit. "And so I was forced to climb the wall and spend the day in the bathhouse." She saw Dracula give an appreciative cock to his head while Kelene stared at her in blatant astonishment.

"You . . . climbed the walls?" Her voice had risen almost five notes and her face was white.

"I did when I got out of the convent," Fenice reminded her, making light of the effort it had cost her. "This was a bit more difficult, but not beyond me."

"How intrepid you are," said Kelene with difficulty.

"I ran away to sea on my brother's ship," Fenice went on. "I can deal with many problems." She went up to Kelene. "There are so many outside the walls that I hope I will not have to encounter more here."

Kelene looked toward Dracula, who studiously turned away, unwilling to take sides or show any preference for the two young women. "I . . . I . . . I become bored, sometimes," Kelene said with difficulty. "When I try to alleviate it, I do not always conduct myself well. If I have done anything to . . . distress you, I am . . . sorry. I will try not to . . . to do so again." She gave Fenice a hard look. "But you must not forget that I am the first. You should show me deference for that. And," she added with sudden inspiration, "my coffin should be larger than hers. I am the first."

Dracula spoke without turning. "You will have a larger coffin."

"Good." She pointed to Fenice. "And you will treat me with respect."

"As you wish," said Fenice, wondering what she had said or done that Kelene could believe otherwise. "You were here before I was, and I rely on you to help me learn."

"Learn?" Kelene scoffed. "Why should you learn from me when you have books to teach you?" There was so much hurt in her voice that Fenice was taken aback.

"I will read to you, if you like," she offered.

"Do not bother," said Kelene haughtily. She rounded on Dracula. "*Now* can I go hunt? I am hungry."

"Go on," said Dracula, and looked after her as she flounced away, saying thoughtfully, "She has done so well in certain things and so . . ."

Fenice kept silent, knowing Dracula would not want to be reminded of her presence. She heard a distant door slam and it served to break the quiet that had taken hold of them. "How much longer will the gypsies be here?" It was a safe enough question and she did want to hear the answer.

"Through the winter. They have a foundling for Kelene, but some nights

she prefers to hunt." He went and sat in his chair. "There will be no travelers shortly, and she has need of sport."

Fenice thought that this might be an oblique warning, but did not want to ask if it were, in case he had had a different intention. "The snow will be deep here; it is so high in the mountains."

"And we take the brunt of the storms." Dracula did not look at her. "This place can be very dangerous in winter."

Now she was certain this was a warning. "So I thought," she said, wondering if she should say anything more; she kept her guesses to herself. "In Varna, you made me believe I would find adventure here, and freedom."

"Have you earned them?" He sounded very tired and indifferent.

"I did not know I would need to earn them."

"You would have made the same decision. You could not remain in Varna and you could not go back to Venice. It would have been more dangerous to sign aboard another ship." His remarks had a sour humor to them. "Do you deny it?"

"No," she admitted. "But I would have liked to have known about Kelene."

"I told you of her," Dracula insisted.

"Very, very little," Fenice said, making it a reprimand. "Not enough to prepare me for what has happened here."

He considered his next remark. "Do you want to return to Varna? Or to Venice?"

"No." She took a deep breath. "I want to remain here."

"So it would be wise to be careful," said Dracula, then gestured to show he was dismissing her.

Leaving the great hall, Fenice said to him, "I appreciate all you have told me."

Dracula shrugged. "We shall see."

It was more than a month before Kelene attempted anything against Fenice. By that time the snows had girt the mountains in white and the winds howled dirges day and night. Hunting was restricted to those near enough to be reached easily, but not so close to the castle as to cause resentment and rebellion among the peasants. Often left to their own devices at the castle while Dracula ventured much farther afield than they could, Fenice and Kelene did their best to spend little time together. Fenice spent many hours in the library; Kelene wandered the halls like a distracted ghost, fretting and sullen.

Then one night in late December, Fenice left the library, bound for the vault. She was almost through the corridor under the gallery when a sudden sound commanded her attention; a lance came down from the floor above, its point striking sparks from the flagstones as it landed and clattered.

Fenice stood very still, almost as if the weapon had truly transfixed her as she had no doubt it was intended to do. Then she bent and picked up the lance, leaving it leaning against the wall, its blunted point resting on the floor. She knew no servants had witnessed this attack, for they were all asleep in their rooms, and any complaint of it to Dracula would provide Kelene with the opportunity to protest her innocence, forcing Dracula to choose sides. He had already made it apparent he had no wish to be placed in such a position and would not support either woman. She did not want to be caught by such a ploy, and so, as she closed the lid of her coffin—after noticing that Kelene's fine new one was already closed—she decided to keep the incident to herself.

The next strike was more blatant, as if her lack of punishment for the last attempt had given Kelene the confidence to pursue Fenice more overtly: the two women were out on the battlements during a break in the weather. The moon was almost full and the night sky was gaudy with stars. Those few guards who kept watch did so from the guard towers where they could preserve a little warmth from the fires that burned in braziers there.

"Have you been down that valley yet?" Kelene asked Fenice as they rounded the curve in the wall to the side of the castle over the river gorge. "It is not readily reached, but there is a merchants' road at the end of it and once spring comes, it will offer fine hunting."

"I will keep it in mind," said Fenice. She had put on a cloak with a bearskin hood that kept the worst of the wind off her face.

"You will not go there when I am hunting in that region," Kelene went on blithely. "You will have to look elsewhere for prey."

"Very well," said Fenice. "You have the right to choose the place first."

"Yes. I do," she said with satisfaction. "See you do not forget it."

"How could I?" Fenice's dry intent was lost on Kelene, who skipped lightly along the narrow walkway, taking no precautions on the icy stones.

"You have made me jealous," she announced from the next embrasure of stones. "You want to take my place. I know it. I saw it when you first came."

Fenice, crossing the slippery stones with more care than Kelene, did not offer any protest; she paid more attention to her footing than to Kelene's accusations. When she stopped at a crenelation where she could brace herself, she said, "That's not true."

"It is true. You know it is true. I have visions—did you know that?" She lifted her head proudly. "And my visions showed me you had come to take my place. But that will not happen. Do you understand me? I will not let you do it."

Fenice secured herself against the stones. "You have nothing to fear from me. I have no reason to take your place. How could I?"

"You couldn't," Kelene spat. "But you will try." She rushed out of the embrasure and ran directly at Fenice, striking her shoulder and trying to spin her away from the security of the stones. "Fall!" she shouted, shoving Fenice toward the edge of the walkway; it was three stories to the stones in the courtyard below.

The two women teetered together and Fenice slipped out of her cloak, letting it fall, bellying on the wind like a sail, into the courtyard.

"You should be down there!" Kelene said furiously, and reached to take hold of her again.

But Fenice eluded her. "Stop it, Kelene. This is foolish."

"I am *not foolish*," Kelene shrieked, and lunged at Fenice; she was so overwrought that she no longer considered the danger of her situation. She missed her footing, though she managed to grab Fenice's hand, and she stumbled, falling over the side of the walkway.

Jerked violently, Fenice nearly lost her footing; she fell to her knees, reaching out to hold onto Kelene. She felt the Greek girl's fingers close viselike on her arm. "Hang on," she called out unnecessarily.

"You did this!" Kelene shouted at her. "I know you did!"

"But you . . ." Fenice began, then could think of nothing more to say; Kelene had convinced herself that Fenice had caused this to happen, and this was not the time to debate it, not with Kelene hanging onto her arm, her body dangling over the courtyard in the terrible wind. "Come. Let me pull you up." She hoped she would have the strength to do it.

"No. You will drop me," Kelene said, her fingers digging into Fenice's arm as if to clutch the bones.

"I will not. I am going to hold out my other arm. Catch my hand." She made herself as secure on the stones as she could, then she extended her other hand to Kelene.

"I won't let go," Kelene said as she grasped Fenice's hand.

"No. Don't let go," she replied as she strove to pull the Greek girl up. Her back was growing stiff from cold and she was not at a good angle to raise so heavy a weight as Kelene, but she would not give up. Slowly, very slowly, she pulled Kelene back to the walkway, so that she could swing her leg up and haul herself onto the narrow stone ledge.

The two lay facing one another for a short while, both panting from exertion and fright. Fenice sat up first, wrapping her arms around her chest in a useless effort to keep warm; Kelene lay still a while longer, then carefully stood up, making sure she was more than an arm's length from Fenice.

"We should go in," Fenice ventured.

Kelene glowered at her. "You could have let me drop."

"No; I couldn't," Fenice corrected her; she did not want to seem lacking in purpose or too soft, so she added, "There was nothing to gain in dropping you."

"You probably should have. I would have let you drop, you know. If I have the chance again, I still will," Kelene said, her eyes narrowed against the bite of the wind and her own suspicions. "I see what it is: you want me to be grateful."

"I don't care whether you are or not," Fenice said bluntly. "I want to get inside; I'm turning to ice. You might not be cold, but I am. I dropped my cloak." She had to keep her exasperation from being too obvious, for Kelene would welcome it as vindication.

"I will not be grateful, no matter what," Kelene said for emphasis. "You are not going to trap me that way."

In the guard tower someone swore and someone else laughed.

Fenice was shivering; she would not be dragged into a contest of motives. "You may stay outside if you like; I am going to get warm."

Kelene laughed. "It will not happen. You might as well take refuge in your little coffin. There is no one in the castle to feed you, not tonight. And the gypsies will not let you take any of them for your sustenance."

"A fire will do for a beginning," said Fenice over her shoulder as she went back along the narrow shelf toward the small tower which had a staircase leading down to the small courtyard.

Muttering under her breath, Kelene followed.

A few nights later, when Fenice had returned from her necessary foray restored and satisfied in body, she went to the library for the opportunity to enrich her mind through reading more of an account of the Huns before she retired. She had been trying to learn the history of the region and had stumbled upon ancient manuscripts written on parchment that told the stories of Transylvania. She was in a chair lighted by a nine-branch candelabra and was engrossed in the description of the horsemen from the east, and did not hear the door to the huge room open, or the soft footfall coming up to her.

"You really are reading," Kelene said, so near to Fenice that she jumped at the sound of the Greek girl's voice; Fenice marked her place in the volume with her finger and closed the book to give Kelene her full attention. "You are reading."

Fenice contained her irritation at this ingenuous remark. "Yes. What did you think?"

"I thought you came in here to impress Dracula and to hide from me," Kelene said with the casual self-absorption Fenice supposed was central to her character.

This was more than Fenice would let pass. "It may be a blow to your pride, Kelene, but I do things that have nothing to do with you." She had to admit that there was an element of truth in the girl's observation, however.

"But you really read," Kelene marveled. "You *do* really read, don't you?" she added with a return of doubt. "You don't just pretend to."

"I really read. This work is difficult because the language is very old and the writing is in an ancient style, but I am able to make out most of it." She opened the book once more. "This passage here says *The men were so wed*—at least I think it's wed; it could be *united—to their horses that often when they fell together in battle, they were left together.*" She glanced at Kelene. "If you doubt me, learn to read it yourself."

Kelene looked away. "I don't know how."

"That much is obvious," said Fenice, doing her best to keep her tone from being too sharp.

"Dracula has not taught me. I used to think he would, but he hasn't." Her voice was very small, like a child who has been reprimanded for some grave error.

Taking the hint, Fenice said, "If you want to learn, I will teach you," she said with confidence, then added, "And if I do, you will not try to be rid of me. If you will accept that bargain, I will spend four nights in seven working with you for half the night. We will have less time to hunt, but you will be able to read after a while."

"How long?" Kelene demanded, her impatience showing without mitigation. "I want to learn right now."

"Well," said Fenice prosaically, "you can't. It took me most of a year to learn the very beginnings." She was not certain that Kelene's enthusiasm was anything more than a whim, but decided to treat her as if her eagerness had some durability.

"A *year*?" Kelene wailed. "So long?"

"We have time," said Fenice. "Does it matter if it takes a year or two or three? You do not have to be concerned with time."

"It *does* matter." Kelene was beginning to pout. "I have already waited decades to learn. Why can't it be faster?"

Fenice had no explanation for that, so she tried distraction. "But think what it will be like when you can write your own thoughts in your own book. Won't that be worth the time it takes you to learn how it is done?"

"You *write*?" Kelene pounced on this information.

Fenice was amused at Kelene's astonishment. "I learned to write when I learned to read."

"And you don't write all the time? You read instead?" She looked over Fenice's shoulder at the old book. "If I could write, I wouldn't bother with any of these things; I would spend my time telling about what has happened to me."

This candid announcement did not surprise Fenice, but she only said, "Then you won't mind the time it takes to learn how, since you will want to do it well."

"And in the meantime," Kelene went on with purpose, "as you teach me, I will tell you what to write about me and you will do it. That will help me to study." She met Fenice's gaze with her own. "I have done many exciting things."

"No doubt," said Fenice, her tone a trifle dry. "Do not forget: while I am teaching you, you are not to make any attempts on my life, or to shut me out of the castle. If you do anything against me, I will no longer teach you."

"Yes, yes," said Kelene with a gesture of dismissal. "That's all settled."

"See that you remember," Fenice persisted.

"I will; of course I will," Kelene said as she took hold of the back of Fenice's chair. "Think how good it will be. I will know how to read, and I will read all these books and—"

"Not all of them," Fenice interrupted her rhapsodizing. "I cannot read all of them."

Kelene glared at Fenice, her distrust returning twofold. "Why not?"

"Because they are written in languages I haven't learned," said Fenice very carefully. "I know Italian and Latin and Greek. Since you are Greek, I supposed that was the language you wanted to learn." She coughed gently. "A great many of the books in this library are in Greek. The book I am reading is." She pointed to a nearby tome on a stand of its own. "That is in Latin."

"Why can't you read the others?" Kelene asked.

"Because I don't know Hungarian or German or Russian or . . . whatever the languages are." Fenice could not tell what effect this confession was having on Kelene. "If you know Greek, you will be able to read many hundreds of these books, and you will be able to write your own."

Kelene was not satisfied. "But you will know more. I will have to know the languages you do."

"Why not wait until you know Greek before you decide about Latin and Italian?" Fenice suggested.

"No. You will know more and that does not suit me," Kelene declared. "I will not have you writing anything I cannot read, or reading things I cannot." There was a determined set to her chin and she put one hand on her hip to show her intent. "I will not let you do anything to . . ." Her voice faded as the door opened and Dracula came into the library.

"I thought I would find you here, Fenice," he said. "You, girl, I did not expect," he added to Kelene.

Kelene swung around to face him. "Fenice is going to teach me to read. And to write," she announced.

Dracula laughed once, the sound cracking like a whip. "Do you think so? It takes time to learn, and dedication."

"Then I will be dedicated," said Kelene.

Dracula ignored this, directing his next remark to Fenice. "Do you think you will do it? She is very flighty and her mind is not so well-honed as yours. You may find the task beyond you."

"I will not know until I try, will I?" Fenice countered, adding to the silently furious Kelene, "Don't let him discourage you before you begin. You and I have to show him that you—"

Dracula cut into Fenice's assurances. "Kelene is a child still; she is not accustomed to study."

"Then her mind is malleable," Fenice said, unwilling to be swayed; she became aware that Dracula did not want the two of them to be anything but rivals. Abruptly Fenice was aware that it was very important that she and Kelene work together.

"If you must," Dracula said, and turned on his heel. "You will discover for yourself." As he left he slammed the door behind him.

Fenice could sense Kelene was shaken; she turned to her and smiled. "Would you like to begin tonight? We have some time until dawn."

In spite of Dracula's deprecatory jibes, the tutorials went on through the winter; by the time the gypsies left their camp at the first hint of spring, Kelene had learned her letters and was beginning to understand simple grammar. Her enthusiasm had increased rather than diminished.

"The novelty will fade," Dracula warned Fenice one night as they rose from their coffins. "You will have wasted your time."

"It is mine to waste," Fenice said, enjoying the minor autonomy her teaching had given her.

"As you wish," Dracula said indifferently.

When summer came, Dracula announced he would have to travel to Pressburg; he hinted at great purpose but would reveal nothing more. "I do not want the two of you chattering about it," he said.

"What danger is there if we do?" Fenice asked. "We have no one to speak with but each other; what is the risk in that?"

"The servants could overhear. Or a traveler," Dracula said darkly.

"The traveler would never repeat it," Kelene pointed out. "No traveler to this place would." She licked her lips.

"I will tell you what my purpose was when I return, at the end of summer," he said.

Fenice went to confront him. "You will return alone. Won't you?"

He scowled at her. "I cannot promise that."

Fenice was not put off. "You will bring no rival. If anyone comes with you, he will be for our use, not to be another bride." She folded her arms. "If you bring another bride, I will not curb anything Kelene may decide to do."

Indignation suffused Dracula's hawkish features. "Are you threatening me? Me?"

"No," Fenice said without quailing under his stern gaze. "I am telling you what we will do."

Kelene, watching this encounter, snickered.

"I will not tolerate such audacity. You cannot dictate to me," Dracula said, his voice like thunder.

Fenice stood her ground. "Perhaps; but if you bring another, it is she, not you, who will pay for your decision. As Asenath and Eudike and Muna have already." For a moment she and Dracula stared at one another. "If you must have another bride, let us choose her. You can hunt all you like, but bring no other woman here. We will decide who is to share this castle."

"You?" Dracula cried. "The two of you? Or you alone?"

"That will not work any longer," Kelene said with such calmness that she commanded Dracula's attention. "You cannot divide us again." She gave him her best seductive smile. "Leave finding brides to us. We will not disappoint you."

Dracula sighed harshly. "I will consider it," he allowed at last. "But I may require more of you in exchange." He strode away, clearly irked.

"Do you think he will comply?" Kelene asked when Dracula was gone.

"We shall see," Fenice answered, and hid the qualms that shook her resolve.

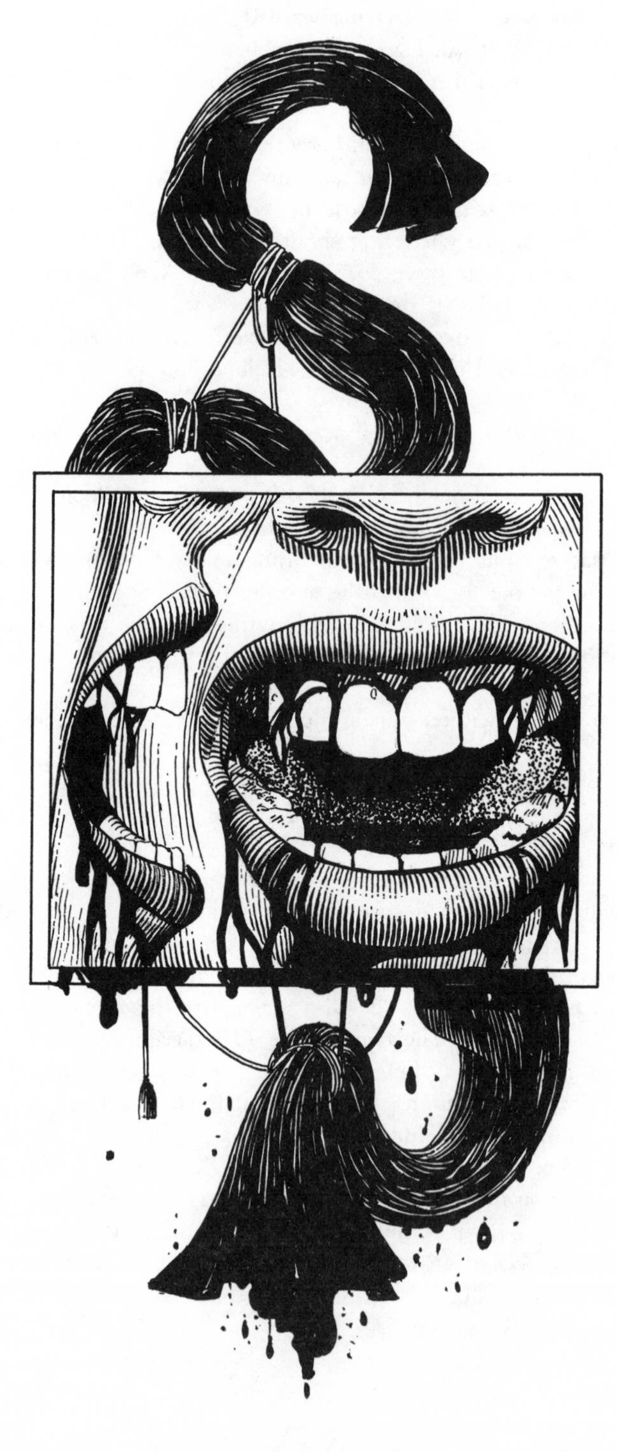

. . . To me she was an angel
In whose steps I could follow:
In giving love, where was my fault?
—Guido Guinizelli

— XXXII —

Dracula came back from Pressburg alone, and endured hearing Kelene read him her first efforts at composition with the air of one asked to listen to an ill-trained musician. When that was over, he told the two women to listen to what he was about to tell them. "I have thought about what you told me before I left, and I have decided to accommodate you, at least for the time being. Later we will have to discuss this again."

Kelene grinned with delight, the fire from the hearth in the great hall making her face shine as golden as her hair. "I knew you would—"

"However," Dracula interrupted her, "I have also decided that if you are to make dictates to me, I have a few to make of you. I am willing—for now—to comply with your dictates. But I am not willing to capitulate without a few concessions from the two of you. Since you would be mistresses of this place, you will have to help defend it." He glanced at Fenice. "I do not plan to put weapons in your hands beyond the ones you possess already." His demeanor showed satisfaction that Fenice feared might bode ill for her and Kelene. "A man is coming here—it was part of what I negotiated. He must not leave, but he cannot be disposed of or ambushed. He must appear to fall into a decline, and, most importantly, he must refuse to leave when the decline begins. You will make him want to stay here; you will make him prefer to die rather than leave you."

"We can do that," Kelene said with delight. "He will never set foot out of the castle once he arrives." She glanced at Fenice, who was frowning. "Why not? Where is the harm?"

"Who is this man and why must we detain him?" Fenice asked. "You expect us to . . . disable him and . . . kill him for you, but you do not say why?"

"When have I ever demanded such an assessment from those you two have used?" Dracula was angry but he masked it with gelid aloofness. "I have made it possible for you to survive, and you question me now?"

"Yes," said Fenice, hoping that Kelene would not be persuaded by Dracula's temper. "Because you have never before made such requirements."

"He has made them of me," said Kelene with a touch of pride.

"And do you know why?" Fenice asked, undaunted. "Who is this man and why do you want him to die at our . . . hands?" She folded her arms.

"He is an official of sorts," Dracula conceded reluctantly. "He is a powerful fellow in a very minor part of Hungarian affairs. He, himself, is Austrian of Hungarian lineage. He must make a report that supports me and that report must be believed. But I cannot have him leave once the report is made. His words must stand unassailably, which they will if he is dead." He laughed at Fenice. "That is as good an account as any."

"Is it true?" Fenice asked, ignoring Kelene's gasp at her temerity. "Or do you tell me a story you think I will believe?" She did not expect Dracula to answer her, nor did he. "Do you think me so credulous that this will suffice me?"

"Kelene will do the work, if you will not; she has done so before. She knows where her loyalties lie. She knows how to show her loyalty. Don't you, girl?"

Kelene smiled and moved a little nearer to Dracula. "I want to do what protects you, and me."

Fenice spoke up at once. "You have served him without question, haven't you? But did it ever strike you that he showed you not his favor, but used you with duplicity? Think, Kelene. Why did he want you to do these deeds for him? Was it because he wanted to show you favor or because he wanted to be able to fix the blame on you if there were questions? Would he show you the same loyalty he has demanded for himself?" She looked directly at Dracula. "My soul is not so wild that I will be led to destruction to protect you."

Dracula regarded her with an expression that showed contempt. "Then what good is it, if it cannot be mine?"

Fenice did not answer at once, and when she did, she spoke to Kelene. "Listen to him. He admits that he keeps us only to serve his ends. He needs us to provide him with servants he can sacrifice to keep him from having to defend himself." She could see Dracula's wrath increasing in every line of his stance. "If he had no enemies, he would have no reason to keep us with him. We are like his guards: oh, a bit more indulged, but as disposable as soldiers." She went to Kelene. "I do not think that you are a scapegoat or diversionary ploy to keep him safe: I think you are a Greek girl who was deceived and seduced into becoming his . . . his decoy. Just as I am." She turned away from Dracula and began to walk toward the corridor leading down to the vault; she did not look to see if Kelene was coming with her.

"He laughed at my writing," said Kelene loudly as she came after Fenice. "I am oldest; I must go first."

Fenice stood aside and allowed her to pass.

"It will not last," Dracula said to Fenice the next night as soon as Kelene had left on the hunt. "She is bound to me and she will do my bidding, in the end. I am her savior and she will never forget that. Once she has tired of learning, she will know you as her rival and my opponent." He reached out and touched her hair. "She does not understand what is between us."

"Nor do I, sometimes," Fenice confessed.

"My blood works in you," Dracula reminded her with great satisfaction. "You are more like me than you want to admit. You accuse me of manipulating Kelene, of bending her to my will. She has followed me since she was a child and she has had no will but mine." He touched Fenice's hair again, more lingeringly. "Tell me that your teaching her to read and write is not simply a way to keep her from trying to kill you. Tell me truly that this is no manipulation you have undertaken. If you can convince me that your teaching is really disinterested, I will release you from any dealing with the man from Vienna and Pressburg." He waited a brief moment. "You cannot, can you?"

"Not wholly, no; at first it was a device, I admit it," she said. "But now I do it because that child knows so little that she is prey to every impulse and superstition that she encounters." With a shrewd glance, she added, "Had she any education, you could never have made her think you were an Angel."

He smiled. "So she's told you about that."

"Boasted of it, I should say," Fenice told him. "Her adoration of you, and her adulation, approaches perfect faith."

"So it does," Dracula said; he gave Fenice a look of indulgent appreciation. "It makes your spirit wild, doesn't it?"

"I will admit it does," said Fenice, then went on, "And knowing you can command her so totally, I am somewhat at a loss to know why you tolerate my resistance."

"Clever, resourceful Fenice, I would have thought you had guessed that by now: I am glad of your resistance *because* Kelene is so wholly my creature." He looked off into the black recesses of the vault. "Such subordination palls after a while, as any other response would—including resistance: when I tire of your obduracy, I will call Kelene to heel and she will be your adversary once again." He put his hand on her shoulder. "You are a perfect foil for her, and as such, I find your contests vastly entertaining, even when you are arrayed against me. But do not deceive yourself that your alliance is anything more than a convenience to Kelene: first and last, she is mine."

"That may change when she has read more," Fenice said, trying to maintain her composure in the face of his condescension.

"Oh, I wouldn't put any faith in that, Fenice. Kelene was suborned early and nothing she learns now will subvert her earliest convictions. And you know it." He patted her shoulder before he dropped his hand. "Still, don't let me discourage you. Your efforts are so admirable and so earnest, I cannot help but admire them."

"How . . . how indulgent of you, to tolerate my efforts." Her sarcasm was wasted on him.

"Many another would not," he agreed, and swung the end of his cloak over his arm. "There is a brigand with a pulled shoulder hiding in the woods below the town at the crossroads: since you are trying to find your prey among those who have preyed upon others, you might find your best sport with him." He offered her a slight bow. "I find your principles intriguing, but a luxury."

"They have guided me thus far," she snapped, vexed that he understood her so well.

"And look where they have got you," Dracula said before he departed.

Autumn came tentatively to the Carpathians, slowly laying down the first, fine swaths of snow and ice as gently as a child's nurse afraid of disturbing the summer plants beneath; the streams, swollen with the bounty of summer, began to vanish beneath the filmy snows, turning their courses to dangerous slush. The roads became rutted, frozen mires. The peasants worried about late-planted crops and complained when ewes and nannies had to be enclosed with their lambs and kids too early for the offspring to thrive. Wolves raided sheepfolds and chicken coops earlier into the fall than was usual, and the creatures of the forest hunted close to humans to keep from starving as winter began to whistle at the back of the wind, promising that by October the cold would be upon them.

Eugen Theiss came to Castle Dracula on an afternoon when sleet was falling mixed with snow. He rode with an escort of five men-at-arms and a carriage filled with his luggage and two miserable servants.

"I am sorry I have not come until now," he said to Dracula when he had been admitted to the castle; he was almost into the great hall and he paused to surrender his hat and cloak to one of the castle's servants and to slap the wet from his boots. "We were late in starting. You know how these things are." He wore traveling clothes: a leather dogaline in worked dark brown edged in sky-blue piping, with vast sleeves turned back to reveal the blue silken lining of the sleeves and the pale silken camisa beneath; his hose were stiff padded blue leather, slashed to gold and edged in brown leather, and his underhose were thick wool in a color between tan and russet; his boots were the same dark brown as his dogaline; he could have been received at the French court in such finery and he knew it; he had intended to overwhelm his host with his fine appearance, even after several hours in the saddle in inclement weather.

"I have some experience of politics, yes," said Dracula, equally impressive in a dolman and mente of dark, dull purple silk, so heavy that it hung like the finest wool. "And I am aware of how uncertain the weather is at this time of year." He stood aside to allow his guest to precede him into the great hall, now alight with all the lamps and candles that could be lit.

"Very fine," Theiss marveled as he paused on the threshold. "Quite magnificent. More than I had thought, to be candid. Most of these remote castles have no elegance about them."

"True enough," Dracula said smoothly. "Your servants will be accommodated with my own, and your men-at-arms will be housed with my guards. You need not fear them being relegated to a common barracks, as happens too often in fortresses." He gave a smile that was as cold as the sleet outside.

"I have ordered a meal for you. My cooks will have it ready shortly." He pointed to the smaller of the high-backed chairs. "I will draw this up to the fire for you so that you may warm yourself."

"That's very gracious of you, Prince," Theiss exclaimed. "Upon my soul, you are as good to a guest as any noble in Paris or Rome."

"High praise indeed," said Dracula, clapping his hands for a servant. When one arrived, he said, "Bring hot wine for my guest, and fried cheese. See that his supper is ready within the hour."

The servant bowed without speaking and went away to do his master's bidding.

"Now then," said Dracula as Theiss settled in his chair, "you are certainly tired from the road. We need not begin our dealings until tomorrow; you may wish to wait a day or more, and if you do, I will be pleased to accommodate you."

Theiss looked at Dracula with increased regard. "That's very good of you, Count. Let us see how these matters progress. The weather, as you have observed, is not promising and I may have to curtail my visit—"

Dracula raised his hand to interrupt. "I do not mean to question your decision, but you may want to consider an alternate plan."

"What might that be?" Theiss said, his cordiality vanishing.

"Why, to remain here through the winter. I would consider your presence an honor. You would have a much greater chance to evaluate our circumstances here and to provide a thorough report to Pressburg and Vienna when you are done. You might make your position more useful in the government through your greater experience and knowledge." This was a deliberate appeal to the man's ambition, direct enough to show the depth of Dracula's acumen; Theiss frowned.

"I will give it my consideration," he stated as the servant arrived with wine and cheese. "In the meantime, I will enjoy what you have offered me."

"It is my intention that you should," said Dracula, bowing to his guest.

Watching from their hiding place in the gallery above, Kelene whispered, "Isn't this exciting?"

Fenice shook her head. "It is a very risky game."

"I know." Kelene giggled softly. "That's what makes it such fun."

Dracula indicated the door to the suite of rooms where Eugen Theiss had been housed. "Tonight I want you only to visit him. Nothing more. Let him think he is dreaming. When he has become interested, we will change the visits." He pointed to Kelene. "There are servants and men-at-arms enough to go around for you both; do not try my patience."

Kelene tossed her head. "I think he would like company."

"He will," said Dracula, "but not yet. And see you approach him together, always together. He will not be able to be your suitor if both of you are with him."

"And it will seem more like a dream, won't it?" Fenice guessed. "You don't want him searching the castle for us."

"No, not yet," said Dracula. "Later on it will not matter, but for now, be his sweet illusions." He tweaked one of Kelene's fair curls. "I know it is hard for you, girl. But your reward will be greater for your obedience." He bent and kissed her on the mouth. "Remember your brother."

Something passed between Kelene and Dracula that Fenice did not understand, but she realized it was important. She said, "How long do you expect us to delay?"

"For as long as it is necessary." Apparently he did not want to speak about this anymore. "You will take your sustenance from the men I have said you may." He made an imperious gesture. "And while the gypsies are here, you, Kelene, will accept what they give you. I will not have you forsaking their generosity because you like tantalizing this guest better."

"I would not do that," said Kelene, not at all convincingly.

"Make sure you do not go to the library until he is asleep. I do not want him to discover you in anything but what he thinks are his dreams." He took Kelene then Fenice by the hand. "You will have to remain together."

"Yes; you said so already," Fenice reminded him.

"In all things," said Dracula to some purpose. "When you find your nourishment, do so as partners; you may choose different men, but find them together."

"What about the gypsies?" Fenice asked. "They bring their foundlings for Kelene. They do not bring them for me."

Dracula considered this for a short moment, then said, "True enough; when that happens, you, Fenice, will find a man among my servants and he will provide what you need." He dismissed them abruptly. "You know what you must do. Make yourselves ready."

Kelene rushed to comply, but Fenice was not in such a hurry. "It is not only to deal with this man that you send us to—" She stopped, sensing she had gone too far. "I will do what you want; one day you will tell me why you wanted it so."

"Or I may not," Dracula said, pointing to the way out.

The man lay asleep under his heavy blankets, irregular snoring promising Fenice and Kelene that it was safe to begin the seduction Dracula ordered.

"I'll take the right side, you may have the left," Kelene hissed. "Let me move first; I am oldest and I've done this much more than you have."

Fenice nodded her acceptance. "I will follow your lead."

Kelene gave a soft purring chuckle. "It will be such fun."

They went to the bed and carefully drew the curtains more wide; then very carefully Kelene took one of Theiss' hands and slowly put it inside her camisa on her breast, motioning to Fenice to do the same; Fenice found Theiss' other hand and slipped it inside her camisa: his listless touch was oddly disturbing to Fenice, though Kelene seemed to like the vague response.

"Now we move near him," Kelene breathed, and did so with a practiced ease that revealed more of her experience than any boasting would have done.

Trying to duplicate Kelene's sinuous reclining, Fenice could not keep from clutching the blanket as she attempted to slide next to the sleeping man as his hand dangled inside her camisa; the whole exercise seemed foolish and comic and annoying. But she had come too far to stop in their endeavors, so she tried to have some of the same delight Kelene had.

Theiss moaned and turned under the covers, his body giving better comfort to Fenice and Kelene; his hands became more animated, reaching and closing on both of them with the roughness of desire found in dreaming. A few incomprehensible phrases escaped his lips as Kelene gestured with her head to get Fenice to slide over his chest; she bent and began to lick his throat.

No matter how silly this seemed, Fenice began to see how it would let them be nourished without killing the man; she began to think she might learn to be willing to do this and not feel smirched by it.

"I go first," whispered Kelene as she bent to nip his throat, and then drank rapturously.

From her place over Theiss' chest, Fenice felt him clutch in response to the brief moment of pain, and then his organ rose up and he began to pant with somnambulistic passion while he pawed at the two vampires.

Reluctantly Kelene gave up her place to Fenice, murmuring, "He is a feast," as she slid out of the bed.

Fenice had to admit the savor of his blood was far more delicious than she had expected, as if the double thrill of his dream had brought out flavors and richness she had not yet known in any of those she had preyed upon. She found it difficult to stop, and did so more irresolutely than she had left any of the others.

When she joined Kelene at the foot of the bed, she said under her breath, "Will he remember, do you think?"

"If he does not, he will be the first." Kelene took Fenice's hand and tugged her toward the door and out of the room; there she danced about in a circle. "Wasn't that perfect? Didn't you love it? Isn't is miraculous how it is so much better together? We were better than sisters: my sisters would never have wanted to do anything with me, especially not with a man."

Fenice agreed that sharing the bounty was gratifying, but with less exultation than Kelene experienced; for the first time she had had no fear, and that terrified her.

The following evening Dracula greeted them upon awakening with ferocious amusement. "He asked me if there were women in the castle. I said there were a few servant women, but he said no, not servant women. He did not want to say whores, but he asked if I had a harem, like the Ottomites do." He looked from Fenice to Kelene. "You are hardly a harem, are you? I do not keep you to give me sons. Of course I claimed ignorance and left him to spend his day wondering." He kissed Kelene. "You did well. And Fenice?"

"She did well for a beginner," said Kelene, relishing the favor Dracula showed her. "She is not as skilled as I am."

Fenice did not let Dracula continue his divisive praise. "How could I be? Kelene has had much longer to hone her accomplishments than I. But with Kelene to teach me, I may develop my abilities over time."

Kelene beamed. "You see? She knows my worth." She clung to Dracula's arm. "Do we go to him tonight?"

"No; he must last a while. You may go tomorrow. Tonight find your nourishment elsewhere." He was stern once again. "He must not know you are more than dreams yet. Do not fail me in this."

"Of course not," said Fenice. "After all, we have a bargain with you."

Dracula scowled. "A bargain?" he repeated, as if it had slipped his mind.

"If we succeed here, you will bring no more women here without our permission," she said calmly with a slight smile. "You remember?"

He started to deny it, then changed his tactics. "Yes; but to have it so, you must succeed with Theiss, and you haven't done that yet, have you?"

"We will," Kelene said, as if desperate for his good opinion again.

"When you do, we will see." He turned and strode out of the vault, leaving the two women behind.

"Do you think he will keep the bargain?" Kelene asked with subdued anxiety.

"I think he is waiting for us to fail so he will not have to," said Fenice with blunt honesty; she saw the shock in Kelene's blue eyes, and went on, "He does not know that we will not fail."

Kelene did her best to sound as convinced as Fenice did. "We won't, will we?"

By the time the second man-at-arms was dispatched with messages, one of his fellows accompanying him, the letter he carried included the news that Eugen Theiss was suffering a decline:

I put it to the severity of our winter, Dracula had written in his note that was included with Theiss' report. *We must all hope that when the spring comes, my guest will improve. I blame myself for urging him to remain here; his little chill has become so much more. I have ordered my servants to care for him night and day; because of this I hope the next news I send you will be happier.*

"You surprised me; I thought you would not be able to resist draining him or you would become careless and reveal yourselves to him before I allowed it. Well, you have managed to accomplish the work I set for you. You need no longer wait until he is asleep to go to his room," Dracula told Fenice and Kelene when the second message had been carried away from the castle in the full obscurity of the first heavy snowfall; they were in the vault preparing for the coming night. "I have what I want from him, and now so may you: I give him to you. If you can resist, wait a while to drain him."

Kelene went to Dracula's side, letting the top of her camisa fall open to reveal the nubile curve of her breast. "He will want this."

"You and Fenice must go together again tonight, as you have before now. Let his dreams be realized—in the flesh," Dracula said. "And Fenice, I do not want you to talk to him except to pleasure him. No questions, no discussions."

"Why should I bother?" Fenice asked. "He will not be leaving, and he has begun to think his dreams are making him mad."

"You have great curiosity," said Dracula. "And you might do it in the hope of learning if he is one you think ought to die."

He had come so close to the truth that Fenice had to hide her confusion in temper. "I have had many chances to urge him to speak in what he thought was his sleep. Yet you did not reprimand me then. You do it now and I do not deserve it."

"Do you think not?" Dracula asked. "When you are through, girl, you tell me how you fared." He brushed the back of his hand along Kelene's cheek. "He is ripe for you. And remember he is awake, not half-asleep."

"We know him well; we will know what to do," she said, beaming up at Dracula. "We will enjoy obeying your orders." She glanced at Fenice. "How is your hunger?"

"Good enough," said Fenice, smiling at Kelene. "You are oldest; you go first." She gave Kelene a short curtsy, which looked out of place in her boyish clothing, though the Greek girl had no complaint, if she noticed the incongruity at all.

Kelene went ahead of Fenice, all but preening with this distinction; she was near the corridor when Dracula reached out and grabbed Fenice's arm. "How long do you think you can fool her with your obsequiousness? She is gullible, but she is not without cunning herself." His voice was as low as the wind soughing through the vault. "How long will your pride stand this unseemly display?"

"It is better than having her trying to kill me." Fenice showed her teeth in a smile as predatory as his own.

"All I would have to do is tell her to turn on you and she would. She is mine." He kissed her mouth without a trace of passion. "As you are mine."

"She is waiting for me," Fenice said, tugging her arm free.

Dracula made a brusque nod to Fenice. "Do as I have commanded you," he told them as they went up the corridor.

Eugen Theiss was pale, with deep marks around his eyes like bruises; were he not so cold, he might have appeared feverish from the glitter in his eyes and the restless way he tossed beneath his pile of blankets. On his throat two reddened marks showed the inflammation of festering sores. His servant had not shaved him in four days and stubble showed on his cheeks; his courtliness was gone and in its place was febrile restlessness.

As Kelene and Fenice drew back the curtains of his bed, he gasped and shuddered. "You!" His voice was hoarse and his tone condemning even as his hands reached out to them. "There *are* two of you. I didn't dream that."

"Unless you are dreaming now," Kelene teased, leaning toward him so that her clothes could hang open to him.

"If I am, I never want to wake," he said, his mouth slack with lust.

"Let your wish be granted," said Kelene, and was on him at once, worrying at his throat before Fenice could get into the bed. When she raised her head, she murmured. "There is some left for you." She began to lick his blood from her lips. "It is good; the heart hasn't finished beating yet."

Fenice did not like the eagerness with which she claimed her share; even as she relished the virtue of Theiss' life-blood she was disappointed with herself for taking it, for succumbing so completely to her need; she had not been able to stop herself, nor had she wanted to.

The door swung open and Dracula stood on the threshold. "So you could not wait," he said with a kind of cynical satisfaction, as if his worst expectations were now vindicated. He strode to the foot of the bed. "I suppose I should have expected it." He laid his hand on Kelene's shining head. "How was it? Did the taste fill you? Did you tremble with the power in it?"

Kelene smiled, Theiss' blood still staining her teeth. "He was good to kill."

Fenice shivered, disgusted for the response she felt within herself. She forced herself to face Dracula. "What about our bargain?"

Dracula shrugged and looked down at Kelene. "What do you want?"

Making a moue of repugnance, she answered. "Why should we bother?"

Fenice shoved herself toward Kelene. "Because we did his bidding."

"We would have anyway," Kelene said, beaming at Dracula. "Look what he gave us."

"For his own purposes," said Fenice, a bit desperately. The joy she had known such a brief time ago was evaporating like the spangles of dew on spring blossoms and she was left with a dead husk and fleeting hope.

"He served our purposes, too," Kelene said, never taking her eyes from Dracula's face.

"You see?" Dracula said to Fenice with a gesture of counterfeit helplessness. "She will always be mine first." He took Kelene's chin in his hand. "Won't you, girl?"

Kelene's only answer was to snuggle closer to him and to kiss his hand.

Fenice watched in dismay; she had lost everything: she was as dead as the corpse of Eugen Theiss now abandoned behind them, but she had not relinquished the burdens of living. She lowered her head in shame. "I was a fool to think you would—"

Now that he had what he wanted, Dracula held up his free hand to silence her. "What would be the harm in keeping the bargain? You would be happier, the two of you."

As Kelene kissed his hand again, Fenice regarded him with suspicion, hating her own resurgence of aspiration. "You mean you would bring no woman here without our permission?"

"Yes," said Dracula magnanimously. Then he added, "For a time."

Fenice wanted to ask how long that time would be, to insist he promise them he would not renege on his bargain again. All she said was, "Then for a time, I am grateful," and did her best to smile at him as he bent to kiss her brow.